Exploration
The Gifted Series

Book Two

USA Today Bestselling Author
Char Webster

Copyright May 2016 © by Char Webster

Copyright notice: All rights reserved under the International and Pan-American Copyright Conventions. No part of this book may be reproduced or transmitted in any form or by any means, electronic or mechanical, including photocopying, recording, or by any information storage and retrieval system, without permission in writing from the publisher.

This is a work of fiction. Names, places, characters and incidents are either the product of the author's imagination or are used fictitiously, and any resemblance to any actual persons, living or dead, organizations, events or locales is entirely coincidental.

Warning: the unauthorized reproduction or distribution of this copyrighted work is illegal. Criminal copyright infringement, including infringement without monetary gain, is investigated by the FBI and is punishable by up to 5 years in prison and a fine of $250,000.

ISBN: 0692718761
ISBN-13: 978-0692718766

Dedication

To my sisters, Chrisie and Kelly, my best friends in the world. I love you both very much!

Acknowledgments

A special thank you to my mom, Arlene Webster, for the incredible encouragement and love you always show me. There would not be any books at all if not for you. My family and friends are unbelievably supportive and I don't know what I would do without you all.

Thank you Dawn Gorman for reading my very rough drafts of pages as I write them. Your enthusiasm about my books is a great motivator. I value your friendship and support.

I want to send out a very special thank you to the bloggers out there, especially, The magic of Books, Wickedly Devine Divas and Readers Heaven. You were the first blogs to take notice of my books and I'm so thankful for your help, reviews and promotions.

A special Thank You to Claire Holt from Luminescence Covers for her awesome work making this book look incredible!

The members of the Gifted Society have been amazing. I am completely humbled by all the love and support you all show me and my books. You are the best group of readers and friends out there. Thank you so much!

Contents

Prologue 1
Chapter One 5
Chapter Two 17
Chapter Three 31
Chapter Four 49
Chapter Five 63
Chapter Six 75
Chapter Seven 87
Chapter Eight 101
Chapter Nine 113
Chapter Ten 127
Chapter Eleven 141
Chapter Twelve 155
Chapter Thirteen 169
Chapter Fourteen 183
Chapter Fifteen 199
Chapter Sixteen 211
Chapter Seventeen 225
Chapter Eighteen 239
Chapter Nineteen 255
Chapter Twenty 267
Chapter Twenty-One 277
About the Author 289

Prologue

1200 years ago

He threw her forcefully into the room with an eerie laugh. She tried to brace herself, but she was unable to do so with her wrists and ankles bound tightly. Hitting the stone floor with a loud thud, the breath was knocked out of her from the jarring impact. For the first time that night, she was thankful for the gag in her mouth because it prevented her moans from escaping the grain sack they had stuffed her into. Her body was already badly beaten from her horrible journey there, so a few more bruises didn't make much of a difference.

The man laughed harder as he watched her weak attempt to sit up within the sack. Her struggling stopped short at the loud metallic clink that rang out through the room. It was the sound of a jail cell closing.

She took as deep of a breath as she could with the gag and through the sack to try to settle her nerves. She had to keep her wits or she would never survive. With slow, painstaking movements, she was able to pull the sack off her, and she threw it aside.

Her cell was in almost total darkness except for the candlelight leaking in from the hallway. Luckily, her wrists were bound in front of her so she was able to pull the gag down from her mouth and take her first lungful of air all night.

Untying her ankles proved to be a challenge, but she was finally able to remove the coarse ropes that bit into her skin and left bleeding burn marks. After several attempts, she realized that her wrists would have to remain bound. Her endeavors only succeeded in causing them to throb even more.

A high window confirmed it was still night, which meant that she had only been gone for a few hours. The cell was surprisingly clean, with a neatly made bed in the corner and fresh smelling blankets folded on the end. Off to the side of the room was a sturdy-looking wooden table and chair.

She was shocked to see a chest with a shelf over it on the opposite wall that held a few books, a water basin, and hairbrush.

She walked over to the chest, opened it, and gasped as she pulled out several expensive-looking dresses. *What kind of a prison has these types of items in it?*

"I see you are getting acquainted with your new lodgings, Edeva," a new arrival said, breaking the silence.

Startled, she ran to the bars and saw a figure walking toward her cell carrying a tall pillar candle. She could see that he was a large man, though his height did nothing to mask his rounded middle. His long, red hair curled at the ends and stood out in stark contrast to the royal blue robes he was wearing. She sighed with relief, before she realized the implication of what he had said. She clutched a bar between her bound hands to support her.

"Chancellor Medric, there has been some mistake," Edeva pleaded. "Please, I've done no wrong."

Chancellor Medric stared at the small young woman in front of him, her long chestnut hair curling wildly down her back. Her face was already turning a nasty shade of purple that made her honey-colored eyes seem to glow.

"I know you have not done anything wrong, my dear," he told her. She suddenly looked hopeful, but he dashed those thoughts easily. "You have not done anything wrong but you could. You could unlock a terrible power and I just cannot have that."

She started shaking her head. "You must be mistaken. I do not have that kind of a gift. I can only feel emotion," she stuttered.

"I wish I were, Edeva." He turned to leave but hesitated. "You will be staying here for quite a long time. Do let me know if you need anything. I will send the guards in with some candles, and to untie your hands."

She stood there stunned, watching him walk away. "Please!" she screamed. "Wait, please! There's some mistake." Medric ignored her screams without even the slightest bit of guilt.

---

200 years ago

She ran blindly through the city. No one paid any attention to a ragged-looking young woman in that part of town. Her long hair tangled around her and her dress was torn in several places. The lace hem dragged the ground and had gotten caught several times, making her lose her measly lead.

The only things that could raise a question to anyone looking were the dogs snarling and snapping behind her as she tried desperately to outrun them and their well-dressed owners. Those people that witnessed the scene figured that a rich lord was having sport with a prostitute or enacting punishment for a wrongdoing. No one was going to help her.

Her lungs were screaming for mercy and her legs felt like they would collapse at any moment. She knew that she could not keep up this pace much longer. Her one hope was that she could make it to the harbor. She was an excellent swimmer and might be able to escape there.

She rounded another corner and her hopes of freedom were crushed. The dogs had chased her into an alleyway with no outlet. She was trapped.

She skidded to a stop next to several empty barrels and wooden crates, and turned to face her pursuers. The dogs stopped to bark madly at her from only a few feet away, but they did not attack. *They must have been well trained.* She looked around for anything to use as a weapon, but there was nothing. The barrels and crates would be too heavy to use.

She gasped when she saw an attractive older gentleman with long, brown hair pulled back with a cord, a dark green greatcoat, and shiny, black knee boots walk into the alley. She cringed when two burly-looking men with their swords drawn came up to flank their leader. The man held his hand up and the dogs immediately quieted and flopped down to the ground.

Escape was useless, so she straightened herself to her full height and stood before them defiantly. "Who are you?" she demanded. "What do you want with me?" Silence filled the alleyway. They just looked at her and smirked. She reached out with her gift, but could feel no emotions coming from them. They were Gifted.

She tried again. "Why are you chasing me? I have nothing of value and have done you no harm."

One of the men behind the leader snorted loudly. "Chancellor, allow me to teach this urchin some manners. She should not be speaking to you in such a fashion." Her whole body stiffened and her eyes grew wide when she heard his title. She had never met the Chancellor, but she had heard many stories.

"My Lord Chancellor, I have broken no Association rules."

The Chancellor continued to ignore her as if she had not spoken. "Thank you, Henry, but I will deal with this young woman." He sighed. She had given him much more of a chase then he had expected. *Too bad,* he thought. She was rather attractive in an unkempt sort of way. Her red hair and porcelain complexion brought out her green eyes. He was tempted to clean her up for some fun, but he quickly discarded the idea. She was far too dangerous.

He addressed her for the first time. "You have been entirely too much trouble." She looked at him in confusion.

"I have caused you no trouble," she said, lifting her chin in even more defiance.

"On the contrary. You have caused me to waste an entire night chasing after you in this disgusting part of town. It stops here." He stepped closer to her in anticipation.

The fire in her eyes grew. "I have done nothing wrong, My Lord."

"You exist. That is wrong enough."

Her body started to shake. Everyone had heard rumors of Gifted people imprisoned by the Association for various contrived reasons. She was going to be one of them. Her legs could barely hold her up so she reached out to steady herself against the crates.

"You will not keep me prisoner," she said in a last attempt to be brave.

"No, I won't. It's much easier this way." He pulled out a gun and shot her.

Chapter One

Kaboom!

The rock exploded into a thousand tiny pieces that rained down on Zach's head. He shook his sun-bleached hair out and the particles flew everywhere.

"Dude! That was AWESOME!" Jason yelled as he ran up to Zach and rubbed some more of the rock debris out of his hair. They both high-fived and chest-bumped. Jason shook out his own light brown hair, which was also full of rubble.

"That *was* pretty awesome!" Zach agreed, smiling hugely. He looked around. The garage was getting cluttered with broken pieces of various objects that had already been blown apart.

"Do it again," Jason urged, but then looked up and said, "Oh no." He turned away with a guilty look on his face. Kate watched him wince a little at having been caught doing something they shouldn't have been doing.

Zach looked over to see what spoiled Jason's mood and winced himself.

Kate was standing at the entrance to the garage with her hand on her hip and that look that all people who work in a school have; the one that all kids, no matter what age, fear. She stared them down for a moment to make them squirm a little and almost ruined the effect by laughing. She turned away quickly to wipe the laugh away, then faced them once more.

"What exactly are you guys doing in here?" Kate demanded. "The entire neighborhood is going to think something weird is going on. Do you want everyone to start asking questions?"

"No," Zach muttered, looking down.

Jason didn't answer, so she turned her wrath on him. "Some role model you are, encouraging him to blow stuff up. Remember, you're twenty-four, not twelve like Zach."

"We were just practicing, Kate," Jason said, trying to smooth things over, but he was holding back a grin as well. "He needs to learn control over his gift."

"Not by blowing up everything you can find and making enough noise that the neighbors start to wonder what's going on."

"Sorry," Jason mumbled quietly, but he didn't look all that sorry.

"Yeah, sorry Kate," Zach said quietly. The looks on their faces made it obvious that he and Jason were both bummed that their fun had ended.

"Clean all this mess up," Kate ordered and turned away before she started to laugh.

She didn't see Jason wink at Zach behind her back.

Kate hurried onto the back porch and noticed Robert lounging on one of the chairs, looking down on a piece of paper. As she got closer, she could see that it was a sketch of a woman's eyes. Robert noticed her approach and quickly put the sketch back into his wallet. He raised his eyebrow at her as she settled down next to him. Kate smiled at him, looking up into his dark brown eyes. Somehow, over the last few months, he had become her best friend. *It's funny to think that he scared me when we first met,* she thought.

"What was that?" Kate asked, curiously.

"Nothing." Robert tried to stare her down, wondering what was going on in her head. She had gotten much better at blocking her thoughts from him. He was also trying to distract her.

"Is that an evil laugh about ruining their fun or are you secretly cracking up about their exploits?"

Kate tried to hide her grin. "I have no idea what you're talking about."

"He's getting good at it, isn't he?" Robert challenged.

"Yeah, he really is," Kate admitted with a smile. "But they can't keep doing that in the garage. They're going to have to find somewhere else to practice."

"At least they're not blowing things up in the backyard anymore," Robert snickered.

"I'm still upset about losing my matching planters out by the pool," Kate threw back. "And they only moved to the garage because it's starting to get too cold outside." She pulled the hood of her sweatshirt closer around her neck.

"We're men. We don't get cold in sixty degree weather," Robert teased back. "They moved to the garage to hide how many things they're really blowing up. Jason's been trying to

slow the explosions down with his enhanced slow-motion gift."
Kate looked at him incredulously. "Are you serious? They're going to get hurt. It's like I have two teenage boys." She threw up her hands and stood.

Robert was laughing at Kate's reaction. She leaned over to him and ruffled his chocolate-colored hair. "You need a haircut," Kate told him.

With that, she walked into the house. Robert followed after her, still laughing loudly, and stumbled into the kitchen. He went right to the refrigerator and started rooting through it, looking for something to munch on.

"Hey Kate, you don't have anything good in here," Robert complained. He frowned at the hummus and veggies that lined the shelves.

Kate walked over and closed the refrigerator door on him. "You do have a house right down the street that you can supply with all the junk food in the world."

Robert pouted and went to the cabinet next to the fridge to look in there. "HA! Found something." Robert was chuckling as he pulled out a bag of hot salsa chips. He smiled over Kate's love of hot foods.

"It's much more fun to be here, though." He grinned up at her with a full mouth of chips.

She shook her head. "I guess you all are staying for dinner again tonight?" Robert, Jason, and Ryan had been eating at her house more nights than not lately.

Robert pouted at her and said, "Kate, you're hurting my feelings. It seems like you don't want us." He even put his lower lip out.

Kate snatched the bag out of his hands. "If you're eating here, no snacking before dinner." She gave him a saucy smile and pushed him out of the kitchen. "Go check on Maddy. She's been playing in her room since she woke up from her nap and now it's very quiet over the monitor." He shuffled off toward the stairs, still moping.

Alex strolled in, bopping her head to the music in her ear buds. She pulled up a stool at the breakfast bar and picked up the bag of chips that Kate had taken away from Robert.

"Hey! Not you, too," Kate scolded, as she took the bag away

and put it back in the cabinet.

Alex pulled the buds out of her ears and looked at Kate. "I just wanted a few."

"Dinner will be ready in an hour, so no snacking," Kate told her. "Did you finish your homework yet?"

"Not yet, but I'll get to it." Alex noticed Kate's look and said, "Okay, I'll do it now." She ran to the other room for her backpack.

Kate followed her. "Alex, you can't play around. You need to be serious about school now or they'll send you right back to eighth grade. You just tested into your freshman year and they're going to watch out for you to mess up, especially after your school record from last year."

"I know, Kate. I'm going to work hard." Alex paused and looked at Kate fondly. "I'm glad you had them test me. The stuff was way too easy."

"And I guess it doesn't hurt that Emily is a freshman this year, too. You know, since she's your best friend and all."

Alex smiled widely and settled back at the breakfast bar to do her homework.

Both Alex and Zach had moved up to the next grade once the school year had begun. They took the placement tests to see if they could skip a grade and both kids were technically qualified to skip two grades, but Kate thought two grades would be too much for them. She wanted the kids to do well in school, but she also wanted to make sure they did okay socially. Zach was now in eighth grade with Emily's brother, Eric, and the boys were inseparable. *It's funny how that worked out this year,* Kate thought. All of the kids were thrilled with the new arrangements.

Kate looked up at a sudden loud giggling and squealing coming from the steps. Robert was holding Maddy upside down with one arm and tickling her with the other.

"Again!" Maddy giggled, clapping her hands.

Kate smiled. She was almost content with her life. *Almost.* Someone was missing, and that was something she tried not to think about.

Robert put Maddy down next to her toy box in the family room and walked over to Kate in the kitchen. "Hey. You have that look again."

"What look?" Kate tried to pretend she didn't understand what he was saying. She pasted on a fake smile and tried hard to not let anyone see how much Nick's disappearance had upset her.

"You know what I'm talking about." He paused and stepped right up to her. "Call him."

"Yeah, I need to find out if Ryan's coming over for dinner. He's been working too hard and keeping really late hours. I bet he's back to living off of takeout again."

"That's not who I'm talking about and you know it." Robert tried to give her the school look, but obviously failed because she laughed. "Seriously Kate, you should call him. Nick misses you."

"He misses me?" Kate got louder. "How do you know that?"

When Robert cringed slightly, Kate got angry. "You've talked to him? When did you talk to him? It's been months, Rob. *Months* and all I get are some text messages and voicemails when he knows I'm at work and can't answer, or when my phone is off. If he really wanted to talk to me, he would call when he actually knows I'll pick up!"

"Kate . . ."

"I don't want to talk about this."

"But Kate . . ."

"Robert, stop. I'm done. I don't want to talk about him."

Kate went back to the refrigerator, pulled out stuff for a salad, and began chopping vigorously. Luckily, she used the cutting board or her countertop would have been very scratched from the force she used to cut up the veggies.

Robert grabbed the knife out of her hand and said, "Are you trying to make your own salsa?"

Kate looked down at the decimated tomatoes and laughed. "Sure, we all like bruschetta. I just need a little bit of fresh basil now."

"Uh-huh." Robert arched his eyebrow at her. "Nice save."

She grinned at him over her shoulder and turned back around.

"You know, it's not like he's been gone that long; it's only been about a month," Robert said, trying to bait her.

Kate whipped around to face him with fire in her eyes. "He's been gone two months and twelve days."

"Really?" Robert drew out the word and shot her a look.

Kate stiffened slightly but remained quiet. She hated when he got the best of her. She began to take more ingredients out of the refrigerator and cabinets. She wasn't paying attention to what she was pulling out.

"What are you trying to make here?" Robert asked. He needed to get her talking. She had progressively gotten quieter as time went by. She laughed and joked around with the kids and Robert, Jason and Ryan, but not wholeheartedly. It was like a muted Kate, and that wasn't good. He needed to help her to get her spunk back, but he was afraid that there was only one person who could really do that—his idiot best friend, Nick.

"I don't know," Kate told him despondently, looking at the various things that she had taken out. None of them went together at all. She laughed a little, but it didn't reach her eyes. "I'm going to pull the pasta sauce out of the freezer and we'll have spaghetti and meatballs."

Jason walked in just then and asked, "With garlic bread?"

"Yes, with garlic bread," Kate told him.

Zach loved that idea. "Awesome! I love garlic bread."

Robert helped Kate make dinner and Jason helped both kids do their homework. It was a similar scene most nights lately. Kate enjoyed having Robert, Ryan, and Jason over. All three of them lived in Nick's house just up the street and helped Kate with everything. They were very entertaining and the kids loved them. She knew they loved being around the kids and her, but she also knew they were sticking around so close to keep an eye out for them.

The summer had gone by without any incidents, which surprised everyone. They all had expected something to happen. Shortly after school started, Ryan noticed a car sitting outside of the middle school that Zach attended. It turned out to be someone who had worked for Brooks, but was not part of his regular team. The man was more like a freelancer who had been trying to get into his boss' good graces. He was now in the custody of the Association, who governed their Gifted race.

A few weeks after that, Alex was approached at her field hockey practice. Jason caught the creeper and turned him over to the Association as well, but before he did, the man confessed that Brooks had put out a bounty for Kate and the kids. Apparently, Brooks' reputation had slid drastically and thankfully, not many people were taking the offer seriously. No one really expected Brooks to follow through with the huge payment promised and no one wanted to mess with Robert, Ryan, and Jason. Luckily, the attempts had been weak and the men that had been trying were desperate.

Jason managed to get a job as the resource police officer at the high school so that he could be around all the time without anyone wondering about his presence. Kate was still trying to figure out how Ryan finagled his way into teaching computers at the middle school. He was more than qualified with his PhD in computer engineering, but she didn't think he had his teacher's certificate. She didn't want to ask him about it, in case he forged his credentials. Ryan was also still running his computer security business during off hours.

Kate wasn't sure what Robert was doing during the day. Every time she asked him, he told her not to worry. It was cryptic and she wondered about it often, but she wasn't going to push him for an answer. He would tell her when he was ready.

Just as they were sitting down to dinner, Ryan rushed in the back door. "You guys were going to eat without me?" He frowned and pulled out his chair.

"Wash your hands!" Maddy scolded him. Everyone laughed, but Ryan ran over to the sink and washed up. Maddy was all proud of herself for reminding him and of course Ryan had to rush over to her for a tight, sticky Maddy hug.

Kate smiled as she thought about the guys who were now a big part of her life. Robert, Jason, Ryan, and Nick, who was still off trying to save the world, grew up together and were all best friends. They used to work together in security for the Association.

Sometimes, she couldn't believe that just a few months ago, she had no idea she was anything but a normal, twenty-three-year-old guidance counselor at the local high school. Sure, she always had a way with people and could tell what they were feeling, but she never thought it was anything out of the norm. It had just been a part of her. That all changed when she decided to help her three kids, who were in the foster care system after their parents had died. Suddenly she was thrust into a completely new world full of special abilities, power hungry lunatics, kidnapping, and danger.

She wouldn't have it any other way.

"You guys are not going to believe what I found out today." Ryan started to pile a huge amount of pasta on his plate.

"Dude, manners," Jason teased. "Ladies first . . . well, even half ladies." Jason winked at Alex who was giving him a look.

Zach laughed loudly and Alex turned her look on him.

Kate tried to ignore them. "What did you find out?"

"Someone broke into the Association's archive library in New York and stole some old books and records," Ryan told them. "Stuff from as far back as their records go."

Robert sat up, very interested, and looked over at Ryan. "How did you find out?"

"A buddy of mine is the historian there. He's been scanning in some of the most important of the ancient documents," Ryan told them. "He also may have been sending me copies of the files." Ryan grinned widely.

"Does he know what was specifically taken?" Robert probed.

Ryan gave him a look that Kate found odd and said, "Information about the original ten."

"Were those documents scanned?"

"Yeah, but they still need to be translated. They're in a few different ancient languages," Ryan mumbled, stuffing a huge piece of bread in his mouth. "I got copies of the scans. I'm running them through translation programs, but it will take some time."

"What was that?" Jason teased. "You just spit bread crumbs all over."

"I did not, Jay, but I'll spit them at you," Ryan told him, acting as if he was really going to spit at Jason.

"Guys," Kate said. She constantly had to stop them from bickering. If she didn't know they were best friends, she would think they were rivals. Most of the time it was funny, but right now, she wanted to know about this break-in. She had a sinking feeling it had something to do with her, the kids, and whatever

Robert was doing during the day.

"Why would anyone want those old documents?" Kate asked. She felt as if they were keeping something from her. "I could see a collector wanting something for a show piece, but no one is supposed to know about that library, right? I mean, the world doesn't know the Association or the Gifted race even exist."

Jason stood up abruptly, looking down at his phone that just beeped. "Ah man, I've got to go."

"You have another date?" Kate asked, not quite believing it. "Isn't that the third one this week?"

Jason flashed her a huge grin. "I can't help it if all the ladies want to get with this." He gestured to himself with his hands, showing how awesome he thought he was, and then left grinning the whole way out the door.

Alex groaned, Zach laughed, and Kate rolled her eyes. Surprisingly, Ryan didn't have anything to say. Kate noticed that Robert and Ryan were unusually quiet, which meant that they were hiding something from her. Now she knew something was up.

The kids finished dinner quickly and asked if they could go next door to their friends' house. When Kate agreed, they ran to the kitchen with their plates and hurriedly put them in the dishwasher. Kate loved that Alex and Zach were happy living with her and that they had good friends nearby.

She turned back to Robert and Ryan. "Okay, so what aren't you guys telling me? I know there's something more to this break-in story."

They exchanged another look, silently agreeing on something. Robert sighed and said, "It's just strange for anyone to break into the Association's archives. We need to keep an eye out for anything unusual that may have something to do with Brooks."

Kate looked at both guys and knew that they were holding something back. She had no choice but to wait until they were ready to tell her. When they closed up like that, no amount of prodding on her part ever worked.

The man with long, stringy hair was on the edge of the roof of the house down the street from Kate's. He watched everything that was happening and kept a log. The people who owned the house were away somewhere warm and wouldn't be back until spring. It was the perfect spot to wait and observe.

He wasn't sure of the reasons, but Brooks was paying him to observe and report. He could grab the woman at any time—it would be easy to do. He didn't know why Brooks told him to only watch.

Nick pulled the wrinkled photo out of his wallet and looked at it for the thousandth time. Kate and the kids smiled back at him and he wished he could reach into the scene and hug them. He missed them like crazy and was tempted to go back home to be with them all, but he couldn't. Making sure they were safe was his first priority.

He flopped back onto his bed in what felt like the millionth motel room he'd had. This week Nick was in Tampa and would be moving on the next day. Tracking down several old contacts that Dawn Johnson had given him had been easy. Dawn had helped out when Brooks kidnapped his nieces and nephew over the summer. She was a very nice lady and had provided the best information he could have received on Brooks' dealings with the foster care system.

Nick looked at the photo again and studied Kate's face. Even though he hadn't known her for very long, she had managed to get under his skin. He looked at his watch and figured she was probably still asleep since it was four a.m. Laughing to himself, he wondered if she still went out to her porch to enjoy the pre-dawn hours. He hoped it was just something that she had shared with him. He decided to send her a text since he was awake and thinking about her.

She used to return his texts right away in the beginning, but as time had passed, she stopped responding. It devastated him when she didn't return his messages, but he knew she was angry with him for leaving and staying away this long. Kate didn't understand that he needed to do this for her and the kids, or they would always be in danger.

Robert had called earlier and told him that Kate was struggling and that Nick had better get his butt back. Robert had no idea how much he really wanted to do just that, but he couldn't yet. He needed a little bit more time.

Nick knew that Kate loved sunsets and loved to take photographs of them in all their colorful brilliance. The sunset off of the Gulf Coast of Florida had been spectacular that night, and he had snapped a photo with his phone to show Kate when he returned. It made him feel closer to her. Thinking about Kate, he didn't want to wait to show her—he needed a connection with her now.

Nick pulled out his phone to text her. Maybe she would respond. He attached the sunset photo and a caption, *Watching this sunset wasn't the same without you.* He waited a while, but she didn't respond.

Detective Martin stared at the smoking wreckage that was once an Audi A4. It had flipped over about six times before hitting a grove of trees and exploding. The investigators assigned to the case were sure that both passengers were killed on impact. Normally, he wouldn't have been called to a crash like this in another state, but this case paralleled the one he had been investigating since the summer. He began examining the unusual occurrences surrounding Dawn Johnson, head of the local Family Services office, and the Taylor kids, with whom she seemed to have a special interest.

The Taylors had been killed in a crash very similar to this one. From what he had learned, peculiar things followed those kids. He was determined to figure out exactly what was behind those strange happenings.

The occupants of the crash in front of him had two teenagers who were placed into foster care, but they had disappeared immediately after being placed into their temporary residence. Family Services listed them as missing and assumed they had run away. The information had hit his desk because before the kids had disappeared, their foster parents claimed that something strange had happened. The lights had suddenly gone out and they had felt like their throats were being restricted, making it almost impossible for them to breath, but when the lights came back on, they could breathe normally . . . and the kids were gone.

Chapter Two

Kate looked at her phone for the eighth time that morning before clicking off her text messages. She forced herself to stop pacing around the house. She needed to find something to do to keep her occupied. If she started thinking too much, then she might begin to fall apart and she needed to keep it together for the kids. She jumped up and went searching for Robert.

"Let's go," Kate told Robert as he lounged on her couch. She shifted Maddy on her hip. She had been building with her blocks all morning.

"Where are we going?" Robert asked, unmoving.

"We're going to the grocery store," Kate told him with a smile.

Kate laughed at Robert groaning like the kids did when she asked them to do something they didn't want to do.

"You don't have to come with me," Kate said lightly, a sly smile on her face.

"Cool," Robert said and put his arm behind his head.

"Yeah, you don't have to come," Kate told him. "You'll have to start cooking for yourself at your house." With a toss of her hair she walked toward the front door with Maddy. Robert jumped up and rushed after her. Kate laughed the whole way toward the car.

An hour later, Kate was rethinking her decision to have Robert join her when she pulled out the fifth item of junk food from the shopping cart. She shook her head at his big grin. He was even getting Maddy to help with his subterfuge.

"Why do we have two bottles of ginger ale in the cart?" Kate asked Robert.

He grinned at her and said, "Oh, because we need them desperately, Kate."

Kate shook her head at him. "Okay. Why do we need them desperately?"

If possible, his grin got even bigger. "You see, I found this really good apple cider whiskey that would go great with the ginger ale to make an awesome after-dinner drink."

She gave him one of her tough school looks. "What

happened to mimosas? I thought you loved them."

"Mimosas are sooo last summer." With that he strutted away to find more junk food.

Robert was thoroughly enjoying himself grocery shopping. He was going to get all the junk food he could manage to hide in Kate's cart; he had just grabbed a jar of marshmallow fluff from the shelf and was attempting to place it in the cart under some veggies when Kate tried to snatch it out of his hands. Robert held it up high while Kate tried to reach it. Maddy was clapping her hands at the two of them playing around.

Laughing loudly, Robert hugged Kate and slipped the jar into the cart behind her back. Kate caught on and said, "Hey!"

Robert started to tickle Kate and she squealed loudly. A store employee looked over and Kate wiggled out of his arms and turned to give him a look. They stared at each other for several moments without speaking.

Unbeknownst to Robert and Kate, their antics had attracted the attention of a woman with short, straight, very blonde hair across the produce department. Her narrow gaze was focused on the trio and their mischief. The woman clenched her jaw and began to flush in anger. She watched their silent conversation and got more upset by the second. She left her own partially filled cart in the middle of the aisle and stormed from the store. She paced the parking lot by her minivan and smacked her hand against the sports car next to her. Finally, she pulled out her phone and dialed.

"Hello. May I help you?" a voice asked politely.

"I need to speak to the Chancellor," she said.

"The Chancellor is an extremely busy man."

"I understand that, but I know he will speak to me. Please tell him Samantha is calling."

"One moment, please."

After a brief pause, the Chancellor came on the line. "Sam, this is a surprise. Is everything okay with your father?"

"Uncle Pete, Daddy's fine. I'm calling about Robert," Sam told him.

"What about him?" Pete asked her, slightly annoyed at having been bothered for such a trivial matter.

"I just saw him with his wife and child in the store."

Pete sighed. "Samantha, I know it must be upsetting for you to see Robert after everything that happened between the two of you, but you're going to have to ignore him and let it go."

"I'm not upset about seeing Robert," Sam snapped. "I'm simply reporting that he has broken the law again."

Pete sighed again. "You really shouldn't get yourself so worked up."

She interrupted him, quickly saying, "She's one of us. Gifted. He went out and married another from our race."

"Are you sure?" Chancellor Pete asked eagerly.

"I watched them have a silent conversation. They were reading each other's minds. I know she's one of us," Sam hissed.

"Thank you, Samantha. We'll look into this immediately," he told her, and hung up the phone.

Sam smiled menacingly and walked back to the store. She rescued her cart from where she had abandoned it and went looking for Robert and his family.

Three aisles later, she spotted him. She watched for a few minutes before deciding to go right up to them.

Robert had just handed Maddy a box of Hot & Spicy Cheez-Its, when he looked up and saw Sam walk toward them. He stiffened and stared at her as she approached.

Kate was eyeing one of the shelves when she felt a wave of negative emotions pouring out of Robert. She looked up concerned, because he hardly ever let his emotions out around her; he was usually very controlled. She saw a pretty young woman walk up, and Robert tensed his whole body.

"I thought that was you, Rob," Samantha crooned.

He didn't say anything, just stared straight ahead. Kate walked to stand next to Robert and Maddy.

"Hi," Kate said tentatively.

"Hello," Sam said as smoothly as she could. "I'm Samantha, Robert's ex-girlfriend. And you are?"

It took every ounce of control Kate had to keep her thoughts and feelings hidden, but she managed to mutter, "Surprised to run into you here at our local grocery store. Do you live around here?"

Sam snorted then said, "My husband and I are staying with his family for a couple of months while our house is being built in Ardmore. It's not ideal, but our son is being completely spoiled by his grandparents." She paused. "Well, it was sure something running into you, Robert." With a smirk, Samantha sashayed down the aisle and away from them.

Kate took a huge breath and let it out with force. Robert still hadn't said a word and she could see that he was shaking slightly. She turned to him and gave him a tight hug. She was trying to take all of his hurt and rage and horrible feelings away and infuse him with as many good feelings as she could. At first he was completely stiff, and then he hugged her back just as tightly.

All of a sudden, Kate couldn't feel anything at all from Robert. She was just about to kid him about blocking her when he yelped, "What the heck?" He pulled back and looked at Kate in confusion.

"What's wrong?" Kate asked, concerned.

"Tell me what you're feeling right now!" Robert demanded.

"What?"

"Seriously, Kate," Robert pleaded. "You feel badly for me, right? And you're now feeling confused and thinking I'm losing it, right?"

"Basically. Why?" Kate asked, even more confused.

"You can't feel me, can you?" He asked.

"No, and you need to stop blocking your feelings from me," Kate scolded.

"Kate, I'm not blocking you. I probably couldn't if I tried right now. I'm too emotional to block anything," Robert told her. "I think I somehow got your gift."

"What? That's crazy."

"Walk away and see if you can feel someone else's emotions," he told her. "Go ahead and try." He gave her a slight nudge to get her moving toward someone else instead of standing there looking at him like he was crazy.

Kate walked toward a group of people waiting in line at one of the registers. She stood there for a few minutes and then turned away in frustration, looking even more concerned.

Robert was now smiling. "You can't feel them can you?"

Kate looked at him in horror. "No, I can't."

Robert passed her and went to stand where she had just been

only a minute ago. He turned to her and smiled in triumph. When he reached her side again, he whispered. "The guy in the back of the line was feeling annoyed that he had to wait. The lady in front of him was getting frustrated because she was trying to get the man in front of her to notice her, but he was feeling quite amorously about someone else."

Kate looked at him in horror. Robert continued, "The little girl was feeling very excited about getting ice cream."

"How did this happen?" Kate asked, devastated. She loved her gift and couldn't bear the thought of not having it.

"I don't know," Robert confessed. "When I was hugging you, I was thinking that I really wanted to know if Sam felt even slightly as horrible as I did."

Kate took a deep breath and said, "Let's finish up here and go home to figure this out."

Kate watched Robert try to get as close to people as he could so that he could use her abilities on them. She saw his expressions as he took in the feelings of an older gentleman who looked annoyed and a teenager who seemed bored, and wondered if she looked like that when she accessed her gift.

Steering him into the checkout lane, Kate thought he acted much like an unruly toddler who didn't want to do something.

On the way back to the car with their purchases, Kate suddenly got her ability back and she could feel the emotions of the people around her once again. As she passed an old station wagon, she could feel the annoyance of the old man sitting in his car waiting for someone in the store.

"Oh, thank goodness, I can feel emotions again," Kate said relieved.

"Well, I'm glad you have your gift back, but it was kind of cool using it."

"It was sort of like you absorbed it from me," Kate explained.

"Yeah, and it lasted for about fifteen minutes." Robert got a gleam in his eyes.

"Oh no, I know that look," Kate told him. "What do you have planned?"

"I have to test this theory," Robert told her with a grin. "What if I can absorb other abilities on a temporary basis?

Maybe this is my enhancement. The others have had their gifts strengthened being around you and our group. Nothing had been different about my gift. Maybe this is it." Kate knew that Robert had been disappointed that the guys' gifts had increased while his had not changed.

"That's a scary thought," Kate muttered.

The first thing Robert did when they got back to Kate's house was hug Jason and wish he had Jason's slow-motion gift. Jason looked at Robert like he was completely nuts and said, "Dude, I know everyone loves me, but this bromance you have going on here just isn't going to work."

Robert smirked and walked a few feet away. He then picked up Jason's glass of ice water from the breakfast bar and threw the contents at Jason. Jason put up his hand, shot Robert a very arrogant look, and said, "Really? You think that . . ." He didn't finish his sentence when he was hit in the face with the contents of the glass. Ice cold water dripped from his hair and nose. "What the hell?"

Robert pumped his fist in the air. "Oh, yeah!"

"What did you do?" Jason demanded and attempted to stalk forward, but Robert had other plans. He put his hand up like Jason usually did and froze his friend in place. Jason looked back at Robert in horror. "How the hell did you do that? Let me go and give me back my gift," Jason yelled, struggling. "You stole it from me!"

Robert was enjoying himself more than he had in a very long time. "Don't like it when you can't move like you want to, huh?" he taunted.

Kate walked into the kitchen, took in the scene in front of her, and put her hands on her hips. "I guess your theory about absorbing gifts was correct. Now let him go." Robert frowned at her.

Jason looked like he was going to clobber Robert. Kate knew she had to defuse the situation. "Relax, Jay; you'll get your ability back in a few minutes. Robert did it to me at the store." Jason still didn't look happy, but he was less upset than he had been when she first walked in the room.

"I can't believe it worked," Robert said with a laugh. He released Jason and sat down at the breakfast bar.

"Is that why you hugged me?" Jason asked.

"Yeah. That's how I got Kate's gift at the store."

"You did this to Kate?" Jason asked in shock.

"Yes, he did. But that time it was an accident," Kate told him. "Now he's on a mission to see if he can absorb everyone's special abilities."

"I wonder if you have to hug someone to steal their gift," Jason asked. Though still irritated that his slow-motion power was taken from him, he was warming up to the idea.

"I don't know. I'll find out." Robert hopped off the stool and was just about to go looking for Zach and Alex when Kate blocked his path.

"We don't know anything about this new ability of yours. We need to be careful. You don't know how you will react to the different abilities and you don't know if anything bad will happen if you try to absorb more than one at a time," Kate told him.

Robert frowned, but he nodded. He needed to understand his new ability and he knew he had to be careful as well, so he spent the next few minutes experimenting with Jason's slow-motion and freezing abilities. He could see why Jason was having so much fun with Zach lately. It was a cool gift to have.

Jason kept checking to see when his gift would return, so exactly fifteen minutes later Jason froze Robert in place with a huge grin on his face. "Baby, I'm back," he shouted. Jason kept Robert frozen for a few minutes before letting him go. "No more stealing my gift," he warned.

When Robert was finally free, he went to search for his next victim. "Wait up, dude," Jason called after him. "I want to watch."

Kate shook her head. Robert was going to be impossible to deal with for a while, especially with Jason's encouragement.

Louise Brooks was pacing around the den in her house right outside of Baltimore. It was a house that her husband, Richard, didn't know she had. The house was owned by a private corporation so that it would be difficult to trace. The brick front colonial was smaller than she was used to, with only five bedrooms and a three-acre plot of ground, but it served her purposes. Other houses in the neighborhood looked just like the one she was living in, but she didn't care. The community was still gated and no one paid too much attention to what was going on.

It was too small to hold all of the children she wanted to keep with her, so they were staying at another estate. She did keep her favorite, Emma, with her. Louise never let the petite girl with shoulder-length, reddish-brown hair out of her sight. Emma had a lovely gift of prediction. Right now her gift worked only in dreams, but it would continue to develop since the girl was only twelve.

Louise was waiting for Ray to get back from his latest trip. They needed to be very careful. There were too many people after the same thing she was—the Key. Even her idiot husband was after the Key, but he didn't know how important the girl was to everything. Louise wasn't sure what Brooks knew anymore. She had been effectively avoiding him for months. The only thing her husband had been any good at was collecting those with strong gifts.

She was worried about the other people who would be after her Key. She needed to get all the pieces in place before collecting her, but time was running out and she may have to grab her sooner than expected.

She also needed to find a way to keep her husband out of her way. After all the years they had been together, Louise finally stopped pretending to be the quiet, mousy wife, and could finally put her plans into action. Brooks had been so accommodating to her wishes that he find children with specific gifts. He had no idea there was a reason behind it; he just thought she was asking for things on a whim.

Ray walked in and sat down on the couch against the wall. He put his arm along the back of the sofa and pulled his right foot up to his left knee. He looked relaxed, and that just made Louise angry.

She turned toward him and said, "Well?"

"I have some of the documents you wanted, but one of the

men we used was sloppy and got caught," Ray told her too nonchalantly. Louise thought he should be more upset.

"So now they know we're looking for the information?" Louise demanded.

"No, he didn't know who was paying him. He also was instructed to take more documents than just the ones we needed. It won't get traced back to us."

"And the others that will be looking for the Key?"

"So far we are the only ones who know who she is. Well, maybe one other person." Louise knew who that one person could be, and she didn't like it. She wanted to be the one in control of the Key.

"Where are the documents?" Louise inquired.

"I'm having them translated. It will take a while."

"Why?"

"Several different ancient dialects and some of them are extinct," Ray explained. "It's going to take some time. I have an expert working on it."

"Is that wise? What if he leaks the information?" she asked.

Ray laughed. "I have him sequestered and I'll take care of him after he serves his purpose."

"Good. Make sure all the loose ends are taken care of." Louise left Ray lounging on her sofa.

She walked out of the room to get away from him. She didn't like being in the same room with him, but for now he was a necessary evil.

She would have to get rid of him as well.

A few days later, there was a knock on Kate's front door and Robert got up to answer it. He came back into the room with Cindy, Kate's best female friend and work colleague. Cindy was smiling and had a bounce in her step. "Hey guys! How are you?"

Ryan choked on his drink and fidgeted in his seat. He managed to mumble a quick hello. Kate loved seeing Ryan get this way around Cindy. She suspected he'd had a little crush on her friend for a while now.

The first time Ryan met Cindy had been a little before school started, and Cindy had just gotten back from vacation with her boyfriend, Mike. They had been in Florida for a few weeks. She had decided to stop by and surprise Kate and the kids, and did her best to sneak up on them in the backyard.

Just when Cindy was about to jump out at them, Ryan, thinking she was someone working for Brooks, sneaked up on her and attempted to detain her. He was just about to grab her when he found himself flat on his back and Cindy kneeling on his chest. She had flipped him over her shoulder and knocked the wind out of him. Ryan hadn't expected tall, skinny, gorgeous Cindy to be a black belt who competed nationally. He had looked up at her with awe after that and then in embarrassment as the kids cracked up, laughing at both him and the situation. He'd been a mess around her since.

Kate jumped up and gave her friend a big hug. "Hey. What are you doing here?"

"I wanted to make sure you're still good to go for Friday night?"

Ryan found his voice finally. "What's going on Friday night?"

Cindy turned to him with a huge smile. "Girls' night."

"What do you mean girl's night? Why wasn't I invited?" Ryan whined.

"Oh, so you're a girl now?" Cindy asked.

"That's not what I meant. I was just saying that it wouldn't be a party without me there," Ryan finished lamely.

"Dude, just stop. You're sounding really pathetic," Robert teased. Ryan shot him a dirty look.

Kate interrupted any further comments. "We have a bachelorette party Friday night and no men are invited. Well, no men that we know anyway," she said, with a big grin.

"Hey, wait a minute now," Robert started. "What about the kids? What about us?"

Kate laughed. "Zach and Alex are having a sleepover at the neighbors', and Maddy is staying at her friend Jodi's house. Jodi's mom asked for a playdate for Maddy and since the girls are inseparable at daycare, I figured it would be nice." Kate paused. "You boys are on your own."

Both guys were looking at her like she had ten heads. "But . . ." Robert started.

"There are no 'buts.' I haven't had a night out in months and we're going to have a fun night. ALONE."

"Yeah guys, relax. It's just one girls' night," Cindy told them. She pulled Kate into the front of the house and away from the complaining guys. "What is up with them? Are you dating Robert and didn't tell me?"

"No! Why would you even ask me that?" Kate returned.

"Well, they're here every day and Robert just freaked out about you going out. OMG, he likes you doesn't he?"

"There is nothing going on with us and no, he doesn't like me," Kate told her. "I told you this already, Cin. They promised the kids' uncle that they would keep an eye on the kids and help me out in any way they could. They take their promises very seriously."

"I'll say. I still think it's a little weird."

"You think Ryan is a little weird?"

"No. He's not weird." Cindy said quickly, and then thought about it. After a pause, she asked Kate. "Is he weird?"

Kate smiled. If Cindy didn't have a boyfriend, she could see sparks between the two of them. "No, he's not weird at all. Actually, of all the guys, he has the best sense of humor and is the least arrogant."

"He does seem to make me smile a lot when I see him."

"Mmmm, and he's not that bad looking either," Kate added.

"What do you mean not that bad looking? Have you looked into those hazel eyes? The guy is hot."

"Really? I hadn't noticed," Kate told her with a smirk.

"I never told you that the guy wasn't hot. He's totally hot and has a smoking bod, but I have Mike and he's dreamy."

"And is Mr. Dreamy still thinking about moving to Florida?"

Cindy sighed. "He is, but I think that it's all talk. It's hard to find good teaching jobs so the chances of him moving are slim."

"Would you want to move with him?"

"No way. I love it here. You're here, my family's here, and I love my teaching job. I'm not moving."

Kate wondered if Cindy was fooling herself into thinking Mike would stay around here for her.

Cindy bounced a little on the balls of her feet. "Okay, I have to run. I just wanted to stop by to make sure you had the kid situation under control and that you're not going to back out tomorrow night."

"Kid situation is completely under control and I'm definitely going tomorrow night. I can't wait," Kate told her. She was really looking forward to a night out by herself with her friends. Cindy hugged her good-bye, called a "bye" to the guys, and left.

Kate walked back to the family room to face two pouting men.

"Are you seriously going out tomorrow night?" Robert asked her.

"Yes, Rob. I am seriously going out." Kate was readying herself for the fight she knew they would put up. That was part of the reason she had waited until the last minute to tell them.

"You don't think that's dangerous?" Ryan chimed in.

"We're going in a group of about ten of us and we're renting one of those SUV limos. How much safer can you get?"

"Anyone can snatch you in one of those clubs and none of those girls could do a thing about it," Robert challenged.

"Nothing is going to happen. No one is going to come looking for me in a club with a bunch of young women who are having fun. We're going to drink a few cocktails, dance, and have a good time."

"What about the kids?" Robert asked.

Kate put her hands on her hips. "What about them?"

"Do you really think they'll be safe?"

"Are you kidding? Alex and Zach sleep over the neighbors' at least once a week, and Eric and Emily stay over here just as much."

"I wasn't talking about them. What about Maddy?"

Kate laughed. "You're asking if she'll be safe at the chief of police's house? Really, guys?"

"He could be corrupt," Ryan challenged.

"The man volunteers to coach just about every youth sport around, his wife's a kindergarten teacher, and his brother is a minister. Anything else?"

"I don't like it," Ryan complained. "Do you know how many guys are going to be hitting on you and Cindy?"

"That is part of the point," Kate told him.

"What about Nick?" Ryan countered. "You're going to flirt

with some random guy when you have Nick?"

Kate got fire in her eyes. "What about him? He's gone. He's been gone for months and even before he left, he made it quite clear that there wasn't going to be anything between us."

Kate scooped up Maddy and headed upstairs to give her a bath.

"Nice going, moron." Robert turned to give Ryan a look.

"What?" Ryan gave Robert a look right back.

"She's been upset about him enough lately. You didn't have to bring him up."

"I can't believe he's been gone this long," Ryan said, shaking his head. "He needs to get back here."

"Agreed. But he won't until he finds Brooks and takes him out."

"I don't see why Nick is so hell-bent on finding the guy. Brooks doesn't have nearly the power that he once had. When Brooks didn't get the kids last summer, his empire fell apart. He lost too many of his men and he went into hiding. Besides, we've handled everyone else who has come along."

"Don't underestimate the guy. He is ruthless and corrupt and power hungry. He also has an end game that we haven't figured out yet," Robert told him.

"I guess. So, what are we going to do about tomorrow night?" Ryan asked.

"Nothing. What can we do? Kate needs to have a little fun. She's been miserable and misses Nick. She needs to have a good time with her friends."

"We're just going to let her go out alone and unprotected?" Ryan was getting worked up.

Robert smiled slyly. "I didn't say she was going unprotected."

"What's your plan?"

"You'll see tomorrow night," Robert told him.

Char Webster

Chapter Three

Frank was packing a bag when Bret walked into his room. "Hey, Kid," Frank said, using his permanent nickname for Bret.

At fourteen, Bret was still very much a kid, but he had grown up pretty quickly. He'd been on the run from an abusive home and then had to survive the constant torment from Brooks. When Bret helped Frank rescue his daughter from Brooks, Frank decided to repay the favor by helping Bret escape his tormentor.

"You're leaving again?" Bret asked.

"Yeah, and you're going to watch out for Kali," Frank told him.

"I know, or you'll kill me." Bret repeated the threat he had heard a hundred times since Frank saved him. Bret didn't doubt that the big man with bulging muscles and tattoos down each arm would in fact kill him. Frank had probably killed many others in the past. He'd worked for Brooks and did anything the evil man had wanted him to do, no matter what.

Bret also knew that Frank liked him so the threat was only halfhearted.

Bret wasn't worried because he liked Frank's daughter Kali and would do anything to protect the nine-year-old girl. He was even beginning to think of her as a sister. Bret had thought of another girl, Emma, as his sister, but he hadn't been able to save her. Emma had been taken away by Brooks' wife, Louise, before Bret had made the deal with Frank for his freedom. He was still worried about her and hoped that one day he would be able to help her.

"I'll be gone a couple of days," Frank told him, stuffing clothes into his duffle bag. "I got a good lead this time on where Brooks may be hiding."

"Does he know you're after him?" Bret asked. Brooks was not one to hide.

"Yeah, he knows. Why do you think he's hiding?" Frank told him. "I won't stop until he's dead." Frank owed him for a lot more than just Kali; Brooks had killed his girlfriend, Melissa, when he snatched Kali. It was still painful to think about Melissa.

Frank zipped his bag and went in search of his daughter to kiss her good-bye. He had never wanted her to be raised in his world. Before this summer, Kali had not known anything about Frank's business. He wished she still didn't know.

Kali was asleep in her bed so Frank just kissed her on the forehead. He gently brushed her hair out of her face. He would do anything for his daughter, and he intended to. He would make sure that no one ever hurt her again. With one last look, he turned and walked out of her room and out of the house.

Kate had just finished her last student meeting for the day and was completing the endless paperwork required to document each appointment, when there was a knock on her doorframe. Kate always had her door open unless she was meeting privately with a student or parent. She wanted students to feel welcome to talk to her at any time.

Dawn Johnson popped her head into Kate's office and said, "Hi, Kate. I hope I'm not bothering you."

Kate stood up and gave Dawn a hug. "It's so good to see you, Dawn. You're never a bother. Please, let's sit down and talk." Kate led Dawn over to the chairs in front of her desk.

Dawn pulled a stack of papers out of her shoulder bag and placed them on the desk. "I brought the final adoption papers for you to sign." Dawn, the head of the local Family Services division, had originally brought Kate in to help Alex, Zach, and Maddy when they were struggling in the foster care system. Dawn was also the person who had originally discovered that the kids were in danger. Kate owed Dawn a lot for all of her help over the last few months.

"You didn't have to bring them here. I would have come to your office," Kate told her.

"It's no trouble. I wanted to watch Kevin's cross country meet," Dawn told her. "How are the kids doing? Are they excited about this? They won't have to worry about being bounced around again in the foster care system."

"They're very excited, and my parents are thrilled to have more kids to spoil." Kate smiled happily, thinking about her parents when they had met the kids for the first time—they had loved them immediately.

"Kate, I'm really glad that the kids have you. I was skeptical in the beginning because you're so young, but after everything that's happened, I know that you're the perfect person for them," Dawn told her. "That reminds me, I added you to the official consultant list for the agency."

"That's great," Kate told her. "I'm always here to help."

Dawn nodded and changed the subject, wondering about the kids' uncle. "Have you seen Nick?" Dawn knew that Kate and the kids missed him deeply. They had mentioned him a few times during her recent visits.

"He calls and sends text messages, but he hasn't been back," Kate told her. "He travels a lot for work, which was the major reason behind him allowing me to adopt the kids." Kate couldn't tell her that they were still in danger and that Nick was trying to find the man behind it all. Dawn had been through so much when the kids were kidnapped that she didn't need to be dragged into their problems any more than necessary.

Kate signed the papers in front of her and handed Dawn her copies. She was watching Dawn and noticed that the other woman looked troubled. Kate reached out with her gift and knew that Dawn was stressed and worried.

"What's wrong, Dawn?" Kate asked. "You seem upset. What's worrying you?"

Dawn smiled. "I don't know how you do that, but you always know exactly what I'm feeling."

Kate also opened up her other gift. Everyone in her race could read minds, but only what was being thought that moment. Kate didn't like to invade other people's privacy, so she usually kept that gift turned off. She didn't have to worry about it with the guys since they usually blocked mind reading and other such things.

"It's my job," Kate told her vaguely. *It's also my gift,* she thought.

She read in Dawn's mind that she wanted to talk to Kate about the weird things that had happened. Dawn also wanted to discuss some research, but didn't know how to bring it up. The thing that was bothering her the most was that she didn't know if she really wanted to find out.

Kate took a breath and then said, "Dawn, you can talk to me about anything. I'll always be here to listen to you. With that being said, there are some things that are better for you not to know, for your safety and for Kevin's. I never want anything to happen to either of you."

"Do you think that's a possibility?" Dawn asked.

"No, I don't," Kate told her. "But it's still better to be cautious."

"I understand, and thanks," Dawn told her. She pulled out a file and handed it to Kate. "Here, take this. It's more information from the research I was conducting during the summer. I dug a little deeper and ended up with more questions than answers, but maybe it'll make sense to you."

"Thank you. I really appreciate your help."

"One more thing. When everything was happening over the summer, a Detective Martin was investigating the crimes that were related to the kidnapping. He doesn't know anything, but he's suspicious and isn't stupid. I thought he was on to something else and wasn't worried about what had happened, but he stopped by yesterday to see how things were. Just be careful," Dawn told her. She got up and walked to the door. "Talk to you soon, Kate."

"Bye," Kate murmured, but she was already wondering if they should be worried about this detective. She tucked the file into her backpack to take home. She would worry about it later.

Tonight, she was going to have a good time.

He didn't care what Brooks had said, he was going to have some fun with Kate. Watching her did not amuse him any longer. He waited for her in the woods behind the school as she walked out alone. Kate always backed into a parking spot in the last row right up against the tree line.

The students had already left and the parking lot was clearing out. It would only be a couple of steps to reach her car and grab her.

He gripped the knife in his hand tighter in anticipation. She was nearing her car, only a row away. He crouched low, creeping closer.

He watched her shift her backpack higher up on her shoulder. She was not paying any attention to her surroundings, making her easy prey. Kate reached the front of her car and he was about to jump out at her, but a voice interrupted his plans.

"Kate, wait for a sec," a man called out to her. She stopped and turned toward the man approaching her.

"Hi, Ted. Everything okay? "Kate asked him.

"Yes, I just wanted to give you a heads-up about a situation with a student." Kate walked over to him and they began to have a discussion.

Damn, he thought. *Now I wouldn't be able to have my fun tonight.* He slowly made his way back to the woods and away from Kate.

Chancellor Pete was sitting in his office waiting for his men to arrive with their report. The Association headquarters for the eastern half of the United States moved around every few years to make sure no one knew exactly where it was located. Their group always picked large estates in scenic locations, where they could enhance security and keep out of the view of most people in that area. The current headquarters was in Shamong, New Jersey, in the middle of the Pine Barrens. There were trees as far as the eye could see. The Association had to pay an exorbitant amount to the electric company to have them run power lines to the estate, since it was more than a mile and a half away from the end of the electric wires.

The Chancellor looked at the trees he had cut back away from the house for about three hundred yards in each direction so he could see anyone approaching. He had a few other buildings constructed on the grounds but they were separated from the main estate. His security crew demanded that the landscaping be kept to a minimum, but he wanted it to look manicured.

Pete got up to look out at the lawns and shook his head. It was very late, but the grounds were illuminated with so many lights it appeared to be daylight. He had truckloads of rich top soil brought in, but the grass never did well. Even with the sprinklers working overtime, the grass had never been very green.

He wasn't used to having to wait for anything, but this was too important for anyone to rush. The Chancellor paced his office, which was decorated in rich, dark green colors that fit in well with the pine trees in the area. He wanted the furnishings to match the surroundings so he used light, knotty wood for the desk and wall units. Pete liked to reinvent the headquarters each time it moved.

He stopped in front of the mirror on one of the walls. *I am getting old*, he thought, looking at the grey hair that took up more space than the reddish-brown he had even just a few years before. At fifty-eight, Pete was still physically fit. He cared about his appearance and always took the time to exercise and eat well. He usually thought he looked at least ten years younger than his actual age. *Maybe it is time to start dyeing my hair,* he thought.

A knock had him striding toward the door to open it right away. He needed to know what these men had found out.

"Well, Don?" he asked immediately. Two men strolled in and took seats in front of Pete's desk. Both were tall with dark hair and dark eyes. Neither were particularly attractive, but were not ugly, either. They were the type of people to blend in with the crowd and not be noticed—perfect for the assignments that Pete usually gave them.

"We caught one of the thieves that broke into the library archives in New York City. He was on the train to Boston when he was caught. Although we didn't find the documents and scrolls when we picked him up, we know where they're headed," Don told him.

"You didn't retrieve the documents?" Pete slammed his fist against the desk.

"There are several of our team members who should be zeroing in on their location as we speak." The second man, Harry, looked down at his watch and nodded.

"We need to get those documents back," Pete reminded them.

"We know that, sir," Don told him. "The thief was not aware of who had employed him to take the documents, just that he would be paid a huge amount to steal them and then drop them off at a specific location."

"That's it? He didn't know anything else?" Pete asked, irritated.

"Actually, he did have another piece of information," Harry said. "He claims to have heard that another Key has arrived and that the documents were needed to assist the Key."

"Damn it." Pete stood up. "Why weren't we aware of this?"

"We're looking for the Key but we aren't sure who it is."

"You better figure it out soon. We cannot allow the Key to fall into the wrong hands."

Pete paused, lost in thought for a second. He then remembered the other matter he needed to discuss with his men. "Have you learned anything else about the girl? Is she the same girl Nick called me about over the summer?"

"Yes, we're pretty sure that the girl Nick called you about and the one Samantha saw with Robert are the same person. They're together all the time, but we don't think they're married as Samantha claimed."

The second man rubbed his arm and said, "We've been following her and so far there's been nothing out of the ordinary."

Pete frowned. "She hasn't shown any unusual or remarkably strong gift?"

"We're not even sure what her gift is," Don said. "She hasn't revealed anything at all."

She must be hiding her gift, he thought. Pete could understand that. "We need to find out what she's hiding, so please continue to monitor her. Thank you for the information."

The men left his office and Pete walked back to the window. She had to be hiding something. Pete knew that she would have a very prominent gift. The children born of two Gifted parents had unbelievably enhanced gifts; he knew that firsthand. She had a strong gift, and it must be incredibly robust for her to want to hide it. He needed to find out more about her.

Pete walked back to his desk, picked up the phone and dialed a number that he had not wanted to call but was forced to.

It only rang twice before a deep masculine voice answered. "Yes?"

Pete hesitated. "You're correct, there is another Key."

"Excellent. I want her immediately."

Pete took in a deep breath. "I don't know who it is. I'm working on it."

"I don't have to remind you what will happen to you and your position if you fail."

"I'll get you the information as soon as I have it," Pete told him.

"It had better be done quickly." The man hung up and Pete stared at the phone for a moment before he replaced it. He needed to get things together, or he would lose everything.

Kate was flipping through the clothes in her closet, looking for something cute to wear for her night with the girls. It had been ages since she dressed up for a night out. Alex and Emily were flopped down on her bed, keeping her company while she was getting ready. They were having a "girls' moment," as Alex put it. They were also nixing all of her clothing choices.

"Kate, you're not an old lady yet," Alex told her.

"Great. Thanks, Lex. I really appreciate the confidence you're instilling right before I have to go out."

Alex laughed and said, "I didn't mean it like that. You just need to dress young and not like someone old."

"Still not helping," Kate told her.

Alex jumped off the bed and said, "Let me look." She began to rummage through Kate's closet, and pulled out a few different things.

She handed Kate a short, black miniskirt. "Here. This is really cute. You just need a hot top to go with it."

Emily joined Alex in the closet. She handed Kate a bright pink and black patterned top that had two layers crisscrossing each other to create a deep "V" in the front.

Kate just looked at the clothes in her hands, but made no move to put them on.

Alex came up behind her and pushed her lightly toward the bathroom. "Go try them on."

Kate reluctantly went to try on the clothes. She came out of the bathroom and both girls squealed. "You look awesome!" Alex told her.

"Really awesome," Emily agreed.

Kate looked in the mirror. She agreed that the skirt fit her perfectly, accentuating her legs. The top looked great, but Kate wasn't thrilled with how far down the "V" went. "I think I need a cami under this." She ran to the drawer and pulled out a hot pink one that matched the top perfectly. She then slipped into the bathroom to put her outfit all together.

Kate was smiling when she came out of the bathroom. Alex ran up and hugged her. "We did a great job." she said, then handed Kate a really cute pair of high heels.

"Yes, you did," Kate admitted, accepting the shoes and slipping them on her feet. She walked over to the mirror and looked at the whole outfit. It looked good.

Now she just had to fix her hair and add a bit of makeup. Kate normally didn't wear much, but tonight, she would add a little eyeliner, mascara, and lip gloss. She usually just let her hair curl the way it wanted to around her shoulders, but for girls' night, Kate wanted it to lay just right in soft curls.

Twenty minutes later Kate and the girls walked to the family room to wait for the limo.

"We're going to go over Em's now. Have fun. See you tomorrow, Kate," Alex told her as she gave her a hug, then both girls ran out the back door.

Kate was surprised that she didn't see any of the guys. She had thought they would stop by before she had to go, but they must have been pouting because she wouldn't let them tag along. She half expected them to try something to dissuade her from going.

A car horn blew from out front of her house. She grabbed a light jacket and her purse, and headed out the door. She was the fourth one to be picked up. Cindy popped her head out of the moonroof and yelled, "Wooooo! Come on girl, get in here." Kate laughed and slid in.

Half an hour later, all of the ladies were filing out of the limo and into the Roof Top Club, which was a bar on top of one of the tallest buildings in Philadelphia. It had a restaurant, dance floor, and lounge. It was also the hottest place around at the moment.

The ladies went right to the bar area that bordered the dance floor and took seats at the reserved tables. They had called ahead, and the bar staff was thrilled to be having their bachelorette party there. Kate was happy to see that the staff had put up some wedding decorations and banners to make the area festive.

Kate loved the atmosphere. Everyone around her was giving off happy and excited vibes. A few people were giving off slightly naughty emotions, but she tried to ignore those.

Someone in the group had brought all the girls plastic tiaras to wear and Kate had very nonchalantly left hers on the table. She had worked too hard to get her hair just right tonight to mess it up with a plastic crown.

After a round of pink fruity shots in what looked like test tubes, they all headed to the dance floor. The lights flashed and sparkled off of reflective surfaces, making them look like they were pulsating to the beat of the music. One member of the group, a shy girl named Jill, was watching Rachel, the bride-to-be, with unmasked envy as admirers adored Rachel and tried to get her attention. The first beats to Major Lazer & DJ Snake's "Lean On" started to play and several of the girls in their group squealed. Kate was glad that they were not playing techno. She just couldn't get into that.

The tall blonde girl in the group, Jamie, grabbed Kate's hand and pulled her closer to three sexy males who had moved closer to their group. Kate laughed because Jamie was always flirting with someone. It didn't take much encouragement for the men to start dancing with them. Kate was surprised that one of the guys was actually a really good dancer, and admired the way he shook his hips. When he moved closer to her she decided to dance away slowly, and ventured to the other side of the floor closer to Cindy.

Kate got tired of dancing after a few more songs and trying to yell to her friends over the loud music, so she made her way back to the reserved tables. She grabbed her glass of ice water and sipped it slowly, then flopped down onto the nearest stool and watched the rest of her group circling around a few more guys who happened to join them. The girls were having a great time and Rachel was cracking her up. She had on a shirt that said, "Sign Me I'm the Bride-to-Be," complete with Sharpies dangling from colorful strips hanging from the bottom. All the men in the place wanted to sign the shirt.

"Why aren't you dancing with your friends?" a voice asked from behind her. Kate turned to see a man with closely clipped dark hair. His eyes were so dark that they nearly blended in with his pupils. He took the seat next to her at the table. She instantly stiffened because she couldn't feel anything from him. No emotion at all. She concentrated more, but still nothing. He was obviously Gifted. Did he know who she was and had come for her, or was it a coincidence?

"I was just heading back there now," Kate fibbed, and stood up to walk away. "Just wanted to grab my crown." She picked up the plastic tiara and turned away, but he grabbed her arm and said, "What's your hurry? Have a drink with me."

She was instantly terrified. Goosebumps broke out all over. *Is this man going to drag me out of here?* She tried twice to pull out of his grasp, and the second time worked. "Not tonight. It's girls' night." He tried to grab her again but she backed away in time for his hand to come up empty. *If he follows, I am going to scream for help.*

She rushed over to the rest of the girls and decided that she wasn't going to move from the group again. Now she wished that the guys were here.

A girl Kate didn't know meandered over to where she was on the dance floor. She stood about as tall as Kate, but was more muscular—she looked like she worked out, a lot. Kate noticed that her light brown curly hair was pulled up away from her face, and that she had very familiar looking green eyes.

She smiled at Kate and said, "I don't know who that is, but I'm going to have my brother check him out."

Kate gave the girl a long look and laughed. "You're Jason's sister, Jennifer, aren't you?" Kate shook her head, not sure if she should be mad or not. "I knew those guys wouldn't give me one night to myself."

"Hi, Kate. Yes, I'm Jen. Don't be mad. They were just worried and don't want anything to happen to you."

"Yeah, I know, and I should have guessed they would have someone here. I'm just glad it wasn't one of them." Kate was going to have a little chat with them about boundaries.

"They must be pretty desperate because they would never have brought me in on this."

"Why do you say that?"

"They were afraid we'd have too much fun without them," Jen said with a laugh. "Jason told me on more than one occasion that I can always find trouble no matter where I go."

"And they had you keep an eye out for me?"

"I can always take care of the trouble, as well. My gift comes in handy," Jen bragged, and then clarified at Kate's confused look. "I can make a person's muscles freeze up and cramp. Just one little touch and they howl in pain. It works great in a fight." Both of them shared a grin.

"Can you give the guys a little bit of a zap when we get home?" Kate asked mischievously.

"I knew I was going to like you!" Jen exclaimed. "I would love to do that."

Kate looked over toward the tables. The man who came up to her was still there, but had moved closer to the bar. Jen followed her gaze and asked, "Did he tell you his name?"

"No, but I know he's Gifted because he's blocking my ability. I can't feel any emotions coming from him," Kate told her.

"I'm going to ask him to dance," Jen said with a wicked grin. Before Kate could stop her, Jen walked right up to him and pulled him onto the dance floor.

Kate laughed. The girl was completely fearless. Kate wasn't really dancing with her friends, but swaying to the music while watching Jen and the mystery man dance on the other side of the floor. Even though she just met her, Kate felt like she knew Jen from all of the stories Jason had shared, and she didn't want anything to happen to her.

After the song was over, the man stormed off the floor rubbing his arm. Jen bounced back over with a grin on her face. "I don't know why he stalked off. All I did was give him a slight arm cramp when he tried to grab me," Jen said with faked innocence.

That worried Kate. "He tried to grab you?" Kate asked, panicked.

"Don't worry. His name is Don and he was just fishing for information. He works for the Association and was trying to find out a little bit about you because you're the newest mystery. I sent him back home."

"Why would they try to find out information about me?" Kate asked, concerned.

"I'm sure it's nothing. They're just curious about you," Jen told her. "Don't worry. They won't do anything unless you mess with them."

Cindy chose that moment to walk up and Kate smiled at her friend. "Cindy, this is Jason's sister, Jen."

"Oh my!" Cindy exclaimed. "I'm so glad to meet you. I love your brother."

"You do?" Jen teased. "No one likes Jay."

Cindy laughed. "It's quite a coincidence that you're here tonight, too."

Jen laughed and said, "Not really. It's the only place to go in the city right now. I'm just glad you guys are here. My friends ditched me." Jen had her cover story all ready.

"That stinks. You can hang with us," Cindy offered, and after that Jen was just another member of their group. They all danced with her and welcomed her into their circle. Rachel and Jen began to do the same goofy moves, which caused everyone to laugh and try to copy them.

They ventured back to the table for their next round of shots and drinks. There was a tray of purple test tubes waiting this time. Kate raised her purple shot and offered up a toast. "To good times, great friends, strong drinks and hot men. May this night be all about fun! Rach, we love you!"

When Kate followed the group back to the dance floor, she was suddenly assaulted by dark, menacing feelings. Looking around, Kate tried to find the source of these feelings but didn't see anyone out of the ordinary. She couldn't tell where the emotions were coming from.

It was almost impossible to have a good time with someone lurking. Kate spent the rest of the night looking around, waiting for someone else to approach her. She was glad Jen was around, but by the time they all called it a night, she was more than ready to go home.

Jen jumped into the limo with everyone and went back to Kate's house with her. "I'm going to go crash at Jason's house, so I don't have to go back to my place in the city tonight."

"You can stay in my spare bedroom if you want. I wouldn't want to stay at their house. My place is at least clean. I'm not sure when their cleaning service comes and they probably don't have any food there either since they're always eating at my house."

"I'm sold. It would be way better to stay here anyway. I wasn't looking forward to staying with the guys."

"Great!" Kate told her. They walked upstairs to change and then ventured back downstairs to chat. Kate opened a bottle of wine and both ladies sat in the family room relaxing after a fun but slightly stressful night out.

"Thanks again for letting me stay here. I really didn't feel like dealing with Jay and the guys all night. They still think I'm a little kid trying to tag along with them," Jen told her.

"They seem to think all females need them to swoop in and save them from something," Kate countered.

"I'm still shocked that they asked for my help today. It doesn't hurt that they know I can hold my own in a fight with any of them—and that's without my gift."

Kate laughed. "Can you really?"

"Yes. You try growing up with a brother and all male cousins. You learn to take care of yourself really quick."

"I would've loved that. I was adopted so I grew up an only child."

"Not having to share anything, especially a bathroom, and not getting picked on every five minutes sounds heavenly." Jen sighed at the thought.

"You mentioned that you live in Philly. Are you in school or do you work?" Kate asked as she sipped her wine. She wanted to get to know her new friend.

"I'm only twenty-two, but I graduated two years ago from Villanova and have been working in the city ever since. I own my own gym designed for women and I teach self-defense classes there. I could teach you a few things if you would like to learn."

"Absolutely! I would love to learn." Cindy had been bugging her for a year to learn some self-defense but Kate never had time. She was always too busy with work and after-school clients. She wished she had taken Cindy more seriously in the past, because it would have come in handy with everything that had happened.

"I can't wait to start." Kate was just getting excited by the idea when her back door opened. She raised her eyebrows at the two men who walked into her house. *I really need to start locking my doors more often . . . but they would probably break right in.*

Jason stopped short and Robert almost ran into him. "What are you doing here?" Jason demanded of his sister.

"Nice to see you too, Jay," Jen replied back.

"What are you two doing here? It's after midnight." Kate blew out a breath. She loved these guys, but their overprotective bit was getting really old.

Jason continued forward and stood before his sister. "Jen?"

"Jason, Jen is my guest and if you can't be nice, you'll have to come back later."

"ME? You're going to kick me out? I can't believe it. You would tell me to go and let her stay?"

"Dude, what are you, twelve?" Robert teased and sat down next to Jen, taking the wine glass from her. Jen snatched it back.

"Why does everyone keep asking me if I'm twelve?" Jason mumbled. Jen cracked up laughing.

"Is there a reason you guys are here?" Kate asked.

Jason sat down across from them on the chair next to the fireplace. "We got a text from Jen about the dude at the bar. We wanted to make sure you were okay."

"And I specifically told you that I took care of him and everything was fine. I texted you with his name so you could check him out."

"You were supposed to watch out for her, not hang out with her!" Jason scolded.

Kate stood up and faced Jason. "You don't get to dictate who I hang out with. If you didn't want us to be friends, you shouldn't have gotten her to play babysitter tonight." Kate was just getting started. "And don't think for one second that you're off the hook for that."

"Kate, if Jen hadn't been there, you could've been in real trouble," Robert told her. "That guy could've been dangerous and we could be out looking for you right now."

"Yeah, and Kate wouldn't be mad at us right now if you hadn't opened your big mouth and told her," Jason grumbled at his sister.

"Jason, if I didn't love you dearly, I would clobber you right now," Kate told him. "If you guys would actually tell me the truth about what's going on all the time and not try to hide things from me, situations like this wouldn't happen. That has to stop now."

"Robert, tell her that it's not a good idea to hang out with Jen."

"Why can't I hang out with Kate? Jay, you're just jealous that she may like me better," Jen teased.

"Because you get into ten times the amount of trouble a normal person does and you and Kate together would be just dangerous," Jason countered.

Both ladies got huge grins, and that was it. Their friendship was sealed. Kate went to sit on the love seat with her glass of wine.

"Great way to ensure they remain best friends forever, Jay," Robert griped. He snatched Jen's wine glass again and drained it, then handed the empty glass back with a grin.

She didn't take it back but pointed to the bottle of wine on the counter. "You can go pour me another glass."

"If I'm getting up it's to get myself another glass," Robert told her.

"That's fine with me. Take the glass." Jen had a gleam in her eye.

Robert went over to the wine bottle and poured some into his stolen glass. He settled down next to her again and turned to Kate. Just as he was about to say something, Jen grabbed the glass with a grin. "Thanks!" she told him.

She scooted away from him so the glass was out of range. He followed her and moved closer again. She was in the corner of the couch, so she couldn't move away from him any more. He sat up against her and grabbed the glass right back.

Kate watched the two of them fighting over the wine glass and shook her head. She got up to get two more glasses and another bottle of wine. Robert and Jason looked like they were going to stay for a while.

"If you get wine on my couch, I'll clobber you both."

Robert jumped up and yelled, "AWWWW! Damn it, Jen. Did you have to do that?" He began massaging his thigh muscle.

Kate had to turn away because she was laughing so hard. Jen just beamed, completely satisfied with herself.

Robert was still rubbing his leg and said, "That's just mean. It's going to hurt for the next hour."

Jen shook her head and stood up to walk over to Robert. He backed away from her. "Stay where you are. You're not going to do that to me again."

"Stay still, you big baby," Jen told him, cornering him against the coffee table. She reached out and he yelled, "Kate! Make her stop."

Kate and Jason were both laughing at the scene, and were not any help.

"Really Rob, just stop moving. I'm going to help you." Jen put her hand on his leg. He tried to jerk away but ended up sitting on the coffee table. Jen concentrated and used her gift to take the leg cramp away. She stood up and smirked at him. "I wasn't going to let you suffer with it." She mouthed to Kate, *for too long*.

Jason turned to Kate, "See what I mean? She's just trouble."

Kate rubbed the tears out of her eyes from laughing so hard and told him, "I told her she should zap all of you."

"WHAT? You're just mean, too. You really do deserve each other," Jason pouted.

The two ladies sat on the love seat together with a smile.

Robert went to the kitchen to fix himself something else. He was done fighting with Jen over the wine. He wanted his new drink, anyway. After pulling a few things out of the cabinets, he walked back into the room with a smug grin.

Kate looked over at him. "What is that?"

"My new signature drink." He held up the glass and swirled the contents. "Apple Whiskey Ale."

Kate shook her head. "Is that the concoction you were telling me about?"

"Yes. It's good. You all should try it," he told her and then explained to Jason and Jen, "It's apple cider whiskey and ginger ale." Robert handed her the glass and Kate took a sip. She was surprised that it tasted so good.

Robert grinned at her. "See, I knew you would like it. I always make great beverages. Now give it back."

She made a face, but handed him back the glass. "Are you going to drink that all the time now?" Kate asked.

"Of course."

If Brooks could kill someone through the phone, John would be dead at the moment.

"What the hell do you mean you almost had her?"

John began to stutter. "Umm. I thought that if I brought her in, it would save time and I wouldn't have to lie on the roof watching her."

Brooks was screaming, a vein in his neck was pulsating, and his face was bright red. "I TOLD YOU TO JUST WATCH HER. IF I WANTED HER, I WOULD HAVE TOLD YOU TO BRING HER TO ME."

"I thought…"

"I DON'T PAY YOU TO THINK! If you disobey me one more time, I WILL KILL YOU." Brooks banged down the phone and began to pace the room. John had almost screwed up his plans.

Chapter Four

Nick slammed the door of his SUV much harder than he had intended. Once again, Brooks was not at one of his houses. This particular place was not listed on any of the Association files or government records. He had gotten the information from a very reliable source.

It looked as if he had just missed Brooks. There had been dirty dishes in the sink and warm coffee still in the pot. Brooks kept slipping past him. Nick was starting to wonder if there was a spy tipping Brooks off to Nick's location.

He entered yet another hotel room in another city. He was getting tired of constantly moving on to the next place. He wanted to be home.

He needed to talk to Kate, hear her voice, and for a moment pretend things were different. That was what he wanted, but he chickened out and decided to send her another text. After a few different drafts he settled on, *I wish we were sitting on your front porch together, with my arm around you, and two cups of coffee to keep us warm. We would be watching the sun rise and talking about everything and nothing.*

He was shocked when his phone beeped less than a minute later. *I gave up on the front porch months ago.* His heart broke a little bit when he read it. He wrote back, *Don't give up on me.*

She didn't respond.

Monday morning Kate and Cindy were sitting together at the small conference table in the corner of Kate's office, sharing a prep period coffee break.

"This week is going to go so slowly," Cindy complained. "It's always that way when I'm counting down days until a break." She sighed and continued, "Ten more work days and we won't have to go back to work for another ten days."

"I cannot believe it's almost fall break," Kate agreed. "I'm so glad we have an entire week off from school. I'm looking forward to relaxing a bit."

"Oh, don't say that," Cindy laughed. "Remember you said

that last summer and you ended up a mom to three kids."

Kate smiled. "I don't think we have anything to worry about this time."

"You never know," Cindy teased. "Don't answer the phone if anyone calls asking you to help out any kids."

"I promise. No more kids." Kate hoped she was being honest, but if she had the opportunity to help any of the other kids that Brooks had kidnapped, she would in a second. "What are your plans for the break?"

"Mike and I are going to Saint Michael's in Maryland. It's beautiful any time you go, but we're hoping some of the fall leaves will still be around." She was thinking about the incredible time she would be having with her boyfriend.

"That sounds wonderful," Kate told her. "Very romantic."

Cindy took a deep breath and looked at her friend. "When are you going to start dating? It's been a long time since you have even been on a date. It's not good to be by yourself all the time."

"I'm never by myself. I have the kids or the guys around me all the time," Kate told her.

"That's not what I mean and you know it. You need someone in your life that will make you melt. Someone who will make you tingle just thinking about him. A guy who makes your heart pound without even touching you," Cindy told her.

Kate wanted to tell her friend so badly that she had someone like that in her life this summer and that he walked away. *He left me with a heart that feels as if it will never be whole again.* She couldn't tell her because she had been keeping Cindy out of her crazy world. She didn't want to drag Cindy through all of the drama and danger that surrounded her and the kids. Kate never told her about the kidnapping or that she belonged to a different race of people who have gifts. She wanted to protect her friend and keep her as far away from it all as possible.

Kate knew she had to say something to Cindy, so she simply said, "If someone like that comes into my life, I'll let you know." Kate silently amended, *comes back into my life.*

"It's just too bad you never found that blue-eyed hottie you saw on the dance floor of The Deck last summer," Cindy told her. "You said he was really gorgeous. Maybe we should go back there and see if we can find him."

Pain filled her chest. Little did Cindy know that Kate had found her blue-eyed hottie. He's the one who had given her tingles and a racing heart.

Kate was saved from answering when Jason popped his head in the door. "Tell me you have coffee, Kate," Jason said as he waltzed into the office.

"Don't you knock?" Cindy teased.

"Not when I know you two are in here on your prep with coffee," Jason shot back. He started to rummage through the drawer under the table where Kate kept her Keurig. "Ha! Found one. You told me you were all out of the pumpkin spice, but you were hiding it from me, weren't you?"

Kate laughed and said, "Yes, I'm trying to keep you out of my office."

Jason made a pouty face. "I'll forgive you this time if you promise to buy me some more."

"How is buying you more pumpkin spice K-cups going to keep you out of my office?" Kate teased.

"You know you love me visiting you. I make your life fun and exciting," Jason told her and then turned to Cindy. "Don't you think Kate should have a little more fun in her life?"

"I was just telling her that she needed to start dating," Cindy told him "Don't you think so?"

Jason got a funny look on his face and mumbled, "Thanks for the coffee. Got to go." He rushed out of the room.

"Does he like you?" Cindy asked, and then continued to rattle on in her quick fashion, "Or, does he think Robert's into you? You have to admit it's weird that the guys hang out with you all the time and they're not into you. Are you sure you're not just oblivious? You never could tell when someone was interested."

Kate noticed that Cindy didn't mention Ryan being into her. That was telling. "They're just good friends. That's it. You probably embarrassed Jason. Guys don't like having those types of conversations with females."

"Oh please. Jason doesn't get embarrassed about anything," Cindy told her. "He acted weird. Maybe he likes you."

"You do realize that last week he took out three different

women. He's not into anyone."

"I guess," Cindy conceded.

Brooks paced around the revolting hovel that Joel rented. He couldn't even call it a house. It was little more than a shack in the middle of nowhere. He was pissed at the world, and he felt like he was losing control. How could one bitch possibly cause all this trouble? If it weren't for Kate, he would have all the kids he needed for his plan and he would be sitting in his mansion on his huge estate, not in some backwoods shed in the Poconos.

Brooks looked over at Joel and was thoroughly disgusted with what he saw. The weasel-like little man with stringy hair on the sides of a balding head was wearing dirty, wrinkled clothes that looked as if they had been slept in for weeks—which Brooks thought could be a possibility. Even though the other man made him sick, Brooks needed him.

He didn't have many people he could trust at the moment. His wife had made sure of that. As soon as Louise found out about his failed kidnapping attempt, she systematically turned everyone against him. She had made sure that everyone found out about his failure, and made it seem that Brooks had lost his edge and his mind. *Yeah,* Brooks thought, *she made sure everyone questioned my sanity.*

When he found her, he was going to make sure Louise was brutally punished. He was even going to enjoy doing it himself. But that would have to wait.

He needed to take care of Kate Sutton first. Kate and those kids she took from him were his top priority. He was going to take his time inflicting Kate with pain and was going to make sure she screamed the entire time. He would bring her to the point of screaming and begging for death, and then would start all over again. Kate needed to be punished for what she did and what her parents had done to him all those years ago.

Yes, Kate would pay.

Joel noticed Brooks' attention and closed his laptop. "I just heard from a reliable source that Ray is working for Louise and helping her hide from you. They think she's in Maryland somewhere."

Brooks didn't say anything about that news. Louise would have to wait. "Have you heard anything about Frank?"

"Not yet," Joel told him. "He seems to be hiding somewhere that my sources can't find. They're working on it."

Brooks slammed his fist into the wood table. "We need to find that son of a bitch before he kills us both."

Joel put his head down, afraid to look at Brooks. "We're working on it," Joel told him. "At least my source warned us about Nick Taylor closing in on you."

"He's another one who needs to be taken care of."

Brooks walked out the front door and stared out into the woods. He needed a few more resources. Maybe it was time to call his father-in-law. He scowled, hating that idea.

Kate, Cindy, and Jen pushed all of the furniture in Kate's living room against the walls and made a wide area for the three of them to practice self-defense. Jen and Cindy were both thrilled to hear that they shared a love for martial arts. They couldn't wait to teach Kate the basics.

Alex had taken Maddy outside to play in the backyard so that Kate and her friends could practice. They didn't want to worry about Maddy getting hurt by stumbling into the middle of their workout. Zach was in the family room with Eric playing video games. Kate could hear them periodically yelling at the game.

"I've been after her to learn some moves for the longest time," Cindy told Jen. "I'm so glad that we finally convinced her to do it."

The three women spaced out on the area rug and were just about to begin with stretches when Ryan and Jason barreled in and flopped down on the couches to watch.

Ryan shoved Jason and said, "See, I told you that we would miss it if you didn't hurry up."

Jen rolled her eyes, Cindy straightened her t-shirt and smoothed her hair, and Kate huffed. "What are you two doing here?" Kate demanded. "Jay, I thought you had a date."

Jason laughed. "She got too clingy so I had to get rid of her."

"Yeah, Jay's idea of clingy is her calling him the next day,"

Jen muttered.

"You're just jealous because everyone loves me," Jason bragged.

"Okay, either sit there quietly or you can leave," Kate scolded. They both frowned but kept their mouths closed. Kate caught Jason nudge Ryan a couple of times when they bent down to touch the floor. She mentally rolled her eyes.

The ladies continued with stretches and yoga poses until Jen stepped out in front and demonstrated a couple of defensive moves.

"Okay, Kate, move your feet apart a little more and center your weight on your back foot," Jen instructed. "Now thrust your arm up in an angle with the heel of your palm facing me, while shifting your weight forward to give yourself more power."

They practiced a few more moves like that, shifting their weight and moving their arms and legs in fluid curves.

"This is boring," Jason complained. "Go back to the stretching, that was fun to watch."

"You don't have to stay here," Jen told him.

"Why don't you guys help us instead of just sitting there?" Kate asked them.

Ryan jumped up and ran at Jen, who met him mid-run and used his momentum to throw him off to the side, directly toward the curio cabinet.

Everyone froze in place, watching in horror as Ryan flew toward the glass shelves. Jason put up his hand and stopped Ryan in the air before he smashed Kate's display case.

Cindy let out a strangled scream, stumbling back into the wall across the room.

Nick had been waiting at the coffee house for over an hour. He kept looking at the time on his phone even though the numbers barely moved. If he had made the trip to Savannah for nothing, he would be really angry. It was a toss-up between two leads and he made a gamble; if he chose wrong, he wasn't sure what he would do.

His search was taking way too long and he was starting to think he would never find Brooks. He was also afraid that he would find Brooks and then he wouldn't have any other excuses not to go back home. Nick wouldn't have anything else that was keeping him from Kate and that scared him the most. Nick wanted to be with her more than anything in the world. He wanted her so badly that he shook with need, but he couldn't. They couldn't be together. It was against Association laws and he didn't want either of them to face the harsh consequences of breaking those laws. Nick had watched as Robert had been jailed for falling in love with a Gifted girl and he didn't want that to happen to him or Kate.

Someone sliding onto the chair across from him broke him out of his tragic thoughts. Nick looked up to find striking green eyes staring back at him. The eyes belonged to a beautiful young woman in her early twenties who was frowning at him. She tossed her head and her shoulder-length dark hair flipped out in every which way. Nick thought she looked like she was trying to be tough, with her black leather jacket over a tight, red V-neck, black jeans, and boots.

"How did you find me?" she asked without any introductions.

"It wasn't that difficult," Nick countered. He didn't want to give up too much information yet.

They stared at each other waiting for someone to back down. Nick could sit here all day. He would stay there until this young woman gave him the information he needed.

She gave an almost silent huff and said, "Who told you where to find me? I didn't think anyone knew I . . ." She trailed off, not wanting to finish that sentence.

"You didn't think anyone knew that you survived Brooks' assassination attempt?" Nick shot back.

Her eyes got huge and she said quietly, "Yes." She looked like she was ready to run.

"A friend's gift is finding connections between things that do not seem to go together at all." Nick pulled out her old foster care file with a photo from when she was around twelve. "He also has a photographic memory. You were in your local paper for saving someone's life after a fire. He connected the two photos." Nick wished that it had worked as well when he asked Max to help him find Brooks, but he was unsuccessful.

Nick didn't tell her that it was pure chance that he ran into his friend Max. The guy stayed away from everyone. He didn't have a cell phone and he hated technology. There was no way to get ahold of his friend and Max liked it that way. He traveled around helping people find missing items or persons, sometimes collecting a reward and then disappearing. He never stayed in one location for too long because he didn't want anyone to start asking questions about him.

The girl looked panicked and started to get up to leave, but Nick quickly continued. "He isn't associated with anyone and no one knows he has this gift. He uses it primarily on non-Gifted missing persons' cases. He did me a favor."

"How did you get my foster care file?"

"A friend is the head of a Family Services division and she provided me with the information." Nick opened the folder and began to read. "Grace Larkin, from Middleton, North Carolina. Parents killed in a fire when you were six. You were bounced from foster home to foster home until you were taken in by Brooks when you were twelve. Here is a photo of you at that age. It was good enough for my friend to find you."

"Why did you show him my picture? Didn't you think I was dead?" she countered, not trusting him.

"I showed him several photos of people who had been tied to Brooks as children. You were the only one he knew was alive," Nick told her.

"Why did you want to meet me?" Grace was shocked he had so much information about her. She had left the system almost ten years ago.

"You know exactly why I asked you here," Nick countered.

"Why doesn't your friend find him?" She needed him to answer all of her questions.

Nick sighed. "There are no photos of Brooks. Not one that we could find. He doesn't have a driver's license or a passport. I'm sure he has them both but under some other name. It is almost as if he doesn't exist. Every file we were able to pull on the children he fostered or adopted was incomplete when it came to his profile. It seems as if he had someone wipe out the information, or paid people to not include it."

"Sounds like him. He never allowed photos to be taken of

any of us," she told Nick. She paused then asked, "How do I know I can trust you?"

Nick said, "If you're asking me that, why did you meet me?"

She studied Nick for a minute and then said, "Curiosity mostly. I also wanted to know who else knows I'm alive." She stood up and Nick thought she was going to leave, but she got in line to get coffee.

Nick took a deep breath. *This girl is going to be trouble*, he thought as he waited for her to return.

Grace sauntered back and slid onto her seat once again. She looked at Nick expectantly.

He figured he would just go for it. "How did you break away from Brooks? From the information I have gathered, you are the only one who has and survived."

"I almost didn't survive," Grace told him. "He thinks I didn't."

Nick could tell she wasn't going to be very forthcoming with information so he decided to tell her why he needed her. "Brooks is after my family and I'm after him. I'm looking for anyone who can give me information on how to take him out."

She was surprised by his revelation, but it made her relax a bit. "Why is he after your family?"

"He kidnapped my nieces and nephew last summer and he also went after . . . Kate." Nick wanted so badly to call her his, but he couldn't. He even choked on the word *friend* just thinking it, so he simply called her Kate.

"Does he still have the kids?" she asked, concerned.

"No, we managed to get them back, but he vowed to come back for them and for Kate."

"Who is Kate?"

His voice became thick and he got a faraway look. "She's the amazing woman that adopted the kids after my brother and his wife died."

Grace didn't respond. She felt like she would be intruding on a private memory if she did. Instead, she took a deep breath and decided to tell him her story. "As soon as I set foot in Brooks' house I knew that I was in trouble. He collected kids with gifts. It was very clear that the more gifted you were, the better you were treated, but also, the more restricted you became. Those kids had no freedoms and were followed around everywhere. They were never alone. The older we got, the more demand was made on developing our gifts. Those with weak, or what he deemed as useless, gifts were taken to other estates. At least that's what we were told, but not once were any of those kids ever heard from again." She paused for a breath. "He also got rid of the kids who gave him the most trouble unless they had a special gift he wanted."

"So you didn't have a gift that he wanted?" Nick asked "Or were you a troublemaker?"

"Neither," Grace told him. "I never revealed my gift and he was furious. He didn't think I had an active gift. He would beat us to get us to do what he wanted. Sometimes he would have others beat us and he would watch. Still, I never told. He figured I didn't have anything he would want."

"What is your gift?" Nick was curious.

She smiled. "I never told because I was healing myself as he was inflicting pain on me. I can heal myself and I can also heal others. I knew that he would never let me go if he knew that."

"No, he wouldn't have," Nick agreed. "How did you get away?"

"Two of his men took me out to the middle of the woods near one of his estates and shot me in the chest." Grace said it so nonchalantly that Nick could only stare at her, stunned.

Grace continued, "They left me there for dead and I almost wasn't able to heal myself, but I was determined. I knew they were taking me out there to kill me and I knew it was my only chance. It took several hours, but I was able to heal myself enough to escape."

Nick had no idea what to say to her. He was shocked by what she went through. "I never would have expected anything like that. You must be very strong to have been able to survive something that horrible."

She shrugged and said, "You do what you have to do to survive."

"Not many people would have been able to survive something like that, gift or no gift."

Grace didn't answer. She didn't like to think about it. "So, what do you want from me?"

Nick squared his shoulders and went for it. "I want you to tell me everything you possibly can about him, his homes, and anything else that might help. I want to take him out, but I also want to try to help the children that haven't been as lucky as you and are still being abused by him."

Grace was surprised by that. "You want to help the children?"

Nick smiled, "Yes. Kate would never forgive me if I didn't. We saw a couple of kids with Brooks last summer when we were trying to rescue my nieces and nephew, and she wanted to try to help. Unfortunately, they disappeared before we could get to them."

That made Grace's decision to help Nick easy. She had already wanted to help him, but now that he was going to try to help the other kids, she would do whatever necessary to free them. "I'm in. Where do we start?"

Cindy whipped her head from side to side, taking in everyone in the room. They all had varying degrees of horror on their faces, but no one looked as shocked as she felt. Cindy could only watch in stunned silence as Jason grabbed Ryan and guided him to the ground instead of hitting the cabinet. Jen covered her face with her hands and Kate, her best friend, the one person who she felt closest to, looked guilty. She turned to face Kate with a mixture of fear, shock, and anger.

Kate could feel the emotions surging through her friend and was doing her best to calm those emotions. A part of her had wanted Cindy to know about her gifts and her ancestry, but a bigger part was afraid of what would happen if she found out. Now she was faced with that very fear.

"What the hell just happened, Kate?" Cindy demanded, holding out her hand as Jason tried to take a step closer to her. "Don't. Just stay over there."

Jason stayed where he was, but looked ready to freeze Cindy if she attempted to run.

Kate pushed every calming emotion she could at Cindy and stepped toward her. She was happy that Cindy had not told her to stay away. "Cin, it's okay," she began, but Cindy cut her off.

"How is it okay? He did something to Ryan to make him freeze in place. People don't just put their hand up and freeze people, Kate." Cindy looked like she was about to lose it so Kate walked up to her and touched her arm, infusing even more calming sensations through her friend.

"Jason has the ability to slow the motion of things and, sometimes, freeze them in place," Kate told her as Jason nodded.

Cindy leaned away from Kate's touch and Kate tried not to feel badly about it. "Don't touch me. Kate, you're saying that like it's normal. This is so not normal," Cindy stammered. "All of you knew about it, didn't you? I can see it in your faces."

"Yes. We all know about it," Kate started to explain.

"You've been different since the summer. When I came back from Florida things were different. I knew something was up."

"Yes, I found out a lot of things this summer," Kate told her. She gestured toward one of the sofas. "Sit down and we will explain everything to you."

"No! I'm not just going to sit down."

"Please, Cin." Kate begged her friend to listen.

Cindy hesitated, but finally sat down on the edge of the sofa facing Kate, Jen, Ryan, and Jason.

"There are a lot of things that happened over the summer that you don't know. I didn't tell you because I wanted to protect you from our world."

"You just said 'our world,' Kate." Cindy was looking at her with a stunned expression.

"Yes. It all started when I decided to be a foster mom," Kate explained, and continued to fill Cindy in on everything that she learned about herself and the Gifted race of people she belonged to.

"So you're from Atlantis?" Cindy asked.

Kate shrugged. "My ancestors are originally from there."

"And you all have a gift?"

Ryan finally spoke up. "Each of us has a gift that is unique to the individual. I can see better than most binoculars and hear from great distances. You saw what Jason can do."

Jen looked nervous, but walked closer to Cindy. "I can cause terrible muscle cramps if I touch someone. It comes in handy when fighting off attacks of annoying older brothers."

Cindy smiled weakly and turned to Kate. "I knew there was something to your constant need to help people."

"Yeah. I can feel and affect emotions." She didn't need to explain to Cindy about all of the danger just yet. She wanted her friend to be comfortable with everything she had learned so far.

"Wait a minute!" Cindy exclaimed and jumped up with her hands on her hips. "I calmed down way faster than I should have. I feel okay right now. I should be freaking out. Did you do something to me?"

Kate winced. "I just took some of your fear and anger away so that we could explain everything to you before you completely lost it. I really wanted to tell you, but I've been so afraid that you would be terrified and not want to talk to me anymore."

"You can't do that to me, Kate! I need to feel what I'm feeling, not have you change it." Cindy stood up abruptly and walked to the front door. Kate followed closely behind her.

"Don't go, please. I'm sorry. I need you to be okay with this. Cindy, your friendship means the world to me and I don't want to lose that. I love you too much."

"I need a few minutes, Kate. You just told me you belong to some superhero race of people." Cindy watched Kate's face fall and wanted to hug her friend, but she needed to grasp the situation without worrying about what she was feeling. "I'm going for a walk. I'll be back."

Kate watched Cindy walk out the front door, and was petrified that this would be the last time she saw her best friend.

Cindy walked around the block, then the next three blocks, trying to come to terms with what she saw and what she now knew about Kate and her new friends. Her mind raced between being angry at Kate for hiding something like that and being afraid that some people have super powers.

She wasn't really aware of her surroundings even though she had always loved the neighborhood. Her mind was too preoccupied to take in the Victorian homes with their grand porches and vast gardens. The homes were very well maintained for having been built so long ago.

Cindy found herself walking to the swings in the park just a few streets away from Kate's house. She wasn't sure why, but swinging always made her feel better. Settling on the nearest seat, she grabbed the chains and pushed off, allowing the wind to blow off all of her tension. Each back and forth motion drew out more and more of her discomfort. After a few minutes, she decided that she needed to face her friend. She couldn't hide out here on the playground forever.

Finding out like this really freaked her out, but she was slowly getting over her initial unease. It was kind of cool to know that they had special abilities. She, herself, had even wished from time to time for a special power.

Cindy couldn't stay angry. Kate was her best friend and she wouldn't turn her back on her.

Cindy left the playground and walked back to the house. Kate was sitting on the porch, waiting for Cindy to get back; she stood up when she saw Cindy trudging up the steps and gave her a small smile, unsure of what to say. They stood there looking at each other for a few minutes and then Cindy pulled Kate in for a big hug.

Kate squeezed Cindy. "I'm really sorry. I'm sorry I kept things from you and I'm sorry you found out this way."

"It's okay. I'm glad you told me. Just promise you won't use your gifts on me unless I ask you to." Cindy smiled tentatively. They walked into the house and saw that everyone was waiting for them to come back.

"I'm glad I don't have to hide things from you anymore. I was so afraid that one of the kids would do something to give it away."

"Yeah, now we can be ourselves and not worry about scaring you," Jason told her with a gleam in his eye.

Jen grabbed her brother's arm and zapped him. "OWWW. Damn it, Jen."

Jen laughed. "That's for wanting to harass Cindy."

"I didn't do anything."

"Yet. You were going to."

Kate and Cindy just shook their heads. Kate smiled at her friend. "I'm really glad you know."

"Me too."

Chapter Five

Alex opened her bedroom door very quietly and peeked out. The house was quiet and she really hoped that Kate was sleeping. Alex had heard Kate go up to her room about forty-five minutes ago and knew that she didn't sleep all that well. Kate would frequently make trips to the kitchen and to the living room in the front of the house. Alex saw Kate a few times simply gazing out the front window. She wasn't sure why Kate did that.

Alex needed to get downstairs without anyone waking up and catching her. She smiled at her door. She had just sprayed the hinges with oil so they wouldn't squeak. Pushing the door a few more inches, Alex smiled wider at the silence. The oil worked.

As soon as she stepped fully into the hallway, someone grabbed her arm and covered her mouth. Alex was just about to scream her head off when she noticed her captor. Zach was trying to suppress a laugh at Alex's fright, so she zapped him with a really good jolt from her gift.

It was Alex's turn to suppress a laugh as Zach tried really hard not to yell out. He gave her a look that clearly stated he would get her back. Both teens stared at each other, neither wanting to back down. Finally, Alex pulled Zach back into her room and shut the door.

"What the heck is wrong with you, Zach?" Alex demanded in a strong whisper.

Zach was rubbing his arm and trying to control his anger. "You zapped me!"

"You deserved it for scaring the crap out of me!"

"Where were you going?" Zach asked.

"That's none of your business."

"It is my business if you're going to do something that will get Kate to want to kick us out," Zach told her.

Alex grumbled. "She can't kick us out. She adopted us."

"It doesn't mean she can't get mad at us and change her mind."

Alex paused. Zach was usually her fearless brother, but he was worried. She wasn't going to give him a hard time about it.

They had all gone through too much.

"Kate loves us, Zach. She isn't going to change her mind."

"She might if you do something to change it."

"I won't."

"You were trying to sneak out, weren't you?"

Alex couldn't tell him the truth, so she shrugged and said, "I was just going downstairs for a bit. I'm not tired yet."

"It looked like you were sneaking out. You've been acting weird lately. What's up?"

"Nothing. I promise. Don't worry. I'm not going to do anything to upset Kate."

Zach gave her a funny look but let it go. "Okay. Night, Lex."

Alex watched him walk back to his room before closing her door. She couldn't try to sneak out again tonight. Zach would be waiting and listening for her to try it.

With a sigh, she pulled out her phone. She texted, *cant meet u 2nite* and then put her phone away and got ready for bed.

Kate was glad it was the end of the day. Cindy had been right. This week was going by so slowly. She had just finished her last student appointment and was stuffing things into her backpack when there was a knock at her door. She normally kept it open, but the last student who left her office had closed the door behind him and Kate hadn't gotten up to open it.

Kate walked across the office and opened the door. She was surprised to see a man standing there that she didn't know. The main office always announced visitors, so it was odd that he was there. The man seemed to be in his early fifties, making him the right age to be a parent, but she didn't think he was. She noticed that his graying reddish-brown hair was perfectly groomed, without a strand out of place.

Kate put on a smile and said, "Hello, may I help you?" She stood in the doorway and had her hand on her door. She didn't have any afternoon appointments and the main office had not contacted her about anyone stopping in to see her.

"Excuse me for the interruption," the man told her. "I've heard numerous things about you and I wanted to meet the woman so many people are discussing."

Kate stiffened. She hadn't expected to run into any other Gifted people at work so her guard was down. She hadn't been actively using her gift and didn't realize that the man standing before her was blocking his thoughts and emotions. She sidestepped slightly to position herself a little more behind the door.

The man noticed and took a half step backwards. "I am not here to frighten you. I just thought we would talk."

"I'm sorry, Mr. . . . ." Kate began.

"Peter Morgan, Ms. Sutton." He held out his hand and said, "It's a pleasure meeting you."

Kate didn't take his hand. She didn't know who he was and she didn't care. He was Gifted and he showed up at her school unannounced.

"Like I was saying, I'm sorry, Mr. Morgan, but I don't have any time this afternoon to speak with you. If you would like to schedule an appointment for another time, I'm sure the school secretaries could do that for you."

She never had them schedule her meetings for her, but they would realize that something was up immediately when he went to them for an appointment. Hopefully, the principal would step in and insist he leave. She wished she hadn't left her phone locked in her desk drawer. She would have to keep it on her at all times now.

He reluctantly dropped his hand, but Kate thought he looked like he wanted to grab her hand anyway and yank her out of her office. She wished Jason were around, but she was glad he was at Alex's field hockey practice. At least Alex would be safe.

"This will only take a moment," Pete insisted, trying to catch her eye. For some reason, Kate didn't want to look him in the face.

"The main office is straight down that hallway on the right. I'm shocked that they didn't announce you when you came into the building. You should have gone right by there when you entered." Kate was trying to keep her cool. She didn't want to reveal any of her thoughts to him. Sometimes, when she became emotional, her ability to block her thoughts slipped, and right now, she was starting to get very nervous.

"It doesn't look good for you to avoid speaking with me," he said, taking a half step forward again. "Someone might think it's because you have something to hide."

"And someone might think you're rude and presumptuous to barge into my office without an appointment or an invitation," Kate countered, holding her own and finally looking him directly in the eyes. She might be worried about this man, but she wasn't about to back down. "I have things to do. Good day, Mr. Morgan." Kate managed to push the door closed in his face and turn the lock. Hopefully, he wouldn't try to enter her office.

She ran over to the desk and picked up her office phone. The secretary answered right away. "Could you please have someone stop by my office? I had an uninvited guest who wouldn't leave when I told him he had to make an appointment."

"I'll send a couple of people right away, Kate." Kate heard her yell for someone before she even hung up the phone.

Less than a minute later, there was a knock on her door. At first Kate tensed, but she relaxed when she heard her principal call her name. She opened the door and her principal and the janitor came rushing into her office.

Ted Burk, her principal, noticed Kate was alone and seemed unharmed, and said to the janitor, "Please check the hallways." The man hurried off.

Ted turned to her and asked, "Kate, are you okay? You look really shaken."

She took a big breath and said, "I'm okay now. The man really creeped me out."

"How did he get to your office?" Ted asked. "He didn't walk by the main office. I've been with the two secretaries by the glass window for the last twenty minutes. We would have seen him come in."

"I don't know. I usually have the door open, but my last student closed the door when he left," Kate told him.

"I'm going to pull the video from the cameras and have Jason evaluate security around the school," Ted told her. "I have never seen you rattled in any way, even when you've dealt with horrible parents. The man must have really scared you."

"I was just startled more than anything." Kate tried to give him a smile. "Thanks for coming so quickly."

"You never have to thank me for that. I take care of my

school family just like I would my own family."

"Well, thanks again," Kate said to him. She picked up her purse and backpack and headed for the door. "I have to go pick up Maddy from daycare."

"Let me walk you to your car," he offered.

"Thanks." She searched around her the whole way to her car and the entire drive to the daycare center.

Kate was still a little shaky as she walked up to the reception desk. "Hi, Miss Maggie. How are you today?" Kate asked, trying to be as normal as she could.

"Kate, hey. Wow, you're a few minutes late. You're never late," Miss Maggie told her. "We laugh about it here. Some parents seem to never pick up their kids on time, but you're always one of the first and always at the exact same time."

Kate forced a laugh. "I guess I'm getting too predictable."

"No, no, not at all. You just love that little one and want to get her as soon as you can. That's one of the reasons we can tell you're a great mom."

Kate smiled for real this time. "Thanks."

Maddy ran out to Kate and gave her a huge hug. The toddler squeezed her around the neck as Kate picked her up. Maddy looked at Kate and said, "Don't be sad," then kissed her on the cheek.

Kate gave her a gentle squeeze and said, "How can anyone be sad around you, Maddy?" Maddy just giggled, and Kate felt better.

By the time Kate and Maddy got home, she was feeling much more like herself. She was still worried, but she didn't have the panicky feeling she had before.

None of the guys were there. Both kids were still at soccer and field hockey practices with Jason and Ryan watching out for them. Kate decided to call Robert.

He answered right away. "Hey, gorgeous."

"Are you around?" Kate asked.

"I'll be there in two minutes."

Robert hung up and ran out the door of his house. When he got to Kate's front door, he tried to run right into the house, but she must have locked the front door when she came in with Maddy. Kate had to have been frightened to do that.

Just as Robert was about to ring the doorbell, she opened the door.

"Where's your key?" Kate teased.

"Left without it," Robert told her as he pulled her in for a hug. "You scared the hell out of me."

"How? All I said was, are you around?" she replied.

"I could hear it in your voice," he told her. "It's also no big secret that you like a few minutes of alone time after you get home from work to unwind before everyone invades your peace."

Kate pulled away and smiled up at him. He knew her so well.

"What happened?" Robert asked as he walked back to her family room with her.

"Nothing really. I was just a little freaked out before, but looking back, I might have overreacted." They sat down on the couch.

"Kate, I know you." Robert reached out to turn her to look at him. "You don't get upset over 'nothing,' and you rarely overreact unless, of course, there is a huge bug."

"Funny," Kate muttered. "I don't freak out about bugs."

Robert gave her a smirk. "You screamed like you were being murdered when a cave cricket jumped near you."

Kate laughed. "I only screamed a little."

"Are you going to tell me what happened?" he prodded.

She sighed. "A Gifted man showed up at school today."

That got Robert's attention. "Who?" he demanded.

"He said his name was Peter Morgan," Kate told him.

He grabbed her shoulders again and said, "Tell me everything that happened."

His reaction scared Kate. She explained her strange and scary encounter with Peter, and Robert got up to pace around the room.

"Did he have any men with him?" he asked.

"Not that I saw," she told him. "I closed the door on him before he could say anything else. You know him?"

"Kate, that was the Chancellor for this region."

"The Chancellor that told Nick to bring me in for an evaluation?" she asked.

"Did Nick tell you that?" he asked.

"Yes, he told me when I first found out about his relationship with the kids. I had been angry with him for keeping things from me and he admitted that the Chancellor wanted to evaluate me because I was a potential danger. He told Nick that because both my parents were Gifted, my gifts could be out of control and . . ." Kate didn't finish. It was still too difficult for her to think about it.

"He told you why marriages and relationships between the Gifted are banned."

"Yes. He told me that people have gone insane in the past."

Robert pulled her to him. She rested her head against his shoulder. "Are you worried about that?"

"I try not to think about it," she said sadly.

"I don't believe any of the things the Association preaches about those types of relationships," Robert told her.

"What if it is true? What if I go insane?" she asked softly. She was terrified to think that she could eventually become crazy.

"Hey. None of that. Nothing is going to happen to you." Robert was going to make sure nothing happened to her. "Come on, let's order pizza tonight." He pulled her toward the takeout menus on the breakfast bar. "You know you want bacon, mushrooms, and jalapenos." Somehow that pizza had become everyone's favorite.

Ryan and Zach came home first and Zach went right up to shower after spending the afternoon at soccer practice. Ryan walked into the kitchen in search of a snack. Kate didn't say a word when he pulled out the chips.

Ryan looked at Robert. "Is she okay?" he asked.

"I'll tell you when Jay gets here," Robert told him.

"Great. This should be good." Ryan continued to munch on chips as they waited for Jason and Alex.

A few minutes later, Jason strutted into the room with a giggling Alex.

"Hey Kate, one of the moms asked Jason out and grabbed his butt at practice," Alex said with glee. She had been so excited for practice to be over so she could tell Kate about what had happened.

Ryan jumped on it. "Was she hot?" he asked. "Did she give you the two-handed butt squeeze?" Ryan demonstrated with both his hands up, making opening and closing gestures with his fingers.

"Eww, gross, Uncle Ryan," Alex squirmed.

Robert started to laugh. "So tell us about your hot date, Jay."

"There's nothing to tell. I had to gently turn her down," Jason bragged. "I can't help it if all the ladies love me."

Kate shook her head. "One of these days you're going to meet a girl who won't give you a second look and you're going to be crushed—or fall hard for her."

"It'll never happen, sweetheart," Jason confirmed.

"He already met someone who didn't give him a second look, Kate," Ryan told her. He continued when she gave him a confused look, "You seem to be immune to his charms."

"Oh, but, I beg to differ," Jason corrected. "I seem to remember a certain young woman throwing herself into my arms the moment I met her."

Kate laughed. "Would that be when I literally ran into you trying to escape from Tony?"

"You still threw yourself at me," Jason smirked.

"Oh yeah, Jay. I want your bod," Kate teased.

"I know, I know. Every female does," Jason teased right back. "It's a curse."

Kate laughed and shook her head. The guys were definitely funny. She turned to Alex. "Jump in the shower and then you and Zach need to finish your homework before dinner."

Zach came down the steps and asked, "What's for dinner?"

Robert answered him. "We ordered a couple of pizzas."

"All right! What's the occasion?" Zach asked. "We don't have pizza very often."

Ryan bumped his shoulder. "Dude, don't question it or we'll get stuck with something like lima beans."

Kate laughed again. "Since when have you ever had lima beans at this house?"

Ryan shrugged. "It could happen," he told her.

Robert stepped in to change the subject. "We need to chat, guys. It's important."

They all settled around in the family room. Maddy was off to the side by her toy box. She had all her babies out and was having a tea party. Zach and Alex went up to their rooms to get everything done before dinner.

Robert filled Ryan and Jason in on what happened and then turned to Kate. "We've been speculating for a few weeks on why the Association would be interested in you. After the break-in at the archives, we did a little more research."

"Okay," she mumbled. She was a little worried about what they were going to say to her.

"We'll tell you what we suspect, but we don't have any proof, just some theories," Ryan told her.

"Okay, now you're worrying me," Kate told them.

"Kate, do you remember when we told you that no one has had the gift of enhancing and diminishing gifts since our people left Atlantis?" Robert asked.

"Yeah. What does that have to do with anything?"

"We're getting to that. Do you know the story about the first ten family lines that left Atlantis?" Ryan asked.

"Yes, ten couples were selected from the most powerful family lines and they were sent out to establish territories and lead the others who would join them. One couple turned evil and all the others got together to bind their gifts so they could never use them again."

"Yes, but there's more to the story," Robert told her. "That couple lost the ability to use their gifts, but, so did every generation after that."

"Wow. So there are people out there today that know they have a gift because they can feel it, but they're unable to use it?"

"Yes," Ryan confirmed.

"That's horrible. Nothing like punishing the whole family for hundreds of years for something an ancient ancestor did."

"More like thousands of years," Jason corrected.

"So, for thousands of years, that family has been punished for what someone else did, who they only know about by legend?" Kate asked skeptically.

"Yes. They have broken off from both the Division and the Association," Robert added

Kate could understand not wanting anything to do with either group.

"A few generations back, a branch of that family petitioned the Association to reinstate their gifts. The Association denied their request. Periodically throughout history, the family has pleaded for their gifts to be returned. The Association has always claimed to not know how to return the use of their gifts," Ryan explained.

"There have been rumors that the family has tried everything to restore their gifts and nothing has worked," Jason told her.

Kate turned to Ryan. "You said 'claim.' Do you think the Association lied?"

Ryan looked uncomfortable. "We're not sure. So far, all of the information has been rumors and speculation. It happened so long ago, no one is sure what even happened."

"Okay guys, what are you leaving out?" Kate asked. "What does this have to do with me?"

"Kate, the one piece that has consistently been missing throughout our race's history is no one has . . ." Jason didn't get to finish.

Kate interrupted, "No one has had my gift until now."

"Yes," all three of them said at the same time.

"That we know of," Robert added. "That's a gift that the Association would notice, so we would probably hear about it."

"Why can't we help them, then?" Kate asked.

They all hesitated. *That's not good,* Kate thought.

"Throughout history, this family line has caused all kinds of mischief and, in a lot of cases, truly horrendous violations and acts," Ryan told her.

"Almost every maniac throughout history that tried to take over the world or committed mass murders could be traced to that one family line."

"Okay. So we don't help them all. There could be a few good ones in the group," Kate told them.

"It doesn't work that way," Jason told her. "That family could be after you right now."

"Jay, don't scare her," Robert scolded. "We don't know that. We don't know if anyone even knows about Kate's extra gift."

"What does that have to do with the Chancellor?" Kate asked.

"He wouldn't want you to return their powers or the

Association would have chaos on their hands," Ryan told her. "I'm sure that they are just being cautious. No one has had that gift for such a long time, that I'm sure no one would even think about it."

"The Association hasn't had to deal with anyone who has had two Gifted parents. They are going to be cautious around you," Robert told her. "They are probably just making sure that you're not going to be a danger."

"Should I have talked to him?" Kate asked.

"No," Robert said quickly. "He should have never cornered you like that."

"So, we just keep my extra gift a secret," Kate tried.

"It's not that simple, Kate. People at the kidnapping last summer saw us use enhanced gifts. Word of it is bound to get out," Jason told her.

"Great," Kate mumbled. "More people after me."

Robert walked outside as soon as Kate went upstairs to get Maddy ready for bed. He knew that they took a few minutes with their bath-and-reading-books routine. He needed those few minutes away from Kate to make a phone call.

The phone only rang once before someone answered. "Hey!" Nick exclaimed, happy to hear from his best friend.

"We need to talk, buddy," Robert told him.

"Is Kate okay? Did anything happen to the kids?" Nick sounded panicked.

"The kids are fine . . ." Robert didn't get to finish what he started to say.

"What happened to Kate? Tell me," Nick demanded.

"Dude. I'm trying to . . ." Robert started again.

"Rob! What happened?"

"I'm going to hang up," Robert told him. He could hear Nick grumbling on the phone. "I'm trying to tell you, but you keep cutting me off. She's fine. Pete showed up at Kate's work and scared her. He tried to go into her office for what he said was just a chat. He told her he'd heard lots of stuff about her and wanted to meet her."

"But she's okay, right? She wasn't hurt?" Nick pleaded with

Robert for answers.

"She was just a little scared," Robert told him. "It seems like you filled her head with all kinds of crap about him wanting her evaluated. She's terrified that he's going to throw her in some room and do experiments on her."

Nick sighed. "Damn. I shouldn't have told her all that stuff before," he told Robert. "I just wanted to be straight with her, since I wasn't in the beginning."

"It's true? He wants to examine her?" Robert asked incredulously. He was afraid of the answer.

Nick hesitated. "He told me to bring her in because he wanted to make sure she wasn't a danger to everyone. I never got back to him and I haven't spoken to him since. I thought he would let it go."

Nick heard Robert swear loudly. "I know. I screwed up. I shouldn't have told him. But that was before I knew her."

Robert shook his head. "Haven't you learned yet?" he questioned. "What's it going to take for you to believe they're not the good guys here? They may have been at one time, but not now. Not Chancellor Pete."

Nick released a breath and said, "What do you want me to do?"

"Get your ass home and help us protect Kate and the kids," Robert told him bluntly.

"Do you think I should call Pete?" Nick asked.

"No, I don't think you should call him," Robert snapped, exasperated. "So that answers my question. You haven't learned a damn thing. I have to go and check on your family." Robert hung up the phone. He didn't know what it was going to take to get through to his best friend.

He walked back into the house, trying to get rid of his anger at Nick.

Chapter Six

Nick slammed his fist into the brick wall next to the motel he was staying at this time. He looked down at his knuckles that were already swelling and bleeding. He wondered if he had broken them. At least he hadn't used full force. He couldn't believe that Robert hung up on him. Nick knew that he hated the Association, but Robert wasn't very objective when it came to them. He still blamed the Association for wrecking his life.

Nick paused. *Maybe they did wreck Robert's life.* They shouldn't have thrown him in jail like they did. Yeah, he'd broken the rules and fell in love with the wrong person, but was it worthy of jail? *No. No, it wasn't right*, Nick thought. Couldn't the same thing happen to Nick if he continued to let his feelings for Kate grow? *Yes, it could.*

"Hey, you okay?" Grace asked, glancing down at Nick's battered hand.

Nick turned around to face Grace. He wasn't sure how long she had been standing there.

"Yeah. Great," Nick said sarcastically.

"Want to talk about it?"

"Not really," he muttered. "After we check out the lead on another of Brooks' hidden estates tomorrow, we need to head back to South Jersey."

"Is your family in trouble?" Grace asked, concerned.

"Yes, and I caused some of it."

Grace grabbed his bloody hand. "Here. Let me."

He tried to pull out of her grip. "I don't deserve to be healed," Nick told her.

"If your family's in trouble, you might need to use your hand," Grace told him, and then closed her eyes and concentrated.

Within seconds, the bleeding stopped and the swelling disappeared. Nick looked down at his hand and was surprised to see that it was completely fine.

"Thanks," he told her. "I bet that comes in handy."

She smirked. "I have a feeling it will with you."

"I hope not." He walked toward their motel rooms.

Kate was lying in her bed unable to sleep. The guys had left about an hour ago and the kids were all in bed sleeping. The house was way too quiet, which gave her way too much of an opportunity to think. Her mind seemed to work overtime at night, making it impossible for her to keep her emotions inside. Tonight was way worse. She needed someone to hold her and tell her everything would be okay. She wanted someone else to help her deal with all that had been happening.

That someone left a couple of months ago.

Kate's phone rang, which startled her, making her whole body jump. It was sitting on the nightstand next to her head. She reached for it and looked at the display. *Nick.* She hesitated. Should she answer? Kate wanted to desperately. Her whole body tingled just thinking about it. It rang again. Kate didn't want to answer. Her heart might not be able to handle it. Her finger hovered over the green answer button. It rang again.

"Hello," Kate said quietly.

"Did I wake you?" he asked.

"No."

"You didn't know if you wanted to talk to me." He said it as a statement because he knew she was angry with him for leaving and for not staying in better touch with her. She just didn't know how much it hurt him to hear her voice and how much it hurt him to stay away from her.

"I'm still not sure," she whispered.

He sighed. "I miss you."

"Don't."

"Don't what? Don't tell you that I lie here every night and think about you? Don't tell you that I start off toward home several times a day? Don't tell you that I'm scared to death to come home because I don't know if I am strong enough to stay away from you?"

"Nick." She wanted to hear more, but she wanted to yell at him, too. She was so conflicted. Her heart was aching.

"That's all you can say? My name?"

"What do you want me to say? You want me to tell you that I miss you so much my chest aches when I think about it? You want me to tell you that I'm so mad at you for leaving the way you did?"

"Yes. I want you to talk to me, yell at me if you have to, but it's been awful how you've ignored me for the past month!"

"You've been doing that since you left! Only calling when you know I have my phone off."

"It hurts to hear your voice sometimes," he told her. "And my chest tightens up too much when I think about you."

She sighed. "So, why are you calling me now?"

"I wanted to make sure you were okay."

That made Kate angry. "Great. Robert called you, didn't he? You only called me tonight because he told you what happened. I'm such an idiot. I really thought . . . I have to go. Good night, Nick."

"Don't hang up, please." He was begging her, but he didn't care.

"Why?"

"Because ultimately we miss each other and it's been months since we actually had a conversation," Nick told her. He heard her take a breath to interrupt him so he rushed on. "And you don't have to say it's my fault. I know it is, but I don't care right now. You can be mad at me later."

She gave him a small laugh. "It is your fault," she muttered.

"Tell me what happened today," he told her.

They talked for a few more minutes about the Chancellor. There was so much more to say, but it wasn't the right time. Nick would talk to her when he got back and he would work hard to make things up to her. That might even be fun.

"Okay, Beautiful, you have work tomorrow and I have a long drive ahead of me in the morning. I'm following up on a lead. Sweet dreams, Kate."

"Good night, Nick." Kate set the phone on her nightstand and turned out the light. Suddenly, she was very tired.

Right before she fell asleep she heard a voice in her head. *You're mine now, Kate.*

Kate sat up abruptly and turned the light on. She jumped out of bed and looked out into the hallway. Everything was quiet. She rushed over to the window and searched the yard and street. There wasn't anyone around.

Her head felt weird, almost like she wanted to scratch the

inside of it. She shivered. Maybe she had imagined it. She tried to convince herself of that the rest of the night.

Frank crouched down beside the minivan that was parked at the Hamilton train station. It was definitely one of Brooks' vehicles. He had tracked it to the station, but had yet to see who was driving it. Brooks knew Frank was coming for him, and he was hiding, *the coward*. Frank placed a small tracking device under the vehicle so that hopefully the driver would lead him to Brooks.

Frank moved farther into the shadows to observe the man walking toward the vehicle. For a second he thought he was seeing Joel, but as the man got closer, he could see that it wasn't Joel, but someone who looked very much like him. That had to be Joel's brother, John. He had met the man a few times but had not been too impressed. Both brothers were weak-minded, weasel-like men who would turn on anyone for the right price. It was interesting to see him driving Brooks' minivan. John had left years ago to work for someone on the West Coast. Frank hadn't thought he was back in the area. John would definitely lead Frank back to Brooks.

Frank smiled and turned to go back to his car. Brooks would be his in no time.

Kate was still shaken from the night before. She couldn't get that voice out of her head. She had been unable to fall asleep and when she finally was able to rest, she kept waking up and looking around. The voice had really freaked her out. She was exhausted but knew that the kids would be up soon so she pulled herself out of bed and into the shower. She stood there leaning her head against the wall for several minutes, letting the warm spray slowly wake up her senses.

Kate. She heard someone call her name.

She whipped upright and slipped on the wet shower floor, sliding into the shower door. It buckled and vibrated noisily. She quickly turned off the shower and looked around the bathroom. No one was there. Wrapping a towel around her head and sliding her arms into her bathrobe, she walked into her room. It was empty as well. She checked on the kids and they were all still sleeping in their beds. No one had called her.

She sat down heavily on the chair next to her bed. She must be more tired than she thought. She must have been thinking of the voice from last night so her mind conjured it up, but her head felt itchy again. She was trying to convince herself of that when Maddy walked into her room.

Maddy had a funny way of knowing when Kate needed a hug. She crawled up into Kate's lap and snuggled close. "Morning!"

"Hey, little one. Why are you up so early?"

"I had a bad dream."

"Oh, no. Do you want to tell me about it?" Kate asked her.

Maddy shook her head no, but said, "The bad man was trying to take you away."

Kate pulled her tighter, hugging her closely. "No one is going to take any of us away."

"Good."

Kate sat with Maddy for a little while until she started to squirm and wiggled down off her lap. "I want to play with my doll."

Kate smiled and watched Maddy take off after her baby doll. She hoped that Maddy wasn't going to start to have bad dreams again. She had had them after the ordeal this summer, but had been nightmare free for some time now. Kate hoped it wasn't another thing she had to worry about.

Ray stalked closer to the man who was sprawled in the corner of the lab, cowering from him.

"Please, no more. I beg you," the man pleaded.

Ray smiled menacingly and reached out with his gift. The man instantly howled with pain and began to shudder violently. Ray let up for a moment and the man quieted. Just when the shivering stopped, Ray zapped him again with his power. The man screamed out louder this time and then fell silent.

Damn, Ray thought. He hadn't expected the man to be so weak that he'd passed out. He would have to wait for him to wake up to get the additional information he needed. He hated to wait. It was probably for the best anyway, since he needed to go check on Louise.

Ray walked into the den with a sly grin on his face and a flash drive in his hand. Louise looked up from her laptop, annoyed that he walked in once again without knocking. He really was getting entirely too bold.

"You are going to be pleased with the first of the translations. It is very much like we had thought. We just need to find the correct combination of gifts and binding ritual," Ray told her.

Louise sighed dramatically. "We already knew that. What do you have to tell me that is *actually* useful?"

Ray gave her a nasty look but quickly wiped it away. "The documents list exactly which gifts were thought to be used in the original binding."

"Why didn't you say that when you walked in?"

"It has not been completely translated yet."

"Bring it to me as soon as it is completed. We need to collect the kids from the other estates to prepare."

"You are getting a little ahead of yourself," Ray began, but Louise cut him off.

"Who do you think you are, speaking to me in such a way? Do not push me, Raymond. You will not like the consequences."

Ray gave her another brief glare before smoothing his features into a blank expression. "I misspoke. I was merely attempting to caution you that the translations are taking much longer than we originally thought."

"Just get it done." Louise stormed out of her den.

Ray picked up his cell and dialed. The man picked up on the first ring.

"You are correct. Louise is becoming a problem. She thinks she's running things and not you, sir."

"Continue to monitor her and report back to me." The man hesitated, "And Raymond, do not hurt her or you will have me to deal with. Have I made myself clear?"

"Yes, sir. Crystal."

Kate decided to shake off her bad mood and enjoy her Saturday. Even though all she wanted to do was hide in her bed, she had to hold it together for the kids. It was a beautiful autumn weekend and the county was holding its fall festival. She decided that the best way to chase away dark thoughts was to have as much fun as possible.

After breakfast, she told the kids to get ready to go out for some fun and called the guys to see if they wanted to tag along. After what happened to her last night and this morning, she needed them around. Kate wanted them to distract her from her worries and make her feel safe for a little while.

The fall festival was held at the historic Smithville mansion, an 1840s estate and village that was surrounded by beautiful parkland. The Rancocas Creek cut through the grounds and a scenic lake bordered one side of the park. The grounds were littered with multicolored tents and vendors selling all sorts of things. Happy people strolled through the festival with giggling children running in and out of the crowd.

Kate's group walked toward the creek where the county was offering free canoeing. It was a little chilly but the guys couldn't resist dragging everyone over to the rack of life jackets.

"It's too cold out to be on the water," Alex complained.

"Don't worry, brat. I won't dump you in the creek," Jason said, grabbing her and throwing her over his shoulder. Alex squealed as he carried her to the edge of the creek, pretending to dunk her in head first. The man who was helping people with the canoes gave the pair a nasty look. Jason noticed, but wasn't fazed. He simply put Alex down and whispered something in her ear.

"Oh yeah!" She yelled, fist-bumping Jay. "It's on."

Ryan was quick to figure it out and grabbed Zach, and the pair headed to one of the waiting canoes. Kate shook her head, knowing that a canoeing contest had just been declared.

"Do you want to canoe?" Robert asked.

Kate shook her head. "I promised Maddy that she could get her face painted and jump in the big blow-up castle."

Robert scooped up Maddy and put her on his shoulders. "Let's go get Kate's face painted, cutie."

Maddy clapped her hands and said, "Yay!"

Soon, both Kate and Maddy had their faces painted. Maddy had her whole face made up to look like a cat and Kate selected a small butterfly for her cheek. Maddy tried her best to get Robert to have his face painted, but he wouldn't do it. She had such a cute pout that Robert found himself promising to get her a stuffed animal from one of the venders.

Kate laughed. "You do know that she just conned you, right?"

"What can I say, I completely fall for demanding women." He grinned at her and tossed a giggling Maddy into the air.

Kate watched the two of them have some fun, but her smile began to fade. "When are you going to start dating again?"

Kate's question startled him enough to almost drop Maddy. He turned to stare at her.

"I'm serious. You need to start dating again and get that witch out of your head. It's been long enough."

He didn't pretend to not know who she was talking about. "I don't need to start dating someone to have Sam out of my head. She's not important enough to give another thought."

"Rob, I saw how you reacted when we ran into her."

"I don't want to talk about this, Kate. I'm over Sam. It's done. She is a lying, manipulative bi—uh, creature, and I'm glad I'm free of her."

"Yeah, but . . ." Kate didn't finish her sentence because Zach, Alex, and Ryan came running up to them. Alex was soaking wet, looking miserable, and Zach and Ryan had a look of horror on their faces.

"Oh, no. What happened?" Kate asked, looking concerned.

"We have to go now," Ryan told them, pulling the kids toward the parking lot.

Robert still had Maddy in his arms so he carried the little girl quickly to the SUV. He looked at Ryan and asked, "Where's Jason?"

"Doing damage control. I'll tell you guys in the car."

Neither Zach nor Alex had said a word yet and both kids looked as if they were going to be executed.

"Guys, it's okay. Whatever happened, we'll fix it and deal with the situation," Kate told them. She knew they would both be afraid of having to move to another home. No matter how many times she had told them they were stuck with her, they were still scared.

The kids moved to the third row of the SUV and Kate climbed into the middle seat with Maddy to strap her into her car seat. She turned to face the kids, but Robert became impatient.

"What the heck happened?" he demanded.

Zach and Alex were both looking down and kept silent. Kate looked at Ryan who had just climbed into the middle row with her and Maddy.

"We were racing in the canoes and everyone was having fun. Alex and Jason were going to beat us so Zach leaned over and tipped their canoe really hard. Alex freaked out and overcompensated, and Jason and Alex ended up getting thrown into the creek. It was seriously funny," Ryan told them. Alex folded her arms over her chest.

Zach was trying to stifle his laugh, and Ryan continued. "Thankfully we were in a deserted area because Alex crawled out of the creek furious. She turned her wrath on Zach, who wouldn't stop laughing at the situation. The kids exchanged a few words and then Alex got even angrier and lashed out with her gift, which, by the way, has enhanced."

"Oh, no. What happened?"

Zach couldn't contain his laughter. "She set the scarecrows on fire!"

Alex pushed Zach. "Not all of them, Zach. Just two."

"You can set things on fire now, Alex?" Kate asked gently.

Alex got a funny look on her face, but nodded.

Robert got a big grin on his face. "That is really cool, Alex! You're going to have to let me try that out."

"Not helping."

Ryan looked as if he wanted to continue the conversation Robert had begun, but one look from Kate stopped him. "No one was around when she set them on fire and Jason stayed behind to clean things up. He swiped a pack of cigarettes from a vendor and was going to leave them next to the charred remains."

"Alex, did you know that you could produce fire?" Kate asked.

"I don't want to talk about it," Alex said so quietly that Kate struggled to hear her.

"We don't have to talk about it now, but when we get home, we need to sit down and discuss what happened. I'm not angry with you guys, but I am concerned. Someone could have seen your gifts and we could all be in serious trouble," Kate told her. "I love you guys and I worry. I don't want anything to happen to you."

Kate caught Robert and Ryan exchanging an odd look and was going to question them when Jason jumped into the front passenger side. "My work here is done. Let's go home. I'm hungry."

When they got back to the house, Alex ran upstairs to shower after her dip in the creek, and Jason ran to his house to do the same thing. Zach went up to his room and Kate put Maddy down for a nap.

When Kate returned to the family room, Ryan and Robert were huddled closely in a deep discussion. As soon as they noticed her walk into the room, they stopped talking. She was getting tired of all the secrecy from them and was so stressed from the near disaster at the festival that she snapped at them.

"What are you guys keeping from me?"

Ryan looked pensive but Robert was resolved. Kate could tell he was finally going to talk to her.

Robert sighed. "Fire-setting is not a good gift to have."

"Besides the obvious reasons like setting things ablaze, you're acting like it's bad for another reason. What is it?"

"Almost every fire-setter in history has ended up in some kind of trouble. There have not been many that we know of, but the ones we do know have been nothing but trouble. They tend to acquire big egos and think they are unstoppable, which, considering their gift, they probably are close to being," Ryan told her.

Kate fell into the chair, feeling deflated. "Great. Just another thing we have to worry about."

"She probably doesn't know any of this history, which is a good thing. We'll just have to keep an eye on her and teach her how to control her gift," Robert said, trying to comfort her.

Kate was just about to say something when Ryan shifted in

his seat, partially getting up, but settling back down. He shifted again, nervously.

"Ry, just say whatever it is you're thinking." Kate didn't think there was anything else that could bother her today.

"You could always concentrate on her gift and try to minimize it."

Her eyes got wide and she let out a huge breath. "I don't want to have to do that. I can't do that to her. It's just not right."

"It may be the only way, Kate," Robert added. "She may not be able to handle her gift."

"We don't know that that she can't handle it. Alex is one of the strongest girls I know. She has been through so much and she has come out of it all amazing. I know she wouldn't have been given an ability like this if she couldn't handle it."

"Okay, but we're going to have to keep an eye on her," Robert relented.

"Of course we are going to watch out for her, but we're also going to help her learn control and make sure she uses it only with the best intentions."

Kate escaped to the back porch for a few minutes of privacy. Once she was out of sight, she covered her face with her hands and took a few deep breaths. She stayed like that for several moments until she could push her panicked thoughts away. She couldn't lose Alex to the darkness of her new gift.

Kate went back into the house with her smile in place. *Just another challenge to face,* she thought.

Char Webster

Chapter Seven

After her shower, Alex flopped down on her bed and pulled out her iPad. Her phone was all wet and Kate had put it in some rice to hopefully dry it out from the unexpected dip in the creek. Luckily, Kate told her that she would get Alex a new phone if they could not successfully save that one. Until it dried out or she got a new one, she was without a phone. She never used messenger—only older people did—but it was still better than nothing. She pulled up the app and found her contact, 2Gifted. The message she sent was short.

ur right. It happened.

Hopefully, it would reach him quickly. She needed to find out what to do next. Alex rested her head on her arm, waiting for a reply, needing to know how to deal with her gift. He had told her that fire starting was bad and that Alex would end up killing her family. She didn't completely believe him before, but after today, she was scared. Alex didn't want anything happening to her family. She loved Zach and Maddy, but she had also grown to love Kate and her adopted uncles, even though they were a little annoying.

Her messenger beeped, letting her know she received a new message.

Sorry. I can help u. Meet 2nite?

Alex looked at the screen and sighed. There was no way she could sneak out to meet anyone tonight, even though it was really important. Kate was in worry mode, which meant that she would check on Alex every few minutes all night.

Cant 2nite.

She would chat with him after she talked to Kate and things calmed down. It was still early and they hadn't even had their dinner yet. Kate would be coming to talk very soon.

Talk ltr.

She closed the app. 2Gifted had been chatting with her for a few weeks. He had started following her on Instagram and Twitter, and liked almost everything Alex posted. He started to comment on photos and then sent her a message on Twitter. After that, they started chatting and texting almost every day.

She was shocked that he was Gifted. She had thought that the name was just a coincidence, but it wasn't. It was there for everyone to see. He had told her his name was Rick and he was fifteen. He seemed to know everything about the Gifted world, and she thought that was really cool. Even though Alex liked to be as normal as possible, it was still hard sometimes, hiding things from her friends. With Rick, she didn't need to hide and she could tell him everything.

Alex was just about to see if he had posted anything on social media, but Kate knocked softly and opened the door to her bedroom.

"Hey. Are you okay?" Kate asked gently, sitting on the bed next to Alex. "You don't have to stay in your room. You're not in trouble."

Alex smiled slightly. "I know. I'm just upset that it happened."

Kate pulled Alex in for a tight hug. "Things happen, Alex. You're young and learning to control a really difficult gift. Most kids your age have trouble just being a teenager, without having to deal with all the extra stuff you do."

Alex gave her a half laugh. "Yeah, I guess you're right."

Kate quirked a brow at her and said with a big smile, "I'm always right."

They both laughed and Alex pulled back. "Come on downstairs. I conned Robert into cooking honey mustard chicken on the grill," Kate said.

Alex rolled her eyes. "He thinks he's the grill master."

Kate smiled wider. "I know. Which is why it was so easy to con him into doing it. I'm just going to have to figure out how to convince them they love cleaning up the kitchen afterward."

Alex laughed. "We need to find someone who has that gift."

"Every woman on the planet would want the gift of making their men love cleaning up the kitchen."

Joel walked into the room and began to rummage through the cabinets looking for something to eat. Brooks turned to him with a look of disgust.

"You cannot possibly be hungry again. You just had three

sandwiches," Brooks said with distain.

"That was just a snack," Joel grumbled. "When are we getting out of here? I want to go back to your place with that hot cook. She said she wasn't interested, but she would always give me whatever I wanted to eat."

"She was paid to cook for everyone, you imbecile. She was *not* interested in you." Brooks could not imagine anyone being interested in Joel. He was disgustingly unattractive, with a belly that hung over his pants. Brooks flinched at the thought.

After a moment, Joel found a large bag of cheese curls and brought it over to the table where Brooks had been working. Brooks watched Joel struggle with the bag and then, when it opened, it ripped halfway down the side, spilling bright orange cheese curls all over the table and the papers Brooks had stacked neatly.

With a deep breath, Brooks yelled, "What the hell is wrong with you? You're a disgusting mess. Clean that crap up and I don't want to see a speck of orange anywhere."

Joel quickly cleaned up his snack, but not before smearing orange fingerprints on just about everything. Brooks was about to throw the man across the room when his iPad beeped.

Brooks smiled as he read the message and quickly responded. Seconds later the next message came but he was slightly disappointed at what it said. *Soon,* he thought. *Very soon.* He closed the app and turned off his tablet. It was going to be way easier than he had thought. Kids would believe anything their friends said on social media.

"Joel, you and I are going on a road trip."

Nick waited impatiently for Grace to come out of her motel room. He paced back and forth between his room and the SUV. He had already put his bag in the vehicle and had even gotten them coffee and pastries. He wanted to get on the road and he would have been an hour ago if he'd been alone. He hated waiting for people, and he hated things not working to his schedule. Grace seemed to hate any type of schedule, and she was routinely late for everything. He had only spent a couple of days with her, but already he was picking up on her lackadaisical personality. It drove him nuts.

He sighed and leaned against the wall outside of Grace's door. He was being grumpy and he knew it. It was occurring a lot more lately and there wasn't anything he could do about it.

Put simply, he missed Kate.

She was the exact opposite of Grace in every way. Kate was sunlight where Grace was more like an overcast day. They both had dark hair, but where Grace's was layered and flipped wildly around her head, Kate had soft waves down to the middle of her back. It was hair he had run his hands through several times, loving the silky feel of it. Grace had dark green eyes to Kate's beautiful honey-colored eyes.

Nick shook his head. He really needed to get it together. He needed to just head home and figure out what he was going to do about her.

"Hey. Snap out of it," Grace said, waving her fingers in front of his face. He hadn't seen her approach.

"What?" he grumbled.

"Are we leaving or what?"

"Yeah. Let's go."

Four hours later, Nick pulled off the winding road they had been on for a while, onto a dirt lane that disappeared from the view of passing cars. He turned off the engine, grabbed the binoculars from the center compartment, and got out of the SUV. Grace followed behind Nick as he pushed through underbrush and low tree limbs. He emerged from the woods on to a flat area that overlooked an estate below. For once, his information had been correct. This was the perfect location to spy on the mansion and extensive grounds.

"Is that one of Brooks' estates?" Grace asked.

"Yes. This one is not in his name but in a corporation that we have linked to him."

"How did you find it?"

"I have the best computer guy in the world," Nick told her with a smile. Ryan *was* the best tech guy in the world, and could break into almost every system he attempted.

"So, what are we looking for?"

"I'm trying to see if there is any activity around the house and what kind of a situation we will have when we get there."

"If he has any kids there, I'm getting them out," Grace told him fiercely.

"Absolutely."

"If there are any kids there, what do we do with them?"

"I know of a few families that would love to take in kids." Nick thought back to a time when he and the guys had been on their first assignment and found a teen that was in all kinds of trouble. He had needed a place to live and Robert had taken him to his parents. They were thrilled to have another child to spoil, especially since Robert had already left their house to be on his own. Jason's parents had also told them that they would have taken the teen as well.

Nick and Grace watched the estate for several hours but saw no one on the grounds. There was absolutely no activity, and it appeared to be deserted.

They walked back to the vehicle in shared silence. Both were afraid that when they reached the estate, they would find it empty.

The drive to the estate took longer than Nick had thought it would but they used the time to review the blueprints and plan how they would enter unseen.

A high iron fence surrounded the entire property, which consisted of approximately twenty-three acres. There was a large main house that had twelve bedrooms, fifteen bathrooms, two kitchens, and numerous other rooms for entertainment. An Olympic-sized pool graced the backyard, along with several gazebos and a pool house larger than Nick's house back home. A guest house sat along the fence toward the rear of the estate. They would have to check each of the locations to make sure no one was there.

They knew the gate was closed and probably locked, but that wasn't how they intended to enter the estate, anyway. They drove along the side road that led to the barn. The dirt road didn't look like it had been used in some time. They parked near some trees by the entrance to the stables and Nick pulled a backpack from behind the driver's seat.

Grace went to pull at the door to the stables, but Nick stopped her from opening it. He held up a small device. Grace arched an eyebrow at him and Nick whispered, "It is a scanner for security frequencies. Ryan created it." The scanner registered an alarm. Nick pulled out the laptop that Ryan had given him and started up the program that would connect to the alarm signal and disable the call out function. This way, if the alarm managed to go off, it would not be able to call out for help or make any outgoing calls to anyone. It would also disable any sounds if the alarm did go off.

Grace wasn't concerned. "No one is here and there isn't a house for miles. Let's just go in."

"There could be guards in the main house or anywhere inside that we didn't see. We need to be careful and not tip anyone off that we're here."

The computer beeped, alerting Nick that he now had access to the alarm system. He shut it off and cautiously opened the door to the stables. They walked slowly along the stalls, noticing that there were no animals anywhere.

Together, they headed toward the pool house, Nick watching closely for any movement. They entered it easily from the back and continued through the house, looking for anything that might tell them when it had been last used. Nick looked out of a side window and noticed that the pool had been drained, and had dried leaves at the bottom.

"Hey. Here's a newspaper," Grace said, picking it up from a coffee table. "It's from the summer."

"He cleared out all of his estates after the kidnapping situation. Wonder why?" Nick muttered. "Come on, the house is probably empty as well. Maybe there will be something in his office."

When they entered the house, they quickly split up to check each room and found that they were all deserted. A few of the bedrooms still had clothes and a few personal items from the kids that had lived there. Surprisingly, the master suite had been completely cleared out. There was not a single personal item in the room. The bathroom was also completely devoid of anything.

They met back at Brooks' office, but did not expect to find anything useful. The drawers had been emptied and the shelves held nothing but leather-bound books. Grace pulled each book off the shelf and shook them out. Nick gave her a quizzical look and she smiled. "I saw this done in a movie so I figured I would try it out. You never know if something might fall out of one of the books."

"Yeah, let me know how that works out for you," Nick said with a shake of his head. He went back over to the desk and checked for anything hidden under the drawers, or for any hidden panels. He was just about to give up when he noticed a tiny flash drive under the desk in the shadows, up against the side. It blended with the color of the carpet so he had almost missed it.

"Grace, I think I found something," he told her, holding up the memory stick. "Hopefully we'll find something on the drive. Let's get out of here."

"I'm not done looking through the books yet," Grace complained. Nick gave her a look and she said with a slight pout, "Oh, okay," and followed him out of the room.

They were almost to the back door, when a man stepped out of the shadows of a nearby doorway with a gun pointing directly at them.

"Stop right there. What are you doing in this house?" The man kept himself away from the light.

Nick and Grace stopped abruptly and stared at the partially hidden figure. Nick arched his arm back, pushing Grace behind him and away from the gun that was facing them.

"Hey, buddy, we were just looking for someone to help us. The girl here used to live in this house and she just wanted a few of her things." Nick spoke slowly and calmly, and stepped closer.

"Don't move and hold up your hands. I *will* shoot you."

"Easy. We're not a threat to you." Nick took another step closer to the man. He needed to be able to reach him or the gun. Nick knew his speed would be far faster than that of their assailant. He tensed, ready to strike when he got the opportunity.

"You're trespassing here, that's enough of a threat."

Grace knew she could heal most gunshot wounds, but if the man was lucky and hit the heart, there wasn't much she could do. She needed to try to defuse the situation enough so that Nick could take the man out. She hoped her acting skills were good enough.

She wailed and cried out, "Please don't hurt us."

Her outcry was just the distraction that Nick needed. The man whipped his head to look at Grace and Nick rushed him, focusing all of his energy on speed and then strength. Nick grabbed the gun and forced the man's wrist to bend backward.

The man screamed in pain and Nick punched him with all of the force he could, knocking him out. Nick shoved the gun into his pocket, grabbed Grace's hand, and ran for the door. He knew that the man would be out for a few hours, but he didn't want to take any chances. They ran all the way back to their vehicle.

"Come on, Kate. Do it again. You're not trying," Jen complained. "You're not going to hurt Ryan."

"Pffft. She can't hurt me," Ryan bragged, and swaggered around the living room. They had been training again and Ryan, Jason, and Robert were helping this time instead of getting in their way and making jokes about their efforts.

Cindy slyly watched Ryan strut around the room, waiting for him to get closer to her. He was so busy bragging about his prowess that he was not paying attention to her. That would end up being a problem for him. With a huge grin, she stepped out in front of him and knocked him to the ground with one fluid sweep of her leg. Robert and Jason began to laugh uncontrollably.

"Haha! Nice one!" Jen rushed over and high-fived Cindy. The ladies were so busy basking in their triumph that Cindy didn't notice Ryan coming up behind her until she was lying on the floor, looking up at Ryan grinning at her. Robert and Jason were laughing even harder.

Cindy smiled back and offered her hand for him to pull her up. Kate watched the two of them and wondered how long it would be before they finally admitted that they liked each other.

"You would be dangerous if you had a gift," Ryan told Cindy.

"Yeah, well she can kick your butt without one, Ry," Jason chimed in.

"What, I'm not dangerous now?" Cindy said, with a gleam in her eyes. She looked like she was going to show him exactly how dangerous she could be.

"Oh, you're dangerous, all right. I was just thinking how out of control you could be with a gift as well. We all use our gifts to help in a fight," Ryan told her.

Cindy got a funny look on her face and turned to Kate. "That's it!" she said excitedly. "Kate, when you go to attack someone or break free, focus all your negative energy and feelings toward the person. Make them feel worthless, weak, confused, and any other debilitating emotion you can come up with."

Robert gave Cindy a big hug and said, "Honey, you're brilliant." He kissed her forehead and Ryan gave him a hard look.

"Kate, I think Cindy is right," Robert told her. "Try it out on me now. I'm going to come at you and you need to throw some emotions at me."

"I can't do that to you," Kate told him. "I don't want to hurt you that way. Emotions are much harder to heal than physical injuries."

Jason stepped up with an arrogant look. "I have a thick skin, baby. Lay it on me."

Kate hated when he called her "baby" and figured that was why he had done it. She took a deep breath and threw some emotions at Jason. She wanted him to feel self-conscious; she figured his ego could take some of that.

She concentrated and noticed that he faltered slightly as he was coming at her.

She stopped immediately, not wanting to really upset him. He suddenly grinned and picked her up and twirled her around. "That was amazing. I could completely feel what you were pushing at me. It made me stop and think for a second, which is all you might need in a situation. Great job, gorgeous."

Robert motioned her forward. "My turn. Let's go."

"Robert, I'm not doing that again. I don't like making people feel badly," Kate told him.

"We need to see if it will work. We need to practice," Robert told her.

"I can't."

Ryan was just about to open his mouth to argue with her when Robert ran over to Kate and hugged her. He let her go with a mischievous look on his face.

"Robert Tate! Darn it. You did it again, didn't you?" Kate demanded.

Robert just grinned widely and motioned Ryan to attack him. "If you won't try it out, I'll test it for you."

Cindy looked confused, but Jason jumped up and said, "Oh, yeah! Let's check this out.

Kate looked at Jen. "Zap him, Jen. I can't believe he did that." She turned to Robert. "You promised you wouldn't do that to me again."

"What is going on?" Cindy asked, watching the situation unfold.

"He can absorb people's gifts for a short time, so he took my gift and is going to try your theory. They love to pummel each other for fun. He knew I would never really test it out and figured he would have some fun with it."

The ladies knew that their practice time was over, so they left Robert, Jason, and Ryan to play with Kate's gift on their own.

"Sir, we figured out which scrolls were taken."

Chancellor Pete looked up from his laptop to see his two most trusted men, Don and Harry, walk into his office. He had been waiting for his fears to be confirmed for a couple of weeks now. He took a fortifying breath and motioned for the two men to be seated. "Which ones?"

"A few ancient documents, but the one we're concerned about is the one that described the ritual."

Pete's shoulders slumped. "Are you sure?"

"Yes. We scanned the scrolls and translated them before they were taken."

"So it's true that we have a traitor?"

"It looks that way," Harry, who had been silent up until that point, said quietly.

Pete sat forward. "Did you figure out who it is?"

Don frowned. "No, but it has to be someone within the Library and Archiving Department."

"Everyone knows that, you idiot." Pete slammed his fist again. "Of course it has to be someone in that department. Who else would it be?"

Harry shifted in his seat. "It could be someone in your administration as well."

Pete glared at him and was about to say something when Don spoke up. "There have been a few other breaches lately."

"Find the traitor." Pete got up and walked out of his office, leaving the two men there.

Pete walked onto his back patio and looked at his grounds. He pulled out his phone and dialed the number he didn't want to call.

As usual, it only rang once and was answered briskly. "What is it?"

"Did you have your people steal scrolls out of the archives?"

The man on the line sounded even more annoyed. "Why would I go through the trouble to have my people steal something from you when all I would have to do is call you and tell you to bring it to me?"

"If that is the case, then we have a problem."

"Why is that?" the voice said patronizingly.

"Because that would mean that someone else is after the Key."

Silence. For several long heartbeats, Pete waited for the explosion he knew would occur.

"Did they get the ritual?"

"Yes."

Another long silence. "I'll take care of it."

Pete slumped down on a wicker chair and ran his hands through his hair. He finally rested his head in his hands. He was playing a very deadly game and if he didn't watch, he would lose everything. He needed to take care of things himself.

Kate was at the sink washing a few pots from dinner. She pulled them out of the dishwasher after the guys had stuffed them in it. She couldn't figure out how they had managed to shove all of the dishes and pots from dinner in there. It was amazing that the door had closed.

She was enjoying a quiet moment. It was rare for her to be completely by herself. Maddy had just gone to bed and both teens were in their rooms.

Jason had another date. Kate thought that he was trying to see how many women he could date within a month. Ryan was working his second job, doing some top secret computer stuff that she was glad she didn't understand. She had no idea where Robert was; she hadn't seen him since their defense practice the day before. He was getting more secretive. She was going to have to figure out what he was up to soon.

Soon, Kate. I'm coming for you soon.

Kate dropped the pot she was washing. It hit the edge of the counter and crashed to the floor. Her breathing became harsher and she broke out in goosebumps. She looked around the room but knew that she would find nothing.

Kate was hearing voices.

She slumped down to the floor next to the soapy pot, drawing her knees up to her chest. A couple of tears slipped out of her eyes. Was she going crazy, like Nick said happened to the other people who had two Gifted parents? She didn't know what to do and didn't want to tell anyone. Even though she could tell Robert, Kate didn't want him to be concerned about anything else. He worried about her enough and already had a bad relationship with the Association.

She was so afraid that she would be locked up and would lose everything. Kate wrapped her arms around her legs and rested her head on her knees, a few more tears escaping from her tightly closed eyes.

After a couple of minutes, she straightened and stood up. With a deep breath, Kate decided that she was not going to let this scare her. She was a strong young woman and could do anything. As a licensed psychologist, Kate dealt with issues like this all the time. She would just keep track of it and see what happened. Kate wouldn't be beaten down by anything.

"Damn it!" Nick yelled. He pushed away from the desk in the hotel room and paced the small space. He was muttering to himself when a knock sounded on the door that joined the two hotel rooms. He rolled his neck to relieve some of the tension but walked over to the door. *At least she knocked before she opened the door,* he thought. The key to the doors was on Grace's side.

"What happened?" she asked. "I heard you yell."

"You heard that?"

"You were not quiet, and you yelled a few times." She sat down on the bed that he was not using. "Want to tell me?"

"The flash drive is encrypted. I can't read anything on it."

"Can't that super laptop do anything?" Grace asked, pointing toward his desk.

"That super computer is only as good as the guy who is operating it."

"Or girl," Grace added with a smirk.

Nick moved aside with a sweeping hand. "Go ahead and give it a try if you think you can do it."

"Oh, I'm not good with computers. I was just pointing out that it might not be a guy who is working on it."

Nick decided to ignore her, or he was going to say something to her he shouldn't. "We need to head home so I can get Ryan to work on this. If it's encrypted, then it probably has some good stuff on it."

"Why can't we just mail it to him? I want to go looking for another estate to find the teens Brooks has hidden."

Nick almost growled. "Grace, we can't just mail something this important. We need to bring it to him. Anyway, we are all out of locations to explore. The Association checked all his listed properties already. This one was the last of the unofficial residences that I uncovered. There could be more, but I can't get the information off this damn drive."

"Fine. So where does this guy live?"

"He is actually living in my house in South Jersey. We are going to head home. We leave in the morning. It will probably take a good two days to get there."

"Great. Can't wait," she muttered sarcastically.

"You don't have to come."

Char Webster

Chapter Eight

Kate was in her office, just about to go find Cindy for lunch, when she came storming into her office.

"Hey, what's wrong? You're screaming all kinds of negative emotions."

"Gee, you think?" Cindy said sarcastically. She flopped down on the chair in front of Kate's desk. "And I don't want you to try that emotions stuff on me right now. I want to be mad and I don't want you to take that away."

It took all of Kate's training for her not to laugh at what Cindy just said. "If you don't tell me what's up I will do my 'emotions stuff' to you."

Cindy stuck her tongue out at her.

"Oh, that's real mature. What happened?"

Cindy sighed really loudly and Kate knew she was fighting tears. "Mike's moving at the end of this semester. He already signed his contract. He didn't even talk to me about it. He sent me a text! A TEXT! Can you believe that, after dating for over a year, he decides to move to Florida without talking to me about it and then sends me a text saying that he is so excited to have found a job in Florida?!"

Kate went to open her mouth but Cindy continued, "He expects me to quit my job and move down there with him. He was upset that I'm not being more supportive. He doesn't care about me."

Kate got up and hugged her friend. "He wants you to go with him, so he cares about you," she said gently when Cindy didn't say anything. She also pulled some of the negative emotions away and changed them out with calming ones. "I know you're upset and I'm so sorry, but he did warn you that he wanted to move to Florida."

"Yes, he did, but he didn't tell me he had applied anywhere and he didn't tell me he interviewed. He flew down there last week and didn't tell me. He flew there and back in the same day. That's sneaky."

"Maybe he didn't want to get you upset until he knew for sure what he was going to do," Kate offered.

Cindy looked at her friend. "Kate, you're doing your counselor thing."

Kate laughed. "Okay, he's a big selfish jerk and has always been a big selfish jerk and you should be glad he's leaving. Feel better?"

Cindy laughed. "No, but you're right. He's always put his wants and needs above everything else."

"I'm sorry. I wish I could say something to fix this for you and make you feel better." That was probably the wrong thing to say because all of a sudden Cindy stood up and glared at Kate.

"You did it, didn't you?"

Kate got a guilty look on her face.

"I wanted to stay mad and upset," Cindy said irritably. "You can't go changing people's feelings. Sometimes they need to feel what they're feeling."

"I'm sorry and I won't do that again. I just wanted to help. It's still there. I only took the edge off for you so you would be okay for the rest of the afternoon. You don't want nasty old Quimby to see you upset. She loves finding any kind of weakness."

Cindy made a face. "It's okay. You're right about her. She's awful. I would love to know who granted her tenure."

"Come on, let's get some lunch," Kate said, leading Cindy toward the door. *Maybe Ryan will help her feel better,* Kate thought.

Can u meet after school?

Cant. Have practice.

Alex stuffed her phone into her bag and shoved it into her locker. She needed to get changed for field hockey practice. She slammed the door closed harder than necessary, but her mind was on her texts.

Rick was really getting pushy about meeting her. Alex wanted to find out what he knew, but she had to be careful about it. She didn't want Kate to catch her and get upset. Maybe she could talk to Kate. She'd been really cool to them and hadn't gotten mad when others would have. Alex didn't know what to do. Rick told her that people would be afraid of her and probably lock her up if they found out. She didn't want people to be scared of her and she really didn't want to be locked up. Would Kate and her uncles protect her?

She stepped out of the locker room and let out a scream when she was suddenly picked up and thrown over a shoulder.

"Haha! Got you," Jason bragged. "And you said I could never sneak up on you."

Alex smacked at his back and wiggled so he would let her go. She gave him a hard look when her feet touched the ground.

"Don't look at me like that," Jason teased. "You've perfected Kate's mean teacher look."

Alex laughed suddenly and Jason joined in as they walked out to the field.

Kate was stuffing things into her backpack to take home when Cindy popped her head in the room. "I just wanted to say thanks."

Kate looked at her quizzically. "For what?"

Cindy smiled and shook her head. "You're so used to taking care of everyone that you don't even realize you're doing it anymore. I was thanking you for making me feel better today and not with your gift. Just you being you. I'm still upset, but I feel a little bit better."

"I'm glad I could help," Kate told her. "Want to come over tonight and hang out?"

"Yeah. We can practice self-defense. The guys are so much fun to knock down." Cindy was already heading out the door when she yelled, "Bye, Kate! See you in a little while."

Kate laughed at her friend. She pulled out her phone and sent a text to Ryan. *Are you coming to dinner tonight? I want to practice after.*

He replied right away. *Yes.*

Kate grinned. It was going to be too easy for her to get Ryan and Cindy together.

She pulled her backpack over her shoulder and grabbed her purse. The parking lot was full of cars, but everyone was at the soccer game. The girls' team was sure to make it to state finals this year. Judging by the cheering crowd, the team must have just scored.

She smiled at the sound and headed toward her BMW. She always parked in the last row because it was great exercise. Most people liked to park close, but Kate loved the walk, even in the cold weather.

Kate had just unlocked the car and opened the rear door to put her backpack on the seat when a man came up behind her. He covered her mouth with one hand and injected something into her neck with the other. It stung for a second and Kate started to slump forward into the car. The last thing she saw before blacking out was the man who had been in the club the night of the bachelorette party.

Robert looked down at his phone and frowned. Maddy's daycare was calling him. That couldn't be good.

"Hello?"

"Mr. Tate. This is Miss Lauren. Kate hasn't picked up little Maddy yet and we're getting ready to close. I've tried to call Kate several times, but it goes straight to her voicemail. It's unlike Kate to be even five minutes late to pick up Maddy. We're worried so that's why I'm calling you since you're the emergency contact."

Robert almost dropped the phone. He sat down hard on the chair near his bed. "I'll be right there to get her. I'm sure Kate just had a problem at school and was delayed. Thank you for calling."

Robert grabbed his keys and ran for his SUV. He threw it into reverse and dialed Ryan at the same time. "Ry! Kate's missing. I'm going to get Maddy now. Daycare called. Grab Zach and head home. Can you call Jay and have him see if her car's there?"

"Oh, crap. I'll grab Zach and call Jay now."

"Thanks. Meet back at her place in fifteen minutes." Robert hung up the phone and dialed again. "Jen, I think Kate's missing. Can you come to Kate's and guard the kids?"

"OH NO! I'll be right there."

Robert slammed his phone down on the center compartment and hit the steering wheel. They should have kept a better eye on her. They should have expected something like this to happen.

Fifteen minutes later, everyone was gathered at Kate's house in the living room to plan what they were going to do. Zach and Alex knew something was up but they didn't know exactly what had happened. Jen whisked them to the kitchen to make dinner and help them with homework. Maddy was already set up with her dolls and a tea party on the kitchen floor. Jen's job was to guard the kids and keep them distracted.

Robert was pacing the room. He was terrified that Kate was gone and they wouldn't be able to get her back. Ryan was doing something on his computer and Jason was putting all kinds of things into his backpack. He had run to their house and grabbed anything he thought they might need.

"Her car was not in the parking lot. Either she drove off on her own, or someone took her and her car," Jason told everyone. He was bouncing with nervous energy.

Ryan looked up with a frown. "The GPS on her phone shows that it is just outside of her school."

Jason jumped up. "Let's go check it out. Although, I looked all around that area before I brought Alex home."

"Whoever grabbed her probably threw her phone out the window," Robert muttered. When Jason paled, Robert said, "We all know she was taken. We just need to find out who took her and how to get her back."

They were just about to leave when there was a knock at the door. Robert pulled the door open hard, throwing it wide. Cindy was standing there looking at Robert oddly.

"Uhh, hi, Robert. Everything okay?" Cindy was looking at him like he was nuts.

Ryan jumped up and ran over to Cindy. He pulled her into the room and kept ahold of her hand. She looked down at their clasped hands and wondered if Kate had anything to do with it. She was just about to ask when Ryan uttered, "Kate's missing."

"WHAT? I just saw her a little over two hours ago. How do you know she's missing? What happened? Are the kids okay?" She was rattling off questions at top speed. It was her turn to squeeze Ryan's hand.

He looked at her with concern and said, "We don't know anything yet. We just know that she never picked up Maddy at daycare. They called Robert when she didn't come to get her and the place was closing."

"I left her office at the end of the day and she was packing up to leave. I should have walked her out. This is all my fault. If I hadn't been in a hurry to avoid Mike, I would have walked out with her."

He pulled her in for a hug and murmured, "It's not your fault. It would have happened either way. You could have been injured or taken with her." He gave her a squeeze then pulled away. "Stay here and help Jen with the kids. We are going to look for her."

She grasped his arm, not letting him go. "You have to find her, Ryan. You need to bring her back," she pleaded.

"I will. I promise I'll find her. Can you help Jen watch the kids? I don't think they're in any danger, but I want to make sure they're protected while we go look for Kate."

Cindy nodded, unable to say anything. She crumpled into the chair, deflated.

"We'll find her."

Robert had stepped outside while Ryan was talking to Cindy. He needed to make a phone call and he didn't want an audience when he did it. He wasn't sure how it would go.

"Hey, buddy! If this is another one of your phone calls telling me to get my butt home, you can save it. I'm on my way," Nick told him with a laugh.

"Good, you need to get here fast. How far are you?"

"What happened?" Nick asked, breathless. He could tell by Robert's voice that it was really bad news.

"Kate's missing."

Nick felt his heart stop and then start pounding furiously in his chest. He was so glad that they had stopped for gas and he wasn't driving, because he would have driven off the road.

"Tell me." He could feel the vein pulsating on his temple.

"We don't know anything yet. Ryan's trying to track her phone but we don't have anything else to go on. He is also trying to tap into security footage right now. How far out are you?"

Nick was trying really hard to keep it together. He wouldn't be any good to Kate if he didn't. "About two hours. I'll push it as fast as I can."

"Just get here. We're going now to the location where we think her phone was dropped."

"Where did they grab her from?"

"We're not sure. She didn't show up at daycare to get Maddy."

"Do you have her car?"

"No, it's missing, too."

"Rob! I can find her. I have a tracker at the apartment in Philly. I can trace her car. I put a tracker on her car when I was watching her and the kids."

"I can go get it," Robert offered.

"No, I'll go right there and get it. There is still a chance that she isn't with her car. You need to focus on any leads we can find. Stay in touch."

"Will do. And Nick, get home fast."

"I'm coming home now."

"It's taken care of," Don said loudly.

Chancellor Pete looked up startled. He'd been lost in thought and hadn't heard anyone walk into the room. "Were there any problems?"

"None. It was way too easy. Are you sure that she was the right woman? She didn't put up any sort of fight. I was able to approach her from behind without her knowing anything was wrong and I didn't sense any power from her."

The Chancellor looked at his trusted guard. "She's the one. She's powerful, but in a different way. Did you use the serum on her?"

"Yes. It knocked her out right away."

"Where is she?"

"I left her in her car in the middle of nowhere. She should be out for several more hours. We'll continue to monitor her closely."

"Good. Keep me informed."

Pete sat back in his seat and rubbed his temples. He hoped he had done the right thing. He was still in charge of the

Association, and as always, their race had to be protected.

"Found it," Jason called out, holding up Kate's purse. "Her phone is here but her car keys are missing." He looked through her purse. "I have no idea if anything else is missing."

Robert took the purse and rummaged through it. "I can't tell either. Her wallet is here and it still has the cash in it. We can rule out ordinary robbery and carjacking. They would have kept the money."

Ryan sighed heavily. "Now what?"

"Now we call in every contact we have to see if anyone knows anything," Robert told them. "Ryan, keep working on the surveillance feeds. Jason, call in every favor we have. Someone has to know something."

They went back to their house so that they could work without the kids figuring out too much.

Nick called an hour later. "I'm less than a half hour out. Did you find anything?"

"We found her purse and phone. It looked like they had been thrown out the window. Please tell me you can find her car," Robert said urgently.

"As soon as I get to my place in Philly, I'll be able to tell you where it is."

"Good. Talk to you soon."

"Later."

Kate's whole body ached and felt like it weighed a thousand pounds. Her head was pounding and her muscles were twitching. She slowly opened her eyes and groaned. It was completely dark outside, except for a little light from the half moon. She was in her car, in the driver's seat, but her key fob was nowhere in sight. Her car didn't need a key in the ignition to start. She had an electronic keypad that she kept in her purse. She looked around. Her purse was not in the car. She was stuck. She reached around the floor and felt under the seats. Still no keys.

Kate had no idea where she was or what happened.

She got out of the car and almost fell. Her knees gave out

and she had to grip the car for support. After a few minutes, she was able to stand on her own. She took a tentative step forward, gripping the opened door for safety. She was able to hold herself up then took a few more steps away from the car.

She looked around, as far as she could see. There was nothing surrounding her but acres and acres of fields. They appeared to have been newly ploughed from the fall harvest, and some had huge bales of grains rolled up in a checkerboard fashion. Kate had no idea where she was. Based on the fields around her, she could be in New Jersey or any other state that had farmland. She had no idea.

Kate also had no idea how much time had gone by. It could be the same day or several days later. It was impossible to tell without her phone or a way to turn on the vehicle.

It had been getting colder at night, but not cold enough for her to worry about freezing. She didn't want to stay in the field until morning not knowing where she was, or if the man who took her would return. Leaving the car was not an option for her in the dark in an unknown location, but staying where she was wouldn't get her the assistance she desperately wanted. She needed someone to find her.

I need Nick.

Kate wanted his arms around her while telling her it was going to be okay. She closed her eyes and pictured his face. She pictured his self-assured smile and the sparkle his eyes got when he teased her. She concentrated on him with all her might, because that was the only thing keeping her calm.

Suddenly, she found herself standing in his apartment in Philly, but she wasn't completely standing there—she could see through herself. She started to freak out and screamed as she looked down at her body.

Nick walked out from the hallway into the living room just as Kate screamed. Nick's knees buckled. He grabbed onto the back of the sofa to keep from falling. "Oh God, Kate, NO! No, you can't be dead, you can't be. Please God, no." Nick put his hands over his head to block out the image of Kate's ghost. *She can't be dead,* he thought. *She just can't be.* He didn't know what he would do if she was gone. *I can't lose her now.* He was coming home to her. He wanted things to work out for them and now she was gone. He kept saying "No, please no, Kate," over and over.

Nick's ranting broke Kate out of her own panic. She knew she wasn't dead because she had woken up in the field and was solid there. So something else weird was happening. At least Nick could see her. Maybe he could hear her as well.

She walked up to him, only stopping a few inches away. She tried to touch him but her hand went through and she shuddered. It felt strange to her.

"Nick, Nick! Look at me. Please look at me. I'm not dead," Kate pleaded, but he was still covering his face. "Damn it, Nick. I need your help and you're falling apart."

He thought, *I must be going crazy because I can hear her talking to me.*

"Nick!" Kate made the frustrated sound that she usually made when she was irritated with him.

That must have gotten through to him because he pulled his hands away and looked at her. "Kate?"

She smiled with a sigh. "Yes."

"How? Are you a . . ."

"A ghost? No. I have no idea what's happening."

He reached out to touch her but she backed up. "Don't. That feels really creepy."

He dropped his hand but still stared at her. "Where are you? How are you here but not?"

"I don't know the answer to either of those questions. All I know is I woke up in the middle of a field a few minutes ago and now I'm sort of here. I have no idea how."

"Are you safe where you are?"

"I think so. No one is anywhere near where I am. All I can see are fields."

"I'm going to find you and we'll figure this out. It must be some sort of astral projection or something."

Kate went to reply but was interrupted.

"Nick, can I borrow a toothbrush? I left mine in the last hotel," Grace called out as she walked into the living room.

Kate covered her mouth with her hand, feeling sick. She hadn't even thought about him moving on to someone else. She wondered if astral projections could throw up. "I need to get out of here." Kate started to concentrate on going back to her body with all her might. "I have to leave."

"No, Kate. Don't leave. It's not—" Nick looked around. Kate was gone. "Damn it!"

"What the heck just happened?" Grace demanded. "Who was that? Why did she look like a ghost and how did she disappear?"

Nick punched the wall. Grace jumped back.

"That was Kate. Somehow she managed to astral project here." Nick shook out his damaged hand.

"That was KATE? I thought Kate was some old lady who took in your nieces and nephew when you left." Grace grabbed his hand to heal him without asking. He seemed too upset to think about his injury.

"I never said she was old." He picked up his phone to call Robert. Nick had to let him know that she was okay but still lost. He also needed to turn on the tracker.

Char Webster

Chapter Nine

Kate came back to her body and shuddered. She had somehow astral projected to the one person she wanted to see who didn't want her. He was back in Philly and hadn't told her. He was there and had a woman with him. She wanted to curl up and cry, and she would when she got out of this mess. She needed to get home safely first and then she could fall apart.

Getting help was her priority. She started to concentrate on Robert; he would save her. She kept trying to think about him but all she saw was that woman walking out from Nick's bedroom asking for a toothbrush. Her stomach rolled at the thought. Kate closed her eyes and concentrated on Robert. She felt a tingly sensation and she knew she was doing it again. She opened her eyes and was staring right at Nick again.

She huffed loudly and turned around trying to escape. She hadn't wanted to come back to him.

Nick looked up when he heard her make a noise. "Oh thank goodness, you're back!"

Kate huffed again. "Why do you care? You're obviously busy." She closed her eyes to concentrate on going back to her body again.

Nick wanted to grab her to him so badly. He needed to hold her in his arms. "Kate, please. Don't go anywhere. I'm trying to find you. We all are."

"Yeah, I can see that. You were looking really hard."

"It's not what you think. Grace is just a friend. She came to help us."

"Are you seriously trying that line on me? She's just a friend? Really?"

"Kate, I'm being serious and completely honest. Listen, can we not fight until I find you and get you home safely?" Nick wanted to hug her so desperately, but she wasn't really there with him. Kate looked like she was considering what he was saying when Grace walked out again. The woman had the worst timing in history.

"I don't need your help. I'm going to find Robert. He'll come find me. I don't need you." She closed her eyes and was gone again.

"Are you going to punch another hole in your wall?" Grace asked.

Nick glared at her.

"So, I take it that's your girlfriend."

"It's complicated," Nick muttered.

"And it looks like I just made it even more complicated."

"Yeah. You did." Nick scrolled through the mapping software to find her location. The red dot blinked in the lower right corner of the screen. He picked up the phone and called Robert.

"Tell me you found her car."

"I found a whole lot more than that. She is okay. I talked to her."

"You talked to her? How?"

"It's a long story. I'll tell you later. We need to move out. She is in the middle of a large farmer's field in South Jersey, about five miles off of Route 40. I just sent you the GPS coordinates. We'll meet you there. It should take about an hour to get there."

"How do we know she'll be there when we get there? A lot can happen in an hour."

"We don't know. We just need to hurry."

Robert, Jason, and Ryan jumped into Ryan's SUV and peeled out of the driveway. They flew down the back roads until they reached the main highway. The speedometer hovered around the one-hundred-mile per hour mark. Not one of them said a single thing on the drive. They were too afraid that they would reach Kate's car and she would be gone again—or worse.

Nick drove like a maniac the entire way. He was shocked that he hadn't seen any police cars. Thankfully, Grace had been silent, because he didn't think he could have handled speaking with her. It wasn't her fault, but Grace had made things worse with Kate. He'd wanted to leave her at the apartment, but she insisted that she should come along. Hopefully that decision wouldn't ruin things even more.

If anything happened to Kate, he didn't know what he would do, especially now, when she thought he was with another woman.

Kate tried to concentrate on Robert a few more times but she ended up flickering into Nick's presence and immediately leaving each time. She gave up quickly and decided to wait it out until morning, when she would walk to the nearest road to flag someone down. She had a blanket in the trunk that she would wrap herself in and rest until morning. Kate was tired and scared and completely devastated. She got back into the car and locked the door.

She must have fallen asleep because she woke up to a loud banging on her window. With her back against the driver's side door and still groggy from sleep, Kate thought that whoever had taken her was back to get her. She began to scream loudly.

Kate whipped around when someone tried to open her door. She stopped screaming when she saw Nick tapping on the window and looking helpless. She calmed herself enough to think rationally. *I'm okay.* Remembering her last encounter with Nick, she felt the anger and devastation he caused rise within her. Kate considered ignoring him, but he looked as if he wouldn't go away.

"Come on, Kate, open the door," he pleaded.

With an exaggerated sigh, Kate clicked the unlock button.

She was shocked when Nick opened the door and pulled her to him in a crushing hug. He held on to her tightly for several long moments. She hated to admit that she loved being in his arms. The same familiar tingling sensation filled her when they touched. She tried not to, but she hugged him back just as tightly, basking in the feeling that filled her. Neither spoke. They couldn't. They just kept holding on to each other.

A car door slamming interrupted their moment and reality came crashing back. Kate pulled away and stepped back. The woman from his apartment was standing outside of his SUV, leaning against the vehicle.

Kate was just about to comment on her presence when

another car came screeching to a stop next to Nick's.

Robert jumped out before it even stopped and came running up to Kate, pulling her in for a hug. Kate hugged him back, clinging to him. Robert pulled away and said, "We were *so* worried about you."

Kate hugged him back again quickly, but pulled away asking, "Are the kids okay?"

"Yes, Jen and Cindy are with them," Robert answered, grabbing her again for another quick hug.

Nick looked crushed. "Is that how it is now?" He looked accusingly at Robert, who shook his head at his idiot friend. "Let's get Kate out of here and we can all talk back at the house." Robert was guiding Kate toward his Jeep Cherokee when Nick grabbed her hand. "We need to talk, Kate. Drive back with me. *Please.*" She tugged her hand away.

Jason took that opportunity to pull Kate into his arms and swing her around. "You really need to stop these little adventures. My poor heart can't take it." He made a huge show of clutching his hand to his heart and dramatically falling against the car. He always made her laugh.

"I'm sure you'll survive but I really don't want any more adventures, either," Kate told him.

"My turn," Ryan called as he wrapped his arms around her. "You scared us."

"I know. I'm sorry."

Nick was watching his friends interact with Kate in such a familiar way that his heart ached. He left and they had all created this tight-knit group without him. He should never have left. Was Kate in love with his best friend? Was there even a place for him anymore? He needed to talk to Kate, but he was afraid to find out.

Grace took that opportunity to step forward. Jason took one look at her and slid right up. "The name is Jason," he said, putting his arm around her and maneuvering her away from the group.

She shrugged his arm off and whispered, "I know you're trying to pull me away from that bizarre situation."

"Maybe I want you all to myself," Jason countered. *Wow, she is hot,* he thought.

"And maybe you're full of crap. Does that fake charm work on everyone?"

"Ouch, babe. That hurts. You don't like my skills?"

"Is that what you're calling it?" she challenged. Oh, he was enjoying her. *Game on.*

Jason put his arm around her and pulled her tightly against him, anchoring her to him without letting her go. He pulled out Kate's spare car keys from his pocket and smiled at the guys. "We're going to drive Kate's car back. You guys fight amongst yourselves about who else is driving."

Grace looked relieved to be out of that situation even if she had to put up with the playboy. They settled into Kate's car and drove off, leaving Robert, Nick, Ryan, and Kate still standing in the middle of the field.

Ryan took his cue from Jason and walked over to the vehicle that he had driven there. "I'm taking this one back. You guys can ride in Nick's car." He quickly started the car and left.

Robert smirked. "Cowards," he said under his breath. "I guess we are all riding back together."

He walked up to Nick with his hand out for the keys. "I'll drive. You two need to talk." Nick looked at his best friend and wondered what he wanted them to talk about. Did Robert want them to work it out, or for Kate to break it off with him? He didn't want to find out if it was the latter.

Neither Kate nor Nick looked like they wanted to be near each other, much less talk. Robert smiled as he settled into the Cherokee. *Oh, this should be fun.*

Kate and Nick stood outside of the vehicle facing each other and not moving. Too many emotions were swirling around them.

Finally, Nick sighed and reached for her hand. "Come on, let's get you home."

Pulling away from him, she walked to the car. She opened the back door and slid in, thinking that Nick would take the front seat. He surprised her when he slid in the back with her. Kate scooted over away from him, but he just followed her and grabbed her hand. She yanked her arm but he held her hand tightly, not wanting to let it go. Kate was torn between loving the feel of his hand in hers and hating that he probably had his hands on that woman he brought. Looking out the window saved her from having to look at him. If she ignored him enough, maybe he would give up and let her hand go.

Nick had other ideas. He hated that she was trying to ignore him and he decided she wasn't going to do that to him. He pulled on Kate's arm and she lost her balance, nearly toppling into him. She turned her head to glare at him, but he ducked his head close to hers and whispered into her ear, "You can't ignore me, Kate."

She struggled to keep quiet but she could feel his breath on her ear and it was giving her shivers. She could also feel the tingling electricity surging through her from his touch.

Nick continued his mission. "We've waited too long. *I've* waited too long."

Kate whipped her head around to face him. "Yes! You have waited too long." Kate looked up to see Robert smirk in the rearview mirror. She glared at him and his smirk increased. He was enjoying her discomfort. Robert knew that Kate had been holding her feelings in for so long and needed to let them out. A little argument would be good for her. Robert watched Kate pull on her hand again to make Nick let go, but he just held it tighter.

Nick sighed. "I don't want to have this conversation in the back of a car after you were just kidnapped. Especially with a witness." Robert laughed and didn't try to hide it.

Kate turned away and looked out the window again. Robert took pity on his idiot best friend. He was going to have to help or suffer being around two miserable people.

"Kate, I know you have been through a lot tonight, but can you tell us what happened?" Robert asked.

Kate shifted in her seat to face both of them. "I don't know much. I was getting into the car after work when I was grabbed from behind. He covered my mouth with one hand so I couldn't scream and stuck a needle in my neck with his other hand." Kate rubbed the spot on her neck that still stung.

Nick didn't think Kate realized it, but she was squeezing his hand. "Did you see who grabbed you?" Nick asked.

Kate shook her head, but then stopped. "Yes," she said, remembering a face. "I did see him just before I blacked out. It was the guy from the club."

Robert and Nick shared a look through the mirror, but didn't say anything. They just discovered that the Association was now after Kate.

Nick pulled Kate into his arms and hugged her tightly. She let him hold her. "It's going to be okay. We're not going to let anyone hurt you." Nick was going to make sure of it. He wasn't going to leave her side again.

Kate pulled away and rested her head back against the seat. She closed her eyes and tried not to think about anything.

She woke up cradled in Nick's arms while he was lifting her out of the car.

"I can walk," she murmured.

"Yeah, but I'm not done playing hero," Nick said with an arrogant grin.

Kate rolled her eyes, but didn't struggle. She was just too tired to argue. All she wanted to do was go to bed, but she had to make sure the kids were okay first.

Nick set her down inside the living room as soon as they entered the house. Cindy and Jen ran up immediately and each hugged her.

"You scared the heck out of us, Kate," Cindy scolded. "Don't do that to me. I don't want to lose my best friend."

"You're stuck with me," Kate teased back. "Where are the kids?"

"We're here, "Alex called out as she and Zach flew down the stairs and into Kate's arms. The three of them hugged tightly for several minutes.

"We were so worried, Kate. They wouldn't tell us anything, but we knew something was wrong," Zach told her.

Kate was so happy to see them. "I'm okay. I'm here and I'm not going anywhere."

Kate turned to Cindy and Jen. "Is Maddy in bed?"

"Yes, she didn't want to go to bed, but she eventually fell asleep so we carried her upstairs to her room," Cindy told her.

Just then, Alex noticed Nick and threw herself into his arms. "Uncle Nick!" Zach ran over to him and hugged him as well.

Kate smiled at the family reunion, until the door opened and *that* woman walked into the room. She turned to the kids and said, "You guys need to go to bed, you have school tomorrow. Let's go upstairs."

She didn't notice that Nick had followed them upstairs until she turned to go into Maddy's room to check on her. He walked into her room with Kate and took his turn kissing her good night.

After Alex and Zach were settled in their rooms for the night, Kate moved toward the stairs. Nick grabbed her hand and pulled her to a stop, turning her toward him. "I missed you," he said quietly, gazing at her intently.

"We need to go back downstairs."

"Kate."

"Not now. I can't deal with anything else right now."

He nodded and followed her down the steps.

Everyone was gathered around the family room sharing information.

Jason jumped up. "Kate, I want to introduce you to my new girlfriend, Grace."

Grace walked up to Kate and held out her hand. "I'm Grace, and I'm NOT his girlfriend." She pointed to Jason. "I'm not *anyone's* girlfriend." She looked pointedly at Nick. "I think we got off to a bad start. I'm here to help you defeat Brooks and save the children he is still keeping prisoner."

Kate wanted to hate her, but after watching Grace's interactions with Jason, she couldn't help but think Grace seemed really nice, like someone she would be friends with. "Why do you want to help us?"

Grace pulled off her leather jacket and pushed her tank top off her shoulder to reveal an ugly scar. "There are two more like that one across my chest. He had his goons shoot me and then left me for dead." She pulled her tank top back onto her shoulder.

Everyone in the room was stunned silent. Grace continued, "It took me hours to heal enough to be able to move, but by that time, I had used up so much of my energy and ability, that I couldn't fully heal everything. The scars had formed and there was nothing I could do about them. I'm usually able to heal right away and avoid scarring."

Kate stepped closer to Grace and hugged her, pulling the horrible emotions away that the memories created.

Jason stepped up and hugged them both. "Group hug! Share the love, ladies."

Both women rolled their eyes.

Cindy pulled Kate away to sit between her and Jen on the couch. "Are you sure you're okay?" Cindy asked. Jen was busy talking to Jason and not paying attention to Cindy and Kate.

"Yeah, just tired."

"Who's the hot guy?" Cindy whispered, checking out Nick.

"Oh, that's right. You haven't met Nick," Kate whispered back and then called out to Nick. He sauntered over with a confident smile, knowing that the ladies had been talking about him.

"Cindy, this is Nick Taylor. He is the kids' uncle."

Kate was surprised when Cindy jumped up and hugged Nick. "Thank you for rescuing my best friend."

Cindy noticed that Nick looked longingly at Kate. "You're welcome, but I'll always do anything for Kate." With one more look at Kate, he stepped away from her to join Robert.

Cindy slipped back down onto the sofa and leaned into Kate. "What is going on between you two?"

"Nothing. We spent time together last summer and then he left."

"The looks he keeps giving you are not 'nothing.'" Cindy was studying Kate. "How much time did you spend together?"

"He helped me get the kids back."

Cindy frowned. Kate was hiding something. "He has really nice blue eyes."

"Uh-huh." Kate had a twinkle in her eyes.

"Kate Sutton, is he your blue-eyed hottie from the bar?" Cindy asked a little louder and Kate said, "Shh."

Cindy wasn't giving up. "Is he?"

Kate's smile was mischievous. "Oh, I want details later," Cindy told her.

Kate laughed.

"Hey guys, let's call it a night and let Kate get some sleep. We can all come back tomorrow and figure things out," Cindy told them all.

Jason put his arm around Grace. "You can stay with us. We have a spare bedroom you can use until you figure out where you're going to stay." She looked like she was going to decline, but reluctantly nodded her head and followed Ryan, Jason, and Cindy out.

Robert looked at Jen and she nodded. "I'm staying here tonight, Kate, if that's okay with you."

"I would like that. Thanks." Jen sprinted up the stairs, calling her good nights.

Robert gave Kate a hug. "I'll see you later. You're not going to work tomorrow are you?"

Kate shook her head. "Good night."

Kate was left there standing alone with Nick.

Suddenly, she was nervous. They stayed standing there staring at each other for several minutes, neither knowing exactly what to do or say.

They were interrupted by Robert knocking lightly on the door. Nick groaned and Kate opened the door. "Hey."

"I wanted to give you back your purse and phone. We found them when we were looking for you."

"Thanks. I hadn't thought about them tonight, but I probably would have tomorrow. Did you find my car keys?"

"No, they weren't in your purse. You should take your car to get rekeyed tomorrow."

"Yeah, that's a good idea. Thanks, Robert."

"Yeah, Thanks, man. You can go now," Nick said, pushing him out the door. Robert's laughter could be heard even after the door was closed behind him.

Kate turned to him. "That was rude."

"He could have waited until tomorrow to give you back your stuff. He came back on purpose to tweak me."

Kate turned away and walked toward the family room so Nick wouldn't see her smile. She would be willing to bet a whole lot that Robert did do it on purpose to get to Nick.

She flopped down on the couch, exhausted. Nick settled next to her, only leaving a few inches between them.

"I know you're still angry with me." Nick grabbed her hand and she let him.

"You left without saying anything. After everything we went through, you left with a note." She wouldn't look at him. She just stared at the floor.

"I couldn't say good-bye to you. I tried to, but I just couldn't do it. I've missed you way more than I have any right to miss you."

She took a deep breath. "Why didn't you tell me you were back?"

"I was already heading home when Rob called me today and told me you were missing. I probably busted every speed limit in four states."

"When are you leaving again? I need to know what to tell the kids."

Nick cupped her face with both hands to make her look at him. "I'm not leaving again. I'm not leaving you and the kids. When I heard you were missing I went crazy. The very thing I was trying to protect you from happened and I wasn't here."

"You can't protect me from everything."

"Let me finish. I went crazy when you were missing, but it couldn't compare to how I felt when I saw you in my apartment and thought I was seeing your ghost. My world shattered and my heart stopped beating when I thought you were gone. I don't want to ever feel that way again." He paused. "I don't want to lose you."

She wanted to believe him so badly. She needed to know that he wanted her as much as she wanted him. Kate couldn't risk her heart again so she asked, "So where does that leave us, Nick?" She was afraid to hope and afraid her heart was going to beat out of her chest. "Before you left, you told me that we couldn't be together." She suddenly felt a rush of emotions coming from Nick. He had dropped his guard and let her feel everything inside of him. It was so overwhelming she started to shake.

He was holding her face, and then slid his hands through her hair to curl around the back of her neck. He pulled her closer and murmured, "I want us to be together," before crushing his mouth to hers in a kiss that stole both their breath. He poured all of his longing and loneliness and hope into the kiss, and she could feel every one of his emotions as if they were her own.

She wrapped her arms around him and kissed him back with just as much feeling.

After several minutes Kate pulled away, breathless. Nick rested his head against hers and was trying to settle his own breathing. "What about the Association?" she asked. He worked for them and would never go against the organization.

"How can you ask me that after what they did you to today? I'm done working for them. They can keep their rules."

She smiled widely, but then reality set in. "Nick, why did they take me and then leave me in a field? What did they want? Do you think they did something to me?"

"I don't know, Kate, but we're going to find out."

Nick stood up and pulled Kate with him. "You need to get some sleep." He walked her to the steps. "I'm going to stay here on your couch tonight. I don't want to leave you and the kids alone."

"Jen's here," Kate reminded him.

"I know, but I want to be close by."

Kate smiled and started up the stairs, but turned back to kiss him lightly. "Good night, Nick."

"Sweet dreams, Beautiful."

For the first time in months, Kate fell asleep with a smile on her face. Nick was back.

Ryan closed his laptop and walked to the kitchen where Robert was searching through the cabinets.

"We really need to get some food here," Robert complained. "We missed dinner and I'm starving." Ryan moved past him and pulled out a bag of jalapeño potato chips.

"Why should we buy food when we eat at Kate's all the time?" Ryan mumbled while stuffing chips in his mouth.

"Don't let her hear you say that. She will ban us from eating there again." Robert grabbed a handful of chips.

"Yeah, she said we should be able to take care of ourselves. I tried to tell her we could, we just don't want to."

Robert laughed, then stopped and became serious. "Why did the Association take Kate and then let her go? What did they do to her?"

Ryan stopped eating and put the bag down. "I think I know but it doesn't make sense with what happened."

"What do you mean?"

"A buddy of mine works in research and development for them. He was working on a serum that can render gifts useless. The serum doesn't work on everyone, but when it does, the person can no longer use their gift—and it's permanent. The Chancellor asked for a vial of the serum a couple of days ago."

Robert closed his eyes. "How long does it take to work?"

"That's just it. It's immediate. It should have taken effect by the time she woke up."

"With Kate's abilities, could the serum have a different effect?"

"Like what?"

"She astral projected. She never did that before and I don't think it was a gift she had before. Kate concentrates all the time and it would have happened before now. I think maybe that serum caused her abilities to strengthen and mutate."

"Hmm. That's a really interesting theory. I'm going to ask my buddy if it's possible." Robert gave him a hard look. "Don't worry, I won't tell him why I'm asking. We can trust him. He hates working for them."

"Yeah. Ask him. We need to know what we're dealing with. Also, see if you can get some of it so we can have it tested."

Ryan nodded. "Did you happen to notice the sparks flying tonight? Things will definitely be interesting now."

Robert grinned. "You should have seen his face when I walked back there. It's going to be so much fun messing with him."

"Do you think he will give in and date her now?"

Robert grinned wider. "Without a doubt. He just learned what the Association is really like. There isn't anything that is going to keep him away from her now."

Char Webster

Chapter Ten

A light knock on the door very early the next morning startled Kate. She figured one of the guys had forgotten something since they had just picked up Alex and Zach for school. She was calling in sick for some much needed rest.

Kate was shocked to see a detective at her door holding up a badge. She didn't want him to come in, so she spoke to him through the doorway.

"I'm sorry to bother you, ma'am. I'm Detective Martin. Are you Kate Sutton?"

"Ummm. Yes, I am. Can I help you with something, Detective?"

"I'm here to follow up on a call we received yesterday from the Sunshine Daycare Center."

"Oh? What call?"

"A Miss Lauren called us because they were worried that something had happened to you. She told me that you are always on time picking up your daughter, but that you didn't show up yesterday. Miss Lauren told me that she called a Robert Tate who was the emergency person on the list and that he seemed extremely upset when he got the child."

Kate wanted to panic, but she controlled her emotions and focused on his, trying to pull the suspicion and disbelief from him. She also opened her other ability and read his thoughts.

Something fishy is going on here. Too many weird things have happened around those kids.

Kate took a deep breath to calm herself even more. "I'm sorry they were worried, but as you can see, I'm completely fine."

"Would you like to tell me where you were yesterday instead of picking up your child from daycare?"

Kate stiffened. She didn't like anyone questioning her like this. "I really don't think it is any of your business, Detective. Nothing has happened. I appreciate your concern, but it is unfounded."

She's hiding something. I know it.

"Well, I'm glad you seem to be okay, Miss Sutton. If you

want to tell me about where you were last night, give me a call."
He handed her his business card.

"Like I said, I appreciate your concern, but really, I'm fine. Nothing happened. Good day." Kate closed the door and slumped against it. She really didn't need another complication.

After her encounter with the detective, she was really glad that she had called Miss Lauren earlier. She went over the call again in her head, to make sure there wasn't anything that could get her into trouble.

"Hi Miss Lauren. It's Kate Sutton, Maddy's mom."

"Oh, Kate, we were so worried about you."

"I'm so sorry I worried you. My car's computer chip died and I lost all power. That will teach me to not have my phone charged, too. I was stuck with no working vehicle and no cell phone. It was really stressful and a little scary being stuck like that."

"Oh, that's terrible."

"It was. I managed to flag someone down so that I could call for help. Roadside assistance took two hours to get to me. I also called Robert to go get Maddy, but you had already called him."

"How awful. You should complain to someone about that."

"I'm planning to." She paused. "I don't want you to worry again, but I'm going to have Maddy's Uncle Jason drive her today since I don't have a car."

"Of course. Thank you very much for telling us. Good luck with your car."

"Thanks. Good-bye."

Kate quietly walked into the family room since Nick was still sleeping peacefully on the couch. It had been a long, emotional night for everyone and she wasn't surprised that he was still asleep. She knew that he had stayed up most of the night checking on her and the kids. She had heard him moving around and considered going to join him, but she had too much on her mind. She had missed him like crazy and needed his comfort after everything that had happened, but she knew that her anger would resurface at some point. Kate was just going to take his comfort and support and worry about the other feelings later.

She pulled the blanket off the floor and covered him. He still didn't wake up. He hadn't heard the kids come downstairs, or the guys making a ruckus when they picked Alex and Zack up for school. Jason had even taken Maddy to daycare for Kate so she could have a day to rest.

So much had happened in the last twenty-four hours that she was still trying to process. She looked at Nick lying on his back with one arm bent above his head and the other arm thrown over his stomach. She wanted to smooth his hair off his forehead, but she didn't want to wake him. She also didn't want to know if he had changed his mind about them being together.

She moved to the back door and looked out at the yard. She wasn't really seeing it, but lost in thought. Strong arms circled her waist and pulled her tightly against a solid chest. He nuzzled her neck, whispering quietly in her ear, "Good morning, Beautiful."

Kate leaned back against him and turned her head to look at him. "Good morning." Her smile was brilliant. He hadn't changed his mind. "Want some breakfast?" It felt so good to be in his embrace.

"Are you going to make me pancakes again?" Nick whispered in her ear. His breath was making her shiver.

"Maybe you should make me pancakes." She stepped out of his arms and reached for his hand to pull him toward the kitchen.

"You really want me to cook?" He gave her a slight grin.

"Are you that bad at it?"

Nick shrugged. "I can make the kind you add water to and shake the bottle."

"That's cheating. Come on, you can help me make real ones from scratch." Nick went to kiss her but she ducked and continued to the cabinets.

"Hey, I was doing something there." He tried to grab her again but she evaded him.

"You think that you're always going to get your way?"

With a gleam in his eyes, Nick stalked after her, backing her up against the counter. He boxed her in with his arms and leaned down to her. "I've really missed you."

She couldn't stop her hands from running up his chest to rest around his neck. "Oh yeah? How much?" she asked.

"A lot," he whispered, capturing her lips in a slow and easy kiss that was meant to show her just how much he missed her.

Loud laughter interrupted their moment. "You two sure didn't waste any time."

Nick growled and Kate slipped under his arms and over to the refrigerator to pull out ingredients for breakfast. "Hi," she called out to Robert, slightly embarrassed.

"Dude, what are you doing here so early?" Nick asked, annoyed that his plans for breakfast had been ruined.

Robert grinned and slapped Nick on the back. "I came to make sure you two weren't killing each other."

Nick rolled Robert's hand off his shoulder. "As you can see, we're fine, so you can leave now."

"Be nice, Nick."

"Yeah, Nick, be nice," Robert agreed. Nick shot him a hard look, but went over behind Kate and wrapped his arms around her.

"So have you two stopped being stupid?" Robert asked Kate. She giggled and Nick gave her a squeeze.

"Don't tease my girlfriend," Nick murmured against her neck.

She twisted out of his arms to face him. "I don't remember you asking me to be your girlfriend."

"Dude, do you need lessons? Are you that out of practice?" Robert teased.

"What did I miss?" Jen called out as she walked into the kitchen. She was wearing sweats and her hair was in a ponytail, obviously having just rolled out of bed.

"Nothing," Kate said quickly. Nick mumbled something under his breath but Kate couldn't figure out what he said. He stalked over to the breakfast bar stools.

"I thought you were going to help me." Kate looked pointedly at Nick.

He smiled brightly and went over to her side. She loved how he pouted when he didn't get his way.

Jen took a seat at the breakfast bar and Robert joined her.

"Kate, I know you and Boy Scout are all into your newfound ridiculousness, but we need to talk about what happened last night."

Nick threw a spatula at Robert, who caught it and set it on the counter. "Is that all you've got?"

"Oh, bring it on."

"Guys." Kate rolled her eyes. They were as bad as Jason and Ryan.

"Do you want me to take care of them?" Jen asked excitedly.

Robert jumped out of his seat and yelled, "NO." Nick backed up several steps to put a lot of space between him and Jen.

Jen and Kate both started to crack up. "That was easy." Kate went over to high-five Jen.

"You two are just mean," Robert complained. "Nick, you haven't had to deal with these two and when they get together with Cindy, it's just bad."

"You guys are such babies," Jen shot back.

Kate needed to steer the conversation back to a safe topic or nothing would get done. "What did you want to discuss about last night?"

"You said that the guy who took you was the same guy from the night of the bachelorette party. Are you sure it was him?"

"Wait, the guy I zapped?" Jen asked, stunned.

"Yes, he was the one from that night."

"So it was definitely an Association guy," Robert stated, turning to Nick. "He works directly for the Chancellor."

"What aren't you saying?" Nick asked him

"Ryan's buddy told him that the Association has been working on a serum to neutralize gifts. He thinks that is what they gave Kate last night and why they let her go."

"No . . ." Kate began, stunned. She couldn't bear the thought of losing her gifts. They were a huge part of her life now, and losing them would be devastating.

"Kate, it would have worked right away. Ryan's friend said within the hour. Can you feel anything from us? Hear any of our thoughts?" Each of them dropped their guard and allowed their feelings and thoughts to flow.

"Yes, I can hear and feel each of you." *I also used my gifts on the detective earlier,* she thought. Kate blushed at what Nick was thinking. Robert smirked at what Nick had been thinking, and thankfully Jen turned away. "So what does that mean? Maybe they didn't give me that serum."

"We think they did give it to you and that it had the opposite effect," Robert told her.

"That makes sense, Kate. You did astral project to me. Maybe it mutated your gifts and gave you extra abilities. Have you tried to project again?" Nick asked.

"No, I hadn't thought about it."

"You should try it again."

She looked embarrassed and muttered, "I could only project to you when I tried before."

Nick got the biggest, most arrogant smile on his face when she said that.

"Great, give him an even bigger head," Jen complained.

"So you don't think I have to worry about my gifts being taken away?"

"No, you'll be okay," Robert told her. "But, we think you could still be in danger." He looked at Jen. "How would you like an internship?"

"What?" Jen asked, clearly confused.

"Kate needs twenty-four-seven protection right now and until we can figure out how to get the Association to back off. We can't be with her when she's at work, but you could if you were her intern."

"Great idea!" Jen squealed. "We could have so much fun."

"This isn't play time, Jen. This is serious," Nick told her sternly.

"I know that, Mr. Grumpy, but hanging out with Kate and Cindy is always fun."

Kate stood there with her arms folded across her chest. She hated when they made plans for her without asking what she wanted first. It was a good idea to have Jen there, but they needed to stop treating her like she was helpless. "Are you guys done making plans without asking me?" she snapped.

Jen winced. "Kate . . ."

Robert and Nick both looked determined. Nick grabbed her and pulled her into his arms again. "I could be your intern."

"No way. Not happening." Kate tried to back away from him but he tightened his hold on her.

"So, Jen it is," Robert jumped in.

"I'm not opposed to having Jen around; like she said, we have fun together. I'm not happy that once again you guys are making all kinds of plans without even asking me about it."

Nick hugged her tighter. "We'll try harder to include you in all the plans from now on."

"Don't be condescending."

"I swear to you I wasn't. I was agreeing that we should include you in all the plans."

Kate went back to making pancakes, still annoyed, and tried not to worry about the Association.

"Where's Grace?" Kate asked Robert. He smiled because it was Kate that asked and not Nick. His friend hadn't even thought of the woman he had brought home with him. *It's good to see them so happy*, he thought.

"She was still sleeping when I came here. I left her a note to swing by when she was awake," Robert told them. "She and Jason were playing video games until very late. I was surprised he was able to get up for work on time."

"Sooo, big brother has a crush," Jen said with a grin. "Nice."

They were just finishing breakfast when there was another knock on the front door. Kate hesitated, hoping it was not the detective again. She probably should tell everyone about her early morning visitor.

"Hi, Kate. Robert told me I should stop by. I hope that's okay," Grace explained.

"Yes, of course. Come have some pancakes. We just finished up and there are plenty left over. Probably because Ryan and Jason aren't here." Kate led her into the kitchen and started fixing her a plate.

"I can't believe you stayed at the frat house last night," Jen said to Grace.

Grace laughed. "It wasn't that bad, but I should probably look for a place to stay around here."

"Don't you have a place where you're from?" Kate asked.

"Sort of. Since I escaped from Brooks, I've moved around a lot. I kept waiting for his goons to catch up with me and take me back there," Grace explained. "I have an apartment that I was sharing with two other girls. We all worked at the local hospital together."

"Are you a doctor or nurse?" Kate asked.

Grace frowned. "No, I'm a nursing assistant. I didn't want to risk Brooks finding me. When you go to school, you have to give them your real identification and social security number. I was so afraid he would track me down through that information. I've been using fake names and social security numbers to take jobs. I never stay long at one place so I don't get caught."

"We have great medical schools around here and with all of us around, you wouldn't have to worry about Brooks," Kate mentioned. She could feel that Grace wanted to settle down and go to school, and to belong somewhere so badly.

"You know, the lease on my place in Philly is up and I was thinking about letting it go and finding a place around here, especially if I am going to be Kate's intern," Jen told everyone. She looked at Grace. "Maybe we should find a place together?"

Grace's face lit up. She was afraid to get too excited about the prospect of belonging somewhere, but Jen's offer was too good to resist. She also really liked Kate and the guys, so staying in the area was very appealing. She clicked with them immediately, feeling as if she belonged with their group. She had never felt like that before. "Sounds good to me," Grace agreed.

"I love the idea. This way you guys will be close by and we can hang out more," Kate said happily. She knew that Grace would fit in with their group and that they would be great friends in no time.

Robert rolled his eyes. "Great, another one of you guys to cause all kinds of trouble." The ladies each gave him a hard look.

Nick quietly watched things unfold. He didn't want to say anything at all. Kate had been upset when she had seen Grace at his place in Philly and he didn't want to say or do something that would cause her to think that he had any feelings for the woman.

After Grace finished eating her breakfast, she and Jen took off in search of a new place to live. Jen also wanted to check on the gym she owned and make sure her manager was okay to take on more hours since she would be interning for Kate.

"I'm going to get a shower. You boys play nice now," Kate

called over her shoulder as she ascended the stairs.

Nick faced Robert and braced himself with what he knew was coming. He knew that his best friend would not stay quiet—it just wasn't in Robert's nature.

"So, I see you've finally stopped being an idiot."

"That's it? That's what you are going to say to me?"

Robert laughed. "Do you really need me to say 'I told you so?'"

Nick slumped against the counter. "I can't believe they did that to Kate. I can't believe I blindly trusted them for so long. Look at what they've done to Kate and what they did to you. I'm sorry, man." Nick pulled Robert into a man-hug.

"It's done. I'm just glad you know the truth now. We're cool. You don't have to say anything else."

"I feel like I do. I'm not usually wrong. I can usually tell when people are lying to me, so how did I not see this?"

"They don't feel like they are doing anything wrong and they feel justified with everything they do. Your lie detector wouldn't register anything."

"Maybe." Nick was going to beat himself up over this for a while. Robert knew that he would have to work things out for himself before he could get past the Association's betrayal.

"You know that if you openly date Kate, you both will be a target for the Association."

"I don't care anymore. Let them try something. I'm not losing her again. When she appeared at my apartment and I thought I was seeing her ghost, I completely lost it. I felt like my entire world stopped and I was being crushed to death. I knew I cared for her, but I had no idea how much until I thought I lost her. I will fight everyone in the world for her."

Robert smiled widely. His best friend was back and he was finally accepting the truth about the Association. More importantly, he was finally going to be with Kate. Those two belonged together and he was tired of seeing them both hurting. "I'm glad you guys are going to be together. She's been so miserable without you."

Nick took a deep breath. "I need to know if there is anything between you guys. You seem really close."

Robert laughed. "She's the sister I never had. I love Kate,

but only as a really good friend and the love of my best friend."

"Are you sure?"

"Absolutely. We have gotten close, but only as friends." Robert didn't know if he would ever love a woman again. He had given his heart to Sam and that turned out to be a disaster. He didn't think he would ever trust his heart with anyone again.

"They're not all like Sam." Robert knew that he was still blocking his thoughts, but Nick knew him really well.

"I know. I'm just not interested in anything like that right now."

Nick wasn't going to push, but one of these days Robert was going to find someone who turned his world upside down, just like Kate had done to him.

Ryan pushed Zach into the house with his hand fisted in the back of his t-shirt. Zach wasn't struggling, but was dragging his feet, not wanting to enter. Kate and Nick had been curled up on the couch watching a movie, trying to relax while they were waiting for everyone to come home from work.

Kate and Nick immediately stood up and faced the scene. Robert quickly followed, wanting to know what was happening. It looked like Ryan was literally holding Zach up by his t-shirt.

"What is going on?" Kate demanded.

Zach looked at his feet and remained silent. Ryan nudged him. "Tell her."

Kate was concerned because Ryan never corrected the kids and he got along almost too well with Zach. Sometimes Ryan and Jason would even get into trouble for having too much fun with Zach.

Zach mumbled something no one could hear. Kate could feel the dread coming off of him. He'd obviously done something bad enough that Ryan drove him home before soccer practice was over.

Ryan sighed and let go of Zach. "I caught him terrorizing Mr. Hubert. He was waiting for the man to turn his back and was then moving things on his desk, and other things around the room. He could have been caught by any of the students, or Hubert himself."

Nick turned around quickly to hide his laugh, but Robert wasn't quick enough. He laughed loudly before exiting the room. Zach looked up for a second and smiled, until he caught Kate's scowl.

"Zach?" Kate said with exasperation. She knew this would happen at some point, but she hadn't expected it to be so soon, especially after the events of last night.

"No one saw."

"If no one saw, then how did Ryan catch you?"

"I don't know."

Ryan was not happy with Zach. "Hubert came and asked me to install cameras in his classroom because he thought someone was breaking in after he locked up for the day and was touching his stuff. He told me that all of the things on his desk were being moved around and turned upside down."

Nick laughed and decided to join Robert when Kate glared at him.

Ryan continued. "Hubert also claimed that he made sure the room was locked up, and even went so far as to not allow the janitorial staff into his classroom. The man became so paranoid that he put paper in the door to show if anyone entered. Apparently it has been going on for several weeks."

"Zach!"

Zach glanced at Kate with a very guilty expression. "The guy is an ass."

Kate narrowed her gaze. "Zach, language."

"Sorry. But, he really is, Kate. He's mean to all of us. He gave Eric a zero on an assignment because he didn't double space his work and then when Eric tried to argue, he gave him a detention."

"That doesn't mean you use your gifts on your teacher, or anyone else for that matter."

"But Kate, the guy is really horrible. One kid asked a question that Hubert thought he should already know the answer to and gave the whole class a zero for the day for not paying attention."

"Then you should have come to talk to me about it, or to Ryan. You don't use your gifts in public. Ever. Zach, if he'd recorded you using your gifts, you guys would be taken away from me, and God knows what would happen then."

Zach dropped his head in defeat, but uttered, "They wouldn't have caught me. I was doing it from outside of the window."

Ryan looked impressed. Nick and Robert walked back into the room. They had apparently been listening to the whole thing, just out of sight. "You did that from outside the closed window?" Nick asked. He was impressed as well.

Kate glared at the three of them. "You're not helping."

Zach tried to hide a smile, looking proud of his accomplishments. "Yeah. It was pretty easy." He quickly hid his grin when Kate turned her look on him.

"You cannot use your gifts in public. You know that," Kate said unhappily. "You're grounded."

"Grounded?" Zach said, stunned.

"Yes, grounded. No hanging out with Eric and no practicing powers with Jason."

"But fall break starts this weekend!"

"You should have thought of that before you pulled a stunt like this."

"So not fair," Zach said as he headed to his room to pout.

They heard his door shut loudly, and the guys all burst out laughing. "It's not funny," Kate scolded.

Robert laughed louder. "Wow, you really sounded like a mom just then."

"I am a mom."

"Yeah, but you really sounded like it. You're usually the cool mom. Today you were scary strict mom."

"Someone could have caught him!"

Nick wrapped his arm around Kate's shoulders, pulling her into his side. "Don't tease her. She's right. We're all taught from a young age that if we want to be around normal people, we need to hide our gifts. He knows that. We're also taught that it's against our laws to use our gifts on regular people."

Kate smiled widely at him. She loved that he stuck up for her.

"You're right. It's just pretty funny," Robert agreed.

Ryan laughed. "It really is funny. If you knew how pompous the guy is and how horribly he treats the kids, you would think Zach was justified. He shouldn't have done that, but I can understand why he wanted to."

"Nick turned to her. "How long are you going to keep him grounded?"

She shrugged. "A few days to make my point, as long as he doesn't pull anything else."

Nick kissed her head. "It's never going to be dull is it?"

She looked at him with an odd expression. "I used to like dull. Now I don't remember what dull is like."

Kate walked upstairs to her bedroom to call her mother. She needed to hear her voice and she needed the comfort that only a mother could provide. She couldn't tell her mom about what was happening, but she could still soak in the motherly love.

Her parents were traveling around the country, visiting inner city clinics. Both retired doctors, they had volunteered their time since selling their practice two years ago. After the holidays, they would be returning to Africa to continue their work setting up medical facilities.

Her mother's phone rang several times and then went to voicemail.

"Hi, Mom. I'm just calling to catch up. Call me back when you get a chance. I love you. Tell Dad I love him, too."

Char Webster

Chapter Eleven

"She didn't go to work today so we couldn't monitor her like we wanted to," Don told the Chancellor.

"That was to be expected. I want to know immediately if she shows any signs of a gift," Chancellor Pete told him.

"Nick Taylor is back in the area and stayed at her house last night."

"Taylor is back? Hmm. I wonder why he didn't check in."

"It was late when they all got back to her house, but he should have had plenty of time to call in." Don was fidgeting. He'd never liked Taylor; Nick was the golden boy of the Association and always got whatever he wanted. Don would like to show Taylor just who the "in" guy was now. "When was the last time the guy gave you a report?"

The Chancellor scowled. He didn't like hearing that Nick Taylor might not be his loyal agent anymore. "Watch all of them." He started to leave the room but turned around and said, "Don't embellish any of your reports, Donald. I'll know if you do."

Don glared at the Chancellor's back as he left.

Louise paced aimlessly around her den. She was tired of hiding and sick of the cramped house. She needed to get back to her friends, her social engagements, and her projects. She also needed to find where Brooks was keeping the others.

Ray was lounging on one of the chairs with his feet on the upholstery. She hated when he did that and she glared at him as she passed by. He probably did it on purpose because he knew she despised it. Louise was starting to detest him and couldn't wait to end their association. Normally, she had people take care of problems such as Ray, but she would enjoy ending him herself. She couldn't wait to watch that smug look on his face turn to shock and then horror. She grinned at the thought.

"What devious thoughts are you entertaining now, Louise?" Ray asked condescendingly.

She turned to glare at him. "Shouldn't you be checking on

the translations? I want that information as soon as possible. We've wasted enough time here."

"And I already explained to you that it's taking time. We are dealing with a lost language and several ancient dialects. You're going to have to be a little more patient."

She shrugged with annoyance and he continued. "Besides, you don't have all the pieces in place yet and from what I have heard, your husband has been impeding those efforts."

"We need to put an end to his interference."

"We won't have to worry about him for too much longer."

"What do you mean?" Louise asked suspiciously.

"Oh, nothing to worry about right now." Ray pulled himself off the chair and strutted out of the room.

Loulouise stared after him, wondering what he was planning.

Jason carried Maddy into the house after picking her up from daycare. He also carried a new stuffed animal that Kate had not seen before. Alex trailed behind and went straight up stairs to shower after practice and do her homework.

Jason shifted Maddy into Kate's arms and flopped down on the chair in the family room with an exaggerated sigh.

Everyone had been waiting for him to come back from Alex's field hockey practice so that they could start their meeting.

Jason sighed again louder to gain a reaction from everyone, but no one said anything. It was driving him crazy that he couldn't get a response, so he groaned instead.

Kate took pity on him and said, "Okay, let's hear it. Why the theatrics?"

"You don't understand what I had to go through for you, babe. But don't worry, I took care of everything, because I'm the man."

Kate rolled her eyes, but curiosity was getting to her. "What happened?" She put Maddy in her play area.

"Daycare grilled me today. Those ladies in there are out of control. They wouldn't leave me alone. As soon as I walked in there this morning, they flocked to me and were hanging on my every word. It's tough being this awesome sometimes."

"Yeah, Jay, you're awesome alright," Ryan teased Jason, punching him in the arm. "An awesome pain in the butt."

Kate ignored them. "Where did this stuffed animal come from?"

Jason pretended he didn't hear them. "They wanted to know all about me and if I was single. I had to let them down easy, although the one girl was very cute."

Robert walked up. "How exactly was that strenuous?"

"You're just jealous because all the ladies love me," Jason boasted, but changed his attitude when he noticed Grace in the room. "But of course all that has changed. I don't need a trail of women behind me. I'm becoming a one-woman man."

Nick, Ryan, and Robert all broke out laughing. "Yeah, sure, Jay," Nick said, cracking up. They all knew about Jason's dating history.

Grace just raised her eyebrow at him.

"Anyway," Kate said quickly. "Did they seem suspicious?"

"Are you doubting me?" Jason got up and hooked an arm around Kate's shoulders.

"Of course not, how could I ever doubt *Jason the Great*?"

Robert groaned. "Don't encourage the ego."

"It's not an ego if it's true."

"Hopefully it worked, because they had called the police last night and reported me missing."

Stunned expressions faced her. "It's okay. I spoke with the detective and assured him that I was okay and that nothing was wrong."

"Kate, we need to discuss this," Robert began, but Kate cut him off with a look.

"We will talk about all that kind of stuff later," she said, looking over at Maddy. "Okay, back to the story. Where did the stuffed animal come from?" Kate asked.

Maddy must have been following along with their bantering because she walked over to Kate while hugging the new stuffed rabbit. Kate scooped her up again and cuddled her close.

"Uncle Jay gave it to me," Maddy told her.

"Why did Uncle Jason give that to you?" Kate asked her.

"I wanted it and said please."

"Well, that was very nice of him to get it for you." Kate

squeezed her again and set her down. Maddy walked back over to her toys and began to play, ignoring the adults in the room.

Kate turned to Jason. "She conned you, didn't she?"

"I guess so. We stopped at the grocery store for two seconds and she saw it. I can't say no to her when she looks at me like that and says please in her cute little voice."

Kate shook her head. "You can't keep doing whatever she asks. Maddy will end up completely spoiled."

"Oh, like you can say no to her?"

Maddy chose that moment to walk back up to them and climb into Nick's lap.

Nick cuddled his niece and suggested, "Let's order out for dinner and we can all talk when the kids go to bed."

Later that evening after the kids were in bed, everyone gathered around to discuss the situation and compile all of the information they each had. Cindy had rushed in right after the kids had gone to bed. Her eyes were puffy and it looked as if she had been crying. Kate wanted to pull her aside to find out what had happened, but too many people were around. Cindy had probably been fighting with Mike. Kate smiled when Cindy sat down next to Ryan, who seemed to inch closer to Cindy each time he moved.

Kate went to her hideaway desk and pulled out the file that Dawn Johnson had given to her before. She hadn't found the time to look through it since things had been so hectic. *Maybe something in the file will help,* she thought.

Robert had disappeared after dinner to get the information he had been collecting. Kate was finally going to discover what he'd been doing during the day. He had been secretive about it, so she figured it was about her somehow. Everything lately was centered on her and the kids.

Nick handed Ryan the flash drive that he and Grace had found at Brooks' estate. He was excited to find out what was on the drive and needed Ryan's computer expertise. "Here. It's encrypted and didn't respond to the normal programs that we run for situations like this," Nick told him. Ryan grinned. He loved a challenge.

Kate paced the family room, busying herself with fixing people drinks and putting out snacks. She was nervous about what all the information would reveal. She was also scared to find out what the guys had been hiding from her. She felt as if her world was about to come crashing down around her, and she just hoped that she was strong enough to survive it.

Grace was sitting on the floor in front of the coffee table, which had maps spread out across the entire surface. She was marking the areas where Brooks was known to have property and how many estates had been searched. Jason had moved to her side to watch what she was doing but she continued to ignore him completely.

The back door flew open to reveal Robert with an armful of documents. He quickly entered and dumped the contents onto the coffee table, covering the maps that Grace had been working on. "Rob, the lady was working here," Jason scolded. Grace glared at Jason. "Why are you looking at me like that? He's the one who dumped this crap all over your maps."

Robert ignored him and began to shuffle through the documents.

Kate was still pacing around the room when Nick came up to her. "Hey. Things will be okay," he whispered, brushing some hair away from her face. "All we're doing here tonight is figuring out what is going on. Nothing more."

"I know. I'm still worried."

"Don't be. We're in this together now and I'm not going to let anything bad happen."

Kate smiled and gave him a confident look. "As much as I love having you back, you do know that I am very capable of taking care of myself."

"Yeah, but I'm better at everything," Nick winked at her.

Kate smiled and somehow felt a little bit better. She went to sit on the love seat and Nick joined her there. He wanted to be close to her because he knew she was going to hear some things that were going to bother her.

Robert stood up and faced everyone. "Okay, let's start with a little recap."

Jen burst into the room. "You guys were going to start without me? Seriously? I'm like a few minutes late and you don't even wait."

"We don't wait for tagalong little sisters," Jason teased. Jen passed Jason on the floor and kicked him as she passed.

"Oh, whoops." Jen grinned and settled down next to Cindy and Ryan. "Okay, now we can start."

Robert cocked an eyebrow at Jen but continued with what he was saying. "For a while now I have been researching some of the older documents and legends that surround our people." He looked at Ryan and motioned for him to begin.

Ryan looked at Kate. "A couple of weeks ago, there was a break-in at the Association's archives in New York. The intruders targeted specific documents that raised all kinds of alarms with the Association and even the Division. They took ancient scrolls and copies of tablets that specifically mentioned the original lines binding the gifts of the rogue couple."

Everyone glanced around at each other, not knowing what to think.

"Okay, why?" Kate asked.

Ryan looked toward Nick, who nodded. He took a deep breath and continued, "Because of you, Kate."

"ME?" She tried to stand up but Nick held her hand, anchoring her down.

"Yes. We'll explain in a moment," Ryan told her, and looked toward Robert.

Nick squeezed her hand and she gave him a confused look.

"There have been rumors for hundreds of years that the Association had imprisoned and in some cases killed women who possessed certain gifts in combination with their ancestry."

"Meaning what exactly?" Nick asked. He was afraid of where this was going.

"It seems that women who have been born from specific family lines with the ability to feel emotions and manipulate them have been targeted throughout history. These women have also been linked to the ability to enhance or diminish gifts."

Kate was starting to feel sick. "Feel emotions," she uttered. Nick put his arm around her and pulled her against him.

"Kate, we believe that you may be from one of the original lines," Robert told her.

Kate didn't want to hear any more but she needed to find out what she was up against. "So, they're after me like they were the other women who had my gifts?"

"It looks like it."

Nick frowned. "Guys, that's not making any sense. I get that the Association is after Kate because it fits the pattern you just told us about. What does that have to do with the burglary and documents you mentioned?"

Ryan took a deep breath. "Because we believe that the Association is not the only one after Kate."

Nick ran his free hand through his hair. He had been afraid of that.

Cindy and Jen both looked as shocked as Kate felt. Cindy shifted closer to Ryan and asked, "Are you sure? How do you know?"

Ryan regarded Cindy compassionately. "We're almost positive," he paused. "We've been researching this for a while now."

"I still don't understand what I have to do with anything." Kate was getting a headache, and she could tell it was just going to get worse.

Robert tried to help everyone understand. "The family line that had their gifts bound have been trying to get them back for centuries. They've tried just about everything to reverse the binding ceremony so that they can access their gifts. Some of them have become obsessed with retrieving their abilities."

"Why can't they have them back?" Grace asked, wanting to make sure that the family was not being unjustly persecuted.

Jason shifted closer to her. "Almost every crazy dictator, evil ruler, or maniac terrorist can be traced back to a branch of that family line. We don't know if they went crazy and it's hereditary, or if they become crazy with the obsession to restore their gifts."

Grace looked at everyone. "Great, so basically, we're up against the evil empire, Darth Vader, and the Emperor?" Jason grinned at her, loving the *Star Wars* references.

"I'm sorry, I don't speak science fiction geek," Robert said sarcastically.

Jason rolled his eyes. "Come on. It's so easy. The Association is the Evil Empire. Brooks is Darth Vader, and the head of the crazy family line is the Emperor. It's so not funny when you have to explain it."

Robert shook his head. "Grace, to answer your question, yes and no. We know that Kate is on the Association's radar. We also know that from the events that happened this summer, people witnessed Kate's gifts, so others are now aware of what she can do. We don't know if that information has gotten to anyone from that family line, but we have to assume so since the documents about the ritual were stolen. Brooks has been after Kate since before she was born."

"Is there anyone not after you?" Grace asked.

Kate slumped back on the love seat. Part of her wanted to take the kids and go hide somewhere, and the other part wanted to go fight the world. "So what do I do?"

"We learn everything we can and go from there," Nick told her. "We're all here for you, Kate."

Robert started to pick up copies of scrolls and tablets off the coffee table. "Ryan was able to get these copies from a buddy of his who works in the archives. They had already been scanned and translated before the burglary. Basically, they outline what we think happened in the original binding ritual. It's unclear exactly what occurred because they are from hundreds of years after it had happened."

"What does it all have to do with me?" Kate asked.

"There was a woman who had your gifts who was the central person in the ritual. She was able to combine all of the other gifts and abilities to bind the couple. It looks like there were specific gifts needed, elemental ones: earth, water, fire and wind. Two sensory gifts. There was no explanation for that. Energy, again no explanation. Telekinesis, and one other that was not listed."

Nick sat up. "Was that list available anywhere else?"

"What do you mean?" Robert asked.

"Could the bound family have had that list?" Nick asked.

Grace blanched. "Brooks was collecting Gifted kids. Could that be related?"

"I don't think so. He has a gift so it wouldn't be something he would concern himself with."

"What are some of the last names of the bound family? Do we have any of the leaders' names?" Nick asked.

Ryan began to read off names that were connected to that family. Kate yelled, "Stop!" when he read Santos.

"Wait. I've heard that name," Kate muttered, trying to remember. Nick pulled out the file that Dawn had given him last summer and flipped through it.

"Here." He pointed to a sheet from the file. "Damn. We could have missed this. Louise Santos Brooks."

"So Louise is the Emperor?" Jason asked.

"Looks like it," Nick told him. "She probably targeted Brooks because he had been already collecting Gifted teens."

"Wonder if he knows she has a gift but it's bound?" Jason added.

"No idea. But I bet not," Nick told them. "Well, at least we know who we are up against."

"That makes sense," Grace chimed in. "She would tell him about specific gifts that she felt would help them and he would look for children with those abilities."

"So now what?" Cindy asked.

"We need to make some plans, but I think we have covered enough for one night," Robert told her. "Let's meet back here after dinner tomorrow night." Kate gathered up all the information and placed it in her desk. She closed the roll-top and locked it.

Kate didn't get to look at the new file from Dawn, but she didn't think she could process any more information.

One by one everyone gave her a hug and some encouraging words before they filed out.

When Cindy came up to her, Kate hugged her closely and said quietly, "Are you okay? Your eyes were a little puffy when you came in. Were you fighting with Mike?"

Cindy gave her a squeeze. "I'm okay. I'll talk to you about it tomorrow." She looked pointedly at Nick. "We'll talk about a bunch of things." Kate rolled her eyes and Cindy grinned deviously.

Kate crumpled down on the love seat with exhaustion. She didn't want to move or think any more that night.

Nick pulled her against him and stroked her hair. He wished he could take away her worries and make the whole mess disappear.

"What am I going to do?" Kate asked.

"*We* are going to figure things out together. You're not in this alone. You agreed to be my girl so you're stuck with me now."

Even though she was mentally exhausted, she couldn't resist bantering with him. "Actually, we already established that you never asked me to be your girl."

Nick growled and nipped her ear with his teeth. Kate shivered. He kissed the area below her ear and she shivered some more. He kissed a slow path down her neck, and she leaned her head to the side to give him better access. "So what were you saying about not being my girl?"

She closed her eyes. "Hmm?"

He kissed up her jaw toward her mouth. "Say it."

"What?"

"Say it. Say you're my girl." He skipped her mouth and kissed a trail back toward her ear. He whispered softly, "I want to hear you say it, Kate."

She didn't want to give in, but he was making it almost impossible.

He pulled her earlobe into his mouth and she made a sound that he thought was very much like a purr.

"Kate," he whispered.

"Yes."

"Yes, what?" he prodded.

"Yes, I'm your girl," she admitted.

He abruptly stopped his teasing, leaned back with his hands folded behind his head, and grinned at her with a triumphant smile.

"Oh, you brat! I can't believe you did that."

He gave her his most innocent look and said, "What are you talking about?"

She gave him a halfhearted glare, but he pulled her closer and captured her lips in a scorching kiss.

———◆———

Alex was stiff all over from lying completely still on the floor at the top of the steps. She had wanted to listen to what was going on and knew that they wouldn't fill her in even though both she and Zach were old enough to know. She looked over at Zach, who was on the other side of the stairs listening in as well. She mouthed, "Let's go before she comes up here."

They quietly stood and made their way to Zach's room. Zach motioned for Alex to go to her own room, but she followed him anyway. Once they shut the door quietly, Alex turned on him with her hands on her hips.

"What the heck is wrong with you? Why would you risk everything to harass a teacher like that? Mom and Dad would have thrown a complete fit!" Alex was furious. She had been holding it in the entire time they were listening in to what was going on downstairs.

"You're not my mother, so back off."

She was just getting started. "You could have gotten us all caught. After all the crap you've been giving me about getting Kate mad at us and you pull this? Why didn't you tell me you were doing it?"

"You've been keeping secrets from me. You haven't been talking to me and you've been acting bitchy lately."

"Me? I haven't done anything!" Alex challenged.

"Oh really? The fire starting?" he paused. "I know you're texting and messaging with someone and I caught you trying to sneak out."

Alex slumped on Zach's bed. "What's happened with us? We used to tell each other everything."

Zach sat down next to her. "Things are changing and we let all kinds of stuff get between us."

"Yeah, you're right. We can't let that happen. We've got to stick together."

"How long do you think I'm going to be grounded?"

Alex smiled. "Knowing Kate, a couple of days as long as you don't do anything else."

"It's really going to stink if I'm grounded the whole break," Zach mumbled, more to himself than Alex. "What's going on with you? Why the sneaking around?"

"I'm really freaked out about the fire stuff," Alex admitted.

"You don't have to be. The guys will help you get it under control. It's a cool gift to have. Your abilities are changing just like mine did. I bet Jason would love to work with you."

Alex shrugged and didn't respond.

"Hey? Lex?"

"Haven't you heard about the fire starters from the past?"

Zach shook his head.

"Most of them caused all sorts of trouble and some couldn't ever get it under control. There have been a few famous fires throughout history that could be traced to a fire gift."

"That won't happen to you. The guys will help you and Kate knows all that 'emotions' stuff. She'll help you learn control and how to keep calm. You'll be fine. Don't worry. You need to talk to Kate."

"I can't talk to her right now. You just heard all that stuff tonight. She has enough to deal with."

"You need to talk to someone."

"I'll see how things go."

"Who were you sneaking out to meet?"

Alex gave Zach an annoyed look. "That's none . . ."

"Don't even try to tell me it's not my business."

She shot him a dirty look. "It's just some kid I've been chatting with"

Zach was suspicious from the way she said that. "From school?"

"No. I met him online."

"Lex. You don't even know the guy and you were going to meet him?"

"I wasn't going to meet him. I just wanted to talk to him in private. He has been bugging me to meet him though."

"You can't go meeting someone you don't know."

"I know that but he says he has information about fire gifts."

"YOU TOLD HIM YOU HAVE A GIFT?"

"Shh. You're going to get Kate up here. He's Gifted, too. He told me about his gift first."

"You still can't trust someone who randomly comes up to you and tells you he is one of us. Haven't you learned anything?"

"I'm not stupid, Zach. I just really want to know what information he has. He doesn't trust sending me the information in case someone else finds it."

"It sounds wrong, Lex. I'm worried about you."

Alex smiled and hugged her brother. "Thanks. Love you, Z."

"Love you too, Lex."

They opened the door a crack to listen. They wanted to make sure it was safe for Alex to go back to her room. It was very quiet downstairs so Alex figured it was safe to dart into her room. Right before she closed her door, Zach and Alex heard Kate giggle. Alex smiled but Zach made a gagging face. He hated it when Kate and Uncle Nick kissed and from the sound of things downstairs, that was exactly what they were doing.

Char Webster

Chapter Twelve

Frank followed the minivan to a neighborhood that he didn't think he would ever be in again. It was the same neighborhood where he had grabbed those kids last summer. He parked off to the side of the road down the street from where the van pulled into a driveway. Frank watched John get out and walk up to the porch. He expected him to enter the house, but instead, he pulled himself up to the roof of the house and flattened himself along the peak. He was watching the kids from the summer. Apparently, Brooks hadn't given up on them. That made Frank really worried about Kali.

He pulled out his phone and dialed Bret, who picked up immediately.

"Hey. What's up?"

"Kid, you need to be extra careful with Kali. I think Brooks may be looking for you guys."

Bret stiffened and took a deep breath. "I'm always careful. You know that."

"Don't screw this up, Kid, or I will kill you. If something happens, grab Kali and run just like we planned."

"Got it. How do you know he's after us?"

"I don't know, but he's having the Taylor kids watched. I'm down the street from their house now."

"You mean Alex and her brother from the summer?"

"Yeah. That's them. Watch Kali and I'll be back soon." Frank hung up and continued to watch John on the roof. He wasn't sure what to do about that situation. He felt like he owed them for his part in their kidnapping.

"You should get some rest," Nick told her. He didn't want to let her go from his arms, but he knew they couldn't stay on the couch together all night. He wanted to, but he knew Kate wouldn't want the kids to see them like that.

"You can't keep staying on the couch," she said quietly. He wasn't sure if she was inviting him up to her room, which was probably wishful thinking, or if she was trying to kick him out.

Kate almost laughed at the emotions she felt raging through him. She could tell exactly what he was feeling. He wasn't hiding it very well. She wanted him to stay with her and hold her all night, but it wasn't something that the kids should see.

"Don't look so panicked. I'm not telling you to leave." She needed to finish before he got too excited. "And no, you're not staying in my room either." She thought he looked so cute when he pouted. "You can stay in the spare bedroom."

He pulled her closer to him and tried to kiss her neck. She jumped away from him. "Oh no, you don't. You're not doing that again to get your way."

His smile was brilliant. "Why don't I hold you for most of the night in your room and then go back to my room before everyone gets up? This way we both get what we want."

"Is that right?"

"Absolutely." He grabbed her hand and pulled her toward the stairs.

Brooks slammed the iPad down on the table. The girl had not responded to any of his messages and he was getting really angry. He left her three text messages and a couple of posts on social media. She had been less and less responsive lately and he needed to get her attention back. It had been so easy to lure her into thinking he was the only one who understood her.

"No answer from the girl?" Joel inquired.

"Not yet." Brooks hated admitting any kind of setback.

"Maybe we need to find that kid Bret. He was the social media wiz. Didn't he set up all your accounts?"

"Yes, but only after I hurt that one girl he always tried to protect. That kid was nothing but trouble. I'm glad I don't have to deal with him anymore. Frank can have him. Useless gift. So what if he could control water? It's never really helped me with what I wanted done."

"John called a few minutes ago. There was some commotion last night at the woman's house and tonight they seemed to be having some sort of meeting with everyone there. The Taylor guy is back and has been staying at her place."

"Interesting. I wonder why he gave up pursuing me," Brooks

pondered.

"Maybe he got tired of all the false leads the Association was feeding him?" Joel laughed.

"No. Something else had to have happened. Find out what it is."

Brooks wondered if someone had gotten to the man he was paying at the Association. He was a valuable asset, and Brooks didn't want to lose him. Now that he thought about it, Brooks realized he hadn't heard from the man in several days. That would be a serious setback if he lost that connection.

Brooks left the room to get some time away from Joel, who was getting on his nerves. Brooks had moved them from the shack he was sharing with Joel to a bigger—and thankfully cleaner—place much closer to the girl and Kate.

He would have Kate and those kids soon, and then he would start his collection all over again.

Jen had a bounce in her step as she walked into Kate's office for her first day as her intern. She was actually excited about it. Jen loved that she was going to be spending time with Kate, but she also loved that her brother, Robert, Nick and Ryan were taking her seriously enough to give her this important assignment. She hated being thought of as only Jason's tagalong sister.

"Hey, Jen," Kate greeted her. "How are you?"

Jen took notice of Kate's happy expression and slight glow, and smiled. "You seem very happy, especially after last night's meeting. Could that have to do with a certain dark-haired, 'blue-eyed hottie?'"

Kate's grin lit up her entire face. "It's completely crazy to feel this way when there is so much happening."

"You're allowed to be happy, Kate. Especially now. You need to grab whatever happiness you can because who knows what can happen." Jen hoped that someday she would find a guy who looked at her the same way Nick looked at Kate. She wanted to feel that kind of magic.

"Okay, I cleared your internship with my principal. I told him that you needed the hours desperately and that your other assignment abruptly ended and you were stuck in the middle of a semester. He feels for students, so he will help us get you approved. I gave him the background report Ryan created for you and he requested an official one from the state. Ryan said he would handle that. Ted told me that you can work provisionally until the board approves you at the meeting next week. All you need to do is fill out some papers, meet with him real quick and we'll be good to go."

Cindy rushed into Kate's office during her morning prep period. She called out a quick hello to Jen, who was changing a bulletin board on the wall of the office, then flopped down in one of the chairs in front of Kate's desk and said, "Well?"

"Well, what?" Kate asked.

"Oh, don't even try to avoid my question. I've waited almost two days to get the details from you."

Kate smiled. "There isn't anything much to tell you."

"I want to know what I missed over the summer and what is going on with you and him now. You're glowing and after what was revealed last night, I half expected you to have bags under your eyes from crying. You don't, by the way. You have that 'I woke up with a hot guy' look."

Jen wandered over to join them. She wanted to hear this story as well. Kate couldn't help but smile wider.

"You did, didn't you?"

"No, we didn't wake up together. He stayed in the spare bedroom."

Jen chimed in. "Notice how she didn't mention falling asleep." Kate's blush told them everything they needed to know.

"Did he do the 'sneak out' thing this morning?" Cindy asked.

"I'm not talking about this."

"Aww. Come on, Kate. I need to live vicariously through you since my love life stinks," Jen told her.

"Me too, since I dumped Mike."

"You haven't told me about that either. What happened? You came in last night looking upset. Tell me."

"Okay. I'll tell you but you have to tell us about Nick first," Cindy challenged. "So is he the hot guy from The Deck last summer?"

"Yes, he is."

Cindy squealed. "I knew it." Jen looked confused so Cindy filled her in. "Kate had noticed a really gorgeous guy with incredibly sexy blue eyes staring at her across the dance floor at a bar. She lost sight of him and he disappeared, and she became very interested in finding him."

"So, you guys just happened to see each other one night?" Jen asked.

"Not exactly," Kate told them, and then explained the details of her relationship with Nick.

"Wait a minute. He left you after all that with a NOTE?" Cindy exclaimed. Jen shook her head.

Kate was done with the interrogation so she turned to Cindy and said, "Your turn."

Cindy's shoulders slumped. "I broke up with him. He's going to Florida with or without me and said that he didn't mind if I came along but hadn't expected me to."

"Ouch," Jen said, flinching. "That's horrible."

"Oh, Cin, I'm so sorry." Kate felt so badly for Cindy. She knew that Cindy really liked him, and Mike didn't deserve her feelings.

"It's okay. I'll get over it."

"Maybe Ryan can help you get over it," Kate teased.

"Kate!" Cindy screeched, but started turning pink.

"What am I missing?" Jen asked.

"Ryan has a little crush on our girl here," Kate explained.

"He does not!" Cindy was even redder.

Jen sat up straighter in her seat, clearly excited. "He does watch you every time you're around and he gets a very goofy expression on his face."

"Okay. Prep period is over. Got to go!" Cindy jumped up and hurried from the room.

Kate and Jen both started to laugh.

———●———

Nick walked into his house down the street to meet Robert. They had plans for a little excursion that would, hopefully, generate more information.

Nick noticed that Robert was looking down at a piece of worn paper. Robert shoved it into his wallet quickly and nodded to Nick.

"Hey, man. You still have that old sketch? It's been like five years since you found that. Why do you still have it?" Nick asked, concerned about the look of melancholy his friend was wearing.

Robert shrugged. "It's just a cool sketch. No big deal."

Nick knew the look Robert was giving him. His friend didn't want to talk about it. Robert never wanted to talk about that sketch.

He and Robert had been on their second assignment out of the Association Academy and were sent to Rutgers University to investigate some experiments being conducted around research into extrasensory abilities. They had been about to enter the science building where the lab was located when Robert stopped to help a girl who had fallen. His friend had taken on an odd, faraway look after helping her pick up her books, which had scattered all over the sidewalk.

When she scurried away, a piece of paper fell out of one of her books. Robert watched her hurry into the next building. He walked over to it and picked up the sketch. It was a detailed drawing of the girl's eyes, and it seemed to hold him captive. Robert folded it in half and shoved it in his pocket. He'd had it ever since, and Nick would catch him staring at it occasionally.

Robert noticed Nick's approach. "Are you ready to go?"

"Yeah."

"You don't sound ready," Robert teased.

Nick sighed. He wanted to have a little fun with Robert but he was worried about Kate. "Do you think we need to worry about this detective?" Nick asked Robert.

"I don't know. We need to figure out if he is the same guy who was asking questions this summer. If he is, then we need to do something about it."

"Yeah," Nick said, running his hands through his hair. "I feel like everyone is after us right now."

"They're not after us. They're after your girl."

Nick rubbed the back of his neck. "I don't know how I'm going to be able to protect her from everyone."

"You won't have to. We're all in this together. You need to stop thinking you have to do all this alone. We're your best friends and we're a team. That's how it is and always will be."

"Thanks."

"Now let's go spy on the Association."

Both of them were dressed in camouflage clothing, since they were going to be hiking in the woods and for obvious reasons didn't want to be seen. Hopefully, they wouldn't run into any hunters. Nick picked up both backpacks full of the supplies they would need and headed for his SUV. Robert climbed in with a few of Ryan's tech gadgets.

"Does Ryan know you're borrowing his toys?" Nick teased.

"He's working and what he doesn't know . . ." He trailed off.

"He's going to clobber you if you break anything."

Thirty-five minutes later, they pulled off of the main road and onto a dirt path that looked more like a trail than a street.

The compound was about two miles to the east, on another dirt road. They purposely chose the road they were parked on to conceal the Jeep Cherokee, and to be able to approach on foot without being seen. They needed to know what kind of security the facility had and how many people were there.

They hiked through the woods slowly, taking in everything that was surrounding the compound. Nick made note of any security measures they witnessed and Robert mapped out the locations of any guards and potential hazards. They were both enjoying themselves.

"It's good to be working with you again like this," Nick told him.

"Let's have some more fun then." Robert pointed to a building on the outer edge of the property. It didn't look like the other buildings and it seemed to have more security around it. "Let's check it out."

They crept up toward the building that was painted in greens and browns to partially camouflage it. It was two stories tall, with very few windows. They circled to the other side of the building to see if there was anything else interesting about the structure.

"One door in the front and a garage door on the side toward the back," Robert commented. "Looks like two guards are stationed in front and two in back."

"It's a prison or holding facility," Nick guessed.

"Probably."

"Wonder who they're holding there?"

"It was listed as a barn on the official documents on this compound," Robert read from a sheet he pulled out of his backpack. "No way that's a barn."

"We're not going to be able to get close enough in the daylight to check it out properly," Nick told him. "Let's come back another time."

"I want to check out something else first," Robert called quietly as he sprinted off into the woods.

"Where are we going?"

"You'll see. Come on."

Robert came to a tower that he knew the forest rangers had used for a fire lookout in the past. He grinned. "Are you up for a climb?"

"There are ladders on both sides." Robert's grin was contagious. Nick was having so much fun. "Race you to the top."

Robert suddenly got a sly look on his face. He clasped Nick's hand and forearm in a friendly challenge pose and started to concentrate. "No using your gift to gain speed, Taylor," Robert called out as he used Nick's gift to his advantage.

They both took off at a run toward the tower and started climbing as fast as they could. Nick was falling behind and tried to use his gift to catch up but he couldn't use it. He couldn't even *feel* it. He started to panic and almost fell but managed to grab on to the tower ladder to catch himself. He held on tightly, trying to calm down, resting his forehead on the rungs.

Nick looked up and Robert was already at the top of the platform, with a cocky grin on his face. He managed to pull himself together long enough to continue his climb to the top. When he swung himself up onto the platform, Robert was leaning against the railing.

Nick sat on the floor and continued to regulate his breathing. He couldn't panic. There had to be an explanation as to why he couldn't access his gift.

"Dude, are you okay?" Robert asked, concerned.

"No." He paused. "Rob, my gift is gone. I can't feel it." Nick was miserable.

Robert started laughing. "So you tried cheating on the way up, is that it? How else would you know your gift was gone?"

Nick stood up and faced Robert, suddenly suspicious. "What did you do? You asshole! I almost fell off the damn tower!"

Robert laughed but stopped himself. "Dude, I didn't mean for you to almost get hurt. It was just a joke. I swear I didn't mean any harm." Robert put his hands up in surrender.

"What did you do to take my gifts? They will come back, *right*?"

"You'll be back to normal in about ten minutes. Promise. But for now, I'm going to check out your gifts."

"You took my gift from me? How? How could you possibly do that?" Nick demanded.

Robert shrugged. "My abilities have developed while you've been away. I can now absorb someone's gift for a short period of time. Usually it only lasts for about ten to fifteen minutes."

"And you're just telling me this now?" Nick complained.

"I wanted to screw with you." Robert shrugged again.

"Well, it worked. Please tell me you already did this to Jay and Ry."

"What do you think?"

"Good. At least I wasn't first. Who was first by the way?"

"Kate," Robert told him but quickly continued at Nick's scowl. "It was a complete accident. I didn't know I could do it at that point. It just sort of happened. I thought it was completely cool. Although, Kate wasn't too happy about it until she got her gifts back."

"That's a cool thing to be able to do. I'll give you that."

Robert laughed. "I really am sorry. It probably wasn't the smartest idea to do that to you on a climb this high. I hadn't thought that part out."

"It's okay." Nick shook his head and gave him a guilty laugh. "I wouldn't have tried to use my gift if you hadn't been beating me so badly."

Robert got another guilty look on his face. "You were cheating!" Nick yelled. "Just wait until I get my gifts back."

"Hopefully, we will be on the ground by then," Robert teased. "I had to see how your gifts worked."

"Yeah, uh-huh. So besides, stealing my abilities, why are we up here?" Nick asked.

"Didn't you read the sign as we were jogging up to the tower?"

"No, I was too busy racing you."

There were a bunch of signs that said "Private Property" and "Do Not Trespass" with one of the corporation names that the Association used to hide things. "This used to be a public fire station and now it's an Association tower," Robert told him.

Nick pulled out the maps from his backpack. "On the maps of this area, it looks like another fire tower was newly constructed about two miles from here."

"Makes sense that the view from here would probably show something the Association wouldn't want anyone to see."

"Absolutely, but what?" Nick asked.

"We need to figure that out. Too bad we don't have Ryan's vision. Even these binoculars aren't as good as he is at seeing far."

"Why do you think no one is guarding this tower?" Nick asked.

Robert looked at one of his documents. "It shows that the tower was demolished. They probably only have people swing by in shifts to check on it. Hardly anyone ever comes out here in the middle of nowhere."

"We should probably get out of here and come back with the rest of the team and do some night surveillance."

"Yeah. We need to make some plans to come back." Robert nodded. "Right now I'm going to check out your gifts before I lose them." He started to climb down the tower, and Nick followed at a slower pace. When Nick reached the bottom, Robert was trying to bend a metal sign to see if Nick's strength could do it. He wasn't completely successful.

"It takes a lot of practice to master the energy flow. It does make you stronger, but you have to learn how to focus it."

"That's too much work. I thought your gifts were supposed to be way cooler."

"Hey. You take my gifts and then you disrespect them. Not cool." Nick smiled because he could feel his gifts returning. "Ha! They're back."

"I want to try them again another time," Robert muttered to himself.

"Let's go, the girls should be home from work soon and I want to find out if Kate still has her gifts, and make sure that serum didn't take them away. Since Kate's gifts are so much stronger than anyone else's, it may take longer to affect her."

"Does Kate know you're worried about that?"

"No. She has enough to worry about."

"Yeah, she does. Let's go."

Alex threw her phone into her locker without even looking at it. Rick was texting her more and more. It had been sort of cool in the beginning, but now he was starting to concern her a bit. Maybe Zach had been right about the guy. Maybe she shouldn't text him anymore.

"Hey, Alex. I've called your name five times. What are you doing?" Emily said from a locker a few down from hers. They were both getting changed for gym class.

"Oh, sorry. I didn't hear you."

"I know. I asked you about the homecoming dance this weekend. It's the last school event before fall break."

"I don't know. Do you really want to go?"

"Yes! I really want to go and you're coming with me. Brian asked me to go with him today."

"WHAT!" Alex screeched. "Why didn't you tell me?"

"He just asked me before this period."

"Oh, okay." Alex was a little disappointed that no one had asked her to go.

"Don't give me the pouty face. Brian told me that Josh wants to go with you and that he was going to ask you after school."

Alex beamed at her friend. Josh and Brian were best friends and a couple of the cutest guys in their grade. The homecoming dance suddenly became a lot more interesting.

"You're going to go with him right?" Emily prodded.

"Yeah, if he asks me."

"He will," Emily was bouncing. "We need to go dress shopping!" She was very excited about it, but then mellowed. "My mom's sick and can't take me. She has a really bad head cold."

"I'll ask Kate when I get home from practice. I'm sure she'll take us both."

Emily was back to bouncing and both girls headed out to the gym for class.

———⬥———

Don stood in the tree line by the parking lot of Kate's school, watching for her to come out of the building. If she stuck to her previous schedule, she was due to exit the school soon and then go pick up the little girl from daycare. Sometimes she came back to the school to watch the older girl in a game, or she would go to the middle school up the street to watch the boy play his sport.

He wanted to catch Kate doing something, anything that would allow him to bring her in again. She was an abomination, and she should be locked up. No one with the amount of power she had should be allowed to walk free. The Chancellor was taking a huge risk trying to render her abilities useless. They should have just gotten rid of her.

Don watched her walk out to the parking lot with her friends. They were probably not going to leave her alone for a while, which would make things harder for him. He took a couple of photos of the women getting into their vehicles. Don was still pissed at the one who had given him a massive muscle spasm at the club that night.

She needed to have a little payback.

———⬥———

Alex couldn't wait to get home from school. She needed to talk to Kate about homecoming. Alex hadn't yet mentioned the dance to Kate, but since Kate worked at her school, Alex was sure that she knew it was that weekend coming up.

She was still smiling from how Josh asked her to go. He had come up to her right before field hockey practice began. She was lacing her cleats and he sat down on the bench next to her. "Hey," he said quietly.

She tried really hard not to smile too broadly as she said, "Hi." She could tell he was nervous because he kept kicking the dirt with the toe of his soccer cleats. He should have been on the other side of the school beginning his own practice.

An awkward silence stretched between them while Alex waited for him to ask her. She couldn't take the quiet anymore so she blurted out, "Emily's going to homecoming with Brian."

He let out a deep breath. "Yeah, he told me he was going to ask her to go. I had already told him I was going to ask you so he thought it would be cool if we all went together."

Alex was still waiting for him to ask her to go. "That's cool. She was really excited about going."

"He is, too. He even asked if my dad would drive us all in his Lexus SUV." Alex's coach blew his whistle to signal the beginning of practice. Josh got up and said, "Well, I'll text you later."

Alex couldn't believe he didn't ask. She was just about to be crushed when her mouth had a mind of its own. "Are you going to ask me to the dance?"

Josh's eyebrows shot up and he got a huge grin on his face. "Oh, whoops!" he said, then walked over to her and asked quietly, "Will you go with me?"

"Yes," she said a little too loudly, and ran onto the field. She hadn't stopped smiling since.

After practice, Alex ran into the house and went right for the kitchen where Kate was usually making dinner. "KATE!" she yelled.

"Hey. Everything, okay?" Kate asked, concerned—until she spotted Alex's huge grin.

"We need to go shopping! I have a homecoming date and I need a dress. OMG, Josh asked me to go!"

Kate loved seeing Alex so excited. "That's awesome! I'm so happy for you. You're going to have such a good time."

"We're going with Emily and Brian. Oh, that reminds me. Can we take Emily shopping with us? Her mom's sick and can't take her and we need to look fabulous!" *Alex was talking really quickly. Cindy must be rubbing off on her,* Kate thought.

"We can all go Friday after school or Saturday morning."

"YAY!" Alex squealed. She threw herself into Kate's arms and hugged her tightly. "Thanks, Kate." Alex ran upstairs to text Emily.

Char Webster

Chapter Thirteen

Once again everyone was gathered at Kate's house. They had a bunch of things to discuss because they hadn't gotten to a lot of the information the night before.

Kate also wanted to talk to them about her astral projection, or whatever it had been. Her questions kept piling up. She was worried that it could happen to her again when she didn't want it to. Kate wanted to know what happened to her body when she left it. Was she is danger when she left? Why could she only go to Nick? Was it because of their connection or was there a different reason? Now that the stress of her ordeal was over, she needed more answers.

Nick and Robert were telling everyone about their trip to investigate the Association headquarters in the Pines. All of the guys were planning to go back another night for more information. Ryan was disappointed that he missed out on the fun.

"Yeah, it was fun until I almost fell off the tower," Nick complained.

Robert laughed. "I didn't know he would freak out like a little girl when he couldn't cheat to win our race."

Kate settled on the chair next to the fireplace and pulled out the file that Dawn had given her. She started flipping through it, scanning for names and places, while the guys busted on each other. One name, David Sanders, caught her attention.

There was a man named David Sanders who had inquired about a lost baby dozens of times in every Family Services office and adoption agency in the region. He had even offered a reward for information about the lost child. This man was her birth father's older brother, her paternal uncle. Her mother had mentioned him in her journal.

Kate leaned back in her seat, stunned. Her uncle had looked for her. He searched for her for years and had even made many more inquiries during what would have been her teenage years. The file stated that he specifically asked if any teens had been difficult or had unusual behavior or strange things happening around them.

She had an uncle out there who would probably want to meet her. He had looked for her. She was scared and excited all at the same time.

"Hey, everyone. You need to hear this," Kate began. "Dawn Johnson pulled some more information from her agency's records for me that related to the kids and any other cases that seemed similar. There are a bunch of cases we should look into, but one in particular caught my attention. My uncle David was looking for me for years! It even says here he raised suspicion because he kept asking about troubled teens and unusual occurrences."

Cindy walked over and sat on the arm of the chair. She squeezed Kate's hand. "You have always wanted to know about your family and here's your chance. Does the file have contact information?"

"Yes, but it's several years old," Kate told her. Everyone was watching the exchange. Kate started to feel a little self-conscious. What if her uncle no longer wanted to meet her, or had given up and moved on?

Nick knelt down in front of Kate. "We have ways of finding contact information for people. We can get it for you if you want."

Kate smiled nervously. "I'll think about it." Still feeling a little self-conscious, Kate wanted to turn the conversation to the current information and not her past. "There are about a dozen cases in here where weird things happened with foster children. We should check them out."

Grace spoke up first. "If you don't mind, I would like to research them. I was one of those kids and I know how lost and helpless I felt. I want to be able to help some others that could be in the same type of situation as I was in with Brooks."

Kate loved the idea. "That sounds great. I'll give you the information."

"I'll help her," Jason told everyone. "She shouldn't go out on her own. It's not safe."

Grace said something to Jason under her breath but Kate couldn't hear what it was. From the look that Grace gave Jason, it probably wasn't very nice.

Nick turned to Ryan. "Any luck on that flash drive?"

"Not yet. It has some sort of encryption that I haven't seen, but I'll get it. Don't worry," Ryan assured him.

"I know you will, Ry. That's why I gave it to you."

Jason stood up abruptly, rubbing his hands together. "Okay, now that Kate is over her ordeal, let's talk about her cool new ability. Have you tried it again, Kate?"

Kate knew they were going to ask her about it, and she wanted to talk about it, but she was nervous about it. "I still don't know how I did it, or if I can do it again."

Nick was still on the floor in front of Kate's chair. He turned sideways and grabbed her hand. "All of our gifts have strengthened and morphed into additional abilities. It makes sense that yours would as well."

Robert jumped up. "DUDE! Let me try it out. I can tell you if it works or not." Robert stalked over to Kate's chair, but Nick blocked his way.

"Not now," Nick told him, grabbing his shoulder to keep him away from Kate.

"It's the easiest way. Look at her. She doesn't look like she wants to talk about it or try it again. I would love to try it out."

Kate shook her head. She was going to have to face it. "Robert, you're not trying out my gifts." He got a pouty look and went to sit back down.

Jen came over and pulled up a chair from the dining room. She faced Kate. "Nick, could you please move out of the way so that I can try something with Kate?"

"I'm not moving anywhere," he told her stubbornly.

Before Jen and Nick got into a heated debate, Kate spoke up. "Nick, please. Jen and I have been working on other things together and she has a great method for tapping into gifts." Nick grudgingly got up and walked into the kitchen.

Everyone stopped to watch what Jen and Kate were doing. Robert and Cindy had already watched them go through the exercises before, when Jen was trying to teach Kate to focus her gift into self-defense moves.

Kate got comfortable and closed her eyes. Jen began speaking in a soothing voice. "Okay, Kate, remember how we have been working on breathing to connect with our gifts. Let's breathe deeply, inhaling and feeling the connection with our energy, filling our lungs with air and our center with our gifts. Exhale and release all the negative emotions, and push our gifts to the surface."

They practiced breathing for several moments, letting their gifts fill them. "Can you feel your ability to astral project?" Jen asked.

"I don't know. I feel a different energy, but I don't know if it is the astral projection."

"That's okay. If it's a different energy, then that's probably it. Focus on it and concentrate on the living room. See if you can picture the living room in your mind."

After a couple of minutes, Kate became frustrated. "I can't do this with everyone watching me."

Jen stared everyone down until they all filed out of the room and headed toward the living room. They wanted to be close by when Kate succeeded in projecting. Nick stayed in the kitchen, leaning against the counter with his arms crossed over his chest. He was not about to move too far from Kate. He needed to know she would be safe.

Jen gave Nick a look and he challenged her right back with one of his own. He wasn't going to back down to his friend's sister.

"Okay, Kate, everyone's gone. Let's try this again." They both closed their eyes and began breathing deeply again.

Kate focused on the new energy she felt and concentrated on the living room. She wanted to be in the living room with everyone. She could feel the energy flowing and just when she was about to release some of her energy, Maddy screamed. Kate immediately found her projected self standing in Maddy's room. Her daughter's eyes got huge and Kate was quickly pulled back into herself. She jumped up and ran up the steps.

Kate pulled Maddy into her arms and hugged her tightly. "Shh. It's okay. You just had a bad dream. You're okay. I've got you." Maddy squeezed Kate and didn't let go. Kate's heart broke when she saw tears in her eyes.

"Tell me what happened in your dream," Kate prodded.

"The bad man wanted to get you and Uncle Nick."

"No one is going to take us away from you." Kate was sitting on the bed with Maddy on her lap. She looked up and saw

Nick hovering in the doorway.

He walked over and sat next to his girls, putting his arm around them both.

"See, here is Uncle Nick. Everyone's okay."

The three of them sat quietly for a few minutes while Maddy settled down. She soon started to fall back to sleep so they tucked her in, each kissing her forehead.

Robert was waiting at the bottom of the steps for Nick and Kate to come back down. "Is she okay?" he asked, concerned.

"She had another bad dream," Kate told him. "She's had a few of them in the last couple of weeks. She also had quite a few right after the incident this summer, but that stopped after only a couple of weeks, and she's been fine since. I'm not sure what is causing them now." She went and flopped down on the love seat. Nick sat next to her and rubbed her back.

"We'll figure this out," Nick told her. "She's probably just picking up on the stress from everything that's been happening."

"I guess."

Jen interrupted. "You astral projected, didn't you? Right before you ran upstairs to Maddy? You suddenly slumped a little in your seat, but only for a few seconds. Then you inhaled deeply and took off up the steps. Where did you go?"

"I ended up in Maddy's room. I was so afraid that I was going to scare her. Plus, I couldn't hold her like that."

"I knew you would be able to do it again."

"Yeah, but I don't know exactly how I did it. I was thinking about the living room but ended up with Maddy."

Nick hugged her shoulder tightly. "You went to the place you needed to be in that instance. Just like you came to me that night. Maybe it's like your other gifts and it's tied to your emotions."

"Great, so I need to be upset in order to use it?"

"No, but maybe that's how you can start to access it."

Jen jumped up. "Awesome. Let's start practicing this tomorrow."

"Good idea. I'm suddenly really tired," Kate told her.

Everyone said their good-byes and left Kate and Nick alone at the door, watching them leave.

"Are you ready to go up?" Nick asked.

"I am, so I'm going to say good night to you now."

Nick looked confused. "You can say good night to me upstairs."

"No. I'm going to say good night right here and you're going to go back to your house down the street."

Nick got a stunned pouty look on his face. "Why? I'm staying right here to make sure you guys are protected."

Kate made sure he was looking at her. "We don't need anyone to stay here, Nick. I really appreciate that you stayed the last two nights, because I really needed your support after what happened to me, but now I need to be on my own." It had been too easy to completely lean on him after what had happened to her a few days ago, but now she needed to be able to take care of herself. She didn't want to solely rely on him for everything. She needed to remember to be strong for herself.

"Are you breaking up with me?" Nick asked, shocked.

Kate wanted to laugh but she kept her expression completely neutral. "No, but we just got together, Nick, after you walked out on me a couple of months ago." He started to protest, but she cut him off.

"Wait. Let me finish. You told me before that we couldn't be together and that everything in our world was against us being a couple. Then, we started to have feelings for each other but things were crazy with trying to get the kids back. After everything settled down and we had an opportunity to really talk about us, you left. Nick, you left without saying good-bye to me. You said it with a note. Then you were gone for months and all I got was a few text messages and a phone call."

"Kate, I'm back now and I'm here with you. We're together now. I'm so sorry I hurt you before. I was stupid."

"Yes, you were, and you did hurt me."

"Are you saying you don't want to be with me?"

"No. I want to be with you."

"So we're good." Nick tried to pull her into his arms but she stepped back.

"I didn't say that, either. I'm saying that things are not just completely fine. You need to build trust with me again. We also need to build a relationship, not jump right into something serious. We've never actually been on a real date."

"What do you mean then?"

"Do I really have to spell it out for you?"

From the look on Nick's face, Kate guessed that she would have to tell him exactly like it was. "Okay, you're in the dog house. You need to show me that you're going to stick around and that you're not going to leave me the next time you decide that we're in danger and you need to go off to chase it. We need to take things slow."

"So that means I'm being banished to the frat house?"

Kate couldn't contain a small laugh. "Yes, it does."

"I can't believe you are making me sleep there when you have a perfectly good bedroom upstairs."

"And exactly how long did you sleep in that room last night?"

"About an hour after you kicked me out of your room."

"Exactly. You sleeping in my bed every night is not 'taking things slow.'" Kate pulled Nick in for a hug. He was stiff at first but then hugged her back tightly.

Nick moved his hands up to her hair and smashed his lips to hers in a demanding kiss. He wanted to claim her lips and remind her of how good things were between them. He began to kiss his way toward her ear when she pulled away and took a couple of steps back.

"That's not going to work." She opened the door. "Good night, Nick."

He mumbled something she couldn't understand, but then grudgingly said, "Good night." She could tell he was pouting the entire way to his house. She closed the door with a small smile.

At the foot of the stairs, she heard the voice again. *You can't ignore me, Kate. You're mine now. No one can save you.*

She grabbed her head with both hands in an attempt to block out the world and crumpled to the floor. She stayed that way for several minutes before going up to bed. It had happened again. She was going to have to talk to someone about it. She just didn't want to tell everyone she might be going crazy.

Bret had spent three hours online looking for the old accounts he had been forced to set up for Brooks. None of his passwords worked, so he couldn't go into the accounts that way to see what Brooks was doing. Bret was searching for any reference to the screen names and any comments that those screen names had made. It was much harder than he had originally thought.

"Damn," Bret muttered to himself, but had said it louder than he had planned.

"You're not supposed to curse around me. Daddy told you so," Kali reprimanded him.

"Well, he's not here."

"I could tell him," she teased.

Bret picked her up and flipped her upside down. "Oh, yeah? How are you going to tell him now?"

Kali squirmed and giggled. "I wasn't going to tell Daddy. You know I wouldn't tell on you, Bret."

Bret set her down but decided to tickle her just a little. She giggled louder and screeched, "Stop!"

He let her go and expected her to go back to playing but she sat next to him at the table. "What are you doing?"

"I'm looking for something." He was being vague on purpose. He didn't want to worry her and he really didn't want to mention Brooks' name. Brooks had terrorized Kali so brutally that she still had nightmares. "I'm just doing some research."

"To help my dad?"

"No, to help a girl I know."

Kali looked at him oddly. "You're looking a little pinkish with some black. You're usually orangey-red."

Bret tried to distract her with teasing. "You and your colors. I bet your coloring books look like rainbows all the time."

She continued to study him. "You only get pinkish when you talk about that girl from the summer."

"Kali, you're silly. You have no idea what the colors you see mean. You told me they change all the time."

"I don't know exactly what they mean, but I do know that they change at certain times and they are always the same colors. You get pinkish when you talk about her. When you get mad and talk about Brooks, you get darkness around you. When you tell me about what you want to do when you grow up, you get light purple.

Bret was really surprised that nine-year-old Kali was that observant. "Okay, maybe I was looking for Alex online."

"Is that man after us again? Is he after Alex again?"

"Hey. You're safe. Your dad and I are going to keep you safe. He won't get you again. He doesn't know where we are."

"Is he going to get Alex?"

"I'm going to try to make sure he doesn't."

Nick begrudgingly trudged back to his house up the street. He couldn't believe that Kate had kicked him out. After spending last night with her in his arms, he was going to be sleeping alone and worse, in a house with the guys. He really hoped they were sleeping, or at least in their rooms. He didn't need the comments that they would surely make as soon as they saw him.

He stomped up the porch steps and opened the door.

As soon as he took a step into the house he heard Robert.

"Ha! Pay up, both of you." Robert had a huge grin on his face.

Ryan and Jason both groaned, but pulled out their wallets.

"I think you cheated," Jason complained.

"I didn't cheat. I just know these things," Robert shot back.

Nick tried to act like nothing was wrong, but he had a feeling that he was failing miserably. He was trying to ignore their bantering, so he began walking toward the stairs.

"Are you sure Kate didn't tell you what she was going to do?"

Nick stopped abruptly and turned around. "You guys bet on me?"

Ryan laughed. "No, we bet on Kate getting her fire back and kicking your dumb butt out of the house. Robert took tonight. I gave it until the weekend. Jason said she wouldn't kick you out at all but would want to. He thought she would feel bad about it."

"You guys are dicks," Nick muttered. He didn't think the night could get any worse. "I'm going to bed."

He heard roaring laughter from the guys as he climbed the stairs. He turned left to go to his old bedroom but stopped short.

No. Robert didn't, he thought. *There's no way I am getting kicked out of Kate's bed and out of my old bedroom, all in one night.*

Nick turned around to head back downstairs, but Robert appeared at the top of the steps.

"Are you kidding me?" Nick complained, pointing to his old room.

"Hey, you left and your room had the clear view to Kate's place. It made sense to switch. Plus, it was the best room," Robert explained with a grin.

Nick growled, but didn't comment. It was clear that his leaving had caused more damage than he had thought it would. Maybe Kate had a point about him needing to make amends.

"I'm going to bed. You're vacating my room tomorrow, so live it up tonight." Nick could hear Robert's laughter through the closed door of the bedroom.

———•———

Cindy flew into Kate's office five minutes before her prep period was supposed to begin.

"Hey. How did you get out of class early?" Kate asked. Jen looked up from a stack of papers that she was filing for Kate.

"Hey, girl. What's up?" Jen asked.

"I CANNOT BELIEVE YOU DIDN'T TELL ME!" Cindy nearly shouted.

"Tell you what?" Kate was confused. Jen was intrigued.

"You made Nick go home to his house last night. That's what!"

Kate turned a little pink and smiled contritely. "How did you find out already?"

It was Cindy's turn to look embarrassed. "Ryan told me," she explained quietly.

Jen jumped up. "Wait! When did you talk to Ryan?"

Kate got excited as well. "Yeah, Cin. When did you talk to Ryan? What's going on there?"

"No, no, no. You're not turning this on me. I want to know about Nick."

"Well, I want to hear both stories," Jen said. "Who needs coffee?" Just as Jen went to the Keurig, Jason breezed into the room.

He was all smiles as he joined them at Kate's conference table.

"What are you doing here, Jay?" Kate asked, exasperated. She should have known that the whole crew would bombard her with questions today. Apparently her love life was the topic of everyone's discussions.

"You know why I'm here. I want to hear the story. It looks like I was almost too late. Did I miss anything?"

"Once again, big brother, your timing is miserable. We can't have girl talk with you around."

"Sure you can. Just pretend I'm one of the girls."

It was obvious that Jason was not going to budge until Kate told him what he wanted to know. She sighed. Sooner or later they would find out anyway. She needed to figure out how to turn everyone's attentions elsewhere.

"It's really not that big of a deal, guys. He has a house and I have a house and I suggested that we both use our own houses."

"Aw, come on, Kate. There had to be more to it than that. The guy looked crushed when he walked in last night."

Kate had mixed feelings upon hearing that. She didn't like him being upset, but he needed to know she was serious and that their relationship was important.

Jen pulled her brother up from his chair. "Okay, you heard her, now out so we can have girl talk."

"You can't kick me out, too." Jason gave a fake pout look. He turned to Kate. "When did you get mean all of a sudden?" He winked at them.

"Good-bye, Jay," Kate called out.

"Fine. I'll go, but you guys are going to miss my company." He grabbed Jen's coffee and left the office. A second later he popped his head back in and said, "Eww. You put too much sugar in it."

"It was *my* coffee, Jay, not yours."

"Next time not as much sugar." He left again, but the ladies waited a moment to see if he was going to come back in to annoy them again.

Cindy rubbed her hands together. "Okay, so what is the real story?"

"I want to hear about you and Ryan," Kate challenged.

"You first!" Cindy would make sure that they talked about Kate and Nick the whole prep period.

Kate sighed. "Okay. When he first came back it was the night I had disappeared and things were out of control and my emotions were completely raw. I had missed him so much and suddenly he was back and wanted me. Wanted a relationship. I was still scared about what had happened and I needed him. I wanted to feel safe and protected. I needed him near me." Kate paused. She was still trying to make sense of everything she was feeling.

"Then things began to settle down. I still want to be with him, but some of the hurt and feelings of abandonment came back. I want to be in a relationship with him, but I need to know that I can trust him with my heart. I know he'll protect the kids and me, but will he protect my heart and feelings as well? After telling me he wants a real relationship, I can't go through him leaving again like he did before."

Cindy and Jen both came up and gave her a hug.

"That guy loves you," Jen told her. "You can see it in his eyes every time your name is even mentioned. Don't doubt that."

"I think he loves me. I just need to know that he's not going to run off again if there is another situation like before."

"Kate, I don't know Nick that well, but even I can see how much he cares. You just need to give it some time," Cindy agreed.

"I told him I wanted to take things slowly and that he was in the dog house and needed to make things up to me," Kate told them with a slight smile.

Cindy loved it. "Oh, that's awesome."

"How did he take that?" Jen asked.

"He pouted the whole way home last night." The three of them burst into laughter. "Okay, now spill, Cin," Kate commanded.

Cindy knew she was defeated. She was going to have to tell them. "He brought me coffee this morning and told me."

"*What*? He brought you coffee? Where did he bring it to you?" Kate asked.

"He brought it to my classroom."

Jen looked at her slyly. "This wasn't the first time he brought you coffee, was it?"

"Well, um, no."

Kate's eyebrows shot up. "Really? You've been holding out."

"It's just been a few times. He's been helping me practice for an upcoming tournament."

Jen didn't look convinced. "And neither of you mentioned it? We've all been teaching Kate self-defense and you two never said a word about it."

"It's not that big of a deal," Cindy assured them, but they clearly didn't believe her.

"You could've asked Jen to work with you since she has similar training," Kate challenged.

"He has a different fighting style and I wanted to get a guy's perspective."

"Yeah, uh-huh," Kate teased.

"Okay, got to go back to class." Cindy hurried out of the office.

Kate and Jen laughed as they watched her leave.

Char Webster

Chapter Fourteen

"Has she shown any signs of her gifts?" Chancellor Pete asked his two guards.

"It's unclear, sir. Her gift was not a directly visible one to begin with. It's almost impossible to detect her using it," Don answered.

Pete slammed his hand down on the desk. "I want you to find out today, not give me some half-assed answers. I shouldn't have to tell you how important this is."

Don started to argue but thought better of it. He would fight his battles with Pete at a later time. He didn't want to fight with Pete in front of a witness. When he made his move, no one would be around.

Pete watched Don closely. He wondered if Don was the leak in his organization. Maybe he needed to stop putting so much trust in him.

"You can leave now." Pete phrased it that way so that both his men knew he was still in charge and needed to respect him. He was going to have to put a little fear into Don.

The two men left quickly and Pete began to plan his next moves. It had been a calculated risk abducting the girl to inject her with the serum. If the wrong people found out what he had done, his life would be over.

Dawn had already had a tough day at work and it seemed that things were about to get worse. She had a haphazardly piled stack of new files on her desk, ready to fall onto the floor. Sheila, her secretary, had just returned to work from a long absence. Over the summer, she had been severely beaten and ended up in the hospital, but while she had been there, Sheila had experienced some sort of mental breakdown. Since her return, she was very heavily medicated, and this was causing her to have delayed reactions and slow processing skills. Dawn hoped that Sheila would eventually fully recover.

Picking through the files, she managed to create some order to the mess. At the bottom of one of the piles, a file caught her eye. It had more hand-written notes and bright yellow tags than all the other files combined. She could only remember one other file that had that many notes in it. Leaning back in her chair, she was unable to believe what she was reading. The similarities were disturbing.

This case involved two teens, both girls: Sara, age twelve, and Holly, age fourteen. Their father had been killed in the military and their mother had been missing for about a year and a half. Neighbors and friends had said that she never would have left the girls. There was an aunt who had taken them in but she was mugged and killed in Philadelphia six months ago.

Sara and Holly had been sent to an elderly grandparent who could not care for them. Authorities had taken them away from him, claiming signs of dementia. He had been telling people all kinds of farfetched stories about the girls and had claimed that they were all true, even when faced with losing them.

Sara and Holly were then sent to a series of foster homes, all resulting in them being thrown out for unexplained occurrences and violent outbursts.

Dawn closed the file with an exaggerated sigh. Should she call Kate? She had promised Kate that she would let her know if she found any other children with similar situations to those of her kids, and this situation screamed "Taylor kids." There was something weird going on with Alex and Zach—and even Kate and her friends—but Dawn couldn't deny that since going to live with Kate, Alex and Zach had been thriving. Maybe Kate could help these girls as well.

She picked up the phone and dialed.

"Hey, Kate, it's Dawn."

"Dawn, how are you? How's Kevin?"

"I'm doing well, and Kevin is still doing really well."

"Oh, that's so good to hear. I see him sometimes in the hall and he seems to be happy."

"He is, but that's not why I'm calling." Dawn took a deep breath to steady her nerves. She wasn't sure how Kate would react. They had been through a great deal in a short amount of time and Dawn didn't want to add any more to Kate's worries.

"I didn't think so. Dawn, why am I suddenly getting flashbacks from last summer?"

"You're far too perceptive for your own good sometimes."

"Now I'm scared," Kate laughed, but she was really intrigued.

"I have a case I think you might be interested in. Two teen girls. They have a file that looks an awful lot like the one your kids had."

"Really?" Kate paused. She had suspected that was what Dawn was going to say, but she hadn't really been prepared to hear it. "Do you want me to meet with them?"

"Yes. I think you might be the perfect person to work with them," Dawn told her. "Right now, they're with a new family, but if their pattern stays the same, they should be at the end of their welcome in about three weeks, possibly four."

"Do you want me to meet with them now, or wait until something else happens?" Kate asked.

"I think we can wait. They haven't done anything at this new place yet. We have a little bit of time. I'm going to send you a copy of their file so you can get familiar with it before meeting with them."

"That sounds good. I look forward to reading it."

"Thanks, Kate. I really appreciate it."

"Anytime, Dawn. We owe you so much."

"Good-bye." Dawn hung up the phone and hoped that she had done the right thing. There were too many similarities to ignore.

Kate hung up the phone and looked at Jen. "I think Dawn Johnson just found a couple more kids like us in the foster care system."

"Oh, no. We need to get them," Jen insisted.

"I agree, but we can't be too pushy with it. She wants me to meet with them in a couple of weeks. There isn't anything we can do until then without looking suspicious."

"I hate to think of Gifted children out there, alone and scared, and not having anyone around to help them with their gifts."

"I agree. She's going to send me a copy of their file. When she does, I'll have the guys check them out. They could be just regular, troubled teens."

"It's possible. What are we going to do with them if they are Gifted?"

"Not sure yet. I guess we'll figure that out after we meet them."

After finding the badly beaten and broken body of the professor who had been working on the translations thrown into the corner of the basement lab, Louise knew that she had to leave. She hadn't told Ray to get rid of him yet, but it seemed as if Ray was taking it upon himself to do things without her knowledge. *How long will it be before Ray turns on me?*

Louise hurried through the house and out into the garage. She needed to leave as quickly and quietly as possible. She didn't want Ray to find out she was going anywhere without him. He had slowly changed from her employee into what she felt was her jailer. She had a feeling that he was no longer taking her instructions, but being controlled by someone else.

She was too afraid to think about who could be issuing commands. She couldn't think about the possibility that he was pulling strings again behind the scenes. He had promised her that she would be in control. How foolish of her to have actually believed him. All of her hard work the past few years could be destroyed if she was not careful.

She pulled the emergency handle on the garage door to open it manually. The electronic opener was much too noisy and Ray would hear it in a second and come out to investigate it. She raised it slowly, releasing the rope inch by inch. Once it was open, she moved silently to the car.

Louise opened the door to the Mercedes as quietly as possible, sliding into the seat and shutting herself in the car. The push button start immediately revved the engine to life and she cringed at its loudness in the confined space. Throwing the car in reverse, she stomped on the gas pedal and flew out of the garage and onto the quiet street. Luckily, it was still early enough that most people were still asleep.

She watched for signs of Ray in the rearview mirror, but he did not appear. Finally, Louise let out the breath that she hadn't realized she had been holding. She was free of him, and free to plan her next moves. She hated leaving Emma there with Ray, but she had no choice. Louse couldn't take the girl and escape like she planned so she would go back for Emma when her other plans were in place.

Suddenly her phone rang in her purse. She let it ring until it stopped, figuring it was Ray wanting to know what she was doing. It started to ring again, so she pulled it out and looked at the display.

"Damn," she muttered to herself. She watched it ring a few more times, and then stop. Her worst fears were coming true. Another loud ring vibrated through the vehicle. Louise knew he would continue to call until she answered. She thought about throwing the phone out the window, but he would just send someone to track her down.

"What?" she answered abruptly, trying to sound confident and annoyed, even though she was nervous.

"Is that any way for you to speak to your father?"

"The term father usually refers to a person who shows some sort of affection to their child."

"You were coddled too much as a child. Look at you now."

"What do you want, *Father*? I'm sure you didn't just call to criticize me."

There was dead silence on the line and Louise wondered if she pushed him too far. She was just about to apologize when he said, "It's time for you to come home."

She half laughed, but it was empty. "I'm not a child that you can command anymore. I have the information and I'll be the one to decide how and when it's used."

"Do you really think Ray gave you all of the information that you asked him to steal?"

She paused. She figured that Ray had shared the information with her father, but did he withhold some of it from her? She forced herself to sound brave and convincing. "I have everything I need. Good-bye, *Father*."

She hung up the phone and prayed that she did have all the information she needed. She hated to think she might have to go crawling back to her father.

Detective Martin decided to pay another visit to the Sutton/Taylor house. He had a report about a house on her street that had been broken into while the owners were away on vacation. The couple's nephew had gone into the house to check on things and discovered that someone had been using the house, so he had immediately called the police.

Normally, the detective would have left the situation to the uniformed police, but they had discovered one piece of evidence that made his visit to Kate Sutton necessary. Her photograph had been sitting on the counter. It would not have raised any concerns for a typical investigation, but it had a date and time stamp on it from only two days before. It looked as if it had been taken from somewhere close and that she had not been aware it was taken.

Detective Martin knew there was something going on with that family and now he finally had something that he could use to force her to speak with him.

He decided to stop by her house for a short chat. Martin knew that she worked at a school and went to get her adopted daughter immediately after work. The nice ladies at the daycare had filled him in on her routine. Kate should have had enough time by now to get her daughter and return home.

He knocked on the door, determined that she would speak with him and not avoid him like she had done before.

Kate wondered who was knocking on the door. It seemed like just about everyone had a key to her house or used the back door. She looked out the window next to the front door and groaned. It was that detective who had questioned her about her disappearance.

Kate put on a fake smile and opened the door. She stepped out onto the porch to make it clear she was not going to invite him inside.

"Hello, Detective. What brings you here?" Kate asked politely, but with a cool edge. She did not want him to feel too comfortable at her house.

"Ms. Sutton. I have something I need to discuss with you. Would it be okay to go inside and sit down?"

"I'm sorry, Detective, but I need to make dinner. My kids will be home from their practices soon and they are usually starving." She hated to use her mind reading gift, but she had to know what he was really interested in finding out.

He was suspicious of her, the kids, and the guys. He knew something had happened over the summer, but didn't know what it was. He had also been investigating cases with similar patterns and reports of odd occurrences.

Great, Kate thought. *Just what we need, someone else we have to worry about.*

"This will only take a few moments, Ms. Sutton. It's for your protection and that of your adoptive children."

She continued to look at him, waiting for him to continue. She wasn't going to budge from her spot and she sure was not going to let him in her house. Who knew what would happen? With her luck, Maddy would suddenly display a gift in front of the man.

He sighed heavily, pulled out a photograph sealed inside a plastic bag, and pushed it toward her.

Kate couldn't control her gasp as she saw herself in the photo. It showed her inside her house, and it looked to be from close range. Someone had to have been right outside of her house, or have a high powered lens, to take that photograph. She glanced up from the photograph to a smug look in the detective's eyes, daring her to ignore the evidence in his hands.

"Where did you get that?" she asked in a very calm voice. She was impressed with how steady it sounded.

He sighed again, realizing that she wasn't going to invite him inside. He motioned to the two wicker chairs on the porch.

"Please have a seat. I'll be right back. I need to check on Maddy." Kate dashed into the house and went straight for the family room.

"Jen," she called. "Please watch Maddy while I talk to a detective outside. If I'm more than ten minutes, come get me with some excuse, just don't make it too over-the-top."

"Of course. What does he want?" Jen asked, concerned.

"He's fishing for information." Kate headed back toward the front door, and called over her shoulder, "Don't call the guys. They'll make this worse. We'll fill them in later."

Kate pulled the door closed and walked over to the chair next to the detective.

"Is everything okay?" he asked, gesturing toward the house.

"Yes. Everything is fine," Kate murmured. "So, you were just about to tell me where you got the photograph."

He narrowed his eyes at her, but decided to indulge her. "We found it on the counter at the Carters' house."

"I don't understand." Kate was confused. She knew that the Carters wintered in Florida every year. This year, their winter escape started in the beginning of October.

"The Carters had their nephew check on things for them. When he went into the house, he noticed that someone had been staying there. The house was a mess; the kitchen had dirty dishes in the sink, trash was piled everywhere, and several items of value were missing. When our guys went to investigate, they found this photograph along with the mess."

He wasn't going to tell her about the notebook they had discovered, filled with notes on her and her children. He would keep that to himself for the moment, and use it later as leverage to get her to cooperate. She was hiding something and he was going to find out what it was.

Kate tried to keep her expression neutral, but it was almost impossible. She had heard everything he was just thinking, and she couldn't believe it. She needed to get the information from him, but not reveal anything. Kate tried to calm her emotions. Maybe he would think she was upset over the photograph, which she was.

Kate knew she had to say something. "Why would someone have my photograph?"

"That is the question I have for you. Why would someone who broke into your neighbor's house have a photograph of you?"

"I just asked you that," she said a little impatiently. "How would I know why some crazy person who broke into a neighbor's house had my photograph?"

He gave her a look that clearly showed that he didn't believe her. "I don't know if you've noticed, but it's got a time and date stamp from two days ago. Did you know this was taken?"

She was actually glad that it was only from two days ago and that someone was not stalking her for very long. She chose not to answer that question, but to ask one of her own. "Did you catch the guy?"

"No. No one was there when we got to the house and no one has come back. We've been watching the area."

Kate wondered if she should have the guys check the neighborhood. *No, she thought, they would be even crazier with my protection.* She couldn't even move without someone being with her at all times. She was going to leave the guys out of this one.

"Ms. Sutton, I find it awfully odd that your daughter's daycare was concerned enough to call us when you didn't show up to pick her up after work and now, the same week, we find your photograph at a crime scene."

Kate stood up and glared at the detective. "I don't like your tone or your insinuations that those two completely unrelated incidents had anything to do with each other. Since when does having car trouble and being late to pick someone up equate to a crime? Maybe you should focus on who broke into my neighbor's house."

"You aren't worried about someone having your photograph? A photo, I might add, that was taken without your permission?"

She started to infuse him with calm, accepting feelings. "Of course that concerns me. Maybe he wanted to break into my house next. He obviously knew that the Carters were away. Maybe he stalks his victims," Kate rattled on. "What concerns me more is the fact that you are here and not out looking for the burglar. Please let me know when you catch him. Good-bye, Detective. I need to make dinner for my children."

"I'll be seeing you again soon, Ms. Sutton." He took his time walking off her porch and out to his unmarked police car.

Jen was in the foyer as soon as she heard the door close. "So?"

"Someone has been spying on us from a neighbor's house down the street. The detective had a photo of me in my house. I'm closing all of the blinds now and keeping them closed."

"Oh, yuck. That's really creepy." Jen shivered thinking about it.

"I know. What's worse is that there was some sort of log about the kids and me. The detective didn't tell me about it. He thinks he's going to hold it as leverage against me to get information."

"Oh yeah? Like that'll happen. We need to get a copy of it."

Kate could see the calculating look in Jen's eyes. She was definitely related to Jason. They both got the same look when they were planning to do something they thought would be fun and probably dangerous . . . or illegal.

"We do. The guys will want to deal with the situation themselves. I think we need to be very careful with this detective. He's already really suspicious of us."

Kate walked past the family room into the kitchen. Maddy was playing at her little kitchen set, making pretend dinner for everyone. She rushed up to Kate and gave her a big hug. "Jen didn't eat her dinner. She was watching you talk to the man on the porch."

Kate and Jen exchanged a look. Jen turned away, feeling guilty about being caught. She scooped up Maddy and said, "It's okay, Maddy. I'll eat my dinner now." Kate gave Jen a stern look before heading to make dinner.

Maddy was getting too observant. People usually spoke freely in front of her, thinking that she was too young to pay attention. She hadn't spoken much in the first few months of living with Kate, but lately, she had gotten much chattier. They were going to have to watch what they said in front of her.

Brooks was furious. He needed to find a way to release some of his fury before it manifested into something much worse. Bad enough he had to deal with the incompetence of Joel, but now Joel's moron of a brother was almost caught breaking into a home.

He wanted to hit something. Hard. Brooks hated waiting for anything and that was all he had been doing lately. He knew that he'd been becoming more and more grouchy and irritable.

It wouldn't get any better until he found a way to eliminate Frank. He would need to find someone to take care of Frank, or he would have to continue to hide in crappy houses in poor neighborhoods.

Looking around the small house with distaste, he couldn't believe he was in his current situation. Thankfully, the four-bedroom home was just enough space to avoid Joel but not big enough for anyone to take notice.

"Joel! Get in here," he bellowed. He could hear Joel shuffle his feet across the floor and knock into something, sending it crashing down. Brooks was completely disgusted with the man. He couldn't wait to get rid of him and his brother.

Joel opened the door to the small room that Brooks was using as an office.

"Yes?" Joel grunted. Brooks glared at him.

"Have a seat." Brooks pointed to the chair in front of his desk.

Joel looked worried for a moment but it quickly faded. He took his seat and then propped his foot on his knee. He was entirely too comfortable for Brooks' liking.

Brooks got up from his chair and walked around his desk toward the man slouching in front of him. Joel tried to straighten up a little but Brooks' hand clamped down on his arm, holding him in place. Joel tried to struggle, but his hold was complete.

Brooks' face slowly morphed into a wicked grin. He loved using his gift, so when he closed his eyes to concentrate, his skin tingled in delight. His whole body welcomed the feelings of fear that oozed out of Joel.

Brooks could feel Joel's fear growing until he finally discovered the one thing that Joel feared the most; Joel was terrified that he might one day be caught in one of the nightmares he inflicted upon people. Feeling almost euphoric, Brooks released Joel and stumbled back to his desk. Joel had a look of complete terror on his face.

"I want you to find your brother and get him in here right now."

Joel scurried from the chair and rushed out of the office. Brooks wandered to the window to look out at the wooded lot. He was going to have to find a way for Joel to experience one of his nightmares, and then maybe he would learn exactly with whom he was dealing.

"Jen, don't tell the guys the detective was here today," Kate told her as she made dinner. "I need to think about the situation before they swoop in and try to take over."

Jen grinned widely. "That's fine with me. Why don't we just come up with our own plan to get the information?"

Kate loved the idea. "Why should they have all the fun? Let's do it."

"Awesome. Let's call Cindy and Grace. We will probably need their help."

"Tell Grace to stop by school tomorrow during our prep period. We can talk there without the guys walking in and catching us planning to steal something from the police station."

"Great idea," Jen told her, and went to go call their friends.

Nick and Robert walked in a few minutes later. Nick stalked toward Kate with a determined look in his eyes. She tried not to smile as she took a few steps backward. She had to stop her retreat when her back hit the counter. He moved toward her until there were only a few inches between them. Nick leaned in closer, resting his left hand on the counter, blocking any retreat to the side. He inched closer and her breath caught in anticipation. His eyes were smoldering and his lips were just a centimeter away. She held her breath waiting for him to claim her mouth in what she hoped was a searing kiss.

She began to close her eyes when she felt him move past her mouth, brushing his lips across her cheek as he reached for a glass in the cabinet behind her. He chuckled as he straightened, glass in his hand, and moved away from her.

"Hey, Beautiful," he called to her, grabbing the filtered water out of the refrigerator. Nick loved to see Kate with fire in her eyes, and her eyes were blazing right then.

Kate turned around to the sink to conceal her embarrassment and irritation. She hated that he could so easily get her all flustered. She tried to ignore her pounding heart and the goosebumps he caused with just a look.

Nick was staring at Kate's back with a very satisfied expression on his face. If Kate wanted to take things slow, he was going to slowly and sensually torture her until she was begging him.

Kate glanced back toward Nick and caught the smug and

arrogant look on his face. *Oh, the brat*, she thought. *He was playing with me. I can play just as well.*

Robert was sitting at the breakfast bar watching his two friends with fascination. They were more fun to watch than some of the shows on TV. He watched Nick's play on Kate and was looking forward to her retaliation. It was sure to be entertaining.

"As fun as it is to watch you two play your games, we do have some things to do tonight," Robert told them.

Kate whipped around. "I have no idea what you're talking about." She then ruined that statement by glaring at Nick when he laughed aloud.

"We need to do some more research and we need to determine if Louise Santos Brooks is the one behind the theft at the Archives," Robert told them.

Nick nodded. "We also need to find out how much she knows and if she's still working with her husband."

Kate shivered, thinking about Brooks. "Is the entire ritual translated yet?"

"Not yet. Ryan's buddy is working on it." Robert played with a glass on the counter, spinning it between his hands. "I feel like there's something we're missing. Something that ties it all together. We need to figure it out before they do."

Nick looked grim. "We also need to figure out which gifts are needed for the ritual. Brooks and his wife have collected children for years. They may have the right combination of gifts already."

Kate went back to cooking dinner and Nick walked into the family room to play with Maddy. He sat down on the floor with her and she climbed onto his lap.

"How's my girl doing?" Nick asked, giving her a tight hug. "Are you going to make me dinner, Maddy?"

With a slight pout, she pointed to a plate on her kitchen set filled with plastic food. "Jen didn't eat her dinner. She was watching Kate talk to the detective outside."

Nick's eyes got wide. He wondered why Kate hadn't mentioned it. "What happened with the detective, Maddy?"

"They're going to steal the police station," she told him with a smile.

It took every bit of training he ever had not to react to what

Maddy had just told him. It didn't take much for him to piece together what must have happened. He wanted to scream. *Was she insane?* he wondered. *Did she really think she could steal something from a police station?* "Did Kate say when she was going to go to the police station?"

"At school tomorrow." Maddy was very proud of herself for remembering what Kate said.

Nick kissed her head and moved her off his lap. He needed to go for a walk before he exploded. "I'll be right back," he called, and rushed out the front door.

Robert crinkled his brow and followed him out the door. Nick was a few houses away when Robert caught up with him. "Nick, what's up?"

Nick glanced over at his friend and opened his mouth to tell him but closed it right away. He was so angry that the words would not come out of his mouth. He stopped and ran his hands through his hair. "I'm going to tie her up and lock her in the house."

Robert laughed. He thought something happened so he ran after his friend, but apparently Nick and Kate were still just being idiots. "Just give in. Believe me, you'll be much happier."

Nick looked at him like he was crazy. "I'm not talking about my relationship with Kate!" Nick yelled. "I'm talking about her crazy-ass plan to break into the police station and steal something."

"WHAT?"

"Yeah, Maddy told me. Apparently that detective came back today. I don't know what happened, but Maddy said that they were going to steal the police station tomorrow."

"They?" Robert asked. "Of course Jen and Cindy would be involved in this."

"Probably." Nick began to pace. "They'll get themselves arrested. What the hell was she thinking?"

Robert laughed.

"It's not funny."

"Sure it is," Robert said, continuing to laugh at the absurdity of the situation. "We can't let them try it, but we can have some fun with it."

Nick stopped pacing and faced Robert. "What do you have

in mind?"

"Let's follow them and let them have a little fun, but then stop them before they cause any real trouble."

Nick loved it. "I can't wait to see their faces when we catch them in the middle of it."

"Exactly."

Char Webster

Chapter Fifteen

They were sitting around Kate's meeting table during the prep period, sipping coffee as if they were just gossiping. Little did the world know that they were plotting an adventure.

Kate was happy with their plan. "Okay, Cindy and I will go into the police station and ask to see the detective. If he's there, we'll keep him occupied, with all kinds of worries I have. I'll make up all kinds of fears." Everyone agreed.

"While I'm crying all over him, I'll listen to his thoughts to see where the notebook is located. When I throw myself into the chair dramatically, Cindy, you come give me a hug and I will whisper where it is."

Kate looked at Jen. "You're going to be in the front of the station and you need to brush by someone, hopefully someone yucky, and use your gift to give that person a bad muscle cramp in his chest. The guy will fall to the floor and everyone will rush over to see what happened to him."

Kate continued "While everyone is distracted and I'm still crying to the detective, Cindy can grab the notebook."

"Grace, you'll need to distract the person who is watching the monitors on the cameras. They can't see what we're doing."

Grace looked uncomfortable. "Wouldn't it be better if Ryan hacked into their surveillance system?"

"We don't need him." Kate picked up a small device that looked like a cell phone. "This will disrupt their cameras for a couple of minutes. It makes it look like a power surge. I just don't want the person monitoring things to get too close of a look at what's going on."

They all smiled. Cindy shook her head. "This plan just might work."

Kate smiled. "If he isn't there, we need to talk to someone who has a work space near the detective's desk and work the plan from there."

Jen was getting excited. "So when do we do this?"

"Tonight. I'm going to set up a play date for Maddy at her friend's house and I'll let Alex and Zach sleep next door."

"Isn't Zach still grounded?" Cindy asked.

"I let him off with a warning. He's a good kid. Three days of being grounded and watching him pout was bad enough. I didn't have the heart to keep him grounded for any longer." They all laughed.

"Big softy," Jen muttered.

"And what do we tell the guys about tonight?" Grace asked.

"We tell them we're having a girls' night out."

Cindy laughed. "We are certainly going to have a girls' night."

They continued to review their plan until the prep period was over. They agreed to meet at Kate's house at seven that night.

Kate and Jen were packing up their stuff to go home at the end of the school day.

"Hey Kate, do you want to add anything to this file before I pack it away for the night?" Jen asked.

You can't get away from me, Kate.

Kate dropped the box of art supplies that she used for her students' groups and grabbed her head with both hands. She crumpled down to the floor holding her hands over her ears. Every time she heard the voice, her head felt as if someone was broadcasting it directly into her brain and it was vibrating throughout her skull.

"KATE!" Jen screamed and rushed over to her. "What happened? Are you okay?"

Once the vibrations seemed to recede, Kate stood up and faced Jen. "Yeah. I'm okay. Just a headache."

"That wasn't a headache, Kate. What happened?"

"Nothing, really. I'm fine now. Don't worry about it."

Jen narrowed her eyes at Kate. "I don't think you're telling me the truth. Something just happened."

"Jen, really. It was just a sharp pain in my head. It's gone now. It startled me. That's all."

"I'll let it go this time, but if it happens again, you need to talk to someone about it." Jen planned to tell Robert about what happed. Something didn't feel right and she needed to keep an eye on Kate.

Kate plastered on a fake smile and tried to sound cheerful.

"Come on. We have a girls' night to get to."

Robert jumped into the driver's seat of his SUV and looked over at Nick, who was already in the front passenger seat. They both shook their heads at Ryan and Jason, who were blaming each other for leaving the front door wide open. They had even begun to push each other. Nick gave in to his frustration and slightly bad mood, and yelled at them.

"I don't care who left the damn door open. Someone go close it so we can go." Nick winced at his own tone. He hadn't meant to sound that grouchy. He still couldn't believe that the ladies were actually considering breaking into a police station. His girlfriend needed her head examined.

"Dude. What crawled up your ass?" Jason shot back, only half kidding as he slid into the back seat.

Nick glared at him and Jason wisely kept quiet. Ryan jogged to the vehicle and hopped into the back with Jason. He was lugging a large black bag filled with computer equipment.

Nick watched the girls on Kate's front porch, laughing and smiling, and he could tell they were joking around. They were all dressed in what Kate called their "go out" clothes, which meant short skirts, heels, and sexy shirts.

Ryan was not happy with what he was seeing. "Do you guys see how Cindy is dressed?"

Robert smirked. "Just Cindy, Ry?"

"Okay, all of them. I can't believe they're going to a bar like that," Ryan complained.

"They're not going to a bar. They are going to get arrested for attempting to break into a police station full of cops," Jason joked. "Did you put the listening device on Kate's purse?"

"Yeah, but then she changed to a smaller one so the listening device is in her closet," Ryan told them.

"Great place for it, Ryan," Nick muttered. Kate and Cindy got into the front of Kate's BMW and Grace and Jen slid into the back. They were definitely not acting like they were going to commit a major crime in a matter of minutes. He could see them rocking out to the music as Kate pulled out of her driveway.

"What are they doing?" Robert asked, pointing to the car. "I swear that looks like they are dancing in the car."

Ryan opened the window and leaned his head out a little to listen. "Their music is blasting. I would say, yeah, they are dancing in the car."

They all laughed. The ladies were sure to be entertaining tonight.

Kate turned up the volume on the radio. "How perfect is this song!" she yelled over the music. Pink's song "Trouble" was either an omen or just a terribly ironic song to come on the radio right as they were starting off on their adventure.

"Guys, you're not going to believe what song is playing on their radio." Ryan shared. "It's called 'Trouble,' by Pink." They all burst out laughing.

"Oh, that's fitting," joked Jason.

Nick really hoped that they would not get into any trouble tonight. Well, trouble with anyone besides him. He planned to give them all a serious amount of trouble.

"Can we stop at Wawa to get a Diet Coke?" Grace asked, yawning. "I need some caffeine."

Jen agreed. "Yeah, I want a French Vanilla cappuccino. Wawa would be awesome right now."

Cindy nodded and Kate said, "Yeah. That sounds like a good idea."

"Now what are they doing?" Nick wondered aloud.

Robert couldn't contain his laughter. "They're stopping for snacks."

"Of course, they need to get something to munch on before stealing something from the police station," Jason joked sarcastically.

"Oh, and who was it that brought coffee and doughnuts to our last stakeout?" Ryan challenged.

"Hey! That was different. We were going to sit outside of someone's house and wait for hours for the dude to do something. That calls for snacks. A quick in-and-out snatch job isn't the same thing."

Nick rolled his eyes at their bantering. He was too busy watching the girls run into the convenience store. Kate really was hot. He loved when she wore skirts. She didn't wear them often enough. Maybe he would take her out to a nice dinner so she could dress up for him. She said she wanted to take things slowly, so maybe taking her out on a few dates would show her that he was serious.

A couple of guys took notice of Kate's group and followed them inside the store. Nick was almost out of the vehicle to intervene when Robert grabbed his arm. "What are you doing? You can't go running in there just because some guy is checking out your girl."

Nick liked hearing Robert call Kate his girl. He closed the door and settled back into the seat. He turned to glare at the chuckles coming from the back.

The ladies took a very long time in the store, but finally came back out with their snacks. They were giggling and looking back toward the guys who had followed them into the store.

"Those guys were checking you out, Grace," Kate teased.

"They were not. That one almost walked into the chips display because he was looking at you," Grace challenged.

Cindy laughed. "There were two guys and each of you had an admirer."

"I'm feeling a little neglected here, aren't you, Cin?" Jen asked. "I guess they liked dark-haired women."

"Hey! Guys usually go for blondes!" Kate shot back. They continued to debate which hair color men preferred until they reached the street before the police station.

The guys were shocked that the ladies pulled over before they had gotten to the police station.

"I thought that they would've pulled up to the first spot next to the door," Nick commented dryly.

Robert laughed. "I did, too. I wonder if they even have a plan."

"If they have a plan it's probably completely crazy," Jason mused as he pulled his backpack into his lap. "Are we going to help them tonight, or are we going to just stop them?"

"We're going to have to go in and get what they came for tonight, or they will just attempt this again another time and we might not be there to save their asses." Nick was torn between being angry with Kate and thinking the entire situation was hilarious.

"Okay, let's circle around and cut them off before they hit the parking lot," Robert told them. "They parked down the road a little. Ry, can you see what they're doing?"

"Well, the mirror is lit up on both the driver and passenger sides, so I would imagine that they are fixing their hair and makeup." They all laughed at that.

"We have plenty of time to circle around and cut them off before they get to the parking lot." Nick got out of the car and motioned for everyone else to follow him.

They stuck to the shadows and crouched low so that the girls wouldn't see them. They managed to sneak up on the car from the side facing the police station before the ladies had gotten out of the car.

Nick crept up toward the driver's side and waited for Kate to step out of the car. He let her take about ten steps before jumping up and grabbing her from behind, and quickly covered her mouth with his hand so she wouldn't yell out. "Hey, Beautiful. Funny meeting you here."

At the same time Nick grabbed Kate, Ryan and Jason jumped out on Jen and Cindy, who both let out a little scream. Grace looked alarmed for a second and then irritated.

Robert stood back and watched the frightened and then seriously angry women react to being startled.

"Nick Taylor! You scared the hell out of me," Kate screeched, and then wiggled out of his arms to face him, hand on her hips. "What are you doing here? Did you follow us?"

"Hell yeah, I followed you," Nick yelled back. "Are you crazy, thinking you guys can break into a police station?"

Kate was shocked and narrowed her eyes in suspicion. "How do you know that was what we were planning? Are you spying on us now? I cannot believe that you would do something like this!"

"Hey! Before you yell at me anymore, I am not spying on you or listening in on any of your private conversations. I wouldn't do that to you." Nick couldn't believe that she was so angry with him.

"Okay. Then how did you find out we were going to do something tonight? Were you guessing what we were doing since we are close to the station?"

Nick couldn't wait to tell her, and was watching her face closely. He didn't want to miss her reaction. "Your daughter told me."

Everyone had stopped to watch Kate and Nick. The group seemed captivated by the show they were witnessing.

Kate wanted to wipe the smirk off of his face. She had forgotten that Maddy was in the family room when she had made plans with Jen. "Maddy told you?" she asked, even though she already knew.

Nick arched a brow. He couldn't believe she was irritated with him. He was the only one who should be angry and he was ready to let her have it. "Yes. She was very pleased to tell me and it's a good thing, too. Do you realize that you could be arrested for pulling a stunt like this? What would you've done if you had been caught? You would have lost the kids and your job and could have gone to jail."

Kate glared at him. "We had a plan and it would have worked."

"Really? And what about the security cameras everywhere?" Nick challenged.

Grace stepped up to them to stop any more fighting. "We would have used this to disrupt the security." She held up Ryan's device that looked like a phone.

"Hey! Where did you get that?" Ryan complained. "I looked all over for it."

Kate turned her annoyance on Ryan. "You left it at my house along with a bunch of your other toys. I happened to remember what this one did."

"Oh." Ryan backed up again and tried to act as if he wasn't listening.

"Okay. The entertainment is going to have to wait for a while. We're in the middle of a street and someone's going to wonder why we're all standing here watching you two argue." Robert needed to break it up, or they would be standing there all night.

"Fine. You guys can leave," Kate said, stepping around Nick.

"And what do you think you're going to do?" Nick asked.

"Finish what we came here for."

"No, you're not."

Once again, Robert needed to intervene. "Guys. Really."

Kate glared at him but moved out of the street. "I'm not leaving here until I get what we came for."

"Are you going to tell me what that is? Why didn't you tell me the detective came back yesterday?" Nick gave her a challenging look.

Kate huffed. "Because I'm tired of you guys swooping in and trying to take over everything. I'm not helpless and I'm not going to sit back while you take all the risks and do everything."

Everyone was silent for several moments. Nick smiled at her. "Okay. Let's go somewhere to figure this out."

Kate stayed rooted to her place on the sidewalk and glared at Nick.

Nick let out an exaggerated sigh. "Please, can we go somewhere to discuss this?"

Kate frowned at him and then looked over at Jen, Cindy, and Grace. "We're going back to the frat house." They piled into their cars and headed back the way they came.

Once settled at the dining room table, Kate explained everything that the detective had told her.

Cindy shifted in her seat. "Do you think that the man who was spying on Kate works for Brooks?"

Jason shrugged. "It's really hard to tell, but it does sound like something he would do."

"Yeah. I agree with Jay. Brooks doesn't do his own dirty work, but he has people working for him to do things like this," Robert added.

Nick started to pace. "Kate, did you hear anything from the detective about the contents of the notebook?"

"No, not at all."

"It might be just a log of your activities. If there was anything in it that was dangerous to us, you would have known. I think we need to hold off on the notebook right now."

Robert agreed. "Yeah. It's too dangerous and there might not be anything important in it."

"Okay. We wait and see what happens." Kate accepted that their plan to steal the notebook from the police station may not have been the best idea.

Jason stood up and clapped. "Okay, now that we got that out of the way and with the ladies all dressed up, we should take advantage of the kid-free night and go out somewhere."

Grace loved the idea. "Yes, we need a night out. It'll be fun."

Nick quirked a brow at Kate. He knew she was still annoyed with him, but he really liked the idea of hanging out with her and the group. "Why not. Well, unless Kate's going to be grumpy all night and decide she needs to stay home and pout."

Kate glared at him and walked up to Jason and said, "I'm in." He picked her up and swung her around. "Alright!"

Frank slammed John into the brick wall of the rundown motel he had been hiding in since the police were looking for him. He was gripping John's throat so tightly that it was sure to make the man nervous.

"I'm going to ask you again. Where is Brooks?" Frank slammed John's head into the wall again. He had never liked him, or his brother. They were slimy, spineless pieces of crap that preyed on children. He was disgusted by them both and thought that the world would be a lot better without them.

John began coughing loudly. "I don't know."

Frank gripped him tighter. "Wrong answer."

John began to turn red and the choking increased. Frank let up slightly so the man could answer his questions. "I swear I don't know. I don't know anything."

"Why were you spying on that family?"

"I was told to watch and report back. He told me not to approach her. I could have grabbed her a dozen different times, but he always said no. It was a waste."

"How do you contact Brooks? Don't shake your head at me." Frank slammed John again. "Tell me!"

John began to twitch. "Cell phone. It's in my pocket." John went to reach into his pocket but Frank knocked his hands out of the way.

"Do you think I'm stupid? Keep your hands up." Frank reached in and pulled out a cell phone and a knife. He glared at John. "Were you reaching for this?" Frank drew the knife across John's cheek lightly, just enough to scare the man even more.

"I wasn't going for that."

"Yeah, sure." Frank pulled out the cell and swiped the screen. It turned on right away. Still gripping John with one hand, he used the other to scroll through the contacts. Finding Brooks, he decided that he didn't need John anymore. Frank punched him so hard that John was completely knocked out.

He dialed Brooks. The phone rang several times before it was answered.

"John, I already told you to wait for Joel to get there and to stop calling me. WHAT DO YOU WANT NOW?"

"I wanted to tell you that I'm coming for you."

There was a long pause. "Frank? How dare you threaten me!"

"I'm not threatening. I'm stating a fact. I. AM. COMING. FOR. YOU." Frank hung up the phone. Brooks hated not getting the last word. It gave Frank a little pleasure.

He needed to find his friend who was an expert in electronics. Hopefully, he would be able to trace the cell to a location. At least Frank had a lead now. Brooks' days were numbered.

Frank made one more call before leaving John slumped in the alleyway. The phone rang twice before someone answered in a clipped voice.

"Sanders."

"It's Frank. I have a scumbag for you to pick up."

"I'll have a team there in fifteen minutes."

"Thanks."

"Frank, remember our deal."

"I haven't forgotten." Frank hung up the phone and pulled John farther into the alley. He secured John's wrists and feet with a couple of zip-ties and duct-taped his mouth. No one would notice him behind the dumpster. Frank considered throwing the piece of crap *into* the dumpster, but it would only cause the retrieval team more trouble than he was worth.

John wouldn't be bothering anyone anymore.

Char Webster

Chapter Sixteen

Robert held the door for everyone as they filed into PJ's, the local pub and latest hangout. The guys loved it because everywhere they looked, a TV had on a sporting event. The ladies liked it because it had good food and a cool atmosphere. Jason went up to the hostess to ask for a table for their group.

Kate watched Jason lean in close to the pretty blonde and whisper in her ear. The girl, who looked barely twenty-one, giggled a couple of times and then swatted his arm. Jason was such a flirt. She wondered if the girl had been a member of his harem.

The pub was crowded for a Friday night, so they figured that they would have to wait awhile for a table large enough to accommodate all of them. A moment later, Jason came back with a cocky grin on his face and was followed closely behind by the hostess. Kate arched a brow at him and he gave her a smirk in return. The hostess led them to a table near the outdoor patio. This area was the least crowded and allowed for more privacy.

Kate had no idea how Jason managed it and was going to tease him about it but her gaze caught Grace's expression, and she decided not to tease him. *Interesting,* Kate thought. *Grace looks ready to clobber Jason.* Jason seemed oblivious to Grace's scowl when he sauntered over and put his arm around her. She shook him off and sat down in a corner seat. He pulled his chair right up to hers and sat down close, crowding her.

Kate figured it was best to ignore that mess, so she turned to Cindy, who was in a discussion with Ryan and wasn't paying attention. Jen pulled her down toward a seat on the other side of the table from Jason. "I don't want to sit right next to my brother," Jen told her.

Nick settled into a seat at the head of the table next to Kate. She was still annoyed with him and was trying hard to ignore him. He grabbed her hand and locked their fingers together. She tried to pull away, but he wouldn't let her hand go.

Robert sat across from Kate and next to Nick. He didn't want to miss any of the drama that was sure to unfold at the table. Nick looked ready to do battle and Kate was trying her best to act like he wasn't next to her and holding her hand. Robert loved the entertainment these two provided. "So, what are we ordering?" he asked.

They settled for a couple of pitchers of beer and two big orders of hot wings to start. The server brought out the beer and some frosted glasses right away and made a point of flirting with all of the guys. Jason flirted back shamelessly, even complimenting her eyes. Grace rolled her own eyes at that and tried to move her chair away from Jason, but he just moved his chair closer again.

Robert noticed and wondered who was going to be more fun to watch, Grace or Kate. "Jay, if you two keep moving your chairs, you'll be both sitting at the end of the table together," Robert teased. Grace was in the corner and Jason was rounding the corner to share her space.

Kate was chatting with Jen and not looking at anyone around the table. They were checking out something that was happening at the bar near their table. Nick followed their line of sight and noticed a couple of men there. He narrowed his gaze and shot Jen a deadly look. Jen smirked at him and turned back to her conversation with Kate.

Nick tried to figure out what they were talking about but it was too noisy in there and Kate had gotten too good at blocking her thoughts from everyone. He liked knowing what she was thinking. He pulled on her hand so she would look at him. "So, Beautiful, what are we doing tomorrow?" Nick asked, trying to get Kate to pay attention to him.

She rolled her eyes and tried to snatch her hand back, trying not to shiver at the feel of his fingers rubbing her inner wrist. It was completely distracting her and she had trouble focusing on what he was saying. "WE are not doing anything. I'm taking Alex and Emily shopping for their homecoming dresses. After that, we are going to get our nails and hair done. It's their first school dance and I want to make sure it's special."

Jen squealed. "Ohhhh! How cool. Can I come, too?" Kate turned her back on Nick again and faced Jen.

"Yes. We'll make it a girls' day," Kate told her. She turned to Cindy, who was still in deep conversation with Ryan. They were both sitting a little apart from everyone else and were almost at the next table. Kate wondered what they were talking about. "Hey, Cindy, Grace? Do you want to have a girls' day tomorrow?"

Cindy looked up right away and yelled, "Oh yeah! That sounds like fun."

Grace shook her head. "I can't. I'm taking a couple of shifts at the senior citizen home in town."

"You got a job?" Kate asked. "That's awesome."

"It's just a part-time thing, but it's cool for right now. I can't wait to start school."

Nick hated being ignored, so he pulled at Kate's hand again and scooted his chair closer to her. "Who's going to watch Maddy and Zach?"

Kate glared at him. "Zach is going to Eric's house and I'm going to bring Maddy with us. She's not too young for a shopping trip." Kate hoped that was the case. If they shopped all morning and went to the salon in the afternoon, she wouldn't get her nap and would be really grouchy. Maybe she would fall asleep in her stroller.

Robert was watching Nick closely. He knew that his friend was going to do something foolish if Kate continued to ignore him. He could see the gleam in Nick's eyes. He tried to distract him with some talk about the soccer game that was on the big screen in front of them, but Nick was only giving him partial answers. He was not interested in sports talk. He was interested in bugging the heck out of his girlfriend.

Nick slid his free hand up Kate's knee under the table and watched her jump slightly at his touch. He loved that he could make her react to him with a light brush of his fingers up her leg. She was still pretending to ignore him but he could feel her slight tremble. He became bolder and moved his fingers up higher and made slight swirling motions to get more of a reaction out of her. He moved them higher still and she jumped in her seat.

Kate whipped around to face him and wanted to wipe that arrogant smirk off his face. The brat knew what he was doing to her. She decided to give him a little payback. Over the summer she had pictured them kissing passionately in her mind and he had reacted just like she had a moment ago. Maybe it was time to try that again, to see if it worked a second time.

Kate opened her mind and began to picture running her fingers up the sides of his face to the back of his neck and into his hair. She imagined pulling him closely to her and teasing the corner of his lips with her tongue, then pulling back just when he leaned closer. She pictured nipping his lip and pulling it into her mouth for a second before letting it go, then teasing him some more before he crushed his lips to hers. Kate imagined him thrusting his hands through her hair and pulling her closer. The kiss in her mind started to get hot and she imagined him sliding his hand down her neck and shoulder and resting it closely to her heart.

Nick spit his beer all over the table. He was coughing and choking on his drink. Kate felt satisfied until she saw the look on Robert's face, which was a mixture of humor and horror.

"Kate, you do realize that we all caught your little mental demonstration?" Robert asked, as he tried to hold back his laughter. He lost the battle and laughed along with everyone else.

Kate was horrified and embarrassed. She immediately stood up and mumbled that she needed to go to the ladies' room. Nick had released her fingers the moment he spit beer all over. She quickly made her way to the restroom. Jen jumped up and followed her.

Cindy had just looked confused and Ryan shook his head at her. She stood to follow them, but Ryan stopped her. He whispered something in her ear that no one caught, and then they walked over to the other side of the pub to the pool tables.

Kate began pacing the bathroom. She was completely mortified. She didn't even want to look at Jen, who was just standing there watching Kate walk back and forth. How could she have forgotten that everyone would hear her? She put her hand over her face and leaned against the sink. She was never going back out there.

"Hey. It's not that bad," Jen began, but Kate stopped her with a look.

"Oh my God. I cannot believe I did that." Kate was back to covering her face. "How humiliating. I'm not going back out there."

"Kate, it was funny and he deserved it." Kate glared at her.

"It was funny and you know it. If it had been me, you would

be saying the same thing." Jen leaned against the counter next to Kate. "Well, at least you stopped before you had him cop a feel." Kate laughed nervously. "Oh, no. You all saw that?"

"It's not like we all don't know that's what you guys have done or will probably be doing anyway." Jen thought the whole thing was awesome.

Kate hung her head.

"Hey. It was worth it to just see Nick's face and watch him spit the beer across the table. I think Robert was completely sprayed."

They began to laugh and couldn't stop. Someone walked into the bathroom and looked at them like they were nuts. That just made them laugh even harder.

"Come on. That deserves a shot. Let's go to the bar."

Nick couldn't believe Kate had done that in the middle of the bar and in front of all their friends. The guys hadn't stopped laughing since Kate and Jen left the table. He knew she had been embarrassed and he should've gone after her, but he had no idea what to say to her. He wanted to drag her out of the bar and back to the house to act out exactly what she had been thinking, only he wouldn't have stopped at the good part. She had done something similar to him over the summer and he had fulfilled those thoughts. He would like to have the opportunity to do that again.

He looked toward the ladies room, but didn't see Kate or Jen. "They're at the bar." Robert nodded toward the opposite side of the room. "I guess she needs a little courage to come back to the table."

Grace shot them a mean look. "You shouldn't have told her we all heard. You embarrassed her."

"Babe, that was the funny part," Jason chided. She gave him an even worse look.

Nick got up and wandered over to the bar. Jen saw him coming and slipped back to the table. He came up behind Kate and put his arms around her. She stiffened at first but relaxed when she felt him nuzzle the side of her neck.

"I loved what you showed me," he whispered in her ear. She

stiffened again but he kissed her neck. He wouldn't let her stay upset about it. "It took everything I had not to drag you outside and do exactly that to you in the parking lot. Heck, I still want to right now."

Kate giggled a little and turned to face him. "Can we not talk about that anymore?"

"Only on one condition."

She sighed. "What?"

"After Alex goes to homecoming and Maddy's in bed, you and I cuddle up on the couch with a glass of wine and a movie."

"Okay," she agreed quickly. That was too easy not to agree to.

"Wait. I'm not done. You have to agree to go on a real date with me."

"A real date?"

"Yes. A real date where we dress nicely and I pick you up for dinner and something after. We'll get someone to watch the kids so we don't have to come home early."

Kate got a huge smile. She loved the idea. "Okay."

"Really? You're agreeing that easily?"

"Do you want me to say no?"

"No. No. Not saying anything else." Nick held her at the bar for a few more minutes until he noticed that the wings had arrived at their table. "Let's go get some wings before Robert and Jason eat them all."

Don watched them from the back corner of the bar. He hated seeing them so happy. So far they hadn't shown anything interesting. Something had gone down at the table but he couldn't tell what it had been. He kept looking for Kate to show any signs of using her abilities, but so far it was impossible to tell if she still had them.

Pete had called him a few times, but he had ignored the older man; he was starting to make mistakes and Don didn't like it. Pete was getting careless and showing weakness. Past chancellors had to make difficult choices for the good of the Gifted race, and Pete shouldn't be any different.

Harry slipped into the seat across from him with a tall beer in his hands. Don gave him a harsh look. "What are you doing?"

"What?" Harry asked, sipping his beer.

"We're working. You shouldn't be drinking."

"Oh, relax. She's not going to do anything. It's been boring so far and nothing is happening tonight. You can enjoy a couple of beers."

Don had to take a couple of deep breaths to calm himself so that he didn't throw Harry across the room. He noticed that the Sutton woman and her friend walked back up to the bar.

"Harry, I want you to brush by the Sutton woman and think all kinds of lustful thoughts, the dirtier the better."

Harry smiled in a lecherous way. He liked the idea too much. Don was disgusted with him. "I'm sure it won't be too difficult for you."

"I've already had some of those thoughts. I'll be right back." Harry stood up and tried to walk away, but Don grabbed his arm.

"Don't touch her. Walk by only. If you put your hands on her, you will have to deal with me."

Harry cursed under his breath but moved along the bar and around the back so he could walk by Kate without her seeing him approach.

Cindy grabbed Kate's hand and pulled her up to the bar and away from the table. "What was that all about back there? Ryan told me that you were embarrassed when everyone heard what you were thinking. I thought you could block them out."

Kate sighed. "I forgot that everyone could hear me when I decided to mess with Nick." Kate was going to try to be vague so she didn't have to relive the embarrassment.

Cindy gave her an odd look. "What exactly were you thinking?"

Kate dropped her shoulders in defeat. "I was picturing us kissing."

"That's all?" Cindy asked, confused, and then her eyes lit up. *"Oh!* You let your mind run away a little didn't you? OMG, I bet you gave them all quite a show."

Kate gave her a look but ended up laughing. "It's not funny."

"Yes it is, and you know it. That explains Nick's expression.

Even though everyone got a show, it seemed to have worked on Nick."

Kate wanted to change the subject. "What is going on with you and Ryan?"

"What? Nothing. We're just friends. He's a really nice guy. He isn't as cocky as the other guys. He's helping me train for another competition."

"Uh-huh. Keep telling yourself that. You like him and you know it."

Cindy was about to say something when Kate caught the thoughts of a man walking up behind them. They were repulsive. The man was a disgusting pig. As he walked by, he nodded at them and said, "Hi."

Kate looked at him in complete disgust, moving closer to the bar and away from him. She didn't want him to touch her.

Cindy caught on to Kate's mood and turned to the man and said, "Keep moving, buddy."

The guy circled the bar and disappeared into a side room.

"Eww. Be glad you can't hear thoughts. He was projecting his and they were really foul. "

"Let's go back to the table."

Harry went back to the table Don was occupying and flopped down in his seat.

"She glared at me, so she probably heard what I was thinking."

"You jackass. Your thoughts were broadcasted all over your face. Anyone could tell what you were thinking. You were also leering at her. It's a wonder she doesn't have someone come kick your ass."

Harry grumbled something unintelligible and downed the rest of his beer. He went to order another but Don cut him off. "Don't bother, we're leaving."

Don wanted to finish this assignment and move on to something else. He hated being so close to Taylor, who was such a straight arrow that it made him sick. He needed to catch him and Kate at something besides hugging at the bar. Hugging didn't prove anything.

Nick stood at Kate's door wanting to go inside so badly, but knowing she would never allow him. It would be hard, but he could wait until tomorrow night. She had agreed to snuggle with him on the couch and he intended to take full advantage of that.

He pulled her into his arms and hugged her tightly. He slid his hand up her back and into her hair. Kate's arms found themselves looped around his neck. They moved closer together, wanting to feel the heat from each other and the familiar tingle that rushed through their bodies. Nick's energy always surged around her and he loved the intensity of it.

Nick's mouth found hers in a scorching kiss that left them both breathless. He pulled away slightly and looked into her eyes. They were cloudy with passion and he knew that it would be so easy for him to pull her into the house, but he wasn't going to do that. Kate wanted to take things slow and he was going to try to honor that.

"Good night, Beautiful. I'll see tomorrow." Nick kissed her again and stepped off the porch.

"Good night, Nick," Kate said quietly. She watched him walk down the street. He turned and blew her a kiss before jogging off toward his house.

Alex and Emily rushed into the house. Kate had just come downstairs and was surprised to see the girls in the kitchen.

"Hey, guys. What are you doing up so early?"

Alex giggled and said, "We wanted to get an early start on shopping."

Kate laughed. "The mall doesn't open for another two hours. You have plenty of time."

"We thought you could take us out to breakfast," Alex said with a mischievous grin.

"Is that right?" Kate asked.

"Please, Kate," Emily pleaded.

"Oh, okay. Let's go to breakfast. After we eat, we'll go get Maddy and meet Cindy and Jen at the mall."

Both girls jumped up and down and ran for the front door. "Come on, Kate," Alex called.

The mall was just opening when they walked through the doors to begin their hunt for homecoming dresses. Alex and Emily walked a few steps ahead of Kate, Cindy, and Jen. Kate was pushing an empty stroller. Jen was holding Maddy on her hip and was laughing at the little girl pointing to all kinds of things she passed.

They stopped at several stores and the girls tried on a number of dresses, not deciding on a single one. The first store that Emily wanted to check out had dresses that were much more appropriate for older girls. She had pouted a little until Kate reminded her that her mother would probably see her in her dress for the dance.

The second store had a few dresses that Alex fell in love with, but none of those dresses were even close to her size, since she was very petite and thin. It was hard to find small sizes. She had insisted on trying on a strapless dress at the shop, but the dress wouldn't stay up without her holding the top of it.

Alex looked as if she was getting disheartened, but Kate gave her a hug and said, "Don't worry, we'll find you the perfect dress for tonight."

"Thanks." Kate could feel a sudden sadness coming from Alex.

"Hey. Don't be sad today. It's your first school dance and your first dance with a date."

Alex wasn't looking up at Kate, but down at the patterns in the carpet. She shrugged but didn't answer.

"You're missing your mom, aren't you?"

Alex shrugged again and kicked a piece of fuzz with the toe of her sneaker.

"It's okay to miss her."

"I wish she was here, but . . ." Alex didn't want to finish.

Kate could feel the melancholy warring with guilt streaming off of Alex. "But you're having a little bit of fun shopping for a dress?"

Alex gave Kate a hug and said quietly, "I would want her to be with all of us. I would want you both."

Kate squeezed her daughter and kissed her head. "I love you, kiddo. Do you want me to call your uncle? He could hang out with us."

Alex looked appalled. "NO! Don't call Uncle Nick. He would make me pick out a little kid dress."

Kate laughed. "Yes, he would probably dress you like you were six."

Alex shivered at the thought, but seemed a little happier.

"Let's go find you a dress." Kate linked her arm though Alex's and led her over to a rack of stylish short dresses.

The girls ran upstairs the moment they entered the house. Their hair, makeup, and nails had been done during their afternoon at the spa, but they still had to put on their dresses.

"Hurry up and get dressed, girls. I want to take some pictures," Kate called to them. She sent a text to Nick to let him know they were back and to come over so he could see Alex all dressed up.

Jen took Maddy into the other room and was sitting on the floor at her kitchen set. Cindy went home, explaining that she had some things to do.

A few minutes later, Nick and Robert walked into the house. Nick was dressed in swishy pants and a long-sleeve t-shirt. He was all ready for their relaxing night on the couch. Kate blushed thinking about them cuddling together watching a movie.

He walked up to her and enfolded her in his arms. "Hi, Kate." He kissed her lightly on the lips and stepped away to tease Jen.

Robert called up the steps to Alex and Emily. "Hey, girls. Get your butts down here so we can take a look at you."

Robert shared a mischievous look with Nick. Kate groaned. They were going to give Alex and Emily a hard time.

A couple of minutes later, the girls bounded down the steps and ran into the living room. Kate smiled widely. "You guys look great. I love the dresses," Kate told them, checking out their outfits. Emily's dress was a light pink tank-style that changed to dark pink at its high waist. The dress flared out to just above her knees.

Alex had a sleeveless teal dress that was about two inches above her knees. It had a halter-style top with a high neckline edged with sparkles. Kate thought she looked adorable.

"No. No. No," Nick said loudly. "She's not wearing that. She looks too old."

Alex was just about to argue with Nick when Kate gave her a look. "Nick, the girls are going to homecoming. Their dresses are completely age-appropriate and are in compliance with the strict dress code." Kate cupped Nick's face with her hand. "Alex is in high school now."

Robert stepped up and shook his head. "I agree with Nick. She needs more clothes on. Why can't you wear jeans?"

Alex rolled her eyes. She knew her uncles were going to give her a hard time, because they gave her a hard time about everything. She faced her beloved uncles and lifted the hem of her skirt a little bit to show them the bike shorts she had under the dress.

Nick smiled. "That's my girl! Make sure you wear a sweater, too."

"Okay, you two, enough with the overprotective uncle routine. I need to take some photos before their dates get here."

Alex and Emily both groaned and Kate realized her mistake. She should have never mentioned the girls having dates.

"Dates? What dates?" Nick demanded.

Robert chimed in. "We need to meet these boys."

Kate rolled her eyes. "They are all going as friends. Wow, you are being ridiculous."

Jen brought Maddy into the living room to check out the girls. "Aww. You two look awesome."

Kate took a bunch of photos and the girls posed in all kinds of silly ways. They were having a great time until there was a knock on the front door.

Nick used his gift to speed to the door first and Kate glared at him. She quickly glanced at Emily to see if she noticed his super-fast approach to the door. Thankfully Alex and Emily were talking quietly and not paying attention.

Nick opened the door forcefully and glared at Josh and Brian standing there. They both took a half step backward but stopped when a man came up behind them. He took in Nick's face and the boys' reactions, and laughed. Nick looked up at the man on the porch and smiled.

Nick let Josh and Brian walk past and clasped the man's hand in a firm shake. "Hey, man, how're you doing?"

"Nick, good to see you. Where've you been? I haven't seen you at the gym in a few months."

"Tom, it's good to see you, too. I've been away for work, but I'm back now," Nick told him, glancing at Kate and Alex.

"This is my son, Josh," Tom told him.

"Hey, Josh. It's nice to meet you," Nick said with a little menace in his voice. Tom laughed at the obvious attempt at intimidating his son.

"What are you doing here, Nick?" Tom asked.

"This is my niece, Alex." Nick pulled Alex into his side with his arm around her. Nick then walked over to Kate and introduced her to his friend. "Tom, this is Kate." Nick said those words with possession in his voice that made Kate smile. He was letting the world know that he and Kate were together.

"It's really nice to meet you, Kate."

Tom turned back to Nick. "What a small world," Tom told him. The guys laughed and Nick forgot about scaring the girls' dates. Nick introduced Tom and Robert, and they went to the side of the room to chat.

Kate and Jen were busy taking photos of the girls and their dates. Finally, Tom looked up and said, "Okay, kids, we're hitting the road. Let's go." Tom turned to Nick. "See you at the gym."

Tom then turned to Kate and said, "Kate. I'll drive both ways tonight. I'm going to be chaperoning at the dance anyway." Josh groaned when he heard that.

"That's very nice of you. Are you sure?"

"Absolutely. I'm going to be keeping an eye on them tonight. Right, Josh?"

Josh groaned again and Kate actually felt sorry for him. She hugged Alex and Emily and whispered to Alex, "Have fun, and if anything happens, call me and I'll be there."

They stepped out onto the porch and Kate noticed Emily's mom standing off to the side, wrapped up in her bathrobe. Her nose was bright red and raw-looking and she was holding a whole box of tissues.

Emily smiled widely. "Mom!" she cried, and went to hug her

mother, but Jessica Bennet stepped back and said, "Don't hug me, I'm still not feeling well. I don't want to get you sick."

Emily stopped walking toward her mom. "You don't look too good, Mom."

Mrs. Bennet laughed. "I feel horrible, but I didn't want to miss you all dressed up." She turned to Kate. "Will you email me some of the photos from tonight?"

Kate smiled. "Of course. I hope you feel better."

Jessica tried to smile, but it looked more like a wince. "Thanks." She turned to leave, but Kate stopped her. "Is it too much to have Zach over at your house?"

"Not at all. He actually keeps Eric out of my hair and I can get some rest. Don't worry, Allen has been keeping them busy."

They laughed and Jessica walked back to her house. Kate hoped she was going to go back to bed.

Chapter Seventeen

Maddy was in bed a little while later and Robert and Jen were hanging out for a few minutes. Kate figured that they would only get to share one drink before Nick kicked them out. He had made it very clear that he and Kate had a date on the couch.

Robert brought out a tray of drinks for everyone. He wanted them all to try out the new Apple Whiskey cocktail he created. He even cut slices of apple as a garnish.

"What's up with the bartender routine you have going?" Nick teased. He took a sip of his drink and had to admit that it was very good.

Robert tried to snatch the drink out of Nick's hands. "You don't have to drink it."

Jen tried hers and smiled. "Ooh. This is good."

Kate was snuggled up against Nick's side and he absently played with a few of her curls. She felt really relaxed, and was enjoying spending time with Nick and their friends. Jen told them funny stories about some of the people in her gym and Robert was interjecting funny comments into Jen's stories.

I'm coming for you, Kate. You can't escape me.

Kate sat up, covered her ears with her arms, and grabbed her head as the words vibrated through her head. The pain got worse each time the voice projected into her mind.

Everyone stopped speaking and rushed over to Kate. "Kate!" Nick yelled. Just then Maddy screamed from her bedroom and Kate stumbled up and ran from the room. Nick, Robert, and Jen were close behind her.

"Kate!" Maddy screamed and cried. Kate scooped her up and Maddy clung to her. Nick sat next to Kate on Maddy's bed, putting his arm around both of them.

"Shh. It's okay," Kate crooned, trying to calm her. She began to soothe Maddy, smoothing down her curls and rocking her.

"The bad man is coming to get you. He said he is coming." Kate stopped and pulled Maddy away from her shoulder to look at her. She needed to understand what Maddy was telling her.

Jen and Robert watched from the door.

"Did you have a bad dream?" Kate asked. "Tell me what happened."

"The bad man was talking to you. He said he was coming to get you."

"Did you hear him say he was coming for me?"

Maddy nodded. Nick brushed some hair out of Maddy's eyes and said, "I'm not going to let anyone get Kate, Maddy. I promise."

She nodded and Nick pulled her onto his lap. He kissed her head and gave her a squeeze.

"No one is going to get me. It's just a bad dream," Kate told her.

After a few minutes, they put Maddy back to sleep and went downstairs.

Kate wasn't sure what to think. It was odd that Maddy had bad dreams when Kate heard the voice. She looked around the room and noticed everyone looking at her, waiting for an explanation. Jen had seen this happen to her before, but no one else had. She really didn't want to confess that she had been hearing voices. What if Maddy was hearing something that Kate was projecting? What if they thought she was crazy? She didn't want everything she had to disappear. Would she lose the kids? Would Nick not want to be with someone crazy? Would she get worse?

She knew she was going to have to say something. They were all waiting.

Jen couldn't handle the silence any longer. "Kate, what is going on? And don't try to tell me it was a headache again. This is the second time I've seen you go through something like this. Something is up with you."

Nick and Robert exchanged a look. "What do you mean this is the second time?" Nick asked, getting upset. "What happened, Kate? It looked like you were trying to block out a loud sound. What's going on?

Robert was clearly upset. "Kate, you need to talk to us. We can't help you if you keep things from us."

Kate took a deep breath, trying to calm her nerves. She needed to tell them. She knew they wouldn't let it go until she told them the truth. Nick had a built-in lie detector, so he would know immediately if she didn't tell them the truth. Would she lose everything?

"I'm hearing voices in my head." She said it flatly, defeated. Nick pulled her into his arms and kissed her head. "Hey. It's okay. We will figure this out. Explain what's been going on."

She felt relieved that he didn't reject her immediately.

Robert looked at her concerned and said, "How long have you been hiding this? Why didn't you tell me?"

"It's been going on for a couple of weeks. It started off with just my name. The first time it happened I looked all around for someone calling me, but there was no one."

"Do you recognize the voice?" Robert asked.

"No, it's a man's voice that I don't know. It's hard to tell exactly."

Nick was rubbing her arm in slow circles. "What does it sound like? What happens when you hear it?"

"There is a vibration that echoes through my head when I hear it. It hurts and feels like something is in my mind."

Kate caught Robert's meaningful glance at Nick. "You guys think I'm crazy, don't you? Because both my parents were Gifted? You think I'm going insane, don't you?"

Robert swore under his breath and glared at Nick. "No, Kate. Not at all. You're not going crazy. Nick, what's the matter with you? Why would you tell her that crap? I don't believe it and neither should you. When are you going to realize most of the stuff we learned as kids is just not true?"

Nick was devastated that he caused Kate so much pain. "I'm so sorry. I never meant to scare you. All that stuff I told you before, about people going insane from having too much concentrated gifted blood, was all speculation pieced together from old stories and ancient documents."

Kate nodded, not completely believing it.

Nick pulled her so that she was in his lap. "What happened with Maddy? You got a funny look upstairs."

"She has had bad dreams a few times when I heard the voice. Tonight she repeated what the voice said. It said, 'I'm coming to get you, Kate.'"

Jen had been silent up until that point. "Kate, I don't think you're going crazy. I think some a-hole is projecting his voice into your head. That's why it feels like a vibration that hurts. If you were crazy, it wouldn't hurt you. Also, I think your brilliant little daughter is picking up that broadcast in your head and it's scaring her."

Robert nodded. "Jen's right. Someone is projecting thoughts that into your head. The vibrations give it away."

Kate felt a little relieved, but also scared that someone could do that to her. "Who would do that?"

Nick gave Robert a long look. Robert nodded, and Nick began, "There have been rumors for years now that the Chancellor has the gift of telepathy, and that he can communicate over really long distances. They have just been rumors, because he always denies the ability, but it would make sense."

Robert rubbed his face. "It *would* make sense, Kate. The guy kidnapped and injected you with a drug against your will. He could be messing with your head."

Kate was overwhelmed with everything she was hearing and burrowed closer to Nick. He was her rock and she needed his strength. She let out a deep breath, soaking up his closeness and feeling a little better now that they confirmed she wasn't going crazy.

Robert stood up and pulled her up into a hug. Nick didn't want to let her go even for a second. He scowled at Robert over Kate's shoulder.

"We're going. Right, Jen? Don't worry about anything tonight. You're not crazier than usual," he said with a smirk. "You need to relax and we'll figure out how to get the Chancellor tomorrow."

Jen gave her a hug and told Kate that she would call her the next day.

Kate sank back down on the couch next to Nick. He cradled her against him again, and they just stayed that way for a very long time.

Alex was so excited for her first real school dance, but she was also a little nervous. She strolled into the school gym next to

Josh, who was sporting a black suit, white shirt, and red tie. Alex thought he looked awesome. She was thrilled to be walking in with him and she couldn't wait for everyone to see them together, especially Clarissa, who still tried to make Alex feel badly every chance she got.

Over the summer, Clarissa had stopped by Alex's house to purposely make her feel horribly about being in the foster care system. She hadn't been nice to Alex since and went out of her way to talk badly about her. Luckily, not many people liked the mean girl. They just tolerated her out of fear that she would turn her venom on them.

The room had been decorated with all kinds of streamers, crepe paper flowers, and other brightly colored hangings that made the place festive. Hundreds of balloons littered the ceiling and ribbons hung down toward the occupants. Tables were scattered around the edges of the room, with the dance floor in the center. A DJ booth was tucked into the corner of the gym, and was surrounded by flashing lights.

Josh looked over at Alex. "You look really good. I didn't want to tell you in front of everyone."

Alex smiled widely. "You look good, too."

Emily and Brian were already on the dance floor and she could tell that they would probably be there for a while. Josh led Alex over to a table with a few of their friends. They sat down and watched the dancers, laughing at some of the moves the other kids were making.

Josh's dad hovered near their table and was trying to look like he wasn't listening to their conversations, but he laughed a few times when someone said something funny. Josh groaned and stormed up to his father. Alex couldn't hear what they were saying, but she could tell that Josh's dad was giving him a hard time.

Josh walked back to the table looking a little weary, and his dad shuffled off toward some of the other parents across the room. He flopped down on the seat next to Alex and said, "He wanted to be near us so he could tell your uncle that he kept a close eye on you."

Alex got a look of outrage and pulled out her phone to tell her uncle exactly how she felt about being monitored, when Josh laughed. "I think he was just trying to give us both a hard time. I don't think your uncle put him up to it."

Alex relaxed again and shoved her phone into her small purse. A song came on that everyone loved and the whole group met up with Emily and Brian on the dance floor. Alex was surprised that Josh was such a good dancer, since he hadn't wanted to dance earlier when Emily pulled Brian onto the floor.

After a couple of songs, Josh leaned in close and asked, "Do you want to get something to drink? It's getting really hot."

Alex nodded and they both walked over to the snack table, but it looked more like an actual buffet. Josh's eyes lit up and he began to pile food onto his small plate. Alex laughed at how high he was stacking it.

Josh smiled sheepishly at Alex but shrugged and attempted to add a couple more hot wings to the heap. Kate must have been rubbing off on Alex, because she had veggies and hummus on her plate. Josh made a face at the healthy snacks and tipped his head toward their table. A few of the other guys had also discovered the food.

Emily flopped down into the seat next to Alex. "Where did Brian go?" Alex asked her.

"He saw Josh's plate and had to go get himself an even bigger one." Emily pointed to Brian coming their way with a mountain of food.

Alex rolled her eyes. "Do you want to go back and dance some more?"

Emily glanced over at Brian and Josh and knew that they would be busy eating for a while. "Yes. I don't really feel like sitting here while they stuff their faces."

They went back to the dance floor and had fun while their dates were occupied. A slow song came on and Josh appeared by her side. Alex's face broke into a huge grin and they began to sway to the music. She didn't think the night could get any better.

Josh was pulling her a little closer when he was suddenly separated from Alex. Josh's dad had sneaked up behind them and pulled Josh back without saying a word. Josh groaned and got an adorably embarrassed look on his face. He tried to move away from his father, but his dad seemed to follow them. Alex wanted to laugh at the entire situation. She could picture her uncles doing something very similar.

"I'm sorry about him," Josh whispered so that his dad wouldn't hear.

"Don't worry about it. I was just thinking that it was good that my uncles weren't here." Josh smiled but Alex could tell that he couldn't wait for the song to end so he could escape his father's watchful eyes.

They ventured back to the table and Emily pulled Alex toward the girls' bathroom.

"Brian is sooo cute. I'm really glad we came with him and Josh," Emily gushed. "I cannot believe his dad was doing that to you guys!"

"It was funny."

"You just think it's funny because it's something your uncles would do. I'm surprised they aren't spying on us right now."

Alex shivered. "Please don't say that. You might jinx things. Now I'm going to be looking everywhere for one of them." Alex half wondered if Uncle Ryan had wired the gym with cameras and they were all watching it from home. She really hoped that wasn't the case.

They walked back toward the table where they had left their dates. About fifteen feet away, Alex noticed Clarissa smirk at her and then fall into Josh's lap, wrapping her arms around his neck and kissing him on the cheek. She grinned at Alex and hooked her arms tightly around him. She wasn't going to give up.

Alex became so angry at the rotten girl that she began to shake.

"Hey, are you okay?" Emily asked. She followed Alex's glare, and saw Josh was trying to get Clarissa off of his lap. "Ewwww, that beotch! Alex, Josh doesn't like her. Look, he's trying to break her hold and get her off of him." Josh tried to stand up but Clarissa was still clinging to him.

Alex wasn't listening. She was just watching Clarissa hang all over her date, making smug faces at her. She was getting more upset by the minute, until the burner under one of the serving trays caught the tablecloth on fire. The flame seemed to leap out of the burner all on its own.

Alex was horrified. She had made the flame jump.

The gym broke out into chaos. Everyone started screaming and running for the exits. A couple of teachers ran over to try to extinguish the flames. Alex fled from the room and into the parking lot alone, tears streaming down her face. She didn't have control over her gift. What if someone had gotten hurt? What if she had injured her friends? She needed to learn what she could about it and how to stop it from bubbling up when she was upset. She needed to contact Rick.

Need 2 Meet ASAP.

A moment later, she received her response.

2morrow nite. txt u ltr w info.

Alex looked down at her screen with relief. She would get the information she needed from Rick.

She was just sliding her phone in her purse when Josh, Brian, and Emily rushed to her. Josh got to her first and squeezed her tightly in a hug. "I couldn't find you and we were really worried."

Emily threw herself into Alex's arms. "I was so worried about you. I didn't know where you went. Can you believe that thing caught on fire?"

Alex shrugged. "Yeah. So crazy that happened."

"They are closing down the dance now. My dad told us to wait by the car while he and the other parents and teachers clear out the gym."

"It's okay, the dance was almost over anyway," Alex muttered. She couldn't wait to get home, but she wasn't looking forward to telling Kate and her uncles what had happened.

Alex and Emily climbed onto the porch after Josh's dad dropped them off. They turned around and waved, and then Alex asked Emily, "Do you want to stay at my house tonight? Your mom won't mind since she isn't feeling well anyway."

"Yeah, that's a great idea. We can text Brian and Josh later." Emily bounced a little bit and flew into the house.

Kate and Nick appeared in the doorway of the living room, wondering why Alex and Emily were home early. "Hey, girls. What's going on? Why are you home early? Everything okay?" Kate asked, concern lacing her voice. She could feel stress pouring out of Alex and knew something was up. She gave Alex a pointed stare.

"They ended the dance early, so we came home. It was fun, though." Alex was trying to be vague so that Kate wouldn't figure out what had happened. Kate was just about to question her more when Emily interrupted her, blurting out, "They closed the dance because the buffet table caught on fire. A fire truck and everything came."

Kate's eyes grew huge. She tried her best to act nonchalant, but it was extremely difficult. Her daughter had just caught the gym on fire. Kate had to put her hand on Nick's arm. He looked like he wanted to flip out.

"Alex?" Nick began. "Want to explain?" He hoped that it had nothing to do with his niece.

Emily jumped in with another answer. "We have no idea how it happened. We were walking back to the table and the flame in the burner under the food leaped out and caught the tablecloth on fire. It was crazy."

Nick and Kate exchanged a look. "Anyone get hurt?" Nick asked.

Alex immediately spoke up. "No! No one was hurt. Just the table was a little charred."

"It got a lot charred. The grease on the tablecloth caught fire and spread quickly," Emily provided. Alex gave her a look to shut her up but Emily continued, "Yeah, the teachers were freaking out because the whole table went up in flames."

"Okay. So what else happened?" Kate asked.

Alex shrugged but once again, Emily ratted her out in her rush to tell the story. "That witch Clarissa was flirting with Josh, sitting on his lap and kissing his cheek."

Nick coughed. "Ohhh. And was Josh flirting back?"

Alex shuffled her feet, completely uncomfortable with the discussion. "No, he was trying to pull her off of him. He even stood up, and she was still clinging to him." Alex pulled Emily toward the steps. "We're going to bed now. Night!"

Kate sank down onto the couch and Nick collapsed next to her. "What else can go wrong tonight?" Kate complained.

Nick began to laugh. "I guess we need to work on that temper of hers."

"You think?" Kate asked sarcastically. "What are we going to do?"

"We need to teach her control. She'll be fine once she learns."

"I really hope so."

"We'll talk to her tomorrow," Nick assured her. "She needs to know that we'll be there for her no matter what happens, but she also has to learn to control."

"She's a teenager, Nick. She's going to be emotional, which can cause her abilities to flare up. You know that."

"Her emotions can get us all in trouble."

"Yeah, you're right." She didn't want to think about anything else. Kate snuggled next to Nick. She just wanted to enjoy her cuddling time with the hottie next to her. She would deal with teenage angst later.

Brooks couldn't contain his excitement from the thrill of the hunt. He was about to capture his prize.

Even his problem with Frank couldn't dampen his good mood, though Frank did worry him a little. How did he get John's phone? Did Frank take out John? That would be unfortunate. John was a waste of a human being, but he would do anything that Brooks told him to do. He wouldn't worry about it. He needed to focus on his prize.

Brooks had to set up a few things before he went to collect her. He had a smile on his face for the first time in months. This would be the first step to getting back everything he had lost. Then he would find his darling wife and make sure she understood who was in control and who would be paying for their insolence. That would be a pleasurable reconciliation, at least on his part. She might not find it that way.

He needed to call Joel and find out how Frank had gotten John's phone. The moron should have been back hours ago. How hard could it be to drive somewhere and back?

The phone rang four times before Joel said, "Hello." Brooks could hear Joel fumbling with the phone.

"Where the hell are you? Why aren't you back yet?"

"Umm. I'm still at the motel."

"WHY?"

"John isn't here. I don't know where he is. I need to find him."

Brooks was instantly furious. "He's probably dead. Get back here." Brooks hung up the phone. *One less problem to deal with,* he thought.

Joel sat down on the bed in the motel room that his brother had rented. All of his things were thrown about, and towels littered the floor. He began to shake. Where was John? Joel had called his phone several times but it had gone straight to voicemail. Could his brother be dead? *If he was dead, it was Brooks' fault. Brooks would pay dearly.*

Joel went to the motel's office. There was a young guy working who didn't look up when Joel entered. Joel walked right up to the desk, and still the kid didn't look up, so he slammed down his fist. The noise and vibrations startled the employee, who glanced up, pulled ear buds away from his ears, and gave Joel an annoyed look.

"Can I help you?" he asked rudely.

"The man who was in 217"—Joel pointed outside—"did you see him leave?"

The desk clerk looked completely annoyed. "No."

"You didn't see anything? Anyone come in looking for him?" Joel wanted to hurt the guy in front of him.

The clerk didn't answer and continued to look at Joel with disgust. Joel was about to begin inserting a horror scene into the clerk's mind when a couple of police officers entered. Joel quickly put his head down and left the office. He didn't need to get entangled with the local police.

Kate couldn't sleep. She had too much on her mind. Were they still in danger? What had that serum done to her? Why was the Chancellor after her? How was he able to get into her head? Would he take her away from her kids?

Thinking about her kids was making her head hurt. She loved them like crazy, but she was so scared. How was she going to deal with two teens acting out with their special abilities? If she couldn't get them to control their gifts, would their whole race be discovered? She hoped she could find some answers.

And then there was Nick. Kate sighed. Nick had left a few hours earlier. She had walked him to the porch, where they lingered over their good-byes. Touching her lips with her fingers, Kate could almost feel his lips on hers. She had been so tempted to pull him back into the house to continue their kissing, and was about to do just that when he pulled away and backed to the steps. He watched her as he made his way down her walk and onto the street. Kate couldn't believe he had worked his way into her heart so easily.

Giving up on sleep, she glanced at the alarm clock on her nightstand. Blue numbers brightened the room, revealing that it was only four-forty a.m. A sudden grin flashed across her face. She quickly threw on yoga pants, a long-sleeve t-shirt, and a hoodie, and then rushed downstairs to the kitchen. Within a few minutes, she had two steaming cups of coffee.

Unable to resist smiling widely, she settled down on the steps and waited for her guy to come. He had always known when she was outside waiting for him. Would this time be any different?

Nick had been lying in his bed with his hands behind his head thinking about everything that had happened lately. He couldn't believe how much his life had changed in only a few months. He never would have thought that he would be fighting against the Association, protecting his brother's children from enemies, and falling hard for a Gifted woman.

Kate. He kept thinking of reasons to check on her and arguments for staying near her. If the guys knew how bad he was getting they would never stop busting on him.

A beeping sound startled him out of his thoughts. He looked over at the monitor and it showed action on her front porch. Nick jumped out of bed with the biggest smile ever. Glancing out the window quickly confirmed his suspicion. Kate was waiting for him. He slipped on sweatpants and his sneakers. He ran down the stairs, pulling on his sweatshirt, and was out of the house in only a couple of minutes. He could see her sitting on the top step with a cup of coffee in her hands and one next to her.

They stared at each other as Nick approached, neither taking their eyes off the other. Nick settled down next to Kate, picked up his mug, and slipped an arm around her shoulders. She tipped her head closer to him and sat quietly for a few minutes.

He kissed the side of her head. "Good morning, Beautiful."

"Hi." She was enjoying the early morning with him when he had to ruin it.

"I thought you gave up on the porch?" he whispered in her ear. "You seem to be enjoying it now."

She swung around to face him, instantly annoyed. "You just had to open your mouth and ruin it, didn't you?"

"Don't be like that. I was just teasing."

"Enjoy your coffee by yourself."

She stood up and stalked back into the house, slamming the door behind her, then turning the lock to make sure he wouldn't come in after her.

Nick just stood there, unable to believe their moment had just been ruined by his attempt to tease her. She must still be upset about his leaving. With a frustrated sigh, he made his way back to his house.

Kate flopped down onto the chair in the family room. How could she want to kiss him one moment and clobber him the next?

Char Webster

Chapter Eighteen

Maddy had just finished her breakfast and was playing nicely in the family room. Kate turned on some cartoons to keep her occupied while she spoke with Alex, since she now knew that Maddy had a habit of eavesdropping on conversations. Hopefully the cartoons would be a good enough distraction.

Kate walked back to the kitchen area. "Girls, after you finish your breakfast, Emily will have to go home," Kate told them. She knew that Alex would try to keep Emily with her all day to avoid their conversation. "You guys can meet up later."

Emily nodded and Alex groaned quietly. Alex knew what was going to happen as soon as her friend left. She took her time cleaning off the breakfast bar and loading the dishwasher. She was trying to prolong the talk she knew was coming. After Emily dashed out the door, Alex tried to run for the steps.

"Hey. Get back here."

"I just want to get a shower and get dressed for the day."

"It can wait." Kate was not going to let her go upstairs. She was also not going to allow Alex to stall any longer.

Alex muttered to herself and sat back down at the breakfast bar. Her arms were crossed over her chest and she had a miserable look on her face. Kate turned away for a moment to stop the smile that was threatening. In seconds, Alex had reverted back to the girl Kate had met last summer. Kate had almost forgotten how grumpy, miserable, and lost the girl in front of her had been; Alex had changed so much since then.

"Start at the beginning and tell me exactly what happened last night. I want to know everything that led up to the fire."

Alex was quiet for so long that Kate was about to tell her to hurry up, but then she launched into the story.

"So you were about fifteen feet away from the buffet table?" Kate asked.

"Yeah, at least that far. I swear I didn't know that was going to happen."

"Did you sweep your arms near it or did you point to something?"

"No."

"Were you concentrating on the flame?" Kate needed to know what the trigger was.

"No. It wasn't my fault. I was just really, really mad at Clarissa."

"That's not an excuse."

Alex huffed. "Kate, you don't know how horrible she is. She is mean all the time."

"You should have talked to me about her. What would have happened if you set her on fire? How would you feel if someone had gotten hurt, or worse? You have a powerful gift that can cause great harm if you let it get away from you, or if you misuse it. You need to learn control."

"I KNOW THAT! DON'T YOU THINK I KNOW THAT?"

"Stop screaming, right now. I'm not yelling. I'm trying to have a conversation with you, and you aren't listening."

"YOU ARE NOT MY MOTHER!" Alex yelled, then quieted a little. "You can't tell me what to do. You're just some lady who took us in." As soon as the words left Alex's mouth, she regretted them. Looking at Kate's face, she regretted them even more.

Kate leaned back away from Alex, almost feeling like her adopted daughter had hit her. She expected that they would have their fights, but she had not expected to feel so awful.

"I may not be your biological mother, but I adopted the three of you and I love you very much. I'm sorry you don't feel the same way." Kate paused, weighing her next words. "Since you can't have a conversation about this calmly and without screaming, you're grounded."

"Kate."

"Alex, I gave you the opportunity to talk to me. I can't have you throwing temper tantrums and setting things on fire. Maybe you need to think about things in your room for a while."

Alex was so angry at what happened and what she had said to Kate. Kate's empty expression made Alex feel sick. Proving her adopted mother correct about her temper, she picked up her phone and threw it across the room, hitting the wall. The phone screen shattered completely and went dead.

Kate looked between the phone and Alex, and turned away. Alex stomped up the steps and slammed her door.

Alex's screaming had alerted Maddy, and she looked like she was about to cry. Kate scooped her up and held her close. "It's okay," Kate crooned. "Alex was just a little angry. She'll be okay in a little bit. Did she scare you?"

Maddy nodded and hugged Kate tighter. "Want to call Aunt Cindy and see what she's up to? Maybe she can come over and we can make brownies."

The incident was forgotten as soon as the word "brownies" was mentioned.

Kate made two phone calls. The first was to Cindy to invite her over. The second was to her mom. They had been missing each other for the past few days and Kate really wanted to talk to her.

"Sweetheart, are you okay?" Kate's mom asked as soon as she answered the phone.

"Yeah."

"Uh-oh. What happened?"

Kate thought she could hold it together but she began to cry. "It's just everything. Everything I do seems like a struggle and I feel like I'm messing up."

"Did something happen with the kids?"

"Alex and I got into a big fight and I think she hates me." Kate cried even harder.

"Oh Kate, honey, she doesn't hate you. She's a teenager and they tend to give parents a really hard time. I seem to remember a teenage girl who screamed at her mother a bunch of times."

Kate gave her a half laugh. "I'm sorry I was like that, Mom."

"I think it's part of growing up. All kids drive parents crazy at times. I would wonder if they didn't."

"I know, you're right."

"Those kids love you and you *are* wonderful with them. You guys are going to fight sometimes. That's just how things are. I'm sure she's up in her room feeling really badly about how she acted. She might not tell you that, but she is."

They spoke for a few minutes about what her parents had been doing and their plans for the upcoming holidays. Kate heard her father calling for her mother. "Kate, I have to run."

"Thanks, Mom. You made me feel a lot better."
"Any time, sweetheart. I love you."
"Love you, too. Bye."

Half an hour later, Cindy walked in and gave Kate a big hug. "Are you okay? I don't have your gift and even I can tell how upset you are. Tell me what happened."

Kate told her about her confrontation with Alex and how much it bothered her.

"Kate, she's a teenager who had a horrible year. She lost her parents, was thrown in several awful foster homes, and had to learn to protect herself and her brother and sister."

"I know and the counselor in me understands, but . . ."

"But the mom in you is devastated that her daughter just crushed her feelings."

Kate shrugged, but said, "Basically."

"Give it a little time and you two will be back to giggling together and making fun of the guys."

"I know you're right."

"I am." She gave a saucy shake of her head and then went to get Maddy. "I thought we were making some brownies."

An hour later, Nick and Robert walked in and went right for the brownies that had just come out of the oven.

Cindy grabbed the plate just as they were reaching for them. They had made a double batch, knowing the guys would eat them all immediately.

"Hey!" Robert complained. "I wanted one of those. Don't be mean."

Cindy ignored him but looked behind them to see if anyone else was coming inside.

Robert watched her looking around and smirked. "Ryan will be here in a few minutes."

Cindy got a little flustered and said, "Why are you telling me that?"

Robert laughed. "Don't pretend you weren't looking for him." Kate bumped him with her shoulder.

"Don't tease her."

"Hey, babe." Nick started to hug Kate but she maneuvered out of the way and ignored his hello.

"Are you still mad at me from early this morning?"

Kate continued to ignore him.

Nick's shoulders slumped. "Don't be mad at me. I was just trying to be funny, but apparently I failed miserably."

Robert's laughter drew Kate's attention. Cindy and Robert were a few feet away and were watching the whole thing. Kate pulled Nick onto the back porch.

"It's not funny, Nick. We still haven't really talked about you leaving and being gone for so long. We haven't discussed why you didn't call me while you were gone. I felt like you abandoned me just when I was trying to figure all this stuff out."

"Oh, Kate. I'm so sorry," he muttered and pulled her to him, crushing her in a hug. "I'm sorry I left. I shouldn't have. I was scared."

"Why?"

"I was feeling too much for you and it was forbidden and I ran."

"Don't you think I was afraid, too?"

"I wasn't thinking about how you felt. I was just wanting you so badly and I didn't know how to deal with it. I'm still not dealing with it very well."

She stiffened and tried to take a step back but he tightened his hold. "Hey. Don't pull away. I wasn't finished. I'm not going anywhere. You're stuck with me."

"Okay. Then what did you just mean?"

"For my whole life I was told that the people in the Association were the good guys and that I must always respect them. It was ingrained in everything I did. I even turned my back on my best friend because he broke the rules."

Kate was captivated by his words.

Nick continued. "And then I met you. Even before we actually met and I was just watching you, I wanted you then. I loved how you carried yourself and how much you cared about people and wanted to help the world. You seemed like the kind of person people wanted to be around."

Kate gave him an encouraging smile. He kissed her forehead.

"When I actually met you, it was so much worse for me because I wanted you even more. I was devastated when I learned you were Gifted. Suddenly, I was faced with wanting someone so badly and not being able to have her. For the first time in my life, I was considering turning my back on everything I knew. It scared me and I needed time to think and to see if what was between us was just a fleeting thing, or something that could become amazing."

"What did you decide?"

He gave her a squeeze. "What do you think?" He kissed her neck. "I'm falling hard."

"I am too." They just stood still and stared into each other's eyes.

"Okay, whenever you two are done making googly eyes at each other, Ryan and Jay are here with some information."

Kate pulled back with a nervous laugh and ducked under Robert's arm to go into the house.

Robert turned to Nick. "You two are going to give me a headache."

Nick just shrugged. "I think we're always going to fight a little."

"No doubt. At least it'll be entertaining."

"Shut up, man."

Ryan and Jason were eating brownies when Robert and Nick came into the kitchen.

"Seriously?" Robert asked. "You gave them brownies and not me?" He began to mutter about how Cindy and Ryan were going to be worse than Kate and Nick, but no one could completely hear what he was saying.

Nick snatched a bite of Kate's brownie and shot her a smug look when she tried to take it back.

"Where's Grace?" Jason asked. "I called her this morning but she didn't answer."

Kate smiled. Jason had taken an interest in Grace. She wondered if it was just because Grace, for the most part, ignored Jason. "She had to work today. She's filling in for someone. In case you're wondering where your sister is, she had a problem at her gym."

"I didn't ask where she was," Jason grumbled.

Ryan interrupted. "Okay, so, my buddy got back to me this morning and had some more information about the ritual."

The fun atmosphere suddenly became quiet and reflective.

"He told me that more of the old scrolls were translated, and the Association discovered that for the ritual to work, some of the original mineral from Atlantis had to be present."

"Well, that's awesome," Cindy said. "Then we don't have to worry about it."

Robert narrowed his eyes. "There has to be some of that mineral somewhere for it to be referenced in the ritual."

Ryan shrugged. "Maybe, but it's been hundreds if not thousands of years since anyone has seen any. I don't think anyone knows where it would be."

Kate had a bad feeling. "If the ritual won't work without some mineral, then why is Louise after the people who have those gifts referenced in it? Maybe they have the mineral."

"If they had it, they would've attempted the ritual by now. I don't think they have it." Nick didn't want Kate to worry, so he pulled her against his side and rubbed her arm.

"I think it's good news," Jason said. "One less thing to worry about. Now the evil empire will never get their powers back."

Nick guided Kate into the living room. "I don't want you to worry."

"I'm not worrying. Not yet, anyway. I'm wondering if the Association has some of that mineral and they're hiding it, just like they hide everything else. They're not exactly open with their information."

"No, but something like that would probably have gotten out or we would've heard about it."

"Maybe." Kate wasn't so sure, but there wasn't anything she could do about it now. "I spoke to Alex this morning. It didn't go very well."

Nick frowned. "What happened?"

"She screamed at me that I wasn't her mother, threw her cell phone against the wall, and then stormed upstairs and slammed the door."

"Oh, it went that well?" Nick said sarcastically.

Kate sighed and shrugged one shoulder. "I grounded her."

"Good. She needs to learn to respect you. I'm going to talk

to her."

"I handled it."

"Kate, you don't have to handle things on your own. I'm here and whatever happens, we'll deal with it together."

"Thanks." She stepped up to him, put her arms around his neck, and gave him a light kiss. He cuddled her closely, wishing he could take her away from everything.

He held her for a little while, loving the feel of her in his arms. He didn't want to let her go, but they had some things to do. "I think we should go see your uncle."

Kate pulled back to look him in the eyes. "What?"

"I've been thinking about it, and we should go see your uncle."

"Why are you bringing this up now?"

"We need all of the information we can get. I looked into him, and it seems that he was pretty high up in the Association for a long time, then abruptly left about ten years ago. He might have some inside information that we could use."

"It's been something I've been thinking about, too, but there's been too much going on lately."

"No time is going to be perfect. He looked for you for years, and maybe he can fill you in about your parents a little more."

Kate was nervous, but decided she wanted to meet him. "Okay. Let's go. I need to get someone to watch Maddy and keep an eye out for Alex and Zach. Zach is still at Eric's and will probably be there all afternoon. Alex will undoubtedly pout all day."

"See if Cindy will watch them. I'm sure Ryan will keep her company." Nick gave Kate a sly grin. Everyone could see that they were interested in each other, but Cindy and Ryan refused to do anything about it.

Louise had driven for hours the night she had escaped. She was headed to her estate in South Carolina, which no one knew about, not even Ray. She had some of her trusted guards move the children she had handpicked to that location, which was listed under a corporation name that was also linked to about twelve other corporations. It would take months to sort out the paper trail for the estate.

She had ditched her car that night and rented a new one with a credit card that was also listed under the same corporation. Louise had set it up several years ago in case she needed to escape Brooks or her father. Now she was going to be hiding from them both.

The night she fled, she'd stopped at a very low-budget motel on the way to South Carolina because nobody would ever think she would stay in such a place. Thankfully, no one had bothered her. She'd thrown her cell phone out of the car immediately after her father had called. Knowing him, he could trace the phone and figure out where she was going. Luckily, she had some burner phones that she could use and get rid of.

She hated that she had to leave Emma behind when she escaped from Ray. Louise would send someone to get her immediately. All she could do was hope that Ray wouldn't take out his frustrations on the small girl. Ray had a tendency to be unimaginably cruel when upset, and Louise was sure she had made him more than upset.

Louise loved her mansion in the South. It was a replica of a southern plantation, but with all new amenities, because she hated not having the best of everything. She pulled up to the gate and punched in a security code. A man appeared as she neared the garage. He relaxed his stance when she rolled to a stop.

"Ms. Santos, welcome back," said the man, who was over six feet tall and heavily built. He was mostly muscle, but seemed to have softened more lately.

"Thank you, Carl. Are all the children here?"

"Yes, most are in their rooms or in the game room. Would you like me to gather them?"

"No, that isn't necessary. I'll see them shortly," Louise told him, and then paused with another thought. "Have everyone tighten security and keep an eye out for things. We could be expecting trouble.

"Should I call in a few more guys?"

"No, that won't be necessary, but I have a little job for you. I need you to go to Maryland to pick up someone for me. It needs to be done quietly and without anyone following you back here. Can you do that?"

"Of course. I'll leave immediately."

Now, Louise needed to begin to form her plan. There was still a lot of information she needed, but she could start. She had waited this long; a few more months wouldn't be a problem.

"I told you Ryan would offer to stay with Cindy as soon as you asked her."

Kate laughed. "Yes, you did. What do you want, a gold star for today?" she asked him sarcastically.

"No, but I will settle for a kiss."

"Oh, yeah, and you think you deserve a kiss for a lucky guess?"

"Babe, there's no luck involved here. You're looking at pure awesomeness."

"Yeah, you're awesome alright." She was sitting in his SUV's passenger seat, clasping his hand. He had grabbed it and held on tightly when she began to fidget from nervousness. *What if her uncle was disappointed? What if he no longer wanted to meet her? What if he blamed her for her parents' deaths?*

"Hey," Nick said, squeezing her hand. "Stop. I can feel your emotions surging."

"That's my gift. How can you feel that?"

"The tingling we feel when we touch gets worse when you're upset. It's almost like I feel your energy surging from you into me."

She looked intrigued. "Since you can manipulate energy, can you control the energy coming from me?"

"Hmm. I don't know. We'll have to play around with it. But, right now, we need to go knock on the door."

Kate hadn't noticed that they had pulled into the circular driveway of her uncle's rather large house. She took a deep breath to settle her nerves.

Nick pulled on her hand to get her attention. "Everything will be okay. I promise."

Kate had put on her mother's charm bracelet. She wasn't even sure why she did. It just felt right. She jingled the silver charms and watched the light reflect off of them. "Okay. I'm ready."

Nick got out of the car and walked around to Kate's side. He liked being a gentleman and helping her out of the vehicle, but he knew she was not allowing him to be gallant. She was stalling. He smiled at her as he opened the door and pulled her out of the car.

"It helps to exit the vehicle, Kate." Nick started to tease her so that she would loosen up. "You might want to fix your hair before you go in."

Kate's eyes got huge. "My hair's a mess? Seriously? You were going to let me go in there with my hair messy?" She was working herself up so much, she didn't notice his laughter.

"You look beautiful."

"You did that on purpose."

"Of course. You're not as nervous now because you're irritated with me." He quickly stole a kiss and then guided her toward the door.

Right before she was to knock on the door, she turned to him. "Maybe we should have called first."

"Kate . . ."

"Oh, okay." She grabbed the knocker and struck the door a few times, then she stepped back with a mixture of dread and anticipation.

A handsome man with dark, messy hair and light greyish-blue eyes opened the door. He was very fit and looked a lot younger than his mid-forties. The man's eyes got larger and he faltered. "My God, you look exactly like Amanda," he muttered, clearly stunned.

Kate was having trouble speaking past the lump forming in her throat. He looked a lot like the photos she had seen of her father, just older.

He shook his head. "I apologize. I didn't mean to startle you. Can I help you?"

"I'm Kate . . . Jim and Amanda's daughter." She stared up at her uncle, petrified to see his reaction.

He grabbed the door jamb tightly, his knuckles turning white from the force he was using to keep himself upright. "You look just like her. I almost gave up on ever finding you. I've looked for you for over twenty years. Please. Come in." He staggered back away from the door so that they could enter.

Nick squeezed Kate's hand in reassurance as they entered the foyer. Kate was looking at the marble floors, but forced herself to raise her eyes and take in her surroundings. Wood panels lined the bottom half of the walls, stopping at a chair rail. A few expensive-looking prints adorning the walls caught her eye and she would have liked to stop and look at them, but she continued to follow her uncle. She also noticed a dark, wooden, skinny table that sat next to the front door and held a small white sculpture. The foyer was empty of clutter, without a knickknack in sight.

Her uncle led them into his study and closed the door for privacy. He wasn't ready to share her with anyone else just yet. The office was done in the same wooden tones as the foyer, with expensive furnishings. He sat down on a leather chair facing a love seat and motioned for Kate and Nick to have a seat.

He took a deep breath. "I'm sorry. I didn't introduce myself. You threw me off completely, but in a very good way. I'm David and you're Kate and . . ."

"Nick Taylor. It's nice to meet you, David." Nick leaned forward to shake the man's hand.

Awkward silence lasted only a second or two when Kate broke it. "You were looking for me?"

David relaxed. "Yes, I looked for your parents after they left. I wanted to find them." He looked uncertain for a second and then asked, "Do you know about our race?"

"Yes. I am aware of our gifts and our race's history."

"Okay, good."

"Why would you look for them? They were breaking your laws. Did you want to turn them in?"

"NO! No. I wanted to help them. I wanted to stand up with them. I never agreed with all of the harsh laws, and frankly never believed the warnings they gave about the consequences of relationships."

"Did they know you were looking for them?"

"Jim knew. He contacted me after Amanda got pregnant. He wanted me to promise that if anything ever happened to him, I would take care of Amanda and you. I never got the chance. I begged him to come home and told him that we would figure it out together, but he said it was already too late and that people were after them. He didn't want to bring the danger to the rest our family. I wish he would have let me help him."

"He knew he was going to die?"

He sighed heavily. "I'm not sure. He was scared and they were running. I think he suspected it was a possibility."

Kate nodded. She didn't expect to become so emotional. Hearing about her parents was way more upsetting than she'd thought it would be. She wiped a tear and her bracelet jingled, drawing David's attention.

He reached out and then stopped himself. He pointed to her wrist instead. "Is that . . ."

"My mom's? Yeah. Nick found it for me last summer. It's one of the only things I have from her. This, and a diary."

"She used to write in that diary all the time. Jim once sneaked a look in it and she freaked. It was all about him, and he bragged about it for weeks."

Kate laughed at his memory.

"Did you have a good childhood? Were you okay? I looked everywhere for you but there was no sign of anywhere."

Kate smiled. "My parents are wonderful people. They love and care for me and have given me everything I could want. I'm lucky they're so great."

"I'm happy for you. I just wish you could have known your real parents and our family. We would have cared for you. I would have brought you up as my own." He looked sad at having missed her life. "I would really like to get to know you, Kate, if you let me. You have cousins. I have a son and a daughter. They're both away at college right now but they would love to meet you."

Kate nodded, but she was starting to feel overwhelmed. He was pushing too hard. She loved her parents—and the life they gave her—very much, and she wouldn't have wanted to change anything.

He could see her growing discomfort and backed off. "I'm sorry if I seem pushy. I'm just so happy you're here finally after all these years. Can we start slowly and see what happens?"

"I'd like that."

They spoke for a few more minutes about the past and her uncle talked about her parents. Nick had been very quiet the whole time, letting Kate and her uncle talk. It was obvious that she loved hearing some of his stories.

A loud knock on the door startled Kate. She looked up to see an attractive young man with blonde hair storm in without waiting for permission. David had an odd look on his face and Nick stiffened.

The newcomer approached David, completely ignoring Kate and Nick.

"Boss, we have a problem. The Association has made a cyber-attack on our systems."

"Now is not a good time, Luke."

For the first time, Luke looked at Kate and then swung his gaze to Nick. "What are you doing here, Taylor? Are you running interference for the Association? Trying to cover their tracks?"

Kate stood up. "You lead the Division?" She started toward the door. She had to escape. She couldn't deal with anything else.

Her uncle was part of the shady organization that everyone feared?

"Kate, please don't leave. It's not what you think. The Division is not what you think."

"I have to go." Kate walked out the door without looking back. She needed some fresh air.

David turned to Nick. "I've heard of you but we've never met, Taylor. So I guess you're the one who has been feeding my niece all kinds of crap about the Division."

Nick stood stiffly. He now knew why her uncle left the Association, but he was now questioning everything else he had ever been taught about the Association and the Division.

"Your silence has said it all. You can leave now, but know this. I *will* tell my niece the truth and I'll protect her even from you."

Nick didn't like hearing that. "*I* will protect Kate. She's mine to protect."

"Do you realize what you are implying, son?"

"Yes, sir. I am no longer under the Association's command."

"If you hurt her, I *will* come after you."

"Same to you, sir."

David nodded to Nick; they had just come to an unspoken agreement.

Nick turned to leave but paused and asked, "Why didn't we know you led the Division?"

David laughed. "What, announce that I control the Division and have every assassin around after me?" David wasn't sure what to make of the younger man in front of him. It was obvious he loved his niece, but could he be trusted? "Taylor, take care of her."

"I will."

Nick left the house and found Kate leaning against the car. He walked right up to her and pulled her into his arms. "Hey. It's going to be okay."

"How is that going to be okay?"

"Because I think it will be. You need to give him a chance to explain."

"This coming from the guy who once accused me of belonging to this group you claimed was evil?"

Nick shrugged. "Nothing has been what it seems. The Association is not what they seem, so it makes sense that neither is the Division. Give your uncle a chance."

"I can't right now. I just can't."

Nick squeezed her. "You don't have to right now. Just think about it."

"Okay. I'll think about it."

Char Webster

Chapter Nineteen

Jason and Ryan waited until one a.m. to leave for the woods. They were going to do reconnaissance on the Association compound that Nick and Robert had begun to explore. They volunteered because they both felt like they'd been left out of the fun lately, and they both needed a little adventure. Breaking into the Association facility sounded like their idea of fun.

"So what's up with you and Cindy? Ask the girl out already," Jason teased.

"There isn't anything going on. She just broke up with her boyfriend and isn't ready for anything right now."

"Do you hear yourself? Have you lost your balls? Do you need to check to see if they're still there?"

Ryan ignored him.

"Dude, seriously, she's going to place you in permanent friend zone if you don't act soon."

Ryan wondered about that, but Cindy had been really upset and trying not to show it. He didn't want to push her and make her more upset, but he couldn't tell that to Casanova next to him.

"What about you and Grace? I see you following her around. You haven't been on a date with a girl since she showed up here. What's up with that? Either you're infatuated with the new girl or you have gone through all of the women in the area. Which is it?"

"She's hot but I've had hotter." Ryan could tell that Jason was hedging.

"So why haven't you been dating?"

"Dude, there's been too much going on," Jason told him

"Since when has that ever stopped you?"

"We're here. Shh." Jason jumped out of the vehicle and reached behind the seat for his backpack.

Ryan shook his head, but grabbed his stuff and followed quietly behind Jason.

Dressed in all black to blend in with the night, they crept up behind a few larger trees to observe the buildings before approaching them.

Ryan could see in the dark without the aid of the night vision goggles that Jason was using. It was a benefit of his gift. There were three guards walking the perimeter of the grounds, but they were focusing on the outermost building. That was the one place that Nick and Robert were interested in getting more information about.

"We need to get into that building or at least tap into their surveillance to see what's going on."

Ryan agreed. "Yeah, my buddy said there were no buildings out here except for the Chancellor's residence. So Pete's hiding something, and we need to find out what."

Ryan pulled out his laptop and began to type at a ridiculously rapid speed. After a few minutes, he turned the screen toward Jason.

"Oh, good. Let's see what Pete is up to."

They flipped through the security cameras on the system, checking out what each one was recording. Ryan set the laptop to record all of the cameras and upload the footage to a secure server. "We'll be able to look at these at any time."

Jason nodded. "Nice." They were flipping through the cameras and angles when Jason told Ryan to stop. "What was that last one?"

Ryan flipped back and said, "Whoa. That looks like a medieval torture chamber."

"That's an interrogation room. The Association outlawed that kind of thing years ago. No wonder he's hiding out here." Jason couldn't believe what they were seeing.

"We need to tell Nick and Rob."

"Yeah, let's get out of here."

Alex had not left her room all day except to use the bathroom. Kate took her a sandwich for dinner since she hadn't come down for any food. Alex had a few granola bars in her room so she had been snacking on those. She couldn't believe what happened between her and Kate. Alex hated fighting with her; she loved Kate and hadn't meant to say those awful things to her.

Zach had even come in and yelled at her. Normally she would have yelled back at him, but she couldn't. She had been so completely wrong. Alex just didn't know how to fix it. It wasn't so bad being grounded; she deserved that, and for more than one thing. She did lose her temper at school and endangered people, but she was horrible to Kate and wrecked her phone. She probably wouldn't get another one any time soon. At least she still had her iPad.

A message flashed on her screen. It was from Rick. He had probably tried to get in touch with her but couldn't. Should she meet him? If he had a way to fix her gift so she wouldn't have to worry, then the risk was justifiable.

U there?
Phone broke.
Meet?
She debated for several moments before responding, *Yea.*
2morrow?
Alex thought about it. She wondered if it would be worth the trouble and risk of sneaking out. It would have to be late after Kate went to bed, but not too late because Kate had an odd habit of getting up in the middle of the night to have coffee with Uncle Nick.

2 AM?
@Boundary Creek Park
Alex knew the park and it wasn't that far if she rode her bike. She would just have to get the bike out of the garage ahead of time and hide it. She hesitated. Things could get way worse if she got caught, but if he could help her, things could get a whole lot better.

Yes.
cu there.
She hoped this worked.

Brooks clicked off his iPad with a satisfied smile. Kate would soon know how it felt to have something taken from her. It was only the beginning of her suffering.

Joel had come back to the house the day before and had been unusually reserved. He was probably pouting about his good-for-nothing brother. He really needed to get over it. The guy was a waste.

"Joel," Brooks called out. Joel took way longer than usual answering his summons.

Joel walked into the room and waited.

"We need to pick up Natalie."

"Natalie? Why? What do we need her for?" The teen gave Joel the creeps, and that was saying a lot. Every time he looked at her, he could see just pure evil oozing out. The kid had had a horrible childhood and Brooks had actually treated her nicer than her parents had, but the damage had already been done.

"She has a gift that might come in handy."

"She controls the flow of things. How can that come in handy?"

"You never can tell. Plus the girl is one hundred percent loyal to me, which is more than I can say for some people."

Joel gave Brooks a look of complete loathing and walked out.

"Damn!" Bret muttered.

"Swear jar!" Kali called out.

"Kali, I'm not putting a dollar in that jar every time you tell me."

"Daddy said you should."

"Your father said that about him, not me. Anyway, I've got some important things to do right now. Can you go play a video game?"

Bret knew the instant the words left his mouth that it had been the wrong thing to say to her. Now she wouldn't leave him alone until she found out what he was doing.

"What are you doing? You're colors are changing." He knew it.

"I found some information for your dad."

Kali lit up. "You're going to call my dad? Can I talk to him?"

"He called you this morning."

"Yeah, but can I talk to him now?"

"Probably not. You'll talk to him tomorrow morning. But Kal, he should be coming home soon."

She lit up even more.

"Can you please go play video games?"

"Ohhhh, okay."

Bret waited for her to start her game in the other room before calling Frank.

"Kid? What do you want?"

"I found him. I know where Brooks will be."

"WHERE?"

"He's pretending to be a teenager and just set up a meeting with that girl from last summer, Alex."

"The girl he made me take?"

"Yeah, her. They're supposed to meet Sunday night at two a.m. in Boundary Creek Park."

"Kid, if this info is correct, you can have anything you want. I'll owe you."

"Frank, I just want you to protect Alex."

"I'll protect her. I owe Kate for taking her. I'll protect us all by taking Brooks out."

"Thanks." Bret was relieved that he could help Alex.

Frank smiled. He was finally going to get his revenge on Brooks and maybe repay a debt. Things were looking good.

Detective Martin wasn't sure what to think, but he knew that a thirteen-year-old girl should not be meeting anyone at two a.m. He wasn't sure it was even a boy the girl was going to meet. He had been searching social media for anything unusual and couldn't trace those accounts to anyone. That was never a good sign. He was going to show up at this meeting to find out what was going on and protect the girl, whether she wanted it or not. Too many weird things happened around this family. Just the day before, the girl's homecoming dance had even been evacuated due to a fire.

Weird things. He was going to discover the truth.

The next evening, Kate opened Alex's bedroom door. "Alex, you can't keep hiding in your room. You've been in here for almost two full days. I know you're upset, but pouting doesn't work."

Alex didn't answer her.

Kate sighed. "I expect you at breakfast tomorrow. This is the last meal I will bring up to you."

Kate walked back downstairs. Nick was lounging on the couch, waiting for her to come back. "Hey. You okay?" he asked.

Kate frowned but didn't say anything.

Nick continued. "She's almost fourteen. Aren't teenagers supposed to be hideous at that age?"

Kate laughed. "Great. I guess I should have expected something like this."

"Things will work out."

Kate gave him a hopeful look. "I know." She snuggled up next to him on the couch.

Detective Martin had been in the park for more than an hour waiting for something to happen. He knew the meeting was not supposed to occur until two a.m. but he wanted to get there early so that he could catch the person preying on a child. Then he would take the girl home and demand answers from her mother.

Alex wasn't pouting anymore, but she *was* hiding from Kate. She knew that Kate would figure out what she was going to do, if Alex talked to her. She had managed to avoid her all day, even when Kate brought her dinner.

Alex had also suffered through a really long lecture from Uncle Nick about disrespecting Kate. She had listened and not said a word because she *was* sorry that she had disrespected Kate. She felt horrible about it, but she couldn't apologize until her situation was all over. She wanted to be able to apologize for everything at once, and Alex knew that she was going to have a lot to be sorry for.

Alex opened her door a crack to listen. There were no sounds coming from any of the other bedrooms. She peeked at Kate's door and she didn't see a light coming from the bottom, so she figured Kate was probably asleep. Alex opened the door the rest of the way as quietly as possible and shut it again with only a slight click. She paused and looked around one more time to make sure no one heard her.

The floorboards at the top center of the steps would squeak, so she stayed as close to the wall as possible. The third step down creaked loudly, so she skipped over that one, too. The second step from the bottom also made a noise sometimes, so that was another one that Alex avoided.

Finally on the first floor, she crept quietly toward the front door. She wanted to make sure that Kate wasn't sitting on the porch. With no one in sight, she opened the door and slipped outside.

She hadn't been able to get her bike out of the garage earlier. Every time she had looked out the window, the guys had been in there. She knew that Kate hid a key to the garage in the planter by the pool, since she wanted them to always have a way into the house in case she couldn't be home to let them in. Alex pulled a few dying leaves out of the way and fished out the small box with the key in it. She quickly unlocked the side door and pulled her bike out, leaning it against the porch, then replaced the key and hopped on her bike. The park was only a couple of miles away, so it wouldn't take her very long to get there.

Don had been completely bored watching Kate Sutton's house. He had no idea why he had to watch a house where everyone was asleep. Nothing was happening and he would never get any information like this. He had to find some other way to prove she still had her gifts.

He was just about to take a nap in his car when he saw the teenage girl creep out of the house. Don sat up, paying attention. Now *this* was interesting. He watched the girl walk around the back of the house and a few minutes later, ride off on her bicycle.

He waited until she had a short lead, then he started the car's engine. Don wanted to know where this girl was going in the middle of the night. It was sure more interesting than watching a sleeping house. He rode with his headlights off so she wouldn't notice; he didn't need to worry, though, because she wasn't paying attention to anything as she rode her bike.

He watched her turn off the road and onto a drive that lead to a county park. Who would she be meeting in a park at two a.m.?

Don parked his car in a driveway half a mile from the park entrance and approached it on foot. He kept to the underbrush so she wouldn't see him follow her. She continued into the park, then took a path to the right that lead from the parking lot around the information building and bathrooms. The path disappeared around a bend and into a wooded area. Don needed to be careful following along behind her so that she or the person she was meeting wouldn't see him.

The anticipation was nearly unbearable, but Frank was trying to keep his emotions under control. His muscles were tensed and he was ready to react. He needed to end things to protect his daughter, and if he admitted it to himself, he was ending things for a few others as well.

Brooks needed to be stopped and Frank was the person to do it.

The location Brooks had picked was almost laughable. The guy couldn't come up with an original idea if his life depended upon it. Parks were always Frank's preferred meeting place, especially government parks. They were always closed from dusk until dawn and, because of government cutbacks, the parks were never monitored as they should be so were isolated enough to provide the privacy needed to conduct this type of business. Brooks gave Frank the perfect spot to take him out.

From Frank's experience, Brooks liked to make grand entrances, waiting until it seemed as if he wasn't going to appear and then swooping in dramatically. This time, Frank was the one who would be surprising everyone, especially Brooks.

Frank walked the trails several times, looking for the best vantage point for his plan. He was also trying to determine Brooks' meeting place. Bret hadn't been too specific, but it didn't matter; Brooks would be in the park and then he would be Frank's.

Alex parked her bike against the fence lining the beginning

of the right trail. Rick had told her that he would meet her at the first observation deck that overlooked the Rancocas Creek. It was at the back of the park, in the farthest area from the parking lot and information building. The hike was only about a mile and a half, but it was completely dark and the trail through the wooded area was not smooth. Alex walked slowly so that she wouldn't fall. She could just imagine tripping, twisting her ankle, and not being able to walk.

Leaves crackled off to her right toward the woods and the creek. She stopped, staring into the woods, but was unable to see anything. She wished she had remembered to bring a flashlight. The moon was really bright, which she was thankful for, but the sounds around her were scaring her. She thought about going home and forgetting about meeting Rick, but if he had a way for her to control her gift, she needed to find out. Everyone could be in danger with her around.

She reached the decking of the first lookout. It was an elaborate, twisting structure that took viewers out beyond the marshes so that they could get a better look at the creek. Kate had taken them to this park for a nature walk. It had been a fun day for them all.

Alex really hoped that her meeting with Rick wouldn't ruin that happy memory of the park.

Someone was approaching her with a flashlight, making it impossible for her to see who it was because the light was blinding in the darkness of the park. Alex suddenly became really nervous. *Was she making a mistake? Was she crazy to meet someone she didn't know in the middle of the night with no one around? Putting it that way, yes, I am crazy.*

The figure drew closer and still, Alex couldn't see anything in the bright light.

"Rick?" she called out.

The person standing before her moved the light to illuminate his own face. Alex froze in her spot on the deck. "Oh my God, what did I do?" she muttered to herself, terrified.

A beeping sound woke Zach up. He rubbed his eyes, trying to figure out what it was. It wasn't coming from his room. He got up and walked toward the sound. It was coming from Alex's room. He was going to clobber her for waking him up. She was probably playing some sort of game on her iPad. He pushed open her door with more force than necessary in his annoyance and stopped short when he saw that her bed and room were empty. Alex was gone.

Her iPad was making the beeping sound. He picked it up and saw an icon blinking. Zach clicked on it and a message popped up on the screen. *Oh my God, Lex. What have you done?* **Rick *IS* dangerous. Not a kid. Don't go.**

Zach rushed into Kate's room, yelling her name. "Kate! Kate! Wake up!"

Kate jumped up, startled, panicking at the look on Zach's face and the terror coming off of him.

"What's wrong?"

"Alex is gone. She snuck out. Look!" He shoved the iPad with the message still showing at Kate. She grabbed the edge of the nightstand as she read the short message.

"No. No, she wouldn't." Kate was shaking her head, unable to accept the fact that her daughter had rushed off toward danger.

"I'll find her. Zach, I need you to stay here with Maddy. I'll have one of the guys stay with you." She pulled a pair of jeans out of the closet and was wiggling into them as she called Nick.

It rang a few times and then a sleepy voice said a soft, "Hello."

"Nick! I need you to get here immediately. Alex is gone. We need to find her. Someone needs to stay with Zach and Maddy."

She heard Nick swear a few times and then he promised, "We'll find her. Be right there."

She pulled a hoodie over her t-shirt and was slipping on her sneakers as she rushed down the steps. Zach was in the living room watching at the window. Kate gave him a hug and kissed his head. "We'll bring her back. Don't worry."

Ryan jogged up the walk with Nick and Robert. "I'll watch the kids for you, don't worry about them."

Nick pulled Kate into a hug and kissed her head.

"Where's Jason?" Kate asked, not seeing him with the guys or outside.

"He wasn't home, and he didn't pick up the call. I'll keep

trying him," Ryan assured her.

Kate handed Ryan the iPad. "Here's Alex's iPad. Can you figure out where she went? Her older messages were deleted. There's only this one left." Kate pointed to the warning. Ryan was already setting up his computer on the dining room table. He plugged the iPad into his computer and started typing.

Nick took her hand. "Before we take off randomly looking for her, let's give Ryan a minute or two to see if there is anything on her tablet."

Everyone looked grim. Kate was in a panic but she was trying desperately not to let it take control of her.

Nick gave her hand a slight squeeze. "It's going to be okay. We'll get her back and then I'm going to clobber her."

"Yeah, Kate. We'll find her," Robert assured her.

"This is all my fault. She's gone because of me. Oh God, what did I do? If anything happens to her I'll never forgive myself."

Robert put his hand on her shoulder. "Kate, this isn't your fault. You didn't do anything wrong."

"Yes, yes I did. She was upset and I was hard on her. We had an awful fight and I let her sulk in her room. I should have made her talk to me. Now, I may never get the chance."

Nick turned to her. "There is absolutely no reason for her to have taken off like this. She should know better."

Kate covered her face with her hands. "This IS my fault. I should have been monitoring her social media better. I should have known something was wrong. I know better than this. I'm a damn counselor."

"Kate, you didn't know," Nick began.

Robert interrupted. "Kate, astral project to her. You can do it. You projected to Maddy when she had a bad dream. You can report back where she is."

"Let's jump in the car and circle the neighborhood to see if we can find her," Nick suggested. "I hate not doing something."

"What about the astral projecting?" Kate was nervous to try it, but trying in a moving vehicle sounded frightening.

Nick looked at her tenderly. "You can do this. I'll hold your hand while you try it from the car. The first couple of times, you projected to me. We're connected, Kate. We will always find our way back to each other."

"Okay, I'll try."

Robert, Nick, and Kate ran out to Nick's SUV. Kate settled into the passenger seat and closed her eyes to concentrate on Alex.

Chapter Twenty

"Jason! Where the hell have you been?" Ryan had called Jason eight times in the last few minutes.

"Sorry, Dad. I didn't realize I missed curfew," Jason joked.

"Dude. You need to get back here right now. Alex is missing."

"What happened?" Jason demanded.

Ryan filled him in and Jason let out a few colorful words. "We'll be right there."

"We?" Ryan asked, but Jason had already hung up the phone.

Kate opened her eyes, and her astral-projected self was standing a couple of feet from Alex, who looked terrified. Kate immediately spun around to search out the danger. Standing in front of her daughter was the most evil person she could imagine. Brooks was holding a gun and a flashlight at Alex.

"Kate?" Alex rushed at Kate but passed through her. "KATE!"

"It's okay, Alex. It's an astral projection. We're on our way. We're coming for you," Kate tried to assure her, but was too terrified herself to sound very convincing.

"Well, well. Kate Sutton." Brooks moved forward. "This is an unexpected surprise. I see you have developed yet another skill. My, my. I knew you would be talented." Brooks circled closer toward her and Alex. "I couldn't have hoped for a better gift than for you to see me take your daughter and you be completely unable to do anything about it."

Ryan's computer dinged. He immediately called Robert, who put him on speaker phone. "Get to Boundary Creek Park fast. This isn't good. Alex's been chatting with some kid named Rick for several weeks. She's been worried about her gift being out of control and this Rick claims he can help. Looks like he has been pressuring her to meet him for a while now," Ryan paused.

"Guys, it's not a kid. It's Brooks."
"We're not far from there now," Robert told him.
Ryan called Jason back. "She's at Boundary Creek Park."
"Got it. We're two seconds from there."

Frank was inching closer to where Brooks was cornering the girl when Kate flickered into sight. He was shocked to see a ghost-like version of her. He watched the girl launch herself at Kate but go right through. Kate wouldn't be any help to the girl; she would just have to watch whatever went down.

"You *will not* be taking my daughter anywhere," Kate commanded with much more bravado then she felt. She was terrified that this evil man would take Alex away and she would never see her again.

"Kate! I'm so sorry. I'm so, so sorry," Alex cried.

"It's going to be okay. We'll come get you," Kate told her.

"Come along, Alex. I don't have all night," Brooks motioned to her, but Alex stayed where she was. "Kate can't help you. She is a shadow, a ghost."

Alex cried out to Kate who was standing very close to her, but unable to really help her.

Leaves crackling caused Alex to look up as two more figures emerged from the woods: a man with long greasy hair over a big balding spot on the top of his head, and a beautiful girl with long, blonde hair who looked sweet and kind. Alex thought maybe they would help her.

"Do you want me to grab the girl?" the beautiful blond asked Brooks. Alex's hopes were suddenly crushed. This girl would offer no assistance.

"Not yet, Natalie, darling. I want your new sister to come to us. We shouldn't have to drag her along." The girl made a loud snorting noise, showing her annoyance at not getting her way.

Brooks was still holding a gun on Alex. Kate wanted to stay with Alex, no matter what, and would follow her wherever she went. Just like she would always be able to find Nick, she would always be able to find her kids.

Kate needed to tell the guys where they were, but she didn't want to abandon her daughter. The best chance Alex had would be for the guys to come to the rescue. As much as Kate hated the thought, she had to leave Alex for a few seconds.

Kate turned to Alex. "I need to tell the guys where we are. I will only be gone for a few seconds. I promise."

"NO! Don't leave me. Please don't leave me." Kate faltered. *What should she do?*

Frank took Alex's outburst as the perfect opportunity to make his presence known. He appeared out of the woods with a gun leveled at Brooks. "Thought I would even out the odds a little."

Brooks stiffened. He hadn't expected Frank to find him tonight. "Frank, you're interfering with some business here. I'm finishing a job that you failed to do last summer."

Frank looked at Kate. "I took your kids 'cause he took my daughter."

Kate was watching the exchange slightly confused. The big guy with tattoos in front of her was the same guy who took the kids last summer, but only took them because Brooks had taken his daughter? The whole situation was becoming much more complicated.

Frank promised Kate, "I won't let Brooks take her."

Kate nodded and flickered out. She returned to her body with a gasp. "She's at Boundary Creek Park!"

Nick squeezed her hand harder. "We're pulling in right now. He won't get her."

Jason and Grace crept up the hiking trail in the park. They could hear voices in the distance and knew that they were near the action. Jason motioned for Grace to be completely silent as they got closer. He could see some flashlights at the bend in the trail and a group of people facing each other closer to the creek.

"I have to go back to her," Kate told Nick.

"Go to Alex. I'll carry you." Nick kissed her briefly and she was gone again.

Nick jammed the car into park and jumped out of the SUV and around the vehicle to scoop Kate out of the car. He nestled her prone body against his chest and he and Robert started jogging down the trail.

Kate flickered back to Alex's side and the girl gave her a thankful look. "Kate," she breathed.

———●———

Jason and Grace entered the opening of the observation deck at the same time Robert and Nick came running up, Nick still carrying Kate. While Jason and Grace had crept up silently, Nick and Robert had run full out and hadn't cared about noise.

"What happened to Kate?" Jason whispered concerned.

"She astral projected to Alex," Nick explained.

"That is so freakin' cool," Jason muttered.

"Okay, let's go. Talk time is over." Robert went to take the lead but paused and turned to Grace. "Are you going to be okay? You know Brooks is around that corner, right?"

Grace glanced at Jason before answering. "Yeah. I've waited long enough to confront him. I want to be here."

"Okay. Let's go." Robert began walking toward the observation deck.

They followed along cautiously, not knowing if anyone was going to appear suddenly.

———●———

Detective Martin was watching from behind the retaining wall next to the observation deck. He saw the young girl waiting for someone and then the man approach with a flashlight. He knew the girl was not expecting to see the man because she looked terrified.

He was just about to reveal himself when he saw what looked like a ghost appear, only this ghost could speak. He rubbed his eyes a few times and looked around to see if he was being pranked. The ghost was Kate Sutton. *What the hell was going on?*

Martin started forward when he noticed a man approaching from the woods and another man and teen hiding slightly off the path. Martin decided to wait a few more minutes to see what was going to happen. He was outnumbered, and also out-gunned.

Kate had been gone for only a few seconds, but it felt like hours. Alex, Brooks, Frank, the man, and the girl were all in the exact locations they had been when she left. It was a complete standoff. She wanted to save Alex, but knew that she couldn't in her present condition. The guys were almost there and hopefully they would be able to do something. The only reason Brooks hadn't taken Alex already was because the man who stole her last summer—Frank, Brooks had called him—was pointing a gun at him.

Kate let out a sigh of relief when she saw Nick, Robert, Jason, and Grace come into view. She waited for them to get closer so she could go back to her body. She didn't want to leave Alex's side, but she needed to be able to do more than just watch. She saw Grace stride forward, leaving the guys behind in her hurry to join the confrontation. Jason quickened his step to stay next to her.

Frank wanted to just shoot Brooks, but he suspected that Joel and possibly the girl both had guns. They were playing things cool, but they could turn ugly in seconds. He didn't want a gun battle. The girl could get hurt and he wouldn't risk it. He owed Kate that much.

"Give up, Brooks. You're not leaving here with the girl," Frank called out.

"You expect me to believe that you'll just let me go if I leave the girl alone? We know each other better than that, Frank."

"I'm not letting you leave here alive. I came here to kill you."

"So shoot me. What are you waiting for? Pull the trigger and kill me," Brooks taunted. "Have you gone soft? Can't follow through? You were always weak, Frank. You never could kill when I told you to."

Frank laughed. "No, I never wanted to kill someone simply because you told me to. But, this is different. You made it personal. You went after my family."

Grace walked directly up to the edge of the second deck facing both Brooks and Frank. Directly across from her was Alex and Kate's astral projection. She watched Brooks and Frank with their guns locked onto each other. She had never seen Frank with such a look of determination on his face. Brooks looked slightly nervous. He was always used to being the one in complete control and it seemed as if Frank was winning the battle.

She was just about to make her presence known when she heard a nasty screech coming from slightly behind Brooks.

"YOU! You should be dead. How are you alive? I shot you myself!" Joel screamed. He raised his gun and fired it at Grace.

Everyone gasped. Jason immediately raised his arm and tried to freeze the bullet. It slowed at first but then sped up again and kept coming at Grace. Without even a thought, Jason stepped in front of Grace and the bullet slammed into his chest. He fell back into her from the impact.

Everyone reacted at once. Kate and Alex both screamed.

Frank threw up his shield to protect Alex.

Kate was pulled back into her body and Nick set her down.

Robert pulled out his gun and fired a shot off at Joel, but Joel had disappeared behind some trees and was out of sight.

Frank fired quickly at Brooks and hit him in the chest, knocking him off of his feet and into the marshy area along the deck. Natalie rushed over to his side, but Frank didn't care what she did. He had fulfilled his mission: he took out the greatest danger to his family.

Frank looked around and determined that there was no more danger so he released Alex and the girl ran over and threw herself into Kate's arms.

Kate was murmuring over and over to Alex, "Shh. It's okay. You're safe now."

Kate looked over Alex's shoulder at Frank. "Thank you."

"I owed you for taking your kids. We're even now." Frank nodded to Kate and left.

Nick and Robert rushed over, but Grace ignored them. She was holding Jason and tears were streaming down her face. "Why did you do that, you idiot?"

She settled him down on the deck and pulled open his button-down shirt. She placed both of her hands on his chest right over the entry wound, then she closed her eyes and concentrated.

The bullet was lodged next to his heart and probably would have been a nearly impossible operation if a doctor was trying to save him. Grace slowly pulled the bullet back out, and healed along the way. She could feel the blood vessels reconnecting and the tissue fusing back together. Jason was still bleeding, but it was slowing down.

Finally the bullet appeared and the skin healed over. Jason's breathing returned to normal but he hadn't opened his eyes yet. When she was finished, Grace collapsed against him.

No one had said a word as Grace worked. They were all afraid to say anything that could jeopardize their friend's recovery. Grace sat up and pulled Jason into her arms, holding him close to her.

Kate put her arm around Grace to offer support and brushed some of Jason's hair from his eyes. She couldn't believe her daughter ran away and was almost kidnapped, a friend nearly died, and the evil man who had been hunting them for the past several months was dead.

Jason gasped and opened his eyes. "Damn, that hurt."

"What the hell were you thinking?" Grace demanded.

"I couldn't let you get hurt."

"Jay, you scared the hell out of us," Robert told him.

"Yeah, man. I thought you were dead," Nick admitted.

Grace and Jason were still staring at each other so Robert and Nick pulled Alex and Kate a little bit away from where they were sitting.

Grace couldn't believe he had stepped in front of that bullet meant for her. "Why? Why did you do it?"

"I told you. I couldn't let you get shot. I couldn't watch you be hurt."

"You don't even know me."

"I've been telling you that I want to get to know you more. You keep pushing me away and blowing me off."

"I haven't been pushing you away."

"Really, so when I showed up at the senior center during

your break to see if you wanted to grab something to eat, you came with me right away?"

Grace frowned at him. He had been showing up everywhere she went, but he was such a player that she figured it was just a challenge to him. Could he really be interested? She had always taken care of herself. No one had ever done anything for her. Ever.

Jason arched a brow at her. "Maybe now, you'll give me a chance."

She gave a short laugh. "You got shot so I would go out with you?"

"Did it work?"

"Maybe."

"I knew you had a thing for me."

Grace rolled her eyes. "Come on. We need to get out of here."

"Yeah, someone probably heard the shots and called the police." Jason stood up slowly and reached out a hand toward Grace. She looked at it for a second and then grasped it. He gave her the smuggest look she had ever seen. She shook her head and they walked over to their friends, who were trying to act as if they had not been listening.

Nick had been flipping between hugging Alex and scolding her. He couldn't make up his mind if he was more angry or relieved.

Robert had taken his turn at both emotions as well, but he left the reprimands to his best friend. He saw Jason walk up and pulled him in for a hug.

"Don't pull something like that again," Robert told him. He thought he had lost one of his best friends, and it was a feeling that he never wanted again.

"Still have that bromance going, I see," Jason joked, but hugged him back.

Nick walked over and took his turn hugging Jason. "No more getting shot."

"You're stuck with me."

———•———

Detective Martin crumpled down on a damp log next to the

retaining wall that he had been hiding behind. He was too stunned to move. He legs would probably give out if he even tried.

Martin couldn't believe what he had just seen. A woman was a ghost and then wasn't, a man moved faster than humanly possible while carrying a woman, and another man raised his hand and erected a shield-type thing around the girl. The most amazing thing was the guy who was fatally shot and the woman who put her hands on him and healed his wound.

Who *were* these people? Was all that an illusion? He wished he had been drinking so he could blame it on the alcohol. Obviously, these people were keeping their abilities a secret, but could they be trusted? Were they a threat? Kate Sutton seemed like a nice young woman. She was a little secretive, but now he understood why.

He needed to speak with her. He needed to speak with all of them and determine if they were dangerous. He waited for what felt like hours, but was probably only a few moments. Everyone had left and it was quiet in the park. He needed to call the coroner about the dead body. He just wasn't sure what to say about how he found the body.

He walked up to the deck and looked over the side. There was no body. He jumped down and saw the place where the man had fallen. There were some marks on the ground, but no body. Martin spent the next several minutes looking around. Where the hell was it?

Don jogged back to where he parked his car. It was a good night. He had proof that the Sutton woman still had her gifts. He had suspected it, but had not been able to prove it. He was shocked to see her astral project. Don was pretty sure that ability was a new development.

The serum he had injected into her should have rendered her abilities useless. It had worked on numerous people, but one of the techs who had developed it warned Don about a possible flaw. The tech had confided that one of the test subject's abilities became enhanced. Sutton's gifts already had the potential to be beyond anything they had seen in years since she came from two

Gifted parents. *Had she just gained even more power?*

He couldn't wait to report his findings. He would also enjoy telling Pete that his star agent was in a relationship with a gifted woman and the object of their investigation. Nick Taylor was going down and Don was going to love watching it happen.

Chapter Twenty-One

Zach rushed Alex as soon as she walked through the door. Ryan told them that Zach hadn't stopped pacing the house the entire time they were looking for Alex.

Ryan was also slightly disappointed to have missed out on the excitement. "Dude, I can't believe you got shot."

Jason still had his bloody shirt on and was pointing out the bullet hole to Ryan. Kate still got chills looking at it.

"So, Brooks is dead?" Ryan asked.

Nick wrapped his arms around Kate from behind her. "Yes, we left him lying in the marsh in the park. One of his teens was with him."

"I can't believe it's over now. He's gone," Kate said quietly.

"He got what he deserved," Robert added.

"Yeah, I guess he did. That guy Frank told me that Brooks had taken his daughter last summer and that was why he took the kids," Kate told them.

"Yeah, I found out Brooks had Frank's girlfriend killed when they took his daughter. Brooks was going to hold his daughter to make Frank do whatever he wanted him to do," Nick explained.

"He underestimated a parent's love for his child," Robert guessed.

"That girl who was with Brooks was really creepy. She looked so sweet and innocent, but she reeked of evil and malice. She was actually disappointed when Brooks told her to wait and not get Alex," Kate told them.

The mention of Alex's name drew everyone's attention to Zach and Alex.

"Zach, you need to go to bed," Kate told him. He didn't argue or protest. His sister was back and that was all he had been worried about.

Everyone decided that it was a good idea for them to go to bed, as well. Jason left with Grace and Ryan. He was filling Ryan in on everything that had happened. Grace was quiet, but she held her gaze on Jason the whole time. Kate wondered what was going on with them. She figured it would be interesting to watch.

Robert gave Kate a hug and ruffled Alex's hair. He walked over to Nick and they fist-bumped and whispered something that Kate couldn't hear.

Alex was waiting for something to happen and the anticipation was horrible. What would Kate do? She knew that Kate wouldn't throw her out, but she probably deserved something like that. She had run away to meet with some kid she had met online, not knowing anything about him except what he had told her. Looking back, that hadn't even been much. And then the boy turned out to be the man who had tried to kidnap her last summer!

She really messed up and she didn't know how she was ever going to fix it.

Kate motioned to Alex. "Sit."

Alex obeyed immediately. "Kate, I'm so sorry. I messed up."

Kate exhaled loudly. She was a trained guidance counselor with a PhD in psychology and she had no idea what to say to her daughter. She wanted to hug her so closely and never let her go and she wanted to yell at her and ground her until she was thirty. Maybe older.

Nick sat next to Kate and grabbed her hand. He was offering her his support and she loved that. He was also letting her take the lead with Alex even though she knew he wanted to yell at her.

"Alex, I need to understand what's been going on with you," Kate began. "You've been secretive and moody and you haven't talked to me in forever without getting upset."

Alex started to cry. It bothered Kate to see Alex cry, but she needed to get her talking.

"I'm going to hurt someone. I can't control my gift and I'm going to burn someone," Alex cried.

"Alex, you just need to learn to control it. It's going to take some time and practice, but you'll get it. *All* gifts can be dangerous without control. *All* of us need to learn how to safely use our abilities and how to keep them from getting away from us," Nick told her gently.

"Fire is a really evil gift. Most of the people who have had it have gone bad, and have caused all kinds of horrible things to happen."

"Who told you that?" Kate asked. She needed to know who Alex had been getting her information from.

"We've all heard stories. And also from some people online."

Nick almost lost his cool. "You're telling people online about your gifts? Are you crazy?"

Kate put her hand on Nick's leg and infused him with some of her calm feelings. She didn't need him flipping out and making things worse.

Alex didn't answer, so Kate prodded. "Alex?"

"There's a forum where some Gifted kids hang out. Mostly just to talk about normal stuff, not gifts. Sometimes someone has a problem or something happens and people talk about it. I didn't tell anyone about the fire thing. It just came up one day and people were talking about the ones who had the gift in the past and all the bad things they did."

"Why didn't you come and talk to me?" Kate needed to know where she went wrong with Alex so that it never happened again.

"I didn't want you to worry and I was afraid that you might make us leave. I don't want to leave."

Kate got up and pulled Alex into a hug. She sat next to her and kept her arm around her daughter. "*You* are not bad. Your *gift* is not evil. It's just something we have to work on. No matter what happens, I am never going to give you kids up. I love you all and I'm not going to lose you. I almost lost you tonight because you were too afraid to talk to me. I never want that to happen again."

Alex's tears were still flowing and she swiped at her cheeks to dry some of them. "I'm sorry, Kate."

Kate hugged her close again. "What happened tonight? Why would you sneak out in the middle of the night to meet someone you don't know?"

"He told me he had a way for me to get rid of my gift. I wanted to get rid of it so I didn't hurt anyone."

Nick had been quietly listening to the exchange, but he couldn't quite let that last comment go. "How did he say he was going to help you get rid of your gift?"

"He wouldn't tell me online. He said it had to be in person."

"And you fell for that?" Kate gave Nick a sharp look, but he continued, "Alex, you should know better than that. We've talked about the internet for years. I know your parents did, too."

Alex sniffled a few times and then muttered, "I know. I was just . . ."

Kate helped her. "Desperate?"

Alex exhaled loudly. "Yes."

"You need to talk to us if you are ever worried or scared. We can't help you if we don't know." Kate hoped Alex was listening to her.

"I'll try to."

"Get some sleep. We'll talk about this more tomorrow and we'll start to practice with your gift," Kate told her.

Alex hugged them both and went up to bed.

Kate fell back against the couch and looked at Nick, who pulled her into his arms. "Hey. You look like you're going to cry."

She nodded as the tears flowed. Everything was crashing down and she needed an outlet. Nick held her tightly as she cried and held on to him. A little while later, he carried her upstairs and tucked her in bed. "Good night, Beautiful. I'll see you in the morning." He kissed her forehead and quietly walked home.

"Hey. We were wondering if you were going to come home tonight," Robert told him as he walked through the door.

Nick looked around and it was just Ryan, Jason, and Robert. Grace must have gone home. He was very thankful to her for saving his friend.

"We were just talking about what happened tonight," Jason began.

"Okay?"

"Something weird happened with that bullet." Jason was fidgeting, which was not something he normally did. He was usually the most laid back of the bunch.

"What, it shot you? That would be weird," Nick teased, trying to lighten the mood.

"No, I was able to slow the bullet down, but then all of a

sudden, it sped back up. A bullet can't do that on its own."

"So, you're saying someone was controlling it?"

"Seemed like it."

"Who? There wasn't anyone there that had that power, right? Was there someone we didn't see?"

Robert sat up and leaned his forearms on his knees. "We don't know. It's strange."

"What about the girl? Do you guys know anything about her?" Nick was a little concerned about this newest information.

"I don't know. I couldn't feel anything from her. She was really young to be able to block that well. Either she is really strongly gifted or she doesn't have any gifts," Robert told them. Since he could always tell exactly what gifts people had and how strong they were, it was unusual to not feel anything at all from someone Gifted.

"We should probably check her out," Ryan suggested.

"Yeah. I'll ask Grace if she knows anything," Jason offered.

"What is going on with you and her?" Nick asked.

Jason got a huge grin. "Nothing. Yet."

They chatted for a few more minutes and then went off to their rooms. Nick really hoped that there wasn't something else to worry about. They could all use a break.

Kate was getting ready for her date with Nick. It had been two days since Alex had nearly been kidnapped and everyone had settled into a routine. Alex was still grounded and now Kate monitored all electronic devices; no electronics were allowed in Alex and Zach's rooms, and they had to be surrendered to Kate when the kids went to bed for the night. She was not about to let something like that to happen again. It was going to take quite some time for Kate to get over the events of that night.

Kate checked herself in the mirror. She was wearing a deep-purple skirt and a black top. Once again, Alex helped her pick out something to wear. Her daughter had good taste in clothes. Kate thought she looked good.

It was funny to think about it, but this would be Kate and Nick's first real date. They had hung out numerous times and had spent more time on rescue missions than she ever wanted to

think about, but they had never actually gone on a date together.
Kate stopped to put on some extra lip gloss before walking down the steps. She heard Nick's voice coming from the kitchen so she headed in that direction. She spotted him before he looked up and noticed her. He looked gorgeous. He had on black dress pants and a blue button-up shirt that made his eyes really stand out. She loved his blue eyes.

Nick smiled brightly as she walked up. "Hey, gorgeous. You look amazing." He pulled her in for a hug and kept her against him. "Are you ready to leave?"

"Yes. Where are we going?" She had asked him that for two days without getting an answer.

"It's a surprise." Nick hadn't told her anything about their night except that he was taking her somewhere for dinner and somewhere else after.

Nick turned to Robert, who had volunteered to watch the kids. "We'll be back late."

"Got it. Have fun." Robert loved seeing his friends so happy. They had both been through so much and they needed a nice night out. Soon enough, they would have to deal with reality.

Nick walked Kate to the passenger side of his SUV, opened the door for her, and helped her inside. He kissed her lightly then closed her door. He wanted everything to be perfect for Kate. She deserved to have the best date of her life and he was going to give it to her. He was also going to be the perfect gentleman, for as much of it as he could manage. He knew how he would like it to end.

He hopped into the car and started the engine. He had flowers for her across the center console that she had just noticed. Kate smiled brightly as she picked the flowers up and inhaled their fragrance. Nick knew that she loved all kinds of daisies, so he got her a huge bouquet of several different kinds. Kate had told him before that they had always made her smile, and Nick loved to see her smile.

"Thank you. They're beautiful."

"You're welcome. I'm glad you like them."

"Are you going to tell me where we're going now?"

"Not yet. You'll see."

Kate got even more excited when Nick turned onto the road that would take them over the bridge into Philadelphia. She loved going to the city, but didn't get the chance to very often with all of her responsibilities.

"Philly?" Kate beamed.

"Yes. It's a beautiful night to walk around the city."

A few minutes later, Nick pulled up to a valet parking line on 16th Street between Market and Chestnut. Kate was so excited. She had always wanted to try the restaurant on the thirty-seventh floor of Liberty Place. R2L had one of the best views in Philly.

"What do you think?" Nick asked her. He wanted her to like the place he selected.

"I've always wanted to eat here. I heard the view is incredible."

"Come on, let's go check it out." Nick grabbed her hand and they entered the building and took the elevator up to the restaurant.

When Nick gave the maître d his name, the man's whole demeanor changed and he suddenly became extraordinarily polite and helpful. He took Kate's coat for her and guided them to a reserved table that was slightly apart from the others, in a section that didn't appear to be in use. Kate glanced at Nick with curiosity, but his smile didn't give anything away.

Their table was against the glass windows overlooking the Philadelphia skyline. "Wow," Kate said in wonder, looking out the window. "That is an amazing view."

"I've seen better." Nick was looking at Kate and not paying attention to the city below.

Kate grinned at him as they settled into their seats. The waiter had been hovering nearby but didn't approach them until Nick nodded. He immediately brought out a bottle of red wine and some sparkling water.

Kate looked at Nick questioningly, but he just smiled. He picked up his glass for a toast. "To the start of something incredible."

Kate couldn't imagine anything being more incredible than right then, but she raised her glass and repeated his words. The wine was so smooth, and tasted perfect. She couldn't stop smiling and knew that her cheeks would start hurting soon if things kept going the same way.

She looked around for a menu but couldn't find one.

Nick was watching her closely the whole time. He wanted to memorize the entire night, every detail of it. "There isn't a menu. I arranged for a chef's tasting menu for tonight."

She arched a brow at him. "Really? And how do you know what I like?" she teased.

"I know what you like."

Kate loved the way they bantered together. "Is that right? Are you sure?"

"Absolutely. I pay attention. You love veggies, but will devour a steak or burger if they're cooked right. You hate heavy sauces and scrape them off most of the time. You love hot food, the hotter the better. You don't like eggplant unless it's breaded and fried. You love seafood but stay away from what you call 'fishy fish,'" Nick told her with a smirk. "How did I do?"

Kate sat there stunned. She had no idea that he knew so much about her preferences. He must have paid attention to everything that she had ever said to him.

"Not bad."

"Not bad? That's all I get?" He winked at her. He loved that he had surprised her with his knowledge, but he still wanted to know everything about her.

She was saved from answering by the waiter bringing their first course.

Their dinner was incredible and Kate loved getting a taste of several different things from the restaurant. She loved their dessert the best. Even though she didn't have much room for it, she wanted to at least sample what they had to offer. Nick had ordered three different things for them to try: a cranberry-apple tart, a chocolate soufflé, and a pumpkin French toast with ice cream. She couldn't decide which one was the best.

After dinner, they ventured over to XIX at the Bellevue Hotel on Broad Street. It was a restaurant and lounge on the nineteenth floor of the hotel. It had incredible outdoor balcony seating that offered a different breathtaking view of the city. The heat lamps kept the chilly night air away from the seating area.

Nick came up behind her and wrapped her in his arms as they watched the city lights.

Nick had one more stop in mind before they ended their first real date. The drive back toward their neighborhood was filled by singing along to the radio and talking about everything possible. Kate couldn't remember ever having more fun.

Nick passed their street and Kate gave him an odd look. She couldn't imagine what he had planned. He pulled down one of her favorite streets in Moorestown, the drive along Strawbridge Lake. Nick pulled off the street onto one of the dirt and gravel lots and turned off the car.

He came around to her side and helped her out of the vehicle and into his arms. Nick gave her a quick kiss, then took her hand to head out to the lake. The water was sparkling from the moonlight and Kate thought the place looked magical. Maybe she was just feeling like everything was magical.

He wrapped her in his arms again and began to slow dance with her to the sounds of the crickets. Kate completely melted. They swayed back and forth for a while until Kate started to shiver.

"Let's get you home. You're freezing," Nick noticed, and rubbed her shoulders.

Kate would have turned into an ice cube before admitting she was cold. She was having too much of a good time for the night to end. When she frowned at him, he laughed.

"Don't frown at me. We can do this again. I'm planning on having all kinds of nights like this with you."

She kissed him by the lake and hoped he would forget about taking her home.

A few minutes later, he was kissing her good night in her foyer. Robert had taken off as soon as they had gotten home, which Kate figured had to have been prearranged. Robert usually lingered there to give them a hard time, but he had jumped up and jogged home. She wondered how Nick managed to get him to agree to that.

"I had a wonderful time. Thank you for an amazing night," Kate told him as she played with his hair.

"Me too, Beautiful." Nick kissed her again and then pulled away and stepped back from her. "I need to say good night before I drag you into the other room and not leave for a really long time."

She grinned at him and he groaned. "Don't look at me like that. I'm trying really hard to be a perfect gentleman."

Kate laughed and kissed him again. "Okay. See you tomorrow."

"Good night." Nick smiled the whole way home.

Kate never felt so wonderful. Her whole body was still tingling from being near him. She wondered if this was what being in love felt like. She'd had boyfriends in the past, but she had never felt anything like this.

Kate jogged up the steps to her room and searched the bookshelf next to her reading chair. She wondered if this was how her mother had felt about her father. She pulled her mother's journal out from the shelf and started to flip through it.

Kate was so busy looking in the book that she didn't realize she was about to walk into the corner of her bed. She stumbled into it, stubbing her foot, and dropping the journal as she hit.

The journal bounced off the bed's footboard and then hit the hardwood floor with a thud. After rubbing her injured foot, Kate bent to pick up the journal and noticed the binding had cracked open.

Picking it up for a closer look, she noticed something shoved in between layers of the back cover. Kate pulled out a folded piece of paper, and a tarnished, silver-looking medallion fell out. It was the size of a silver dollar and had odd markings on one side and a crystal embedded on the other. It looked ancient.

Kate got shivers throughout her whole body. She held the medallion in her hand and felt a slight tingling from it, almost like the sensation she felt when touching Nick.

Why would this be hidden in the binding of her mother's journal?

She opened the paper to see if anything was written on it.

To my baby girl,

I hope that you will never read this and that

you will have a wonderfully happy life never knowing anything about our race. Your father and I tried to hide you as far away from our world as possible, but if you're reading this, somehow you found your way back to it.

There are so many things we wish we could tell you, but there is simply not enough time. People are hunting us and we know that it's only a matter of time before we're caught.

When we were in New York City, we met a couple that had been on the run for several years. They never stayed in one place for more than a month or two. They were not Gifted but ended up finding out about our world. The man was a thief and specialized in stealing rare antiquities. He stumbled upon an Association vault in Greece and took several items that he thought would bring a huge price.

He sold several of the pieces, but for some reason he decided to keep a medallion. He was drawn to it, but he didn't know why. There was an inscription written on the back of it and curiosity got the better of him so he had it translated. He copied down the markings and took it to a university in London. The language was so old and obscure that it raised quite a fervor in the academic world.

That fervor signaled the people he had stolen it from and they began to hunt him. Others had heard about the markings and were also after him. The medallion was an artifact from Atlantis.

He gave us the medallion so that none of the people after him would get it. The partial translation said that this was the source of our race's incredible powers. The man was killed shortly after that and we never knew if he had told anyone who he had given the medallion to.

This medallion is extremely rare and

incredibly dangerous. Keep it hidden and keep it safe.
Baby girl, do not trust anyone.

All my love forever,
Your mother,
Amanda

About the Author
Char Webster

USA Today Best-selling Author Char Webster weaves suspense, mystery, romance and humor into all of her books. She strives to make her fantasy and paranormal worlds fit perfectly into real life, where anything seems to be possible.

Reading and getting lost in a story have always been Char Webster's favorite things to do. She has also had a love for writing, which led her to her daytime career in public relations and marketing. After years of writing for others, Char decided to write something for herself.

Her books fulfill a lifelong dream of creating a world where people can escape reality for a little while. Char Webster loves living in South Jersey because she feels like it is in the center of everything. She loves pizza, hot sauce, French fries, dancing, photography and trying new things.

Made in the
USA
Columbia, SC